DAMAGED DREAMS

KRIS BUTLER

Damaged Dreams
Kris Butler

First Edition: December 2020
Updated and re-edited March 2024
Published by: Incognito Scribe Productions LLC
Kris Butler
Copyright © Kris Butler 2020

No AI was used in the production of this work of fiction.

Proofreading: © 2022 by Owlsome Author Services
Formatting: © 2022 Incognito Scribe Productions
Cover Design: © 2024 Incognito Scribe Productions

 Created with Vellum

blurb

What price would you pay for the truth?

Most teenagers were surprised with a car for their sixteenth birthday. Me...I uncovered secrets that were meant to stay hidden.

My parents weren't my parents.

There was a man after me.

My dream of being an Olympic skater was over.

For five years, I stayed hidden, kept my head down, and worked at my foster dad's ice rink. That was until a job opportunity placed me at the school where I could finally get answers.

The Aldridge School—home of the top elites in the world and where my father told me it all started.

From the moment I landed, I felt more alive than I had in years. Between being back on the ice, connecting with my six roommates, and making friends, I finally felt like I belonged. For the first time in five years, I didn't feel alone.

But with each answer I uncovered, another question emerged, and I no longer knew if the truth was worth the cost—to be used or broken.

My dreams were within my grasp, but my past wasn't satisfied any longer to stay buried. The truth might start with The Aldridge School, but I feared it might end with my life.

foreword

This book has sexual scenes meant for adults. It is a why choose romance that has MM. The steamy scenes are steamy, and apparently insta love on some levels. If that is not your thing, then this book is not for you and that is okay. That is the great thing about books, there are many different kinds and we can all find ones we love.

It has been mentioned that this book may make you laugh out loud, so be careful when reading while drinking or eating or it may cause spewing accidents.

This book highlights mental health in a positive light and the characters have positive coping skills that they will use from counseling. While they may be helpful, this is not a self-help book and if you feel you need help please reach out to someone you trust, or you can find some help here at https://www.samhsa.gov .

content

- Medium burn
- Explicit language (the f word is used a lot)
- Multi-Pov
- Found Family
- Bi-awakening
- Threesomes
- Grumpy/sunshine
- Sex positive
- Mental Health rep
- Queer rep
- No third act breakup, just some angst and mild anxiety about the status of the relationship
- Male virgin
- Second chance
- Friends to lovers
- Enemies to lovers
- He falls first
- A cute dog
- Voyeurism
- Exhibitionism
- Face sitting
- Pierced peen
- Tattoos galore
- Winter sports
- Lots of ice skating
- A fierce bestie

- LOL moments #codeorange
- A FMC with no filter
- Not your average skater, body inclusive
- Twists and turns
- Roomates/forced proximity

sensitive topics

- 'God, Jesus, Hell, Damn' used casually or in a sexual context
- PTSD/panic attacks
- Depression/anxiety
- Alcohol recovery
- Self-doubt
- Negative thoughts
- Sexual abuse (past)
- Parents murdered
- Lied to about birth parents
- Family death
- Past suicide attempts
- Grief
- Human trafficking
- Drug abuse
- Kidnapping
- Jealous ex
- Past trauma

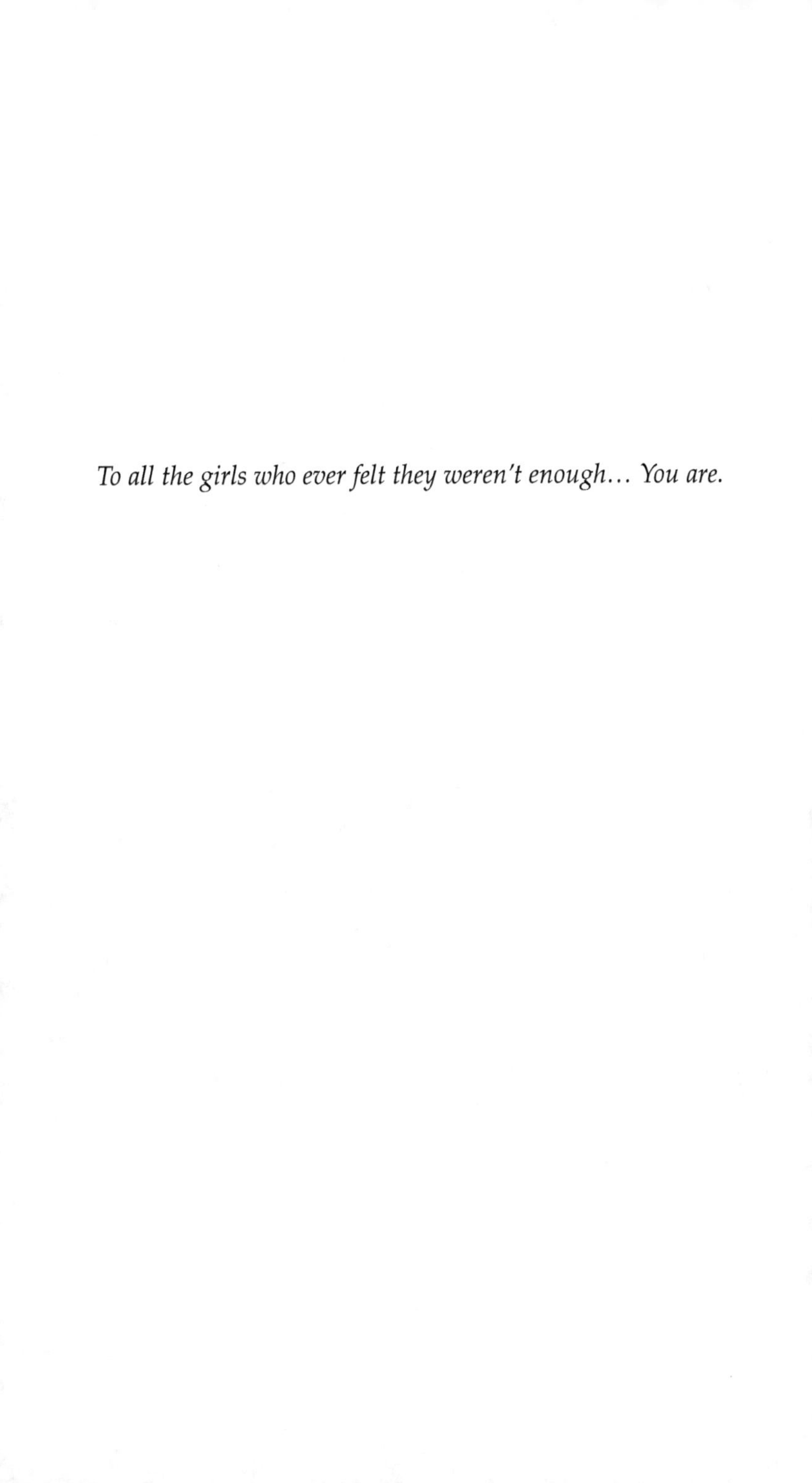

To all the girls who ever felt they weren't enough… You are.

prologue

sariah

I was late, and I hated being late. Rushing around my room, I triple-checked my bag to make sure I had everything I needed for practice. I was paranoid I'd forget something despite never forgetting anything.

"Sariah! Let's go!" my mom shouted up the stairs for the third time.

Rolling my eyes, I knew she wasn't wrong, but it felt like she was always yelling at me to hurry up. But I couldn't leave until I'd run through my list again.

Skates, check.

Extra leggings, check.

Skate guards, check.

Leotard, check.

Muscle cream, check.

Extra scrunchies, double-check.

I could never have too many of those since I was forever throwing my hair up into a messy bun—long hair problems. Satisfied everything was there, I grabbed my bag and finally rushed down the stairs.

"Mom, I'm ready," I grumbled, making my way into the kitchen as I scrolled through social media. Today was my last practice before the pairs competition tomorrow. My skating partner and I were expected to place first, and from there, it would be Nationals. Which would only be one step away from the Olympic Team, my dream.

Giddy excitement bubbled up in me at the thought, but it wasn't only because of being so close to the Olympics, I could taste it. No, each time I thought of my skating partner, Henry, butterflies erupted and I couldn't wait to see him.

Our skating future excited me, but I was eager to see him today because of what happened the other night. My cheeks began to redden with a blush as I recalled the kiss we'd shared. Unfortunately, we hadn't been able to talk about it afterward because Finley had barreled into the room right after.

I loved my best friend, but at that moment, I'd wanted to punch her. Fin had the absolute worst timing. To be fair, though, I hadn't told her about my first kiss yet. Mostly because it was with her brother, and I was nervous about having that conversation with her.

Growing up as neighbors, we'd all been the three amigos since we could walk.

Now, I worried what this new shift in our dynamic would bring. Henry and I were meant to be, I just knew it.

When no one responded, I looked up from my phone and realized neither of my parents were in the kitchen as usual. Glancing around, I spotted my father's sandy head peeking over the back of the couch. That was odd. At this time of the morning, he was typically on his second cup of coffee while he read the paper.

My mother's head of thick chestnut waves sat next to him, so I changed directions and headed toward the living room. Something was going on and I was one determined sixteen-year-old who'd get to the bottom of this. She'd gone from yelling at me to hurry, to sitting on the couch. I didn't buy it. Maybe they had a surprise for me?

"Mom? Dad? Why are you in here?"

When neither answered, I walked further into the living room and immediately noticed my father's typical jovial attitude was missing and had been replaced with a look of fear. It looked wrong, like it didn't belong on his handsome face. My father, Scott Brennon, was forty and apparently considered attractive by my peers. Which by the way, was gross to think about. Except now, his usual clean-cut look was rumpled, and everything about his demeanor seemed off.

It only got worse when I took in my mother's appearance next to him, stopping me dead in my tracks. Kyla Brennon was in her mid-thirties and was considered to be a refined beauty. Her Brazilian heritage gave her features I coveted and kept waiting to develop, but as it was, flat chested and petite were my reality.

My mom's frame was taut with tension as worry lines creased her brow. Most disturbing, though, was the haunted look in her usual cheerful eyes. Both of my parents' postures contradicted their naturally tall frames as they both sat hunched over, tense on the couch. My father's arm wrapped around my mother's waist while she shredded a Kleenex in her lap. They avoided making eye contact as I took in the scene before me.

"What's going on? I thought we had to leave?"

My questions went unanswered, but I caught my father shifting his eyes to the side. That was when I noticed the strange man sitting in our living room, causing my brow to wrinkle in confusion.

"Okay, really, what's going on? I'm going to be late for practice if we don't leave soon. Henry and I need to work on the timing of that last sequence," I said, looking back and forth at my parents.

No response.

"Mom? Dad? Seriously, who is this? Why won't you answer me?" My voice trembled as I asked them, the reality of the situation hitting me as a pit in the bottom of my stomach began to grow. This man had a weird vibe about him, and I didn't like how my parents were responding to his presence like pod people.

Since they weren't answering me, my earlier resolution to get to the bottom of this weird morning had me turning to the strange man instead and taking him in.

He was tall with a medium build, his long legs stretching out in front of him. He had salt and pepper hair slicked back, accentuating his sharp features. His eyes held a sense of darkness that spoke volumes to what he was capable of inflicting. He watched me regard him, his lips curving up in a weird smile like he got off on my uncomfortableness.

Arching an eyebrow in return, I crossed my arms, continuing my observation. He wore a suit that screamed expensive based on the fit, and the gleaming shoes on his feet gave a picture of polished danger. I realized Finley's obsession with fashion had seeped in over the years, apparently giving me an osmosis education on the topic. My focus stayed on his shoes, and I wondered how he kept them so shiny. There wasn't a smudge to be found.

A throat clearing brought me out of my stare-off with those ridiculously polished shoes, and I blinked, remembering something wasn't right here. Not wanting to let my guard down, I pulled out my 'snarky teenager' as Mom referred to it.

"Yes?" I huffed in a bored tone, combined with my death stare. Silence met my question, and my anger rose. "Who are you, and what the fuck are you doing in my house?"

My mom gasped at my foul language, at least letting me know she was present, even if she didn't say anything else. My heart began to race at that fact because she hated when I cussed, and always corrected me by saying, "that's not very becoming of a lady, Sariah!" She acted as if we lived in the era of *Pride and Prejudice* or something. So, her not saying *anything*… not a good sign.

My legs threatened to give out now, so I leisurely walked over to the couch, masking my fear, and took a seat. It was at that moment, I realized I still clutched my phone in my hand. Opening a text to Finley, I typed a 911 message, quickly hitting send before I pocketed my phone.

Fin and I had jokingly created our own code words on the off chance we were ever kidnapped. We thought it would be funny to have a word to send one another if we were in trouble. Mine was "JB girl." It was something I'd never say since I thought Justin Bieber was overrated.

Adjusting my position next to my dad, I noticed he kept his focus trained on the coffee table as if it held the meaning of life. He tensed when my hand brushed his leg but did nothing to acknowledge me. The pit in my stomach grew, and I worried what the news could be at this rate.

The mysterious man decided to talk once I was seated. "Sariah, I've wanted to meet you for a while, or I guess more aptly, meet you again. You see, my dear, I was present at your birth."

Way to drop that creepy bomb, weirdo.

He sat back with his creepy smile, and I pinched myself, almost certain this was a dream now. His eyes flicked to my right as he continued. "But your *parents*," he sneered, "have been troublesome to locate and refused my requests to meet with you."

I raised my eyebrow at that, having no clue what the hell he was talking about now. This guy was bizarre, bordering on terrifying.

"Wellllllll...." I drew out, rolling my eyes. I would have a killer headache at the end of all this if I kept doing that. "Kudos, it seems you've managed to find me. But, unfortunately, I have somewhere to be, and I'm late." I pouted, acting as if I was sad about it, and pretended to stand in an attempt to get him to leave.

I didn't know why my parents were behaving so oddly in his presence, but I knew, whatever the reason, I didn't like it. Maybe he was a vampire and had used compulsion on them? My imagination began to run away with this theory, causing me to be confused when a burly oaf of a man came up from behind me and forcibly shoved me back down, effectively snapping me out of my strange thoughts.

"What...?" I started to ask the psycho vamp, but the look on his face had me shutting my mouth.

"There will be *no* leaving, Sariah. Not until I say you can. Now please, have a seat. I don't want to have to get aggressive," he gritted out, all while wearing his creepy-ass smile. Yep, definitely a vampire. Wrenching my arm away from the burly oaf, my anger reared up in protest.

"So, talk then, Mr…?" I trailed off, deliberately acting uninterested. His smile widened, making me shudder internally at the implications. *Gross.*

"You may refer to me as 'R.' That is all you need to know at this time," he stated matter-of-factly.

Now I worried he was the deranged one since he clearly thought himself to be some kind of *Bond* villain. Seriously dude, this was Indiana. What, was he going to murder me with a stalk of corn? Trying to keep my face blank, I decided to see what information I could gather, since no one else was talking.

"Well, R," I sneered back. "You still haven't explained what it is you want from me? And quite frankly, I don't care that you were at my birth—kind of a weird flex, to be honest. I'm sure several people I didn't know were there like nurses, doctors, and order-lies. So, whoopee freaking doo! Do you want a cookie or something? A high-five? I'm not sure how it makes you anything special," I scoffed, the full sarcasm of a teenager in tow. It was a deadly thing when used, not many adults survived.

Holding his eyes, I didn't blink or break eye contact once. R had no clue how often I gazed into Henry's eyes or had stare-offs with Finley. I was a teenage girl, R; I could go all day. His smile lifted at the corners again, as if he was impressed with my continued abrasiveness toward him.

"Your strength will serve you well for what awaits

you, my dear. Despite your *parents* keeping you in the dark about your heritage, it seems your genetics haven't let you down." R grinned evilly at his words, and he was only a furry cat away from being a TV villain.

Seriously, what was with this guy? And why did he keep saying *parents* like he had a bad taste in his mouth? This was all feeling too much like a bad example of why you shouldn't do drugs. Rolling my eyes for the millionth time, this time it hurt with how hard I rolled them.

"Like I said, the only thing that awaits me, weirdo, is practice. Which, I'm now really late for. You've met me, said your whole creepy spiel, so I'd appreciate it if you were to leave. Tomorrow's an important day for me. So, if you'd please," I said, standing up and motioning to the door.

I couldn't take this whole situation any longer and needed it to be over. I hoped taking charge would help, since my parents seemed to be struck with a case of muteness. They had a lot of explaining to do after this. To my surprise, R stood and followed with his goon to the door.

"Of course, my dear, I'm sure this is a lot to process, so I will leave you to get packed. I'll be here at dawn tomorrow. Goodbye, for now, my sweet Sariah." He bowed his head, leaving on that cryptic message that made my skin crawl.

Like hell would I go anywhere with this loon! For once, I kept my mouth shut, wanting him to leave more than anything. See, teenagers could be polite!

The burly muscle opened the door for R, but he turned back one more time and made a point to stare at my parents, no doubt releasing them from his vampire compulsion. "You know what will happen if she's not here in the morning when I come to collect. *He* will not be happy. You'll be wise to remember that."

The sound of the door shutting echoed throughout the silent house, making the pounding of my heart even more noticeable. I turned, looking at my parents, hoping to finally get some damn answers. The look on their faces sent a sense of fear and foreboding through me. Their usual easygoing expressions and cheerful moods were still nowhere to be found. Dad even appeared to have aged ten years since yesterday.

His face had an unusual pallor, sweat beaded on his brow, and his shoulders held a heaviness. Most troublesome was the hauntingness in his eyes. My mom wasn't faring any better, but her upper-class upbringing allowed her to mask it better. When I peered closely, though, I could see the lines around her mouth, the bags under her eyes, and the fear, vibrating through her body.

"Mom... Dad... What's going on? Who was that crazy guy, and what was he talking about?" My voice shook as I made my way back into the living room. They hadn't moved from the couch other than to look at me. It was Dad who broke first, spilling all the details.

I felt myself go faint as all the blood drained from my face. Thankfully, the couch was still behind me because this time, I freaking fainted.

Apparently, I was a damsel in distress circa *Pride and Prejudice*, after all.

Hello, fainting couch, meet face.

This was not how I had envisioned my day at all. To think my biggest worry this morning had been when I could kiss Henry again… Fuck!

one

. . .

PRESENT DAY

sawyer

The mop swished against the floor, the sound almost soothing. The smell of chemicals swirled around me, and I hummed under my breath as I fell into the easy rhythm.

"Sawdust?" yelled Charlie, my boss and former guardian.

"Yeah?" I shouted as I finished the girl's bathroom. Wringing out the mop, I chuckled at the use of his nickname for me. At this point, I'd accepted it as his way of telling me he cared. Charlie had started calling me Sawdust after we first met when I was seventeen. He said, "you're as annoying as sawdust since you won't go away," and well, the name stuck. He had one thing right though, I hadn't gone away.

Smiling, I recalled the first time I met Charlie Smith after I'd come to the ice rink, nagging him for a job over the course of a week. He was a widower, owned the local ice rink, and was the epitome of curmudgeonly. Somehow, I'd worn him down and he became my guardian and gave me a job. He wasn't my legal guardian anymore since I was almost twenty-two, but it hadn't changed anything in our relationship. I still lived in his house, worked at the rink, and made sure to give him a hard time—out of love, of course.

Charlie had entered my life when I desperately needed to believe in someone, giving me hope that not everyone was out to use me. He'd recognized that lonely person in me and had begrudgingly offered me a place to live along with the job. In the end, the arrangement had been what we both needed.

We worked well together and had developed a routine over the years. I kept him from living alone, taught lessons and clinics, did the scheduling, and assisted with the cleaning. Though, probably his favorite, was that I dealt with all the parents' bullshit so he didn't have to. In exchange, I got a paycheck, a safe place to live, and a companion. We might not always talk a lot, but we had our own way of expressing our affection. He'd become my family, and I'd hate to think what the past five years would've been like without him.

"There's someone on the phone for you," he gruffed. He leaned against the doorjamb, watching me. "She says they've been trying to reach you for a week." He gave me a pointed look, like it was my fault. Charlie was a big old grump, but he was my grump.

Rolling my eyes, I planted my hands on my hips and gave him a look back as I took him in. His old flannel looked worn, and the lines around his eyes were tight in concern. His bushy head of hair and beard were mostly gray at this point, the hairs sticking out all over the place. Charlie had to be in his sixties, but he wouldn't tell me his age, no matter how many times I've asked, so I just called him by what he was—old grump.

"I'm not avoiding anyone if that's what you're implying."

He shrugged, not moving. Sighing, I shrugged back, a tiny smile playing at my lips. I grabbed the mop handle and pushed the bucket toward the door, wondering who could be calling me here.

It was almost closing time, and all I wanted to do was fall into my bed. My body was exhausted after three classes and skating for hours, and I just wanted to sleep. Here lately, things had started to feel suffocating. It felt like I had no way out of this cycle of work, sleep, work, sleep, and repeat.

That was all I'd done for the past three years, and it had been fine. But these past six months, it had begun to feel never ending. If it was a pissed off skating mom complaining about her kid not being a professional yet, or even worse, a creepy hockey dad hitting on me, I might scream.

Charlie backed out of the door, letting me push the

mop bucket through as he headed back to what he'd been working on. Fear and anxiety began to fill me as I approached the office. It was a feeling that never seemed to leave me, even after all these years. Charlie had become my safe place, and after being in the foster care system for a year, I knew the value in that.

Foster care—just the words made me shudder.

It hadn't been all rainbows and puppies like the state would like you to believe. I winced as I briefly recalled celebrating my birthday at my first foster home two weeks after my parents had died. Being a teenager made it challenging to find a home willing to take me, and not all the homes I stayed in had been good ones. Apparently, placing a grieving teen in a home that didn't include a leering predator waiting in the wings to pounce at the first opportunity was impossible. There had been too many close calls, and a few times I preferred not to remember. Meeting Charlie had been the turning point I needed.

Shaking off the unwanted thoughts of a past best forgotten, I shoved the bucket into the closet and headed to the office. It was the only place that still had a landline connection. Charlie was old school and didn't believe in cell phones. No matter how often I spoke of the convenience, he wouldn't get one. Clicking on the light, I entered the enclosed space and picked the receiver up off the desk.

"Hello?" I answered, a hint of exasperation in my voice.

"Sawyer Sullivan?" asked an unfamiliar voice. It

was weird hearing that name even five years after the fact.

"This is she. How may I help you?" I said professionally, since I had no clue who was calling me here.

"Just to clarify, this is 'Sawyer Sullivan' who applied for the junior instructor position at The Aldridge School?"

I sucked in a breath. I'd given up hope on the job when I hadn't heard anything over the summer. To say I was beyond surprised to hear those words uttered to me now was an understatement. The job posting had been in April for the 2020-2021 school year, which now started in just two weeks.

"Yes, this is *that* Sawyer," I managed to state calmly despite my internal freak-out. Was this really happening? It felt like a teenie bopper was jumping all around inside my head at her statement. I even felt like I might pass out. This hadn't been what I'd expected when I'd picked up the phone.

The Aldridge School, TAS for short, was the premier school for winter sports, and I wanted to work there so bad. Student-athletes from all over trained there to earn college scholarships with the hope of making it to the Olympics. It was a college preparatory program that allowed students to focus on studies while they trained and competed at an advanced level over public high schools. It was the Walt Disney of high schools and any athlete would sell their soul for a chance to train or work there.

Most winter sports didn't have the same trajectory

as other sports. There wasn't a national team that bobsled on Sundays, or songs sung about taking you out to the ice rink for some nachos and a root beer. So outside of the Olympics, there weren't many career options for athletes once they graduated, if they didn't go pro. TAS offered injured, retired, and troublesome athletes a chance at a job in something they'd spent countless hours doing and loved.

It was everything I needed at the moment, with the addition of being the one place I could get answers. I'd desperately wanted to be in Utah, and at this moment, it felt like my entire future hinged on her next few words. Taking a deep breath, I prepared for what was to come.

The voice on the line let out an audible exhale, exclaiming, "Oh wonderful! Somehow we'd lost your contact information, but I'd remembered you worked at an ice rink in Iowa from your audition video. I've been calling all the ice rinks in the state for the past week. I'm so overjoyed to have found you, Ms. Sullivan. I'm hoping you're still available and interested in the position at TAS?" She paused for only a second before launching into her pitch, not giving me a chance to say no. "We have a very lucrative starting package for you. The only downside is that it starts in two weeks and there are staff meetings before…" She kept talking, but I no longer heard what she said, stuck on the job part.

I'd wanted to leave this state for the past three years, ever since I'd graduated high school. I knew it was time to uncover the truth and stop hiding. Iowa only served to remind me of what I'd lost, suffocating me in grief and complacency. These past five years have shown me that if I didn't find answers soon, I would be stuck in this holding pattern forever.

So, I worked, planned, trained, and hoped.

I hoped I'd get to feel joy, acceptance, and connection again.

I hoped I'd find myself, and develop dreams again.

I hoped my life would mean something other than this.

My goal became my focus, and it helped to stave off the depression. I was determined not to let the mind monsters win. And for three years, I'd worked in pursuit of that goal.

But the past six months, it had started to feel hopeless. I wondered if I'd be stuck in the ice rink forever, no matter how much I wanted out. My life would amount to stale corn dogs, teaching four-year-olds how to properly fall on their butts, and mopping up the damn bathrooms until I became as old and gray as Charlie.

"Do you accept that offer, Ms. Sullivan?" the voice squawked at me from the receiver, making me jump, reminding me I was on the phone. Panicking, I tried to stall since I had no idea what she was referring to.

"I'm not sure, Ms... I'm sorry I don't recall your name, but, well, it's awfully short notice, and I'd have to rush a lot of things to be able to be there on time. Not to mention, I'd need to give a short notice at my current job, and I would just hate to disappoint my students." Amazingly, it seemed to work.

"Of course, Ms. Sullivan, here at The Aldridge School, we would like to offer a generous salary, housing accommodations, meal planning…," she droned on, but I listened this time. The amenities package they were offering was outstanding. It included a salary, housing, food, and an equipment package. The squawky lady—who still hadn't told me her name—dribbled on about it and I started to feel faint.

This couldn't be real. Things like this didn't happen to me.

When she finally finished, I sat there quietly, digesting her words. Squawky cleared her throat loudly, becoming annoyed at my silence. "*Well*, Ms. Sullivan, do we have a deal?"

I didn't even have to consider it. The opportunity was everything. In fact, I'd have accepted the job for much less.

The lucky break I needed was finally happening. I'd get out of Iowa, and get the chance to pursue a career with skating. My future was finally headed somewhere, and that felt nice.

But mostly, I was moving closer to uncovering the truth. The truth that still haunted me every night.

"Absolutely, do I fucking accept!" I practically shouted. Squawky may not be able to see my head, but it was nodding vigorously, nonetheless. She gasped a little at my response, but cleared her throat, staying professional.

"Wonderful, Ms. Sullivan." I didn't miss how she

sounded like the cat that got the cream now. "Give me your information and I'll email over the contract, travel arrangements, medical information needed, and personal documents you'll need to submit before your move."

After a few more details, we ended the call and I placed the phone back on the cradle. Sitting there in shock, I processed her words again, a weight lifting from me. Slowly, a huge grin spread across my face, and I squealed in delight, doing a happy dance.

Now... to tell Charlie. Crap.

two

elias

My pen tapped against the desk as I looked over the students I would be tutoring this semester. It filled me with excitement to learn who I'd get to mold this year, and I couldn't wait to start on my lesson plans—strategic preparation was my motto. Gathering a general idea of where the pupil was in their studies and what their weaknesses and strengths were helped me to design the best course of action.

Shifting in my chair, I brought my pen to my planner to finish the last student. The sport they played affected when I could meet with them, making sched-uling everyone a bit tricky at times. Tutoring sounded easy in theory, but there were a lot of factors that went into successful student outcomes. Especially when employed at a school that prided itself on both academic and sports achievements. There was no such thing as failure at TAS.

Which led me to my favorite part, individualizing the lesson plan to the student for the best possible outcome. It was the main reason I was hired and part of my doctoral thesis. I strongly believed in looking at the different learning styles and techniques for each student instead of only teaching one way. In fact, I argued traditional school systems failed most students because they were only geared toward one type of learning.

Only having four students from each grade made it possible to complete my thesis while I taught, and combine my theories with real practice. I also loved not having to educate a whole class, but could concentrate on individual students and help them achieve success. This school year was my fourth term and it was almost time to publish my findings to finish my doctorate. I was anxious about finishing, and everything that meant for my future. Familial obligations would soon be calling my name.

Self-loathing burned in my chest at the recollection of what awaited me, and how distracting last year had been. Shame coated everything and I hated how a pretty face, false promises, and thinking I could have it all veered me off course.

That was a mistake I would not make again.

This year I would focus on my career and where I wanted to be in five years, which meant no more distractions.

Speaking of distractions, my phone vibrated with an incoming text message.

Voldemort: I really think you are making this into a bigger deal than it needs to be. It's been over a year. Haven't you forgiven me yet, Eli? It was only one time. I was drunk, and it was a stupid mistake. It didn't mean anything. We are good together. We belong together.

And ignore. Her constant vitriol was not needed in my life anymore. I loved my job enough to stay, otherwise, I would have left a year ago to avoid seeing her everywhere. And she was everywhere.

Voldemort: Come on, Eli, forgive me, and I'll do that thing with my tongue you like. I'll even let you do anal. Just forgive me.
Voldemort: You know you miss these. *Pic Attachment*

I swiped her messages to delete, not wanting to see anything of hers ever again. Fuck, I hated it when she called me Eli. If only I could block her bloody number, but of course, I had to keep receiving her texts on the off chance there was ever a school-related issue we needed to discuss.

Because it would have to be an emergency for me to talk to her. I even went a step further this year and made sure none of my students were in her program.

Voldemort: Fine, be that way, Eli. Don't say I didn't warn you when I'm getting fucked by someone else tonight.

Wow, she really was a class act. Some days, I wondered how I could have been so fooled by her. I could not even bring myself to say her name, the visceral reaction it caused at the pain she had inflicted on my life. If people knew what the true 'Princess of Skating' was like, her popularity would tank with her fans.

Sighing, I turned the volume up on the classical music playing and glanced over at Lucky. He snored softly in his dog bed, and I smiled at the instant comfort he brought me. There was no doubt Lucky had been the one to save me last year when I adopted him after the debacle that my life had become.

He was a Maltese and had become my constant companion, keeping me from falling into a deep depression. Having to take care of and worry about him, allowed me to escape some of the shame I felt after the breakup. Plus, he was adorable. It was hard not to experience happiness when he was around with his cute doggy smile. He was selective about who he gave his affection to, making me feel smug because he loved me. A knock at my door pulled me from my morose thoughts.

"Come in," I called, without looking up from my work. It was probably Rhett, and he was used to my bluntness at this point.

"Hey, man. Did you want to join us for dinner tonight? Soren was thinking of doing something for our last night as five before the new roommates arrive. You down for that?"

I spun around at Rhett's question, taking in my best friend. He was one of the tallest guys I'd ever met, his 6'7" frame making him duck down to peer through the frame. Combined with his dark hair, intense eyebrows, and permanent scowl, most people steered clear of the man. Our friendship was strange to most because we were so different. I could charm almost anyone, and Rhett never bothered, but our friendship worked for us.

Rhett and I were the oldest of our housemates, at twenty-five and twenty-four respectively, and had worked at the school the longest. While Rhett had never left Oak Crest Peek and preferred grunts over words, and I'd traveled more than I'd been settled since the age of five, we'd found an easy friendship through MMA, bonding us together one night during my first year tutoring. His quiet assurance and steadfast nature soon solidified a true friendship.

Nodding, I tossed my pen down, smoothing down my pants. "Sure, I just finished my lesson plans."

Rhett smirked at me, ducking his head back out of the door. He found my anal-retentive tendencies hilarious and often messed with my order to poke at me, not acknowledging his own similarities with fitness and nutrition. I was just posh enough to not comment on it.

Attending boarding school in England had led me to Oxford, which made me the most educated of my housemates, considering the rest were athletes. Thankfully, we all got along and enjoyed living with one another. We had created a family unit over the past few years. They showed me true friendship, and that status, family money, and degrees did not make people more worthy.

If anything, I had learned that all the other things paled in comparison to an authentic friend. My housemates were there for me when the engagement was called off, and my life became gossip fodder. There were things in life that could never be paid back, and it was that way with my housemates.

I followed him into the big living space, Lucky trailing behind me, and found the other guys gathered around the table, dishing out the food. Soren, Rey, and Oliver looked up as we entered and mumbled their greetings around mouthfuls of food before it had even finished hitting their plates. Heathens, I tell you.

"What do you think the new roommates will be like?" Oliver mumbled around a mouth full of food he barely swallowed before asking. Oliver was a big guy, though not as big as Rhett. His ginger hair stuck out of the sides of the toboggan he wore, his chin scruffy with a beard. He was our resident hockey player and a bottomless pit. The guy was habitually eating, and it was rare to find him without something in his hand.

"I only have their names and sport. Mateo, skiing, and Sawyer, skating," I reported, as I prepared my plate like a proper adult.

"I wonder what section of skating," Rey mumbled.

Shrugging my shoulders, I sat down, having no clue on the subject, and attempted to answer him as best as I could. "The information is limited since they were late hires. All I know is to pick them up tomorrow afternoon at the airport. They both land around the same time, thankfully."

The guys accepted my answer, returning to their food. When most of them were done, a quiet conversation started.

"Anyone feel up to a night in town to see if there are any cute tourists? Or is a night chilling here better?" Soren asked.

"I'm leaving tomorrow for that family thing, so I'd rather stay home and not be out late. Plus, I need to pretend to pack," Rey chuckled, a few joining in. Rey was a slob and procrastinator to the highest degree.

Oliver slapped the table when an idea hit him, causing everyone to look. "Rocket League Tournament!"

"Yes! You're on, man!" Soren cheered excitedly, making his way into the game room.

Rhett merely grunted as he started to clean up the mess. He was the house mom, whether he knew it or not. Rhett naturally took care of things for the house and made sure we ate healthily. He checked in with everyone at night and continually made sure we all had whatever we needed. Rhett tended to be quiet in crowds and somehow blended into the background, despite his massive frame. But he was always there, working behind the scenes. He was our protector, even if we were adults. I doubt Rhett knew he did it because it was part of who he was, a product of his upbringing.

Lucky curled up in my lap as we watched the other guys play the game. This game made no sense to me. The players were cars that were playing football, or soccer, as they called it. It was basically bumper car football. It was humorous to watch at least and comforting in a sense.

We might be an odd mesh of guys, but we all understood one another in the ways that mattered. My housemates and I recognized one another's pain, but since we were men, we didn't talk about it openly. Instead, we played video games, punched stuff, and had bro moments to remind one another we were there.

My phone vibrated again, and I was beginning to reconsider my blocking rule, especially if she kept this up—no one needed to be harassed by their ex or continuously barraged with naked pictures. Because yes, she was not above sending them.

Voldemort: Eli, Mommy and Daddy want us to have lunch with them tomorrow. It's about your career path. So, you might not want to ignore me on this one. Lunch is at the club. Wear that blue shirt I got you last year. You look hot in it.
Voldemort: Here's what you're missing out on tonight. *Video attached*

Bloody Hell. There was no way to get out of lunch if

her parents were insisting. They were my bosses, after all.

Fuck, I would have to sit there with her tomorrow and pretend to not hate her fucking guts. She more than likely orchestrated this to get time with me. Nothing was out of the question with her. My ex apparently did not understand what "leave me the fuck alone, you conniving twat. I want nothing to do with you ever again" meant. It felt relatively straightforward to me, but I had also assumed we were in love and agreed to not fuck other people, so maybe I knew nothing after all.

Shoving the phone back in my pocket, I managed to hit the play button on her message. Suddenly, breathy moans filled the room, and I froze. The other guys stopped what they were doing, turning with various looks of surprise on their faces. I had zero interest in seeing whatever she sent, but in my haste to stop it, I fumbled with my phone, unable to get it to do anything other than become louder.

It was stuck half in my pocket and half out—damn skinny legged trousers.

Yanking the phone free, my fingers slipped, and the phone skidded across the room, landing on the floor between Oliver and Soren. We all stared dumbfounded at the device, almost as if it were alive with the sounds we could all hear. Oliver eventually bent over to pick it up, cursing loudly when he saw what was on screen.

"Fuck man, is this who I think it is? Did she really send you a video of her blowing another dude?" Oliver screwed up his face, his tone incredulous, despite knowing better than to be surprised by Voldemort. Raising my eyebrow at him, I said nothing. He shook his head in defeat, sighing as he handed the phone back to me once he stopped the video.

"Thanks, Ollie. I think I could use that drink now," I groaned. The guys gave me reassuring nods, and a couple of slaps on the back as I made my way into the kitchen.

Letting out a deep breath, I shook my head. I hated that it still hurt this much, chastising myself that I should be over it by now. Yet, every time I thought about it, it felt like a glass shard stabbed me, leaving me hemorrhaging everywhere.

I poured two fingers of scotch into a crystal tumbler, tossing it back. The burn slid down my throat, warming my insides in a soft caress. I exhaled the after-burn as it settled in my stomach, relaxing me some.

Remembering her text, I banged my head against the cabinet as I leaned forward. Bollocks!

Lunch tomorrow at the club. With her parents. Bloody Hell.

There was no way I could pick up the new instructors now. I would need to find someone else to get them up in my absence; hopefully, Rhett was available.

sawyer

Packing up my entire life was easier than I anticipated. But to be fair, I didn't have that much to my name to begin with. I signed the contract, completed my physical, and booked my travel arrangements all in a week's time. I'd have three days after arriving to settle in before the term began.

Apparently, the housing arrangement consisted of seven instructors of various sports. I wasn't looking forward to having to share a house with six other females, but at least I would have my own room. Ever since foster care, sleep hadn't felt safe unless I could lock my door, so at least I would have that comfort. It was sharing a house with girls that made me the most anxious, especially competitive ones.

I was the first to admit I was awkward, prone to getting lost in my own thoughts, and had absolutely no filter. When I was nervous or put on the spot, my default response was to be sassy and I frequently blurted out embarrassing things. Charlie had coined it as my 'code orange' moments, and it was aptly named.

In skating, a code orange was when someone had an "ouch" moment that made you cringe, and you knew they were going to need a powerful drug for the pain. Which typically meant I'd gotten myself into a precarious situation and my word vomit detonated. Never a good thing.

My plan over the past five years had been to fade into the background. But it never seemed to work out that way for me. My explosive mouth combined with my awkwardness, and need to protect the underdog didn't lend to making friends easily. And that was why a sixty-year-old man had been my best friend here.

Which, damn, I hadn't expected this level of emotion to hit me at thoughts of leaving the old man.

Charlie had become a surrogate grandfather to me, and I'd miss him. A lot. More than I'd anticipated when I applied for the job, even. Charlie had graciously accepted my news about leaving, surprising me.

"Sawdust, I always knew you were destined for more. I'm proud of you, and your folks would be too."

He tried to hide the tears in his eyes, but I saw them. The depth of the emotion in his words affected me, and soon we both struggled to hold the tears back. I knew no matter what, though, I would always have a home here. It was a level of comfort I didn't realize I needed, or wanted, until that moment.

I knew I needed to leave, but I would miss this place. It was time for me to forge my own way, and I had to believe there was more out there for me. Mostly, I needed to find answers to the night from five years ago that plagued me. The night my whole world shifted on its axis.

Glass shattered around me, and the sound of tires screeching echoed. The smell of burned rubber filled my nostrils, rousing me awake as I came to in an upside-down vehicle.

Where was I? What was going on? Who was scream-

ing? These thoughts ran through my head on a loop as I tried to get my bearings.

"Mom?" I croaked out. No answer.

Why am I upside down?

Hands grabbed me, and a scream escaped me before I realized they were my Dad's.

Shaking me, he started to shout, "Sa……"

I shook off the memory, waving goodbye to Charlie from the curb, as I promised to let him know when I landed. Thankfully, I'd finally convinced him to purchase a cell phone, so it would be easier to reach one another.

Taking a breath, I headed into the airport and headed toward security, wheeling my bag behind me. When I spotted the check bag line, I sighed with even more relief that I didn't need to stop there since I'd shipped most of my belongings ahead.

Once I made it through security, I headed to my gate, the need to be on time riding me hard. There weren't a lot of people at this time of day during the week, so it wouldn't take me long to find my gate. The airport wasn't large, but it was a decent size, with twenty gates providing enough travel for our small town.

Excitement filled me with each step I took, the feeling of being back in an airport enough to boost my mood. I loved flying, but I hadn't gotten the opportunity to in a while. Not really since…

Okay, Sawyer, stop going down that line of thinking.

It wasn't the time to get stuck down memory lane. Inhaling a deep breath, I twirled my necklace for luck and set off toward my gate.

The smile that graced my lips was genuine as I took in all the travelers, shops, and families puttering around the terminals. It was nice to see everyday life happening around me. Spotting a corner bookstore, I decided to grab some snacks for the plane. As I debated between sweet, salty, or sour, I suddenly felt the hair on the back of my neck rise in awareness.

Someone was watching me.

Casually, I chose two random bags and slowly walked up to the register to pay. The whole time I watched my peripherals, looking for the threat, but I didn't find anyone near that looked suspicious. But my intuition had never been wrong.

And someone was there. Watching me. I just knew it.

It only spurred my decision to get out of this town. My awareness of danger had increased over the past six months, amping up my need to leave. Something was coming, and I believed it was coming for me.

The last time I'd felt this, I'd lost everyone important to me. I didn't want to make that mistake again.

Smiling tersely at the cashier, I paid and hurried out of the shop, falling into the crowd of people. Once I left the shop, the feeling of being watched dissipated as the crowd of travelers surrounded me. The creepiness, however, didn't disperse as quickly.

Arriving at my terminal, I grabbed an outward-facing seat with no chairs behind me, giving me a full view of my surroundings. It was these kinds of moves that had become so natural to me now. Putting in my earbuds, I selected a playlist to help distract my mind to pass the time. Now was not the time to lose focus.

When it was time for the flight, I sat down next to the window and watched the other passengers settle themselves, wondering if I would have a seatmate. It was a small plane, considering not many people flew to Utah from Iowa, and I didn't want to be saddled with a talker. When the flight attendants began their flight preparations and safety procedures, I sat back and relaxed.

This was it. My life was about to change. From this point forward, nothing would be the same.

Closing my eyes, I couldn't fight the huge grin that slid across my face. I'd been waiting for this moment for the past five years, and it was finally here. No matter what happened now, it was up to me to figure it out.

Which was exciting, terrifying, and freeing. I'd no longer have to depend on others to make decisions for me.

My future was open, and nothing stood in my way now to make it what I wanted, and I liked that idea a lot.

three

. . .

rey

I jotted down the song lyric that had been playing in my head, humming the tune beneath my breath as I did. A sense of glee at how effortlessly it had come together filled me. I really needed to do this more. A knock at the door had me jumping, and I quickly closed my notebook and shoved it under my pillow. It wasn't something I'd openly shared with anyone, the thought of someone knowing actually sent liquid fear through me.

"Enter!"

Soren stuck his shaggy blonde head into my room, a laid-back smile plastered on his face. "Hey," he greeted as he walked in, dodging my dirty clothes on the floor as he made his way to where I sat on my bed.

Damn, I really needed to pick up my room. It was a

mess, something I never noticed until someone else entered my space and it suddenly all came into focus. I knew my sister would give me hell later too, but I couldn't find the motivation to do it. The familiar heavy fog that encompassed my mind was surrounding me again, and just getting up was difficult enough to wade through it most days. I seemed to only be left with enough energy to train before sleep called me. Lately, it had been coming on more frequently and hanging around longer than ever before. I should be worried about the dark days in my future, but I couldn't muster up the energy to care.

"Rhett just left for the airport to pick up the roomies since Elias had that 'emergency meeting' with the vulture." Soren rolled his eyes as he plopped down onto the bed, stretching out his long limbs. "Too bad you have to wait on your sister, or you could've ridden with him and saved yourself the trip." Soren yawned, his matter-of-fact tone bordering on boredom.

I watched as his band tee rose a little as he situated himself, his arms going behind his head, and I found myself entranced with the little slice of golden skin that peeked out. The knee-jerk reaction to look away was strong, fear I'd be found out if I was caught. It was also too addictive, and the more I stared, the more I wanted. His faded jeans hugged his muscular thighs, causing me to shift in my seat.

Clearing my throat, I looked at the wall as I tried to steer the conversation in a safe direction. "Leave it to her to have a fashion emergency. Some days, I wonder how we're related." I awkwardly laughed.

Soren chuckled under his breath, putting his head on my pillow as he stared up at the ceiling, allowing me to steal another peek. We'd known each other for two years, and he'd become my best friend. He had this wonderful, calming presence about him while also being playful. He was the sunshine to my darkness.

"Are you all packed? Do you need any help?" he asked, rolling his head over to look at me.

"I'm good. Thanks though." I smiled, but it felt a little off and I knew he noticed. One of the greatest things about Soren was the fact he didn't demand things of me, not like my parents did. He would wait until I was ready to share, giving me the choice instead of forcing me.

He rolled his head back, looking at the ceiling before he asked his next question. "Is this that band we heard last month?" His fingers tapped along to the music that I had playing softly.

"Yeah." I grinned, some tension leaving me. "It's Shadows of Mayhem. I'm really liking their new stuff."

"I forgot how good they were," he said, closing his eyes to listen. That was one of the many things we shared, a love of music and discussing the deeper meaning of the lyrics. Soren assumed, though, that my love of music stemmed from my choreography, and was just looking for the next song to use as inspiration. I hadn't worked up the courage to tell him I wrote music yet and wanted to be a songwriter someday.

I knew out of everyone he would understand, but fear stopped me each time. It was becoming harder to keep this from him. Music was in my soul, and I desperately needed it. Without it, I feared I wouldn't even be able to breathe.

I glanced over at Soren again, letting myself look now since his eyes were closed. Over the past year, we'd gotten closer. He was the first person I'd truly connected with, in… well, I didn't want to think about how long.

My feelings had started to morph into more, and I found myself feeling differently around him. I'd started to notice him in a not purely platonic way. It had surprised me since I'd never been attracted to guys before. It had seriously made me question what was going through my head.

Which led me to research my growing attraction, and what it could be. Facts were safe, ambiguity not so much. So, when in doubt, I researched.

It led me down a lot of interesting paths, to say the least, and so I started to test out the questions I had.

When I didn't get a reaction in my pants when I scoped out other attractive guys, I concluded I wasn't bisexual. Adding in the fact I didn't get turned on watching gay porn, I felt it was accurate.

However, I did discover I was aroused by videos of a girl being shared with another guy. Particularly, when I imagined Soren and me as being the two guys. Although, just fantasizing about Soren and me together was arousing. Ultimately, my research led me to believe I was demisexual, meaning it was more about a deep personal connection with a person in order to be intimate with them, and it wasn't based on gender.

It was like a weight was lifted from me, explaining all my prior unsatisfactory sexual experiences too, since I didn't date. I would occasionally accompany the guys to town and hook up with a stranger, but I never felt a connection and always hated myself afterward. Since it had all been physical, it would never be what I wanted. Turned out, I was a relationship guy.

But it was hard to connect with people when your heart already belonged to someone else, maybe two someone else's.

I cleared my throat, pulling myself out of my thoughts. "So, how were the slopes today?" I asked Soren as he continued to stare at the ceiling.

A smile lit up his stunning face as he recalled his snowboarding run this afternoon. I swear, the way Soren described snow at times was almost pornographic. His joy was evident in his words with how much he loved to board. I could listen to him talk about boarding for hours even if I didn't understand half of what he was saying. He just made you want to listen.

"It was perfect, and there was hardly anyone there since the students aren't here yet. Hopefully, I can get in another run before classes start."

Soren was a world-class snowboarder, but he didn't want fame—something we both had in common. He enjoyed the freedom of training others and getting to still do what he loved without having to regularly one-up himself.

"So... are you going to tell me what has been bothering you for the past few days?" Soren asked out of the blue. Sometimes I forgot that just because he was laid-back, it didn't mean he wasn't perceptive.

"I don't know what you mean, man." I shrugged as I fiddled with my phone. "Just the start of a new semester. You know how it gets." I tried to brush off his concern, looking everywhere but at him.

"I'm just worried about you, Rey. The last time you were brooding, you went to a dark place, and I didn't know if I'd get you back," Soren replied, sincerity thick in his voice. He sat up on his elbows, forcing me to look at him. "You're my best friend, dude, and I know that we're guys, and we're not always the best at asking each other to talk about our emotions, but I hope you know you can trust me with that stuff."

Soren stared into my eyes with such care that it caused me to suck in a breath. This was why. This was why I had started to have feelings for this man. He didn't care if he sounded like a weirdo openly talking about his feelings. He genuinely cared about me and wanted me to feel okay. As I continued to gaze into his eyes, I almost blurted it all out. But I didn't feel ready for that... yet. So instead, I decided to start with something equally as frightening.

Clearing my throat nervously, I let out a breath. "Well, there is something... I've never told anyone this before, but..." I stopped, clearing my throat again.

Damn, why was I so fucking nervous? It was just Soren! If anyone would understand, it was him. Slowly, I pulled my notebook out from under my pillow. "The thing is," I started again. "You see...," I stammered. For fuck's sake, I needed to get it together. Suddenly, he grabbed the notebook out of my hand, halting my poor attempts to explain. I began to protest when he opened it, freezing me to the spot.

Someone was reading my words.

No, not *someone*—Soren.

Soren was reading my lyrics, my very essence, the one place where I was myself, without fear of judgment. Writing music gave me an escape, and I could put down all my feelings, fears, desires, and sometimes, my hopes. It was dangerous to think that way, though. Hope made me vulnerable. I stared at my hands, twisting the ring on my thumb as Soren held my heart in his hands... though I doubted he knew that.

Twisting the ring, it brought me some comfort. It was one of those stupid quarter machine prizes. It was made of cheap metal that had tarnished over the years, now a dark metal, though it had been silver once. I'd gotten it as a joke, but now it was one of my most valued possessions. I never took it off, always twisting it when I was nervous. It was soothing.

"Did you write these?" Soren finally asked. Nodding my head in the affirmative, I couldn't look up yet, nor say anything. Sitting there, trying to remember how to breathe, I waited for Soren to rip my heart to shreds and watch me bleed out with his judgment.

"Wow."

Awe, and something unrecognizable, filled his voice, causing me to snap my head up, unsure I'd heard him correctly.

"Why haven't you shared these with me before, man?" Soren questioned curiously. Shrugging in response, I still wasn't sure if I could use my voice.

"These are great. I can't wait to hear the songs. They have a real James Arthur feel to them. Gritty. Raw. Real." He finished looking at the book, glancing up at me and all I could do was stare at him in shock, convinced I'd heard him wrong.

"So, will you?" Soren asked again, his voice taking on a breathy quality I'd never heard from him before.

"Hu-h?" I eventually managed to stutter, still staring at him. Clearly, he'd hit his head today when he was out. Tilting my head to the side, I studied him, trying to gauge him for a concussion. Soren just kept staring back at me in earnest.

"You're serious? You like them? They aren't juvenile garbage?" I challenged him, disdain dripping from my words. Soren shook his head, swishing his hair back and forth across his face.

"Nah, I think these are real. I can't believe you've been able to keep this a secret. I thought we told each other everything." Soren smiled, but I could hear the hurt in his words.

I exhaled deeply, not wanting him to feel that way and needing to get my own insecurity locked down. "I haven't ever told anyone, Soren. You're the first." I managed to get it out without stuttering this time, and the smile he graced me with almost made my heart stop.

It was official. I couldn't deny it any longer—my feelings for Soren were real. And while that gave me a sense of peace, it didn't help me figure out what to do with them. I had no idea if he even thought of me that way. How do you even tell if a guy likes you? Guess it was time to do some more research.

"Cool," Soren answered simply, his smile permanently etched across his lips. "Are these about her?" he asked quietly.

"Yeah. Some of the songs are about her, but not all of them," I admitted, hoping he wouldn't read too much into that answer since some of them were very clearly about hidden desire. My voice had even taken on a heady quality I hoped wasn't detectable. I wasn't ready to bear my whole heart today. Surprisingly, I did feel lighter letting him in on my secret.

"I want to pursue songwriting after I leave TAS."

"You should, Rey. I'd definitely listen to them. You have real talent. I'm sort of in awe of you right now," he said, smiling so big, one of his dimples popped out. His compliment made me blush, and I shifted uncomfortably. Soren, being Soren, noticed and blessedly changed the subject.

He laid back down with his arms behind his head, causing more of his shirt to rise, displaying not only his golden skin and toned abs, but also the light hair leading into his pants. I licked my lips unconsciously, discreetly shifting my cock as I began to get hard. Knowing that Soren didn't wear underwear was all I could think about now. His cock was right there, only inches from me, and I could… I snapped my eyes back up, hoping he hadn't noticed me checking out his junk. Fortunately, he had his eyes closed as he talked.

I tuned back into what he was saying. "So, what do you think the new roommates will be like? Man, I hope they're not assholes. I like the vibe we have in the house right now with the five of us, you know."

"Yeah, me too," I replied. "We'll figure it out. If anything, we can chill together if they're complete douches." I shrugged. I didn't know if I wanted to make any more friends since I had my group here at the house and a few select others. I liked it that way. A small circle was preferable to me.

"Humph. How long do you have until you need to leave?" Soren asked, not worried. He didn't need to be though, he liked everyone. He was friendly and outgoing, so he didn't understand my aversion to new people at times.

"I have an hour. We could watch some Schitt's Creek?" I suggested. We had started watching it last week and had quickly become obsessed.

"Sure," he answered as he grabbed the remote and queued up the next episode and we laughed a lot at David and Stevie on screen. I kept casually glancing over at him, watching his profile more than the episode, laughing when he did. When it ended, I gathered my bags and headed out to my car. I went to wave goodbye when Soren pulled me into a tight hug.

We'd hugged several times before, but this felt different. Or was that just me, imagining it? Please, don't let it just be me.

four

· · ·

sawyer

Stepping out of the airport, I inhaled the fresh air deeply, filling my lungs with the clean mountain air. The rugged, snow-covered peaks in the distance were breathtaking, and I felt something in me settle just by being here. It was nothing like back home, where it was cornfields and flat land for days. The weather here was also strange for September, staying at around 50°F during the day and dropping lower at night. When I'd looked it up to pack, I'd been amazed to learn that while the mountains had snowcaps, the snow didn't accumulate below until October. It was one of the reasons the school year started late September, giving the students plenty of time to train and have fresh snow.

I inhaled again, trying to see if I could smell the snow or taste it in the air. As strange as that might sound when I was a child, my mother would take me outside before a snowstorm and we'd run around in our pajamas trying to taste the air and predict the snow. She swore by this method, always knowing when it would snow before even the meteorologists.

Even now, I couldn't help but try to find the smell and taste of a well-spent childhood in each snowflake. Opening my eyes, giddy excitement overtook me as the reality of my new home sunk in. With the mountains in the distance and the picturesque city around me, I felt very fortunate to be here. This was it, my new beginning.

The Aldridge School was a thirty-five-minute drive from the airport, so I wouldn't have to wait much longer before I stepped onto campus. As I glanced around, my eyes became snagged on another pair of eyes, so intensely focused on me it made it difficult to breathe. *I could get lost in those eyes.* He had the most severe eyebrows I'd ever seen, I wondered if they had their own language.

Seriously, did he practice that look or did it just come naturally?

Right now, his eyebrows strongly proclaimed they were not amused. If "I have no more fucks to give" had a look, it would be *that* look. As I continued to inspect his face, my eyes lingered over his lips that were very distractedly turned downward in a, you guessed it, frown. Yep, it was official; this guy was not amused.

Chuckling silently in my head, I recalled an episode of *Doctor Who*, where Rose and the Doctor kept trying to get the Queen to state, "I am not amused!" Oh, what I wouldn't give to have them here right now to play that game.

Smiling at the thought, I kept up my perusal of this broody man candy. Frowny McFrownerson's jaw was peppered with stubble that was seriously lickable. He had a strong jawline and the plumpest lips. Subconsciously, I licked my own as I examined him further. He was a proper stud that had been bestowed upon me and it was my job to perform my due diligence.

Utah, you were officially my favorite place. Thank you for welcoming me to this beautiful city.

Traveling further down his body, I realized that those dark, dangerous eyes were attached to the tallest man I'd ever seen, and this guy, he was all man. He had to be at least 6'7", which made him more than a foot taller than me!

Granted, I was short, but I bet I would barely come to his abs. Abs that I could clearly see outlined through his skin tight shirt. I wondered if clothing designers advertised their clothes to guys with slogans like "will make all the girls drool at your abs," because if so, pay that marketing company all the money!

It clearly worked. *Dayum*! Wiping my mouth, I made sure there wasn't any drool lingering there. So far, his dark hair, piercing eyes, bronze skin, and muscular body were making me drool. I didn't know if I'd be able to stand once I made my way down the rest of him, but it was a crime not to.

Drifting further down his torso to take in the goods,

I noticed he held a sign down by his side. Peering closer at the font, I realized what it said: *S. Sullivan*.

Oh shit.

rhett

I was frustrated and I'd only been at this damn airport for five minutes. Sighing, I checked my watch again, but it only confirmed what I knew. These five minutes felt like an hour to me. I hated standing around nor was I a patient person by nature. Plus, I didn't like being in crowds of people. My size alone made it difficult to navigate, and I always worried I'd run over someone.

Most importantly though, my schedule had been thrown off and now I was itching to readjust it. I was supposed to be back at the house for my afternoon post-workout cool down and smoothie, but instead, I found myself agreeing to help Elias. I wouldn't want to trade places with him though. His "emergency" meeting with the banshee wouldn't be fun either, so while I'd grumble about it, my best friend needed me and I'd be there for him. Relationships were important to me, and I protected the ones I had.

Shifting on my feet, I rubbed the back of my head, dropping the sign down to my side. A few girls walked by, giving me looks, but I ignored them. In fact, I ignored them all, including the other instructors at the school. They didn't interest me, and I didn't waste time socializing with them. Honestly, I preferred it that way.

The house—along with my roommates—was where I spent most of my time outside of training. It had become my home in the past five years I'd worked at TAS as a fitness trainer. It worked out since I was passionate about fitness and it allowed me to be close to my family in the process. We were locals, and I'd grown up in this town. This job was an easy gig with excellent perks. It was stable, and best of all, predictable. I liked the predictability.

There had been a lot of uncertainty growing up, so now I craved consistency, a schedule, and a routine. The physical aspect of my job was also a bonus. I got to stay in shape and help athletes. The students were alright, for the most part. They were focused and dedicated to their sport, so they typically listened to what I had to say, knowing it could be what gave them the edge over their competition.

Shifting on my feet again, I sighed. Waiting for these two to arrive was driving me crazy. Peering around, I noticed a tiny, curvy woman walk out of the airport doors. She didn't appear to notice me as she breathed in the fresh mountain air, her shoulders relaxing as she gazed around at the city I'd grown up in. I could make out her excitement and appreciation for her surroundings, and for the first time I wondered if she was a tourist or athlete here for training.

The city was well-known to athletes for training

during the off season. And I really hoped she was here for longer than a weekend.

As I watched her, I noticed how her hair shimmered in the sun, cascading around her in gentle waves. Her face was truly mesmerizing, full of hope and fire. She had full, rosy cheeks that squished when she smiled, a button nose, and a pointed chin drawing attention to her lips. I couldn't tell the color of her eyes yet as they were still closed, but I knew no matter what, they'd be magnetic. Taking advantage of her distraction, I used it to check her out thoroughly.

The more I took her in, I felt how odd it was for me to check out a girl. I just didn't do it, generally steering far away from the female sex. Typically, my face screamed "unapproachable" or "stay the fuck away" and people left me alone. It worked since I found people to be exhausting, and I really didn't like meeting them. The amount of energy it took to get to know people was draining. I considered myself a reasonably attractive guy, and the workouts helped keep me fit, but I didn't enjoy the attention I gained from women. In fact, it usually made me uncomfortable how girls would throw themselves at me in some misguided effort to cure me of my grumpiness or, even worse, live out some fantasy like I was some alpha a-hole from a romance book.

In reality, I was the nice guy, or boy next door. I just didn't want to date and wasn't interested in hooking up. That fact didn't stop the female instructors at school from trying, despite my brashness toward them. Elias swore my behavior only made them try harder. I was beginning to realize he might have a point.

Grunting, I made my way down her body and noticed her delicate collar bones as they peeked out of her green top. Her arms were covered by the long sleeves, but her breasts were accentuated by the deep v-cut of her shirt. She seemed to have muscular arms, her frame showing her strength despite her petiteness. Her hips were curvy, and her powerful leg muscles were defined through her black leggings.

If she wasn't an athlete, this girl was at least into fitness based on her build and the way she carried herself. She had an awareness of her body and how to move it that was evident in how she stood. There was a sense of grace about her as well. From her blonde hair, curves, and creamy skin, I found her to be breathtaking.

Shaking my head, I wondered what the hell was wrong with me. I didn't check out girls or talk about them with words such as, 'delicate collarbones,' and 'gracefulness.' Scoffing at myself, I frowned harder. I'd been hanging out with Rey's sister too much lately.

Trying to clear my head of these ridiculous thoughts, when I looked over again I noticed she was looking back at me. Her eyes were the deepest green that pulled me under in an instant. In that moment, I knew I was in trouble. *Shit.*

She gazed back, and it felt as if she was speaking to my soul with her eyes. She slowly started to make her way down my body, and I could almost feel her eyes touching me everywhere she looked. I was unable to scowl or deny her from taking her fill. The confidence in this girl was hot as Hell. She licked her lips as she made her way down to my abs, and the gesture set off a chain reaction in me. Shifting, I worried she was about to get a show if she kept devouring me with her eyes like that.

Abruptly, she snapped her head back to my eyes, a look of shock covering her face. Lifting my eyebrow up higher, a move I'd practiced in the mirror as a teen, I questioned her shocked expression. The eyebrow represented everything I wanted to convey. It was the perfect expression for someone who didn't like to talk. Smirking at her, I tried to gauge her expression, still unsure what had made that shock look on her face appear.

Perhaps I was sporting wood after all? She definitely had that effect on me.

Maybe I had stains on my clothes? After all, I'd just finished a workout before coming here, so who knew.

But why would that shock her? I didn't care about my appearance, and took no time to sort out clothes that weren't athletic wear. It was another way I kept people at a distance, but I was beginning to regret my gray sweats and t-shirt if it made her react that strongly.

Figured. I was finally attracted to someone and they were superficial.

sawyer

Well, shit. The guy I'd been eye-fucking for the past five minutes—like I wanted to lick him all over—was my fucking ride to school. I mean, I did want to lick him all over, but that wasn't the first impression I wanted to make when starting a new job. Leave it to me to get a sexual harassment case before I even stepped foot on campus.

Snapping my head up so quickly hadn't been a good idea either, considering I might've given myself whiplash. Damn, he was tall.

Acting like I hadn't been about to check out his junk, I stared at him sheepishly. But seriously, could a girl be held accountable for her eyes when he was wearing that? Do guys not know the ultimate thirst trap gray sweatpants were to girls? I bet they used the same marketing company as that damn shirt! It should be against the law, or at least come with a warning.

Warning!! Danger!! Drool alert incoming! Walk away now, or you may embarrass yourself!

When I met his eyes, he no longer frowned but instead had an eyebrow lifted—knew they had their own language—and amusement danced in his eyes. He sported a slight smirk, raising one side of those plump lips a fraction. It was as if he was asking, "do you like what you see?"

I decided to roll with it since I couldn't rewind time and stop undressing him outside the airport since I sadly wasn't the traveling companion of Doctor Who. Time to own it.

Sticking out my hand, I placed it on my hip and posed for him. Motioning with the other as if to say, "go ahead, big guy, your turn," I swept it down the length of my 5'2" frame. I swear I heard him laugh. It was so quiet, though, that I couldn't be entirely sure, but I was confident I saw his smirk widen a smidge.

Secretly high-fiving myself in my head at the victory, I made it my new goal to get him to smile more. Because damn… that tiny lift of his lips was breathtaking, and I was sure the whole smile might be life-altering.

As he scanned me slowly, his eyes lingered on my body, touching me gently with their appraisal, and I felt a blush rising to the surface. I wasn't one of those people who could hide it, either. I was fair-skinned with blonde hair and short, which meant my whole body conveyed my awkwardness as my face heated. Not going to let that stop me, I smirked back at him. That's right, hottie frown guy, I could smirk too.

With as much confidence as possible, I sauntered up to Frowny McFrownerson, but my hand decided to go rogue and waved awkwardly. Did I seriously just do that? He kept staring at me, probably in shock as well from my awkward middle school wave, or just because he couldn't believe I was actually walking up to him. He did give off the "do not approach" vibe with that frowny face, probably scaring off most of the population from that look alone.

Unfortunately for him, I'd lived with the ultimate grump for the past three years, so I was All-Pro in all the ways to handle a grumpy soul. And since it appeared we'd be working together, I was making it my mission to crack his shell. I mean, if I got to look at his hotness in the process, I wasn't sure what I was really losing here.

Nothing, that's what.

"Hi, I'm Sawyer," I replied bashfully, my confidence vanishing the second I opened my mouth. He continued to stare at me with those soulful eyes of his. Seriously, this guy should've gone into the CIA. No terrorist would stand a chance against him and his stare. They'd be spilling all their secrets in thirty seconds flat.

"You know, Sawyer," I tried again. This time I motioned toward the sign he held flat at his side. Still, he continued to stare at me with that hypnotic eyebrow arched.

Okay, maybe I'd misjudged this frowny guy wrong. Could he be a typical douchey jock type purposefully ignoring me? Or perhaps he was mute?

Since I didn't feel any weird vibes, I decided to go with mute. That squawky lady really should've given me a heads up. I could've avoided this whole situation where I made a fool of myself. But nope, all I got from her was an email stating, "a representative from the school will be at the airport to deliver you to campus."

Representative my ass, this guy was a fucking

walking hazard for womankind with those delicious… Focus Sawyer! Right.

"Okay," I mumbled, shaking my head in resolve, planning to conquer this and make an excellent first impression with my co-worker. "I… AM… SAWYER," I said slowly, pronouncing each word carefully and then pointing toward the sign.

He continued to smirk at me like it was his job.

Well then, he wasn't going to make this easy on me. That was cool, sexy eyebrows; I would earn that smile again.

I started to repeat my name slowly when I realized how much of an idiot I must sound like. Duh, Sawyer, he was mute. Not Deaf.

I needed to ask yes or no questions so he could nod. Feeling more confident this time with a solution, I grabbed the sign he was holding and pointed. "I'm S. Sullivan. These are all of my bags. Can you lead the way to the car?"

His response wasn't what I'd expected at all. Honestly, I think I broke him. His face went slack, so I waved my hand in front of his face, worried he was stroking or something. The most resounding boom emerged as he bent over in laughter.

Dropping my hand, I stepped back, having never heard such a delicious sound before. It rolled over my body, eliciting a shudder out of me. Oh damn, this man's voice was pure sex.

I was in trouble, *big* trouble.

If I was having a visceral reaction to his laugh, it

might kill me if he said my name. The dark timbre of his voice resonated within my bones, seductively caressing me on the inside.

God, I hoped he laughed often, and I'd get to see him more. I could already tell I'd crave that laugh. It was addictive, and I was officially an addict.

He stood back up, clutching his middle, dragging his hand down his shirt drawing my focus back to his abs. Seriously, superb marketing people. 100% approve.

Yummy.

I licked my lips again, preparing to say something witty and sexy, no doubt, but instead, code orange made an appearance.

Kill me now. Please.

rhett

Her shock faded away to appraisal, and instead of being embarrassed by checking me out, this girl, she owned it.

God, she was fucking adorable.

She cocked out that delectable hip and jutted out her arm. Almost as if saying, "go ahead, fair game" not realizing I'd already checked her out when her eyes had been closed.

Deciding to accept her invitation since I'd been doing it

covertly before, I took my time, taking in my fill of her. The skill of being covert was something I'd learned at a young age. Maybe I should give her a few pointers? I quietly laughed at my joke and her antics when I noticed a blush spreading across her rosy cheeks. Dropping my eyes, I took in the rest of her, confirming my earlier assessment.

Whoever this beautiful girl was, she was exactly my type.

Shaking my head, I needed to clear my thoughts before they got away from me. I couldn't fall for her yet; I didn't even know if I'd ever see her beyond this moment, so there was no point getting my heart involved.

She lightly chuckled, the sound setting my lungs on fire, as she walked over and waved. My smile lifted a smidge at that. She really was adorable. Not to mention the fact that she had some big ovaries, as my little sister would say. Rowan had told me once that it shouldn't be balls since ovaries were tougher, and I couldn't fault her logic.

When most girls approached me, they'd shyly flirt, and when I didn't make a move to approach them, they'd set their sights on easier prey. Except in this situation, I felt like the prey in her sights and I was about to be eaten.

What was even more outrageous, for the first time in five years, I wanted to be consumed by someone. I wanted to be consumed by her.

That thought rocked me to my core, its foreignness

taking me by surprise. Though, not nearly as much as the conversation that followed.

"Hi, I'm Sawyer," she stated, looking at me.

It felt like that was supposed to mean something, so I waited to see what she would do next. But I also didn't want to make it too easy on her, so I stayed quiet.

Really, I liked her sass and wanted to see more of it. Her voice was hypnotic, and I rolled her name around in my brain. *Sawyer*. It suited her—nothing ordinary for this girl.

"You know, *Sawyer*," she huffed this time, pointing at my junk.

I cocked my eyebrow at that. Why was she pointing at my crotch? Was I supposed to know her? Oh shit, did Elias set me up and send me to pick up his booty call again? I was going to kill him. This girl was not a hookup type of girl. I could feel it in my heart that she was different. This girl was the forever type of girl. I wouldn't debase her by letting her go through with it.

I started to devise a plan on how I could convince her to not go on this date with Elias, but with me instead, when she began to speak loudly, aggressively pointing at my dick. Seriously, if she kept giving him all this attention, he would stand up and wave. But why was she speaking so slowly now? Did she think I was deaf?

Realizing I hadn't said anything to her yet, absorbed in my head with thoughts of her, I started to introduce myself when she suddenly grabbed the sign out of my hand, pointed at the name on it, and said sweetly, "I'm

S. Sullivan, these are all of my bags. Can you lead the way to the car?" I stared at her for a minute, my face going blank as I processed her words.

I couldn't help it. The laugh bubbled out of me at full force, and I grabbed my middle as I bent over laughing before I could stop it. I couldn't believe my luck. The guys were going to shit themselves when she walked in the door.

She didn't know it yet, but S. Sullivan was one of our new roommates. And at that moment, I vowed to make her MINE.

I stood back up, straightening out my shirt, mostly just pushing it down over my abs to direct her attention to them again. It might have been awhile since I'd been with the opposite sex, but I could still flirt.

Her face had fallen into a confused frown at my laughter, but the expression looked cute on her. I also happened to notice how her body responded to my voice, her shiver so not weather-related.

Oh, baby, this was going to be fun. A spark I hadn't felt in years lit up inside me, flaring to life.

five

. . .

mateo

Stepping out of the airport, I looked around for the representative the school said they would be sending some guy named Elias—my new roommate. I was hopeful about this fresh start, especially with how things had ended for me at the end of the last circuit. My parents weren't happy with me, but I had to stop living for them and focusing on my needs, my wants, and what I was comfortable with. It was hard for me to switch my brain to think that way, though, when my whole life, I'd been living it for others.

My parents were first-generation immigrants from Guatemala and had sacrificed a lot to come to America. They had settled into a small town in Colorado, Wood-glen Springs. Their sacrifice had been drilled into my siblings and me as soon as we could understand words. Being the youngest of three had left me with big shoes to fill. My older brother was in his first year of residency as a surgeon, and my sister was starting her first year of law school. They'd both willingly followed the path my parents had set for them.

Me, on the other hand, that was a different story. I'd never been the best student , and I was often unfocused in class. I hated speaking up and my anxiety would overwhelm me to the point I couldn't ask questions when I didn't understand something. All of that resulted in me being an average student and, therefore, the disappointment of my family.

That was until I found skiing.

When I was eight-years-old, my only friend, Samuel, had invited me to travel with his family to Aspen. His family was wealthy and had a vacation home there. And while it was only an hour's drive south, it was still out of my family's budget. My parents had felt embarrassed that his family paid for everything, but eventually, they decided it was a more significant slight to reject their hospitality than to accept it.

Considering I was eight, I didn't care about family appearances and was just excited to spend time with my friend, away from my siblings. Growing up, I'd always felt cast in my siblings' shadows, never able to sparkle as brightly as they did. On that trip, I was introduced to something spectacular—skiing.

And I just so happened to excel at it.

When I had strapped on those skis for the first time, it felt like part of me had finally fit. By the end of the week, I was skiing down the more challenging slopes and loving every second of it. I was already craving my next time back on the snow, not understanding the money aspect of the sport.

All I knew was, I'd been good at something and it made me happy.

Fortunately for me, Samuel's parents had a lot of extra ski gear, so they provided me with the necessary equipment in the beginning. The lift fees, on the other hand, were my true hurdle.

I begged and pleaded, promising to work in my parent's grocery store more, do odd jobs in the neighborhood, and stay out of trouble at home. But it still wasn't enough for consistent training and ski time.

When I was ten, I got a lucky break.

Samuel's parents had been supportive of my dream from the start and helped me find scholarships for ski clubs. I didn't know it at the time, but they'd decided to be my benefactor but knew my parents' pride wouldn't accept them paying for everything outright, so they set up a scholarship fund for me to access so I could join in the ski club. The scholarship covered all of my lift fees, club dues, and gave me a stipend for equipment.

Once I made the ski team, doors began to open for me. Initially, I didn't feel the pressure, just happy to enjoy skiing just to ski. On the slopes, I felt free and whole. There wasn't any comparing myself to my siblings.

My family wasn't outwardly negative toward me, but their disdain and contempt were evident in their behavior. School hadn't gotten any easier, and I was constantly compared to my siblings by teachers who didn't understand why I wasn't as 'smart' as them. To my peers, I was the quiet skiing freak who inconsistently attended school. It made it even more difficult to make friends by being a skiing protege, even more than when I'd been an outcast.

Skiing allowed me to shed my feelings of failure, giving me room to breathe.

My parents took notice of my skiing when I was fourteen. This was after I'd won a couple of small competitions and had been recognized in a few prestigious ones that year.

Skiing at an almost level seven, I'd started training nonstop to reach it. Level seven meant bigger competitions and rewards. My parents became obsessive about my training when they recognized the prestige and opportunities it could offer me.

But slowly the one thing I'd had for me... disappeared.

By the time I was eighteen, I was skiing at level nine and made the Olympic team. I competed in the Alpine Skiing and Freestyle categories and walked away with a Silver in Downhill, Bronze in Giant Slalom, and a Gold in Moguls.

I should've felt happy, but I only felt empty inside.

And while I was offered numerous sponsorships from equipment companies to aftershave, it wasn't enough for my parents. *I wasn't enough.*

They wanted me to keep training and win even more medals, specifically gold, at the next Olympics.

Three medals at eighteen, and I felt unworthy.

At the last qualifying events this past season, I buckled under the pressure. I was hounded continuously on how to be better, be more, advance our culture, and bring honor to our family. Somehow, I'd become the representative for all Hispanics in my parents' eyes. Talk about pressure.

Skiing was no longer my safe place. It had become an enormous shadow I couldn't escape, suffocating me to the point it stole away my joy and freedom. I'd become a skiing robot monkey. I couldn't take it anymore.

Unfortunately, I didn't handle it well, making a reckless decision and ultimately bringing shame to my family, proving to them I wasn't the answer.

This job was hopefully a way for me to regain myself. To find joy in skiing again. My therapist thought it would be a healthy environment for me, as well.

Yeah… I had to see a therapist now. It was court ordered after my 'incident.'

Peering around the drop off and loading area, I spotted a giant guy with a tiny girl waving around a sign. She looked kind of cute from here, but I doubted she'd ever notice me with a guy like that around. I glanced at the guy closer, noticing the school logo on his shirt.

Wonderful, this must be my new roommate. I started to make my way over to them when the mountain of a man doubled over and bellowed out a deep laugh. They didn't appear to notice me, so I sucked in a breath to introduce myself.

"Uh, hi… I'm Mateo. I think I'm your new roommate?" I questioned, nervously hoping I had the right guy.

"Wait, you can fucking talk?" the cute girl blurted at the mountain at the same time I spoke. She turned to me wide-eyed and then immediately covered her mouth, horrified.

The mountain straightened, eying me up and down as she frantically tried to dissolve into a puddle. *You have nothing to worry about, mountain. I'm a nobody.* He flicked his eyes back at her, softening his features.

"Sorry, baby. I didn't have the opportunity to introduce myself to you earlier. You know, on account of our mutual eye-fucking of one another?" He smirked, glancing at me again. "But it looks like we can leave now that Mateo is here."

I noticed the blonde's cheeks blushing at his mention of the word fuck. Even mine did a little. I didn't know if I could ever say that word out loud. It wasn't something I'd ever been allowed to say at home.

"I'm Rhett."

He tried to say it nonchalantly, but I could hear the heat and possession in his voice. He wanted her and wanted me to know it. She glanced back, chuckling when she noticed my shirt. Hmph. Maybe this wasn't meant to be my fresh start after all. I was beginning to feel offended by their reaction to me. When her voice washed over me in a warm embrace, though, I quickly changed my mind.

"I like your shirt. I know it's cliché, but Pikachu and Eevee are my favorites," the blonde replied kindly. She had the most captivating eyes and smiled at me softly, making me melt. Instantly, I felt at ease.

"Um, sorry about my outburst. I'm Sawyer. I don't usually scream at people, it's just been a weird few minutes and for some reason, I thought he was mute, and yeah… word vomit," she sheepishly admitted, her cheeks becoming even more rosy.

"I thought it was cute." I shrugged. Apparently word vomit was contagious and my cheeks flamed at my admittance. Back peddling, I stuttered out, "Um, I mean, well, you see, I, uh."

Her laughter stopped my spluttering in my tracks, and I realized she wasn't laughing at me, but at the situation we'd found ourselves in, both unable to control our words.

Sawyer's laughter was infectious and I joined in with her as I felt my anxiety lessen. Maybe I had found somewhere to fit in after all. Making this choice for myself had allowed me to trust my own judgment for once. Plus, if I could learn how to communicate with a girl without embarrassing myself, I'd be further ahead in life than I'd been before arriving.

My therapist was right, and each win I had for myself helped my confidence grow. I knew now that my anxiety wouldn't ever be completely gone, but I could learn to accept myself and maybe, find others who did as well.

Maybe…

I felt myself smile a little at that thought. I could get behind, 'maybe,' especially if she was here.

sawyer

If I were an emoji, I'd definitely be the facepalm one. I was still reeling from the fact I'd shouted at the hot grump, and worse, had a witness to my crazy ramblings. *Abort. Abort.* I was not winning today on first impressions.

I was beginning to believe I needed that blue box more and more in my life. *Doctor, take me away.*

Oh wait, that was Calgon. Shit, I couldn't even get my slogans together.

It seemed to have worked out okay, at least I hope it had. I would really like to be friends with these guys if they didn't think I was a total looney tune. Hottie grump, or Rhett, needed to quit saying things like eye-fucking to me though. My whole mind blanked when that word crossed his lips and all I could do was think, yes, please! So, I blamed him for making my brain short-circuit at the admittance.

The new guy was cute as well with his glasses and nerdy t-shirt that read, *"Gotta catch them all"* with a

Pokeball in the center and *"ultimate thirst trap"* at the bottom. I appreciated his nerd humor. I fist-bumped myself when I didn't say anything else embarrassing, hoping I'd be okay after all. Except, when he told me my outburst was cute, I'd almost melted. His voice was soft and soothing, and he had a slight accent indicative of his Hispanic heritage and upbringing.

Rhett led us to the car once he realized neither of us had any other bags. We were quiet as we made our way there, and I was surprised when Mateo stepped in front of me to open the door. I smiled up at him in thanks. He wasn't as tall as Rhett, but he was still taller than me, and I'd guess around 5'11" or 6 ft.

Matteo blushed, which, you know, made me blush because, apparently, I suffered from reciprocal blushing. He was sweet and smelled nice, even after being on a plane for hours. I tried to covertly take another whiff of him as I got into the car.

Grapefruit. Red Grapefruit. It fit him. Clean, but energizing and fresh.

The butterflies began to flutter in my stomach, and I smiled again at Mateo when he shut the door. The winner for most smiles in the past hour goes to me!

He ducked his head, his raven hair falling over his glasses and I bit back the urge to push it out of the way for him. It was thick and wavy, and I instantly wanted to run my fingers through it. Why did guys have such great hair? Seriously, so not fair! He settled into the passenger seat without another word.

Looking up, I instantly became ensnared with

Rhett's eyes. He smoldered and I felt on the verge of a spontaneous orgasm. If anyone had that power, it would be him. I just knew it.

I was in danger if he ever took off his shirt in front of me and I got to see his abs on full display.

But also, I desperately needed to make that scenario happen. Because if any abs needed to be on display for the world to see, it was definitely his.

He smirked at me before backing out of the parking space, acting like he knew what I was thinking. Shit, I hoped not.

I sat back nonchalantly, trying to throw him off. I couldn't make it too easy on the dude. I smiled mischievously to myself when he started to shift uncomfortably. I hadn't even been in this state for thirty minutes, and I was already lusting after two guys. What was in this mountain air? Maybe I was suffering from altitude delirium or some shit. Was that a thing? It should definitely be a thing. Yep. That was it. *Altitude induced delirium.*

Most of the drive to campus was quiet as we all took in the scenery, each of us in our own worlds. I'd never lived directly around mountains, so everything was new and exciting; it was breathtaking to witness nature's beauty. A sense of peace washed over me, relaxing me even more on how right this decision to come here had been. This job and move were offering me more than I'd anticipated. I leaned against the window, content to watch it all. The car was quiet and peaceful, and I found I felt comfortable with both of them.

When we pulled onto the campus, I was once again awestruck. It was beautiful with all the wood and stone buildings, giant trees, and mountains in the backdrop. There weren't a lot of people on campus yet since only staff had arrived at this point.

I could already tell I would like this place. I just hoped it would lead me in the direction I needed to be as well.

six

soren

Once Rey left, the house was quiet. Between the five of us, it was rare it was ever empty, so I didn't know what to do with it. I decided to head to the living room and wait for Rhett to return with the new roommates. I didn't cope well being alone, so I was glad when I found Lucky sleeping on the couch. He only tolerated me, but it was enough to not feel lonely.

Humming as I lounged back on the couch, I still couldn't get over the songs Rey had shown me. They were so raw and deep. His pain was tangible through his words, along with a sense of longing. Rey's desire for someone and hope for the future had been carefully hidden, but I'd heard it. There weren't as many songs with those themes, but I couldn't help but hope a little that maybe they could be about me.

Rey and I were the complete opposite on the

outside. I had the calm, laid-back surfer thing going on for me, even if my waves were made of snow. I tended to be playful, often making jokes, and playing pranks. Rey had a dark, mysterious soul, ever the broody and passionate one that had girls longing for him. Not that he ever noticed. He tended to walk around in a dark cloud, oblivious to all the people around him.

Rey had a reputation as the bad boy of skating, whereas I was known as the golden boy. Granted, he'd never done anything to earn the "bad boy" title, but in skating, it merely meant to be different, and Rey was definitely that. He pushed the boundaries, taking his choreography to a different level with a darker edge. His own skating was hard, physical, and unforgiving. It always made me feel like he was punishing himself every time he stepped out onto the ice. It had to be why he switched more to choreography. Rey was brilliant at it and had become one of the most sought out choreographers in skating.

On the inside, though, Rey and I were the same. Despite my sunny disposition, I hadn't had the best childhood. My mom saw me only as a moneymaker, conning her way to riches. She started with modeling and then monetized my snowboarding. Pamela proclaimed to be my manager, but in the end, she'd felt more like a butcher, cutting me up to sell to the highest bidder, leaving no piece of me behind. I'd experienced some dark things, but I didn't want to be that guy. So, I quit.

I quit snowboarding professionally, despite being the next big thing in the sport.

I quit my family and made my own.

I quit my agent.

I quit my manager.

I quit feeling sorry for myself.

The biggest thing I quit doing was not choosing myself. I quit caring about others' opinions and started living life the way I wanted. It was freeing when you only had yourself to please. I was tired of everyone else making my decisions and choices for me, so I made one for myself. And now, if I didn't want to do something, I didn't. It made life much simpler. Despite the demons that haunted me at times, I strove each day to chase them away, in the hope that one day, I would have run far enough where they couldn't reach me anymore.

Rey didn't know that I understood what he felt. I recognized his pain in a way that others wouldn't, and I wanted to help guide him out of the darkness he found himself in; to show him there were other ways. He didn't have to accept the path he found himself on, he could change course. He just had to make the first step.

Today was a big leap off that path and onto something new. I'd felt it. Rey had been vulnerable with me in a way he hadn't before. He showed me a new side of him, a real side. It made me love him even more.

I know, I was a total cliché, falling for my best friend.

It hadn't started off that way. Our friendship had

just grown and one day I woke up and realized I was in love with him.

While he wasn't the first guy I'd been with, I didn't often date guys. I hated labels, not wanting to pigeon-hole myself into something, so I never labeled myself. My sexuality fell on the pansexual side of the spectrum. David from Schitt's Creek had said it perfectly for me, "I like the wine—not the label." It was more about who the person was and not their sexual orientation for me.

I've hooked up with both guys and girls, though most were girls. Utah wasn't the most forward of places, but it provided some variety with all the athletes and tourists that visited. The problem was, Rey was straight, or at least I assumed he was. I'd never seen him flirt with guys when out, or talk about liking anyone that way. Which was problematic for my massive crush on the guy.

Ideally, I'd love to be in a relationship with Rey and someone who fit us both. To me, that sounded like the best type of relationship. I just needed to gather my courage to talk with Rey and hope I didn't ruin our friendship.

Lately, it had felt as if something was different, almost changing between us. It made my hope of being with him and the right girl a possibility. Granted, I hadn't met a girl I wanted to be with yet, but that felt like a small detail compared to sharing my heart with Rey. My ploy to wait for him to open up first wasn't panning out as I hoped. His sharing of his songs was a huge step though, and it set my romantic heart soaring.

I'd need to be careful if he ever played music for me. My emotions were always written on my face, and there would be no way I could mask my feelings along with my hard-on. I was a sucker for a musician, and my want would be evident the minute he strummed that guitar.

The hug we shared before he left for the airport replayed through my head, filling me with hope. "That's a good sign, right?" I said out loud. Lucky lifted his head, but rolled over, ignoring me. "It is," I told myself, needing to hear it out loud.

The front door opened a few minutes later, and I jumped up, accidentally scaring Lucky in the process. He scurried down the hall towards Elias' room, away from me. Shrugging, I practically skipped as I headed toward the noise, excited to greet the new roommates.

sawyer

Rhett drove further down the road, informing us that all the houses on this side of campus were for instructors and were divided up by last name. We pulled up to a gorgeous, sprawling, gray house. It had striking light accents, big picture windows covering the front of the house, and a large porch with a swing. It curved around to a garage area and a patio area could be seen in the back.

I instantly felt envious of whoever got to live here. It was facing the perfect direction as well, the mountains starting to show the pinks of the sunset.

"Why did we stop?" I asked, not understanding the reason we'd stopped here.

"I live here," Rhett offered, but said nothing else as he got out.

I shrugged, not mad about getting to spend more time with him and Mateo. They were the only two people I knew and I enjoyed their company. I jumped out of the car after him, hastily following Mateo up the front walk.

Mateo smiled, blushing slightly. He had the cutest grin and I found him adorable in his glasses. I stared into his dark blue eyes that were hidden behind his frames and noticed he had the most extraordinary eyelashes. That was it! It was unfair the level of beauty this guy had, and he didn't even have to try.

But when Mateo held the door for me, I couldn't fault him for it. He ducked his head down again, his hair falling over his eyes. If he kept doing that, the urge to run my fingers through it would win out. I almost wanted to do it to see how he'd react.

I walked into the foyer, amazed even more at the beauty of this house. I'd grown up in a moderate-sized house, in an upper-middle-class family, but this was an entirely different tax bracket.

Rhett led us into a kitchen, a massive island that took up a large portion of the space came into view. It had every appliance you could imagine sitting atop the marble countertop. I mean, I assumed it was marble; I wasn't a design expert, but anything this nice had to be the real deal. A table that could fit ten sat adjacent to the kitchen in a dining area. It was impeccably decorated and staged like it had been on one of those home shows.

The house had a warm vibe, giving it a homey feel despite the luxuriousness, only making me like it even more. Okay, I was beyond a little jealous I wouldn't be living here and had entered full-on envy. I only hoped my place was as lovely, or I would have to become friends with these guys so I could visit whenever I wanted.

Yeah, visiting the house would be why I'd become friends with them. *For the house.* Keep telling yourself that, Sawyer.

Rhett was showing us a new protein powder flavor he just got in and wondered if any of us wanted to try it. Mateo said something that made Rhett laugh. I hadn't caught what they were talking about, but I enjoyed their easy banter, and I found myself laughing with them. Looking around, I turned to ask Rhett where the bathroom was so I could snoop some more. I was halted by a massive guy with golden hair barreling into the kitchen, picking me up, and shaking me in a big bear hug.

What. The. Hell.

soren

When I walked into the kitchen and spotted Rhett smiling, I stopped in my tracks, utterly taken aback by the expression on his face. I became even more confused when I gathered what he was doing, showing off his protein powder, constituted as flirting.

Chuckling to myself, I watched him try to gain the attention of the cute blonde. In the three years I'd worked here, I'd never seen Rhett talk to any girl, much less smile at one. When he laughed, I was positive I was in the Twilight Zone.

Rhett 'the grump' was fucking laughing!

Maybe I should video this for Rey? He'd never believe me otherwise.

My world stopped when she turned.

She was tiny and curvaceous with hair a shimmery gold blonde similar to my own. Hers was long, draping down her back in waves. Her eyes were pools of vivid green that sparkled with amusement at Rhett, despite the topic of conversation. Her face was alight with humor, inviting me in. Her cheeks were flushed, almost as if she were blushing.

She was stunning. I yearned to know her and hear her voice.

Her smile was already affecting me, and I was quite sure her laugh might make my heart take off in flight. I smiled brightly at her as I walked the rest of the way into the kitchen. There was another guy with raven hair and glasses standing next to her. He must be one of our roommates. I wondered where the other guy was, remembering there were two. I looked around but didn't see anyone else standing in the area.

Fear began to pull in my stomach as I wondered if she was our other roommate's girlfriend, making my heart sink.

But why would Rhett flirt with her if she had a boyfriend? I challenged myself.

He wouldn't.

Decision made, I decided to use my happy-go-lucky persona to my advantage. I walked right up to the cutie pie, and before she could even say anything, I hoisted her up in a big bear hug, holding her tight to me.

I inhaled her smell of fresh pears, noticing how perfectly she fit against me in my arms. I squeezed her one more time before I set her down on her feet.

She'd made the cutest squeak when I'd picked her up, setting my heart racing. I had a feeling this girl was about to change everything, and I was ready to board that train.

She could be the missing piece I'd been searching for in my life.

seven

sawyer

A SMALL SQUEAK ESCAPED AS HE SQUEEZED ME TIGHT. I was convinced he'd have swung me around if there had been room to do it. What was with all these awkward encounters today? Did Charlie put a sign on my back? Sounded like something he'd do. I was going to kick that old man's ass if he had.

The cuddly giant put me down, and I was able to look at my captor. Golden eyes smiled back at me; yep, you heard me right. His freaking eyes were smiling. I swear, he must've graduated from Tyra Banks' smizing school.

Didn't believe me? Google it—smize.

He had the happiest face I'd ever seen. This guy oozed sunshine and smelled like fresh laundry. God, I loved that smell. Oh God, he had a fucking dimple! I was done—panties destroyed, type of done. Looked like I had something else to add to my "Sawyer wanted to lick" list.

He was tall, but not as tall as Rhett, probably around 6'4". Mr. Sunshine was toned, with golden skin, and simply built to perfection. He had a whole surfer vibe that instantly created a calming sense about him, and I could tell he was completely comfortable with himself. It was a sexy trait.

His hair was a shade darker than mine, curly, and almost down to his shoulders. He had some slight stubble across his jawline, allowing his dimple to still peek out. Damn. I really needed to see a doctor and get something for this case of Altitude Delirium disorder I had. Here was another guy setting off my hormone meter.

"Well, hello there, cutie pie. I'm Soren. Please tell me you're here to save me from boredom and misery by going out with me tonight?" he asked, jovially. I kind of just stared at him for a moment, dumbstruck, not sure I'd heard him correctly.

"Um..." I started to reply to him, but my words failed me. I wasn't used to guys being this forward and asking me out on the spot. Thankfully, Rhett, of all people, saved me from having to figure it out.

"Back off, Soren, she just arrived and needs to unpack. Besides, you can't go hogging our new room-mate all to yourself."

Rhett said it in a tone, indicating he was bored, but I heard the mischief, and confirmed it by the look of glee in his eyes. Guessing he was used to Soren and his antics, I got ready to introduce myself when something Rhett said registered.

"Wait… did you just say *your* new roommate?"

Embarrassing to admit, but most of my question came out in a high-pitched shriek that only dogs could probably hear. Putting both hands on my hips in a power pose, I channeled all the sass I had into my stare. I might only be 5'2", but I had the attitude of 6'1" Amazonian! There was no way I was letting Mr. Grumpypants and Cuddle Bear intimidate me. *Not today, boys.*

Rhett smirked down at me like I was the cutest thing he'd ever seen and shook his head. "Yes, short stuff, our roommate. It seems the housing office assumed Sawyer was a male and placed you in the guys R-Z housing unit. I inquired on the way home if there were any openings in the single female units, but it's apparently full. The instructor you're replacing was living in married housing, which was overlooked when filling the position. But since we're all adults, it's not a major concern unless you'd feel more comfortable somewhere else. They can relocate you to a hotel room in town, a room in the student dorms, or you can see about bunking up with another girl." I scrunched up my face at that, and Rhett caught it, only smiling as he continued. "You have your own room and bathroom here, so nothing improper to worry about if that's a concern for you," Rhett finished.

I think my brain got stuck on all the words he'd just had tumble out of his mouth; it seemed the other guys were in the same boat as we all stared at Rhett dumb-founded for a few moments. No one made a noise. I was still stuck on the realization I could live here. I didn't want to be in town; that would mean a longer commute, and I'd have to make extra trips to and from campus. Nor did I want to be in the student dorms, and making a stranger share a room with me, when there was a perfectly good room available here, felt rude.

Besides, hadn't I been marveling at this house? This was my chance to live here. Even if it was with a bunch of guys I'd been drooling over—such a hardship. Plus, I tended to do better with guys in general. I didn't want to sound too eager, though, so I nodded, thinking it over.

"Hmm… well, I guess if it's the only option, then I'll just have to get used to it," I uttered sheepishly with a shrug of my shoulders, totally selling the whole "aw shucks" persona I was going for. *Nailed it.*

By the slight tilt of Rhett's mouth, it didn't appear I'd pulled it off quite as well as I'd imagined, though. Mateo and Soren silently chuckled at me behind their hands. Damn! And here I thought I'd get away with it. I'd need to work on my acting skills.

"Well, I'm Sawyer." I awkwardly waved at Soren. Why was I always waving at these hot guys? Seriously! Apparently, my hand wanted to get in on the action and kept inserting itself to get their attention.

Listen here bitch, we needed to play it cool. *Cool.* So, slow your roll. There. My properly chastised hand finally lowered back to my side.

No more going rogue now, you hear me, hand? Geez, I'd advanced to talking to my body parts.

"So, how about a tour, and you can tell me about who else lives here?" I directed, trying to get the attention and focus off my increasingly red face—stupid blush. Soren smiled more prominently at me and took over for Rhett, which he seemed content with. I figured he would head off, but he appeared willing to accompany us as long as he didn't have to speak.

"Well, there's, old man grump here," Soren said, placing his hand on Rhett's shoulder, clapping it. Rhett grunted, shaking it off. Yep, Mr. Grumpy Pants had used up all of his words for the day.

"And I'm guessing you met your other travel companion?" Soren questioned as he looked at Mateo. Mateo ducked his head now that the focus of three gazes were on him.

"Mateo," he replied simply to Soren.

"Well, welcome, Mateo. As I mentioned before, but in case you were entranced by my dazzling smile and have forgotten, I'm Soren, and I'll be playing host today on our tour," he chuckled, using his best host voice.

This guy was a hoot. I liked his easy-going way and his positive aura. I could see myself seeking him out when I needed to decompress. His presence was soothing, and he was wholly himself. It wasn't an act or a mask he used to hide behind, but his authentic self, and that was hot. H-A-W-T, hot.

Soren led us all through the house, pointing out the living room, den, game room, movie room, weight room, steam room and sauna, and even a conference room. Apparently, on days when the weather was terrible and the roads were unable to be plowed, they'd do meetings and training via virtual software. I was in awe of everything this house and school had to offer, and we'd only been to the main floor and basement.

The top floor held all the bedrooms, except for Rhett's. His bedroom was in the basement next to the weight room. I learned from Soren that Rhett was twenty-five and had been at TAS for five years and was actually a local, though he hadn't attended TAS when he was in high school. Soren turned out to be a wealth of information, easily offering it up as he chatted. I'd need to pump him for info on the campus later. Perhaps he'd even be a good source for my other quest.

The first room he showed us belonged to someone named Elias. He was the second oldest at twenty-four and a tutor at the school for four years. Rhett spoke up at this and stated that Elias was his best friend. Elias had been supposed to pick us up but had an emergency meeting, so he'd sent Rhett instead. I noticed a slight blush appearing on Rhett's cheek and I wondered what it was about.

The next room was Mateo's and had a pale blue color that oddly matched his eyes. He seemed pleased with it as well. The last room on this side of the stairs belonged to Oliver. According to Soren, Oliver was twenty-three and the ice hockey instructor/coach. His door was open, so I peeked in as we walked by. It was minimalist in his belongings but was tidy with matching bedding. I caught a whiff of spice mixed with an earthy smell as I walked by. It smelled amazing, and I couldn't wait to meet the guy who smelled like that. Yum. Not that I needed to add more guys to lust after at this point, but hey, what was one more, right?

We crossed over the landing to the other end of the house for the last three rooms. The next bedroom was Soren's, who was twenty-four, and in his third year as the snowboarding instructor. Soren's room was neat with neutral tones and smelled like your favorite blanket. He shared a bathroom with Rey, who was in the room next door to him. He'd apparently just left for a family event and would return before classes started. Rey was twenty-three and in his second year as the speed skater instructor. It kind of amazed me at the variety of athletes we had in the house, but it was exciting to be around people who took it seriously.

My door sat across from Soren and Rey's rooms and had an attached bathroom. I found myself bouncing in anticipation at getting to check out my room. When I walked in, I stopped, looking around in a circle. It was a lot bigger than I'd expected. It had a large open area with a bed along the back wall, parallel to the windows. I noticed I was on the side facing the mountains, and a smile crept over me. I had a feeling I'd never grow tired of that view, waking every morning to it. I could already feel myself falling in love with this place.

My room was painted a soft gray, which would go well with my peach and teal bedroom decor. There was a tall dresser along one wall that matched the wood of the bed. A desk sat next to the window, along with some bookshelves. My favorite thing was the massive round chair that I believed was called a cuddle chair. It sat next to the window, filling my head with visuals of myself cuddled up in it and reading, staring out at the snow and mountains. The room was simple, but it fit my needs perfectly.

I spotted two doors on another wall and assumed one was for the bathroom and another for the closet. I located some of my boxes aligned up against the wall as I took everything in. The last of the furniture consisted of a couple of end tables next to the bed with lamps, an ottoman at the foot of the bed, and a rug placed between the bed and the sitting area. Stepping on the rug, I moaned, feeling the softest material I'd ever felt before. If I didn't love skating so much, I wondered if I would ever want to leave this room.

Rhett walked in, placing my bags by the closet, and I realized I hadn't even noticed him leave as I'd taken in the room. "Thanks, Rhett." I smiled kindly at him, and he shuffled on his feet. Now that we were in my room together, he seemed at a loss for words. Deciding I wanted to try to earn my second smile from him today, I winked.

That poor man apparently didn't know how to handle me yet because his face turned crimson, and I never saw anyone that gigantic run out of a room as if his ass was on fire. Chuckling to myself at his reaction, I was a little disappointed I hadn't earned a smile. Oh well, it just meant I had to keep trying harder. Mateo had already retreated to his room to unpack his belongings, leaving only Soren and me. He smiled at me, enjoying my antics with Rhett.

"I have a feeling that things will never be boring again with you here." He grinned at me, sincerity in his eyes.

"Definitely not." I laughed, knowing if anything, I was always good for a laugh.

"Well, I'm going to let you get your things sorted. We should make dinner later and get to know one another better. I wasn't kidding when I said I wanted to spend time with you, so I hope you keep that in mind."

I felt my cheeks heating at his honesty. "Definitely," I agreed. Even if he wasn't the sweetest, I'd still be interested in getting to know him since he was my roommate.

I wondered if I could get them to not wear shirts for dinner? I mused to myself as he shut my door, leaving me to my lusty thoughts.

Shaking my head, I focused on unpacking, hoping I'd have time to freshen up before dinner. If I was going to be meeting more people, I wanted to look cute. I wasn't a vain person, but every girl wanted to feel her best when meeting strangers. And if they were half as hot as the first three guys, I'd need to carry around a bib to catch all my drool.

I wasn't shy or inexperienced with guys, but there hadn't always been a lot of options around my age living in a small town. I'd lost my virginity to a boy I thought would help me not feel so alone, but it had been a colossal mistake, leaving me unsatisfied and heartbroken because it hadn't happened with who I'd always envisioned.

After that miserable experience, I decided I didn't want emotions and sex to be combined together, but that also hadn't panned out. I wasn't the hook-up with one-night stands type of girl. I needed some level of trust to give my body over to someone else. So, in my junior year, I struck up a bargain with two guy friends of mine on the hockey team. We created a "friends with benefits" agreement that suited us all.

Whenever we were single, we could use each other to meet our physical needs, but there weren't any expectations of romance, dates, or intimate connections afterward. They were guys I trusted enough to get naked with, and it had worked out well for all of us. Our senior year had been a lot of fun as neither of the guys wanted a serious relationship before they left for college, leaving lots of time for me and them between the sheets. There were even a few times where we all ended up together.

Yet, while all those times had been hot, neither of them had ever made me feel the way Rhett, Mateo, or Soren had just from a look.

And while it might not be the best idea to start something with my roommates, I also knew that life wasn't guaranteed, and sometimes you regretted the choices you didn't make the most.

Musing over this as I unpacked, I started to question if I was finally ready to start a relationship with someone. While I was here to find answers about my past, I also wanted a fresh start—no more hiding, physically or emotionally.

Realizing my heart was ready for something more than a physical relationship filled me with excitement. It had been a long time since I had felt eager about a relationship.

In fact, it had been about five years since I'd felt that spark, the rush of excitement, and the joy of connecting with someone.

eight

FIVE YEARS AGO

sariah

THE THINGS MY PARENTS HAD TOLD ME RAN THROUGH MY head on a loop. And now, we had to escape at 2 am. My dad wanted to wait until the guard outside our house either fell asleep or switched shifts. It was our best option to leave without anyone noticing.

I begged my parents to let me slip next door to say goodbye to Finley and Henry, but they'd refused, telling me it was too dangerous. But I couldn't leave without saying anything. My best friends would worry and it would cause more problems in the end, especially if we were trying to go off-grid into hiding. But my parents refused to see reason, not understanding the life of a teenager and how social media worked. They were stuck in their fear and couldn't see any logical solutions.

I understood to some degree, but I needed to say goodbye.

So, at 12:30 am, I snuck out my window and jumped the fence next door. I'd been doing this same path since I was about nine. The three of us would meet in the treehouse and stay up watching the stars, happy to be in one another's company.

I remembered Finley was away at her aunt's house since we were all scheduled to fly out for the competition the following day. She still had to attend public school, so her parents made her stay back. Finley hated the fact that Henry and I were homeschooled due to training. But when you spent most of the day on the ice, or in the training room, you really couldn't be in a classroom.

Earlier, I'd texted Henry telling him I couldn't make it to practice, but to meet me tonight in our spot. I needed to say goodbye to one of them.

"Henry?" I whispered.

"Password?" was mumbled back, and I couldn't help but smile.

"You're killing me…"

"Smalls," he replied, and the ladder lowered.

Holding in my laugh at our password, I reminded myself of my reason for this visit—to say goodbye. I couldn't get caught up in memories, even if we had thought we were so clever back then after watching *The Sandlot*. Henry had loved it so much that he started calling me "Smalls" due to my height.

I despised it in the beginning, thinking Henry was

making fun of my small frame, but here lately, when he said it, it was with affection, and it made me tingle all over.

Over the years, I'd only grown a couple more inches where he'd grown a lot, but it worked well for pairs skating. He just needed to grow a few more inches, and we'd have the ideal height difference for competitive skating. My mood soured at that thought. I didn't know if I'd ever get to compete again.

He was leaning back against the wall as I lifted myself up into the treehouse. "Hey," I said shyly. Henry smiled in that sexy way of his that always made my knees weak, and I knew immediately he assumed I wanted to talk about the kiss.

"Hey, Smalls." He smiled fondly at me, setting off my heart.

Damn him and his tenderness! I couldn't help it after that and the tears burned in my eyes.

"Smalls, what's wrong?" Henry asked, coming over to me in concern. "Is this because of last night? Did you not want me to kiss you? Did you not like it?" he whispered, his voice scared.

Shaking my head quickly, I caused my hair to whip around and smack us both in the face, and we laughed. Henry was no stranger to getting hit with my hair.

Grabbing my arms to steady me, he lifted my chin with one hand. "Answer me, Smalls. Please, I need... I need to hear your words. If you don't want to kiss me anymore, I'll understand." He started to choke up on the last part, and he looked so sad that I couldn't help what happened next.

Lifting up on my toes, I gently placed my lips against his. Henry's breath was still minty from his toothpaste, and his lips were just as soft as I remembered. He stood there, stunned for a moment. I didn't think he expected me to kiss him after seeing my tears.

Slowly, he lifted his hand to place both of them on my jaw, tilting it up further so he could deepen the kiss. I was almost positive that the night before had been the first kiss for both of us, making us equal in our inexperience. Considering we spent 99% of our time together studying for school, training, or hanging out with Finley, I knew he hadn't been around many other girls or gone on dates.

Henry began to lick at the seam of my lips, and I hesitantly parted them enough for him to slide his tongue into my mouth. He hesitated for a second before gently touching his tongue to the tip of mine. It felt foreign at first, but then he applied pressure and swirled it around. I followed his movements, and soon we were in a rhythm as little moans slipped out between us.

One of Henry's hands started to move down my jaw and over my shoulder, sending tingles all down my arm. He wrapped it around my back and pulled me tighter to him. Wrapping my arms around his neck, I tugged his head closer to me. We were flushed tight together, similar to completing a twist lift, only this time was much better.

I could feel every inch of him and how he responded to our kiss, a hardness growing against my stomach. The feel of it made my stomach flip. Pulling back to get some air, we both breathed heavily. Henry rested his head against my forehead, staring into my eyes..

"Henry," I started, and he smiled at the sound of his name from my lips.

"Yes, Smalls?"

"I… well… You see….," I kept tripping over my words and I couldn't figure out how to tell him I was leaving. Not after the kiss we'd just shared.

"I was worried you were coming over to tell me you wanted to be just friends and pretend like the kiss hadn't happened. I've been going out of my mind all day with worry and the other half replaying that kiss over and over. Though now, I think I have something even better to swap it with." He chuckled, his breath tickling me. "Kissing you is like all my favorite things wrapped into one." Henry smiled softly at me as he kissed my nose. My heart began to flutter even more at his sweet words.

"Mine too," I replied just as softly. It was as if we were afraid our voices would ruin the moment we were sharing. "There's something I need to tell you, though," I mumbled. "I have to go away for a while. Something's going on with my family, but I can't talk about it. I just, I couldn't leave without telling you…. without getting to say goodbye." My voice broke, trembling with emotion as my tears started to fall again.

He tensed at my words, lifting his head, and peered

into my eyes, searching for something. "What's going on, Sariah?"

Ouch, he'd used my real name. He only used my real name when he was upset with me. "I can't tell you anything more, Henry. I don't want to put you in danger." I trembled at the thought of "R" getting his hands on my friends if he thought they might know something. That man gave me the creeps.

"Danger? What danger? Sariah, talk to me. Tell me what's wrong. I'll do everything in my power to protect you, you know that, right? Sariah, I—"

Just then, we both heard movement outside, and I turned back with urgency.

"Henry, I have to go. Whatever you do, do not look for me. I will find you when it's safe. I promise. We're leaving tonight to meet someone who can help; that's all I know. Please, promise me," I begged as the tears ran faster down my face.

He hesitated, but eventually, he nodded his head as his eyes began to water as well. "Tell Finley I love her," and *you*, I thought.

With those parting words, I turned quickly and lowered back out of the treehouse. I couldn't look back, or I knew I wouldn't be able to leave.

Darting back across the yard, I barely missed the guard as he did his last walk-through before he switched with someone. I didn't realize I'd been over there for almost an hour, and now I needed to hurry. As I climbed back into my window, I gave in and glanced back at the treehouse, needing to see him one last time.

Henry stood there watching me, tears falling from his eyes, a look of utter heartbreak on his face, breaking something in me.

Whimpering, I hurried back through the window, barely making it inside before I began to sob.

I never regretted anything as much as I did for not telling Henry I loved him.

nine

sawyer

Beep, Beep.

Stretching out my hand, I aimlessly searched for my phone in the pile of blankets I was under. The damn snooze blared to life for the third time, and I needed it to stop. I knew full well I'd set it up that way, but as it shouted at me to get up, I found myself annoyed and grumpy about it. I wasn't a morning person, but setting the alarm to warrant hitting snooze three times seemed to be the best method for me.

Once the stupid noise stopped, I smiled as I stretched my arms above my head. Last night had been fun with my roommates. We'd shared some food, had lots of laughs, and I felt like I'd gotten to know them all a little better in the process.

Soren kept us all entertained, which was useful, considering Mateo and Rhett didn't say much. He was vivacious, and you couldn't help but want to fall into his orbit with him and all the fun he had. Rhett had me in his sight all night, giving me his smoldering eyes, effectively setting my insides on fire. Every time I turned or looked, he was right there, watching and anticipating my needs. I'd never had anyone so focused on me, making it exciting but also overwhelming at the same time.

There was no denying the chemistry brewing between us. Our physical reactions alone were enough to set off any fire alarm. But... I couldn't deny my growing connections with Mateo and Soren, either.

While Mateo was quiet, and I often started our conversations, he was engaged in the topics, becoming animated when it was something he enjoyed and forgot to be nervous. I liked that about him. We'd talked about our shared love of comic book movies and he suggested having a Marvel movie night. I hoped to introduce him to some of my favorite geeky shows, like *Doctor Who*. He smiled when I talked and focused intently on what I said.

It was a nice confidence booster to have all these guys concentrating on me. Every time our knees brushed on the couch, Mateo's cheeks would blush a deep crimson, and he'd duck his head. Eventually, I gave in to the desires of my rogue hand and ran my fingers through his hair. It was as thick as it looked and was incredibly silky. The poor guy almost had a stroke, he tensed so hard at first, but slowly, he melted into my touch.

Soren was by far the most overt flirt of the three, but I found it to be endearing. It was his whole personality and he used it often as comic relief. What I loved most was discovering Soren loved to read as much as I did. He mentioned starting a book club together, and I was all for it, especially if I could enforce the dress code as sans shirt.

It could work. I was sure he'd go for it. Totally.

Soren offered to select the first book, and then we'd rotate. I'd never had anyone I could talk to about books before, so the idea was exhilarating. I found myself looking forward to it almost as much as skating.

The other roommates hadn't returned home while we'd been hanging out in the game room. It hadn't been too late when we all retired to our rooms, but I'd begun to drag, the tiredness of the day catching up to me. With traveling to a new time zone, I wanted to get started on a good sleep schedule.

Thankfully, I only had two meetings today to meet the other skating instructors and get a tour of the facility. I was hoping I'd get some time to skate. It had been a few days now, and my body craved the physicality of being on the ice. I'd need to work out if I didn't get to skate or dance. It was rare to go more than a day without skating back in Iowa.

Stretching, I felt the tightness of my muscles. Actually, I might need to skate and work out for my own sanity, and to build my endurance. I wouldn't deny it would also relieve some of this sexual tension building up. But mostly, I needed to be at elite level to train multiple skaters each day and not seem like I was dying by the end of it.

There was nothing more damning for a coach than not being able to keep up with their skaters.

Walking out of the bathroom, the steam followed me out as I walked in a daze. I still wasn't sure what I'd just experienced. There was a shower… but it wasn't your typical shower, oh no. It was heaven masquerading as a shower. I felt extremely tranquil after that extraordinary experience. Heaven had five showerheads, five! It hit all your muscles at once and was big enough to easily fit four people. Thoughts of what I could do in the space flitted across my mind, causing my face to heat.

Dressing in exercise leggings and a workout top, I was prepared on the off chance I got to skate. Adding a zip hoodie to my bag filled with all my gear, I was ready to go. I mentally ran through all the items, despite knowing they were all there, a habit formed after years of doing it, and started down the stairs.

Rhett had mentioned I could ride with him to campus since I didn't know where I was going yet. Plus, I hadn't checked to see if my baby had arrived.

Noises and smells greeted me as I walked into the kitchen, spotting Rhett blending a smoothie concoction first. Next I spotted Soren fiddling around with a fancy-looking coffee machine, and it appeared like Mateo was eating cereal at the island. He was still in his pajamas, his hair stuck up on one side and was flat on the other, looking all cute. For some reason, it was nice knowing not all guys woke up with that "sexy bedhead hair," especially when they had practically perfect hair to begin with.

A guy I hadn't met had his head down as he ate at the island. He was eating so much food, I worried there wouldn't be any left in the fridge... or you know, campus. It was that much.

Sitting down across from him, he looked up at the movement, his sleepy eyes zeroing in on me. My breath caught when they met mine. Hot damn. It was Oliver Windsor. Charlie and I had cheered for him while he played in the NHL. I'd always thought he was hot, but by the smirk on his face, he knew it.

Damn. Cocky Fuck Boys were not my thing.

Twisting my necklace back and forth, I debated how to play this. I didn't want to disrupt any house dynamics. But when he opened his mouth, all bets were off.

"Don't worry, Bite-Size, there's plenty of me left." He smirked, blatantly checking me out, his eyes lingering on my breasts.

I had on a fitted sports tank with a sweater wrapped around my waist. The v-cut of the shirt, opened in the front displaying my cleavage. I wasn't ashamed of my body, but it had taken me a while to get there. I didn't have the typical ice skater body. I was curvy, with hips and a chest, and I often received insults from online haters over it. While I had the standard—thin, straight, and narrow—frame most skaters had when I was younger, it had changed when I was sixteen. My hips curved out, my ass rounded, and my boobs grew. When everything else had fallen apart in my life, it was another blow to have my body betray me as well.

Granted, most teenage girls were excited to get boobs, but I hated them because it meant I was different. In figure skating, that wasn't a good thing. I was an anomaly. My body type, combined with my career-ending injury to my knee, meant I'd never have the chance to go further. It had been difficult to accept in the beginning. It felt as if everything had been taken from me—my parents, my life, my friends, my hope, and then my skating career.

Skating had been my identity and without it, I didn't know who I was, or what path I was taking. At sixteen, that had been difficult to process.

Thankfully, my third foster home was a decent one, and my foster mom had encouraged me to go to the state-funded therapy after I kept waking up from nightmares. I was still worried about being discovered by R at that point, but wanted to make a good impression on the family, so I complied. It had turned out well, though, and I found I didn't have to give up on anything. Therapy helped me see that my choices were mine to make, and I only had to think about them differently.

Unfortunately, as with most of the good things back then, it didn't last long. One of the biological children in the home, who was a year older than me, crossed a boundary. I woke up with him in my room one night, and I no longer felt safe. I told my counselor how I felt about the intrusion, and she reported it to the state, advocating for me when I didn't have a voice. What I hadn't anticipated was to be blamed for it and punished by my foster family.

After that, I was removed and no longer able to attend counseling again. It didn't matter, though, because in the short time I had with Ms. Mary, she'd taught me valuable skills and that there were some adults I could trust. She'd protected me when I'd asked for it.

Her advice had stuck with me and I no longer hid my body, but embraced it. I taught myself how to skate with my new form instead of against it, simultaneously building my confidence in myself. I was a better skater now because of it, and I could perform moves other skaters shied away from, merely because I'd developed more muscle.

So, I let Oliver look, not bothered by it, and snatched a piece of bacon off his plate as compensation. I didn't want him to know I was equally fangirling on the inside, and checking him out as well. Or that I'd crushed on him. His ego was already big enough by the looks of it.

I'd already taken two bites when Oliver realized what happened, his face scrunching up as he looked from my cleavage to the bacon, and then back at his plate.

Smiling, I licked my fingers. "You're right, it is bite-sized." I took another piece, taking a bite in a dramatic fashion.

"Well played, Bite-Size, well played. This round goes to you. I'm Oliver." He smirked, his megawatt smile lighting up the place. He'd said his name in such a way, he assumed I knew who he was. I mean, I did, but again, he didn't need to know that. So, I played dumb, giving him a confused look to avoid stroking… his ego. Damn, gutter mind.

"Please, tell me you're not with one of these clowns?" he challenged, motioning around the room to the other three guys present. I guess he hadn't gotten the memo that I was one of the new roommates. I glanced up at Rhett, and he slightly shook his head no, his eyes filling with mirth. The smile that started to creep up encouraged me. I could tell he knew I was about to hand this guy his ass, and he was going to enjoy it.

Rhett was merciless, and I liked it.

"What do you mean?" I asked in a faux sweet voice as I twirled my hair around my finger. Oliver responded just as I hoped he would.

Hook. Line. And sinker. Oh, Oliver, you were about to be caught.

"Just that none of these guys are man enough to handle a hottie like you. Let me guess, you're here for vacation with your family and wanted to hook up with a superstar athlete? If you want an experience to tell all your friends about back home, then look no further. I'll rock your world, you bite-sized little hottie." He grinned, sitting back as he crossed his arms, thinking he'd won me over.

Seriously? I laughed internally at his ridiculousness. Did this really work on girls? Ladies, come on! Make him work a little harder for it than that. I get it. He was hot, but it was no excuse to cave to the rugged hotness he had going on. And boy, did he have that rugged hotness down.

Oliver had wavy, auburn hair that sat just above his ears on the sides, a little longer in the back. His eyes appeared to be hazel, and he sported almost a full beard that covered the bottom half of his face. He had a sharp nose and very kissable lips. I couldn't see the rest of him, but I knew from watching him play what was below that counter. His shoulders were broad, and if I hadn't already known he was a hockey player, I would've been able to guess by his physique. He was built to take a hit or two. Hockey players always thought they were the Gods of ice, and he had the cockiness down after years of having puck bunnies throw themselves at him, no doubt.

Deliberately, I licked my lips, drawing his gaze there. Bingo. "Well, according to locker room talk, I'm not the only thing that's 'bite-sized' in this room. So, I think I'll stick with B.O.B., you know, my battery-operated boyfriend. He isn't a… what did you say? 'A superstar athlete' as you put it, but he can go ALL… NIGHT… LONG." I finished by seductively licking my lips, leaving him stunned.

As I talked, I traced along the pattern at the top of my shirt, gently moving across my breasts. Oliver's eyes were laser-focused there, and I wasn't entirely sure he even heard what I said. Consequently, I stole the rest of his bacon. Served him right!

"I don't think you'd be able to keep up with me, dear Oliver. Anyone who doesn't respect their bacon and lets someone steal it away doesn't seem to have his head in the game. Better watch out, Oliver, I'm about to make a breakaway as I deke and dangle out of here with all of your bacon. Might want to lay off the 'roids' there, macho man. Or perhaps, bite-size was accurate? Hm."

I feigned as he sat there, frozen with his mouth hanging open. Had he never been turned down before? I honestly believed his brain was stuck on my use of hockey lingo.

Not just a hat rack, my friends, not just a hat rack.

I might be blonde, but I wasn't stupid. He wasn't the only hockey snob in this house. I'd been a fan for years, and played a lot at the rink with the kids and friends from school.

Grabbing the smoothie Rhett held out for me, I made my way around the island, stopping next to Oliver to leave my parting words. "By the way, my name's Sawyer. Your new roommate. Call me *bite-size* one more time, and I'll take a bite out of something other than your bacon. But I don't think you'll like it as much."

The other guys exploded into laughter as I made my exit. My face flamed some, but I didn't stop. I hoped Rhett could still take me to campus since I was leaving earlier than we planned. It didn't feel as cool to have to walk back in there and ask.

I could still hear them laughing and ribbing at Oliver as I headed to the front door, a shout ringing out behind me. "Marry me? I think I'm in love, sweetheart!"

I chuckled to myself. I couldn't believe those lines worked for him. Peeking around the corner, I saw him shaking his head and laughing with the guys. Okay, good. I didn't have to worry about pissing off one of my roommates on the first day, especially a hot one. Hopefully, he'd realize how stupid he sounded and change up his lines.

Rhett came around the corner with his bag over his shoulder and keys in his hand. He smiled at me and motioned for me to continue through the door. Looked like Rhett got to be my rescue chariot after all. I was completely okay with that.

Not to mention, it was only 7:30 am, and I'd already earned one smile. I was declaring it would be a good day! I followed him out of the house and to the car, a big smile plastered on my face.

ten

. . .

sawyer

Our ride was quiet, but not uncomfortable, as we soaked in one another's presence. This close, I could catch the whiff of his cologne, some type of musk smell that fit him—masculine sexuality. I drank the smoothie Rhett had made, sucking down the delicious ingredients, despite not knowing what odd things he'd added to it. It was just nice to have someone make something for me. If the food kept being that readily available in my kitchen, I'd never want to leave.

I liked the sound of that, *my kitchen*.

Of course, the hot guy making stuff for me was a huge bonus.

I started to run through my day and what I wanted to discuss with the Director when Rhett chuckled out of the blue. Turning at the odd sound that emitted from him, he graced me with another smile. Man, this was a banner day from the verbal sparring and now having two smiles bestowed upon me by Sir Grumps a lot.

I couldn't help but return his smile, even if I didn't know what had been funny.

"I'm just replaying you handing Oliver his ass this morning. I don't think any girl has ever turned him down, much less given it back to him. Especially when you used those hockey terms. I thought he'd spontaneously combust, pass out, or orgasm… maybe even all three at once."

I chuckled along with him, replaying the look on Oliver's face as well. The expression he made when I'd sashayed out of the kitchen clutching his bacon would stay in my head for a while. The man needed to learn to respect his bacon! It should be punishable by law.

Rhett pulled up to the building, and I watched as he began to squirm, his huge frame shifting in the seat, making it look uncomfortable with little space to work with. Turning to him, I smiled, forcing him to spit it out as I stared, waiting.

"I wondered," he said, swallowing, "if you'd like to hang out this weekend? Grab some food, or take a walk around campus?" He shrugged, acting as if he wasn't nervous, but from the way he fidgeted with his keys and bounced his leg, I'd bet a million bucks the silent giant was indeed anxious.

It struck me as odd. He was nervous to talk to me? To ask me out? I couldn't comprehend the fact that this hunk of a man was unsettled because of me. I was so stunned, a soft breeze could've pushed me over.

A rush of heat, along with those damn butterflies resurfaced. He squirmed more when I didn't answer, so I could only do one thing and put him out of his misery.

Besides, let's be honest, there wasn't any way I'd say no.

"I'd like that a lot." I smiled at him, hoping to calm his nerves.

The look he returned about stopped my heart.

I'd thought the others were life-changing, but this one, it was world-shattering. World. Shattering.

I was pretty sure he could thaw the snow with the mega hotness that his face was at this precise moment.

Now, *I* was the nervous one.

Sliding out of the car, I made my way into the building as I added his smile to my ongoing tally in my head—three for today if anyone was keeping track. I barely noticed where I was, only that it was a standard building with big windows. Remembering I was here to do a job, I focused, taking in more of the place. There was an open lobby with hallways leading off in different directions. Most seemed to be offices and meeting rooms.

TAS was founded by two Olympic gold medalists, the Aldridge's. They'd won several medals in the '80s for Russia and then retired from ice skating. They created this school in America for individuals to obtain training by elite coaches while also receiving their education simultaneously. It was a novel idea and TAS's elite program was born, becoming the competitive environment that it was today. The Aldridge's were more hands off nowadays, leaving a board of trustees as the governing body.

After finding the correct room, I took a seat at a round table, hoping the other instructors would be nice. You never knew with ice skaters. They tended to range from the catty bitch type, to the overly sweet, helpful sort, with a little of everything in between. The room began to fill up with an assortment of women and men, though most were women. Quite a few smiled at me with a greeting, making me feel more at ease with each passing second.

When 'she' walked in, however, the whole room changed. Everyone sat up straighter and avoided eye contact with her. And I knew who she was immediately —Adelaide Aldridge. Yep, *that* Aldridge.

Adelaide was a few years older than me, and we hadn't ever competed against one another since she was a solo skater. But I knew of her. Everyone did.

She was known for her attitude and not the skating one. Her parents were gold medalists, so I guess she'd been held to high expectations growing up. However, that didn't excuse rudeness or entitlement. I didn't care who her parents were; it didn't warrant special treatment or the right to disrespect others.

Adelaide walked in with her nose in the air, hair swishing behind her in a high ponytail—that was completely impractical for skating, by the way—cell phone in one hand, and a latte in the other. Almost like a movie, the crowd parted, the music slowed, and people moved chairs for her to take the seat she wanted. It was unreal. Had to hand it to her though, she rocked it like it was a medal podium.

The meeting started soon after she sat, and we were forced to do one of those horrible ice breaker games. Come on, who actually enjoyed those?

No one. That's who. Well, except maybe Smiley McGee up in the front. She appeared to be having the best of times. To each their own.

As my group cringed through the exercise, my mind wandered back to my roommates. They were all so fucking attractive, engaging, and kind... well, for the most part. The jury was still out on Oliver. I'd give him a pass this once, because you know, I was forgiving like that. Ha!

I chuckled at myself—which apparently hadn't been to myself, based on the rest of the room's attention turning to me. Oops, I must've laughed out loud. Crap. Based on the evil glare Princess Adelaide gave me, I'd apparently interrupted her. Double Crap.

"Was there something you wanted to add, Ms. Sullivan?" Director Donnelly challenged.

Deciding I might as well take the opportunity to ask a question, I unknowingly inserted my foot further into my mouth. "Um...yeah, actually. I was curious why the double axel wasn't on the Senior Level program?"

On the plane, I'd reviewed both the Junior Level and Senior Level programs and their criteria for jumps, spins, and difficulty. Figure skating was judged based on levels, requiring different difficulties of spins and jumps in which you had to pass to meet the criteria in front of a panel of qualified judges. Whatever degree of difficulty you were in dictated the teams and competitions you were eligible for. It was a complicated system, but every skater knew it backward and forward, as it eventually led to the Olympics.

To be competitive, a skater had to be able to execute jump sequences cleanly. It would be down to those details that determined their score. While I couldn't compete any longer due to the constant strain and stress on the body training required, I could land jumps. And in fact, I was quite good at them.

Apparently, though, that was not the right question to ask directly after laughing at the Princess. I've never seen a face get that red so quickly, and I was fair-skinned! I almost expected her head to spin around *Exorcist* style. Fortunately for everyone, there wasn't any projectile vomit—just the sounds of my slow dying career.

The Director awkwardly cleared his throat before he answered. "Well, you see, um…. Yes, well, that's not the direction we decided to take as a school. We felt it best as a whole, with the board's approval, to focus on style, grace, and choreography."

Not knowing when to just shut the fuck up apparently, I continued making myself persona non grata. "I don't understand. Skaters earn more points for difficult jumps; it seems irresponsible not to work with them to develop those. Especially if they want to compete at the National level." Steam could practically be seen coming out of the Princess's ears as I continued to dig my grave.

"It's simply not something we're focusing on at this time. We're utilizing the strength of the skills our instructors possess." He closed, thinking it would appease me.

Hello, have you met me? Oh right. This was my first day. Well, time to introduce them to what Charlie called Sawyer's code orange moments.

"That's dumb. You're hindering the students who come here wanting to grow and advance themselves by not including more difficult jumps. Perhaps, you need to hire more advanced instructors then to meet the level of competition the school is known for," I huffed out.

My plan had been to come here, blend into the background, and gather information, but I couldn't stand by and not speak up for what I believed in. It was unfair and short-sighted not to prepare students or provide them with the best possible training to advance them. It was actually a big pet peeve of mine, and probably why I couldn't keep my mouth shut when the topic had come up.

As someone who had to modify moves all the time for their own body and strengths, it didn't sit well with me that they were actually pandering to this.

However, that did not seem to be the consensus. Everyone, and I mean everyone, turned and gaped at me. Mouths opened, jaws unhinged, gaping.

Swallowing my uncomfortableness, I kept my head held up, confident in my assessment. Princess finally couldn't take it anymore, and her head exploded. *Poof.* Brain matter and hair bits rained everywhere.

Okay, so that didn't actually happen, but it would've been cool if it had, right?

Instead, I got Adelaide's verbal vomit directed at me. Yay.

"As if *you* could do better!" she screamed, fury so thick I was worried for myself and her blood pressure. Guess I hit a sore spot for her? Again, oops. "You're a nobody with *no medals. No ranking. No future.* You only got this job because the board was desperate, and you were the only female skater who hadn't signed on elsewhere. So, take some advice, *Sawyer*, and learn your place. You're nothing here, just another bottom feeder thinking they're something they're not. You'll be nothing when you leave TAS. And you'll be forgotten as easily as yesterday's leftover salad."

Visceral hate dripped from each word Adelaide spoke, striking me in the chest with force. The way she'd spat my name felt like I was nothing more than the shit she had her butler scrape off her designer shoes.

Trying not to let her words take actual purchase, I began to build my walls up and blocked them out. I'd forgotten for a moment people were cruel in this world. Meeting my new roommates had made me lax. They were the exception and not the standard. Fortifying myself, I sat up straight. The Director, along with everyone else, appeared too stunned to say anything, and sat watching. That was alright. This wasn't the first battle I'd faced off with a mean girl, and I was sure it wouldn't be my last. I was used to standing up for myself.

Chuckling hollowly, I seared her with my own hate filled glare. "Let me guess, you're the Senior Instructor? Nepotism really is everywhere," I retorted with such nonchalance, you'd think I was merely choosing which bathroom tile I liked the most.

Adelaide's face started to turn purple, her anger turning to rage. I'd never seen anyone ever turn that shade before. Someone should tell her that it clashed with her sweater. I bet that would get her head to finally burst.

Adelaide huffed, also attempting to act unfazed, while sending me death threats with her eyes. It didn't work. "As if you can do better." She rolled her eyes, sitting back with a smug look. I think someone had been watching too much Clueless.

"Actually, I can." The grin that spread across my face was huge.

The gasp and subsequent hush that fell over the room was eerie. I looked around, wondering what I'd just said when the Director remembered he was, you know, in fact, in charge, and took back the conversation.

"I'm not sure if you're aware of this, Ms. Sullivan, but our school operates on a competition style level system. The students move up ranks based on their program difficulty, competition performances, and academic standings."

"Yes, I'm aware. I read that in the manual." I didn't know where the Director was going with this, and that fact alone, filled me with dread. It had seemed like a typical level system all skating programs used to rank the students.

"Well," he continued, clearing his throat. "The board, and the Aldridges, decided a few years back to incorporate the same principle to the staff. It was in an attempt to foster staff to encourage continued growth, advanced ability, and maintain the level of elite instruction. Any instructor, at any level, can be challenged by another instructor, and their position is taken at any time."

Well, fuck. Guess that explained everyone's shock. I'd just openly challenged the Princess of Skating.

So much for this day being off to a great start. Dammit.

After he dropped that bomb, I stayed quiet for the rest of the meeting. When I asked afterward about touring the rink, I was informed it was closed for maintenance, adding to the shit pile I was currently in.

Hopefully, I could work out at home, or I would need to find some batteries. Pronto.

rhett

Sucking down the last of my morning green juice, I was surprised when Elias came into the kitchen, Lucky trailing behind him. I'd been so preoccupied with my own thoughts about Sawyer that I'd forgotten to check on him.

"Hey man, how'd your lunch with Voldemort go yesterday?" I smirked as he shook his head, rolling his eyes.

"You'll never guess what the bloody 'emergency' meeting was about."

"By your tone, I'm scared to ask, man." I grimaced, placing my glass into the sink, rinsing it off.

"That cow-bag told her parents we were back together, and the wedding was on. The lunch was cele-bratory, so I had to tell them that, 'No. Sorry, your daughter is a lying twatwaffle, and I would never marry her.'" He huffed, rubbing his hand down his face in frustration. I grabbed a water bottle out of the fridge, handing it to him. He took it, a grateful smile on his face.

"You know, I tried to save her reputation. I told no one the real reason we called it off. But, this… It was too much. She walks around campus acting like the injured party when *she* cheated on me! The nerve of that fucking tart!" Elias said, twisting off the top of his water, downing most of it. It seemed to calm him some, cooling off some of the anger he'd been previously displaying.

"How did they react to that news about their *princess*?" Disgust dripped thickly in each word I uttered about her.

"Right," he sighed. "I told her dad I respected him, but I could no longer respect his daughter after she cheated on me. I appreciated the opportunities working here has granted me and my career, but I no longer would allow her to treat me this way, as if my feelings were non-existent. If I needed to quit, I would. I understood he needed to be loyal to his daughter, so I would make it easy and walk away." Elias appeared ragged, his shoulders slumping as he leaned against the counter, his head down as he stared at the bottle he held in his hand. Everything to do with the banshee weighed heavily on him, and it was noticeable.

"Wow, man, I'm so proud of you for saying something to them. How'd they respond to that? What was she doing during this exchange?" The realization he could be leaving hit me, and worry sat heavy on my tongue. Elias was my best friend, and I wanted him to be happy, but I'd miss him if he left.

"No, thankfully. Mr. Aldridge listened to what I had to say. He thanked me for letting them know and he would make sure she left me alone. He also acknowledged that he would understand if *I* chose not to work here due to *her* behavior, but hoped I would consider staying on as they valued me as a tutor and the creative take I had teaching students. At first, Voldemort made a scene, but after one look from her mother, she was silent. That part was actually pretty comical."

"That's an unexpected response from them, but a relief, all the same. Maybe now Voldemort will stop sending you so many texts and nudes." We both nodded, absorbing the hopeful resolution of the past year. "What did you do after? I never saw you come in last night. I let Lucky out before I went to bed, just in case."

"Thanks, mate, I owe you. The thought of coming back and having to be perfect Elias felt too much, so I uh, you know," Elias blushed, embarrassed about whatever he did.

"No, I don't know, dude. Spill." I had a pretty good guess, but I wanted to make him say it. Elias tried to act proper all of the time, but there was a naughty side to him. Since the engagement had dissolved, he'd used dating apps to meet women to hook up with so he didn't have to see them again after, not ready for a committed relationship. I'd guess that was where he found himself last night.

"Well," Elias let out a deep breath through his lips, causing a funny sound, "I went to the bar because I wanted to drown out that cow's voice. One drink turned into two. I thought of coming home and meeting the new roommates. But then some girl hit on me and bought me another drink. She was hot and definitely wanting to take things further, so I gave in to the temptation and went back to her room. But... when I got there, I was surprised."

"Now, I'm intrigued." From what I knew, Elias was pretty vanilla. We didn't often talk about his sexual encounters as he was rather tight-lipped on his bedroom activities.

"Well, you see, how can I put this..." he started, pausing. "The girl actually had a boyfriend."

"What... okay, this is not where I thought this story was headed. Damn man, did you get into a fight or something?"

"Not exactly." He stared at me, weighing out if he wanted to tell me. I kept my face blank of any judgment, wanting him to know I wouldn't care. He took a deep breath, draining the last of the water.

"So, you see, this couple likes to bring back strangers to their room to fuck while the other one watches. They enjoy it, and both get off on it. It shocked me, and I thought about leaving, not sure if I could with another man in the room watching. But I was about four drinks deep at that point, and once she undressed and started sucking my cock, I lost focus of who was in the room." Elias blushed, but didn't drop his eyes.

I tried to envision his experience, imagining what it would be like to have sex while someone else was in the room. "Did he touch you or anything? Join in?" I questioned Elias.

"No. He just sat in the chair. But, to be fair, my focus was on the girl, and not him. I believe he only sat there, not even touching himself to get off while I fucked his girl. After I got over my embarrassment, it was oddly empowering having this guy watch me make his girl moan and cum. I could tell he was aroused by it, too. He was tenting his pants by the end. When I finished, I worried he would change his mind, and tell me to bugger off." Elias chuckled, shaking his head. "The guy was accommodating. He got me a beverage afterward and let me shower. I think we might even grab a drink before they leave town!" Elias sat there, a wide-eyed expression on his face over how the event had played out.

I laughed, leave it to Elias to find himself in a peculiar situation and become friends with the couple. He might be bitter about love, but Elias was a good friend. He was the charmer, and typically, got along with everyone, unlike me.

After we laughed together, I gave him an update on the new roommates, leaving out the small detail about how Sawyer was a girl. I wanted to see his expression when he discovered that bit of news after witnessing

Oliver's first impression. Elias was my best friend, but it didn't mean I wasn't an ass to him at times.

Elias left a little while later, heading for the library to work on his thesis for his doctorate. He seemed to always be studying these days, and I missed just hanging out with him and training together. I think Elias had fallen into his research hole as a way of distracting himself from his pain, but he'd stopped doing all the things he loved in the process.

Deciding I needed to pull him out of his room more and back into the gym this year, I made a plan to get him excited about fighting again. I didn't want him to only exist this year and view relationships as meaning-less. Elias had been a hopeless romantic once; I just needed to remind him of who that man was.

twelve

. . .

oliver

Thoughts of the little hottie from this morning plagued me as I skated up and down the rink, running some drills. I loved the hockey rink. The smell of the ice and the chill that settled in my bones comforted me. This campus had three ice rinks: figure skating, ice hockey, and one for auxiliary ice sports such as speed skating and curling. The school couldn't have the next Olympic hopefuls not have enough ice time. No complaints from me, since it meant I always had a place to skate.

After finishing my workout, I decided to head back to the house. I hoped I could catch Sawyer and apologize for my Neanderthal behavior earlier. I didn't blame her for her reaction, I *had* acted like an asshole. Sometimes, I got so comfortable in my fuck boy persona, that it was hard to remove it. My cocky self came out, thinking it could do anything and everything, but I always ended up stepping in it. And boy, did I step in it this morning.

Girls had been easy for me since college, and I'd taken it for granted. Being the star player on a college hockey team and then two years in the NHL had provided me with my fair share of puck bunnies. I had gotten so used to girls throwing themselves at me that I'd forgotten not all girls were that way. Particularly, girls that were worth more than a quick fuck.

Sawyer, now that girl had spunk. I wasn't used to girls turning me down, so it had thrown me for a loop this morning, but I kind of dug that too. It had been a while since I'd had to work to attract a girl with more than my looks. Sawyer had fire and confidence, and I found myself liking it a lot.

She didn't care that I was a hockey god. She wanted me to respect her, and that was extremely sexy. It hadn't gone past my notice that I wasn't the only one checking her out as she sashayed around the kitchen. Every single one of my roommates' eyes had remained fixed on her until she sauntered out with all of my bacon.

Chuckling at her stealing it, I made my way back toward the house, enjoying the fresh air. Everything felt more alive today as hope surged in me. Maybe I could convince the other knuckleheads to do something together tonight. Yeah, I liked that idea. Perhaps a movie or some games. Then Sawyer might see I wasn't such a jerk. I pulled out my phone and opened the house group chat:

Homies group chat:

ME: We should do something tonight with the new roommates

Rhett: Okay

Soren: I'm so there, Ollie! Let's do it! We can order some food and do a bonding activity!

I laughed. Leave it to Rhett to give one-word answers and Soren to want to bond. That dude was one of a kind. I smiled as I walked, and the rest of the guys' messages started to filter through.

Elias: Maybe. I had a shit day. Not sure I would make good company. *Voldemort*. Enough said.

Rey: Screw you guys. You aren't allowed to have fun without me. Don't go erasing my high score either, assholes.

ME: Don't worry, Rey-Rey, you're still my favorite cuddly bear

Rey: HAHA, hilarious jerkface. I'll show you a cuddle with your hockey stick.

Soren: It would be more fun if you were here, Rey. Can't you leave already?

Rey: I wish. Mom is going on and on about what is next for me. Anyone want to switch places?

Rhett: No

Soren: That sucks, bro. You'd like the new roommates.

Elias: Sorry, mate.

ME: Kinky Rey-Rey. Think about my hockey

stick do ya? Okay, for all of us still at the house. Let's say at 6 pm? Anyone have Mateo or Sawyer's numbers?

Rhett: Yes

ME: Be kind and share, grumpy butt.

Rhett: No

ME: What is with the one-word answers? Did you not get enough hugs this morning? Don't worry, I'm almost home and will give you a big sweaty hug to make up for it!

Rhett: No.

Soren: HAHAHA, I want to see that. I'll hold him for you.

Rey: Damn, I miss you guys. Well, not Ollie. Now I sound like a softie. Bye.

Elias: Finalize plans and then get off the group chat. Some of us are busy.

ME: Fine, I'll be home soon. See you all at 6 pm for some "bonding."

Soren: Hell, yes! Roommate party! I'll order some good nom-noms.

Now, time to show Sawyer that I was a nice guy. I wondered if I should get her a gift or something? Would that be weird? Yeah, that would be weird. Shit, not even twenty-four hours, and I felt confused and unsure about a girl. This feeling was new, but I kind of liked it. I think.

thirteen

. . .

sawyer

I DECIDED TO WALK BACK TO THE HOUSE, WANTING THE exercise and I was enjoying the fresh air. It was a beautiful campus, and I cherished the experience of exploring it more. My phone beeped with a message when I was halfway to the house, a smile pulling at my lips when I saw who.

Rhett: Hey, how was your day? Do you need a
ride back to the house?

ME: It was interesting. I'm walking back now
and almost there, assuming I remember which
house it is and don't walk into a random one.
winking face

Rhett: I've been thinking about you

A blush crept up my cheeks, and I was helpless to fight it. It had been a long time since I'd flirted or gotten excited about a man. Okay, let's be real, *men*. I couldn't lie to myself that I wasn't attracted to more than one at this point. They weren't your typical guys, and my heart started to flutter more as the dots danced along the bottom of my screen. Sometimes I hated those dots, but right then, I loved them. I was surprised Rhett was texting me as he didn't seem like a big texter, but I loved it.

Rhett: Hmm… that sounds like you got yourself into some trouble

Rhett: BTW, the roommates wanted to do dinner and an activity tonight. Soren says it is "bonding." Is that okay with you? Do you have plans?

ME: That sounds like Soren, and fun. I want to get to know you all better. And well… let's say I didn't make the best of impressions with someone.

Rhett: That doesn't sound like you at all. You make great first impressions. *winking face*

Damn, Mr. Grumpy was throwing shade at me in the most hilarious way. I couldn't believe it, and a laugh bubbled out of me. He'd texted a wink emoji, making me feel he was definitely flirting with me. My heart raced even more. *Swoon.* My Grumpy Butt was making an effort, even if it was out of his comfort zone. My face was going to be so red by the time I made it to the house. I'd blame it on the physical exertion of walking. That sounded plausible. I changed Rhett's name in my phone and added the Care Bear as his picture, snickering at myself.

ME: HAHA. You're hilarious. Besides, I thought you quite liked my first impression. *kissing face*

Grumpy: Oh, I definitely did. I think you're beautiful, Sawyer.

My heart stopped. Squeeeeee. I couldn't fight the grin any longer that spread over my whole face. How was this guy real? And single? Utah girls were stupid.

ME: Stop, you're making me blush.

Grumpy: I think your blush is sexy. I want to see more of where you blush.

Holy Shit! Rhett was a smooth talker. I hadn't expected that, but I should've known. Anyone with a strong eyebrow game like his, had to be charming.

My assumption was since he didn't talk, he wasn't expressive. But, man, was I wrong. I was learning it was more that he didn't waste his time speaking to very many people, so the fact that he was with me... *Wow*.

Now, I started to get flushed in other areas. I felt myself growing slick between my legs too. It had been a while since I had any "benefits." I wondered how far he was willing to take this. Deciding to be brave, I tested it out.

> **ME**: That could be arranged. But I don't know if you could handle me.

My heart raced as I hit send. This could go well, or really bad. I hoped I hadn't misread Rhett's signals. He did ask me out this morning, so I assumed that meant he was interested, right? Now, I hated those stupid dots as they took forever to show his reply. I was almost to the house by this point, seeing it over the bend. I needed to know if I was racing in or turning around and going for a run.

> **Grumpy**: Oh, baby, I look forward to proving you wrong. How close are you? You're driving me wild with need. Please say you are near.
> **ME**: Hopefully, very close. Otherwise, you might need to bail me out for entering the wrong house.

Hitting send, I jogged up the front steps and decided to take a risk and headed straight to his room. When I got downstairs, though, he wasn't there. I could hear music filtering out from the fitness room, so I moved toward it. I saw him bent over a machine with his phone in his hand through the big window right before I stepped through the door. His head snapped up, carnal desire written on his face as he took me in from head to toe.

I'd never felt such raw heat directed at me before. It was exhilarating. Sucking in a breath, I tried to get my heart to slow. Holy shit balls! I think this man might kill me. But at least it would be with an orgasm.

fourteen

. . .

rhett

Being direct over text was out of character for me, especially since I despised texting. Sawyer drew something from me, making everything with her feel natural and comfortable. Her text came through, and my heart raced as I stared at the message displayed on my screen.

How did I get her to come to me? Or should I go to her? Debating what to do, I was surprised when I heard the door open. I snapped my head up and stopped.

Damn, she was sexy.

Her chest heaved from her walk, or perhaps from being turned on. I hoped it was from being turned on. People assumed I fucked girls all the time, and I could pretend I was confident over the phone, but I hadn't been with anyone since I was twenty, and well now, I was twenty-five. So, yeah, you do the math!

Yet, here was this stunning girl who set every part of

me on fire, and she was standing in front of me with blatant desire on her face. When I realized she was frozen to the spot, I advanced toward her.

That was okay, baby; you got this far, so let me take you the rest of the way.

I had to remind myself I could do this too; because I wanted it so bad, I was fearful I'd blow as soon as she touched me. If I drew this out, I hoped to avoid embarrassing myself.

I towered over her, peering down at green eyes so captivating, it was difficult to escape them. From the moment I'd gazed into them, I'd been hooked. Her eyes held dark secrets, deep emotions, and a magnitude of passion. Sawyer was beautiful, kind, smart, and funny. She had an inner strength I didn't think she realized existed, and a confidence in all the best ways, while being humble in others.

She was as perfectly imperfect as a person could be, beautifully broken, and standing here with me. I placed my hand on her face, and her eyes closed, leaning into my touch.

"You found me, baby, now, what should I do with you?" My voice rumbled with desire, and I felt her shiver. She whimpered, but opened her eyes to look at me.

"Make me feel good. I want you to touch me all over," she rasped.

Fuck, this woman was so damn sexy. She knew what she wanted and asked for it. Her voice was full of need, and I could hear the desperation. Sawyer needed to cum, and I'd been selected to handle the job. I walked her back toward the glass wall and locked the door. I might've entertained someone watching earlier, but not at this moment. This moment was going to be only us—Sawyer and me.

I pushed my hand into her hair and tilted her face up more. She was short, though, and I needed better leverage. Otherwise, I'd end up with a neck ache, and that just wasn't fun. I cursed my height at that moment, but then realized the solution and was grateful with how she responded.

I lifted her up by her ass with one hand. Yep, one hand.

She moaned as her legs locked around my waist, her arms circling my neck. Oh yeah, this was perfect. Sawyer's center matched directly where my cock strained against my joggers. I moaned as she moved against me. Putting my lips against her neck, I breathed her in for a few seconds as I gathered myself. This little vixen didn't take it easy on me, as her hands mussed through my hair and pulled.

"Yes, Rhett." Her moan was liquid ecstasy to my ears.

"Fuck, baby, when you say my name like that, it makes it hard not to cum on the spot," I replied.

No longer able to wait, I smashed my lips down to hers, pressing my cock against Sawyer's center. I pushed her harder against the wall as we rocked against one another. Her lips were the softest silk, and I pressed my tongue against her lips, demanding her to open to me. She complied willingly, and greedily took my tongue into her mouth. The moans Sawyer made as I sucked on her tongue were becoming addicting. I thrusted myself harder against her as she whimpered against my mouth.

Needing to touch more of her body, I dropped one hand from her hair and began to caress down her side. I slipped my fingers under her shirt and slowly moved toward her breast. As I rubbed her nipple, I could feel the stiff peak through her sports bra. As if bras weren't tricky enough, this one had to be the most difficult fucking sport bra ever.

What were all these straps for, anyway? It didn't make sense at all. Deciding to screw the damn thing, I roughly pushed it up over her breasts, scraping against her sensitive flesh in the process. I began to tweak her nipple more as she sucked in a breath. Taking the opportunity, I kissed the hollow of her neck and sucked behind her ear. Her moans grew louder, and she tightened her grip on my hair as she rocked harder against me.

"Gah, Rhett, that feels so good," she moaned, spurring me on even more.

I licked the spot I had been sucking and moved lower on her chest. Taking her breast into my mouth, I gently bit her nipple and licked it. I grabbed more of her ass in my palm as I rocked, grinding myself against her. Deciding I needed both hands free so I could get this damn shirt off of her, I turned, putting my back against the glass and dropped to the ground so she straddled me. I'd never been so thankful for all the squats I'd done until then because it meant I didn't have to move away from her.

Now, Sawyer's breasts were directly in front of my face, and she sat right on my rigid length. She leaned back a little, and I tugged her shirt over her head, throwing it to the side, not caring where it landed. Now, I could access both of her perky breasts.

"Damn, baby, you're gorgeous, and your blush is everything I thought it would be and more. Fuck, that's sexy," I groaned. I didn't think I'd ever seen a more beautiful body.

Sawyer was perfection to me. Her pale skin high-lighted her full body blush with her arousal, and her breaths quickened with my stare. I tweaked one nipple while I sucked on the other, but I missed her mouth too much, so I brought my lips back to hers, moving my other hand lower, brushing against the seam of her pants. Sawyer whimpered into my mouth as she started to dry-hump me like we were randy teenagers. We weren't even naked yet, and it was one of the hottest experiences of my life.

Deepening the kiss, I slipped my fingers beneath her waistband. Thankfully, they were stretchy workout ones and had some give in them, allowing me to reach her wet pussy easily. Slipping my hand into her panties, I rubbed the outside of her lips and immediately coated my fingers in her wetness.

Fuck, that was hot.

Rubbing my thumb against her clit, I slowly pressed

one finger into her hot center. I could feel her tighten around me as I moved it back and forth. Sawyer began to ride my finger harder at that, and I could feel her getting close to orgasming. Adding a second finger, her moans intensified, and she rocked even more on me. My fingers were deep inside Sawyer as she pressed against my cock. I felt myself getting close too, and she hadn't even touched me.

"Baby, you feel so good against my hand. So, wet for me. I can't wait to feel you wrapped around my cock. These little sounds you're making are driving me wild. Can you take more?" I rasped out to her; the level of need dripped from my voice.

"Please, it feels so good. I want more... I need it, now," she whimpered.

Feeling her walls tighten, I inserted a third finger while simultaneously rubbing her clit with the rough side of my thumb. I curved my fingers deep as I continued to kiss the daylights out of her. Sawyer tore her mouth away as she came all over my fingers, spasming around my hand that was buried in her warm, wet pussy. She rocked against me, riding out her orgasm, taking what she needed. She was so breathtaking at that moment that it detonated my release, and I joined her with a moan.

Her pleased smirk on those lips made me feel satisfied in a whole new way. I withdrew my hand as she whimpered, missing it already. I licked my fingers as she watched, her pupils blown, and she licked her lips back at me. Fuck, she didn't even try, and she was the sexiest woman I'd ever seen.

"Baby, that was straight fire. You fucking made me cum without even touching me. Imagining what it will feel like to be inside you, almost has me coming again right now," I said tenderly as I caressed her cheek with my clean hand. Her smile dazzled me as she basked in her orgasmic high.

"That was mind-blowing," her voice had taken on this explicit sexy quality. I kissed her one more time before helping her up and retrieved her top. I didn't want her to get dressed, but I helped her, anyway.

"I fucking hate sports bras, by the way, worse invention ever," I grumbled.

"Oh, you grump. If I didn't wear one, then the girls would bounce everywhere, and everyone would be staring at them. I bet you wouldn't like that," she teased smugly. I hated when the guys called me grump, but it sounded good from her lips.

"Humph. Definitely not. But it would make easier access for me." I smirked back at her. The sound of her laughter set my heart soaring. Two days with this girl and my heart was already a goner.

"Before our texts turned naughty, I was going to let you know that the guys want to make dinner and hang out around 6 pm. Elias should be here too, so you can meet him, only leaving you to meet Rey."

"Awesome. Well, I guess I better shower now so I can rest before then. The jet-lag is catching up with me. Plus, I'm certain if I don't leave, things will keep escalating." Sawyer grinned at me, a naughty look in her eyes.

"You're probably right, and I would like to take you to dinner and more. You're not just a casual fuck for me, baby, I hope you get that."

Her smile set my heart aflutter. I was speaking poetically again, which could only mean one thing… I was falling in love. As much as that should scare me based on my past, for once it didn't, which was almost scarier.

Kissing her on the nose, I left and headed toward my room. I turned back thinking I saw movement, but no one was there. That was when it dawned on me. I'd locked the door to the room, but forgot the mirror was two-way. We couldn't see out, but anyone downstairs would've been able to see what we'd been up to in there.

Shit. I really hoped no one had been down here.

fifteen

. . .

sawyer

RHETT'S WORDS REPLAYED IN MY HEAD AS I WENT UP THE stairs. *"You aren't just a casual fuck to me, baby."* He'd placed a gentle kiss on my nose and left. I heard him get in the shower, and I wondered if he was cleaning up the mess he made in his pants. Fuck, why was that so hot to think about? I'd made a guy cum in his pants like he was a teenager.

I'd hoped to get an orgasm when I'd sent that text, but damn, Rhett delivered and then some. That was the best orgasm I'd ever had. It caused my whole body to shake. And holy hell, that man could kiss! I was getting turned on again just from replaying the way he'd effortlessly lifted me.

With one hand… one fucking hand!

Then he had to go and put me up against the wall like in all my fantasies. But him turning and dropping to the floor with me wrapped around him as if it were nothing, shit, that was erotic. If I'd seen him without a shirt on, I might've stroked out or had a spontaneous orgasm and combusted. Based on the exploration of his muscles my hands had performed as I clung to him like a freaking spider monkey, the man was ripped.

Turning the corner, my thoughts were interrupted by a tiny white ball and a frantic Oliver as he chased after the white blur.

"Stop him!" Oliver shouted, running at full tilt.

Instantly, I sat down in the hallway, blocking the door as the white ball zoomed toward it. The dog saw me too late, and the ball tried to stop, but with the floors being hardwood, his tiny paws caused him to flounder around like a baby deer taking its first steps, making the whole scene hilarious.

Eventually, his momentum plummeted him directly into me, and I scooped up the precious baby, holding him to my chest. I cooed at the white furball as he began to lick my nose in appreciation. I looked up, meeting Oliver's raised eyebrows and confused expression.

"What?" I asked. "You said to stop him, so I did. He wasn't hurt. Promise."

"Sawyer, that's not it." Oliver smiled, squatting down to us. "Lucky doesn't like a lot of people. It's just odd, that's all. I shouldn't be surprised, though. Even Lucky knows when there's a hot girl around." Oliver flirted, reaching out a hand to pet Lucky. When Lucky pulled away from his touch into me, I couldn't help but laugh, happy he wasn't holding a grudge from our showdown this morning.

Standing up, I cradled the little dog in my arms. This house had hot guys and a dog, add in the view, and the shower, and well, it was official… I was never leaving.

"It was lucky I was here to meet you, little guy. What should I do with this precious baby? Hmm? Can I keep him?" As I asked Oliver, I peered up at him with my best puppy dog eyes. Lucky snuggled down into my arms, content to stay where he was. I was *so* going to steal this dog. Whoever's dog this was, I hoped they weren't attached because he was mine now.

"Well, it's Elias' dog. I was just letting him out to go to the bathroom when the rascal escaped the leash and took off in search of freedom. I suppose you can take him with you for the time being. Heaven knows why you'd want to, but he seems content enough." Oliver shrugged his shoulders as he walked closer.

"Perfect." I continued to coo to the fluff ball as we walked further into the house. Mateo was in the game room playing a video game when we walked by.

"Hey Mateo, how was your day?" I asked, smiling at him softly. There was something so endearing about this beautifully quiet, sweet boy. I wanted to know him on a real level.

"It's been good. Thanks for asking, Sawyer. I hope your day was everything you hoped for," Mateo said sincerely. His voice was such a soft timbre that it made my insides feel like a warm blanket each time he spoke.

"It's been interesting. I'd like to hang later if you're up for it?" I questioned nervously. I didn't know why I felt nervous, but Mateo made me feel like a girl with her first crush. He was just so precious, and I wanted to bask in him while protecting him at all costs.

"I'd enjoy that very much." He smiled, and it was so sweet, I melted.

"Perfect, I'll text you later." My face warmed, matching his.

"I look forward to it."

We both wore huge smiles by the end of the conversation, and I was happy Mateo wasn't ducking his head anymore when he talked to me. Those damn butterflies had detonated again. I started to head out of the room toward my bedroom when Oliver caught up with me again. He'd been hanging back while I spoke with Mateo.

"Hey Sawyer, I was wondering if I could talk to you for a moment?" he asked as we climbed the stairs.

"Sure."

"I just wanted to apologize for this morning and the comments I made. I'm not really like that, promise. It's just, um, sometimes I fall into that persona when I see a pretty girl, and the 'cocky Oliver' comes out. I wasn't thinking. It's no excuse, but I am sorry if I came across as disrespectful." Oliver appeared sincere, his face open and genuine, that I couldn't help but want to give him another chance.

"Of course, Ollie," I grinned. He smiled even wider at me, and now those butterflies were having a field day. It must be a 'buy one, get one free' promotion or something on crushes this week. Needing to throw him off my emerging feelings, I pulled out my sassy pants.

"What? Don't be getting all fuck boy on me again, or I'll steal more than just your bacon."

"No, that isn't it." He blushed. "You called me Ollie. I liked it. Only my friends call me that, and I hope we'll be friends."

Damn him and his grin. When he looked at me like that, he resembled Jamie Frasier from Outlander. My cheeks began to flush again. Seriously hormones. You just made out with Rhett and had an orgasm, but you want to go and get all hot and bothered again because of a smile? Horny bitch.

Welp, it was official, I'd lost it. The delirium had taken over entirely now because I just called my hormones a horny bitch. I desperately needed to make an appointment before I started making out with all of my roommates, or my thoughts turned into a cheesy porno from the '70s.

There were so many things to keep track of now. I needed a planner or something. It would be a good idea at this point. I bet I could do one of those cool bullet journals. I had seen a bunch of cute ones—

"Sawyer!"

Oops... lost in my mind again. I stopped abruptly, nearly causing him to crash into me. I turned around quickly. "Sorry, did you say something?"

"You're kind of cute when you get lost in your head, you know," Oliver said with a wink.

"Boy, bye," I laughed as I pushed his face away from me and entered my room. I didn't think he could be serious for long. I wouldn't tell him that I liked the fun he brought—no need to encourage him any further.

"I'm going to grow on you, just you wait!" he shouted from outside my door.

"Yeah, like a fungus!" I bantered back, which only caused him to laugh louder.

"A sexy one, though, right?"

I seriously could not handle this guy. Had to give it to him for not giving up though, and making me laugh.

Sitting my new dog down in my chair, I decided to take that shower I'd mentioned earlier. I was also hoping to have some time after it to start some research. I hadn't been able to find anything yet, but I'd only been here a day.

It had been surprising to meet people I wanted to spend time with, and therefore, had wrongly assumed I'd have loads of free time when I took the job.

Orgasms were nice, okay they were more than nice, especially when delivered by Rhett, but I couldn't lose focus. This was too important. But if the rest of my days felt this amazing, I could get used to it—you know, minus the evil bitch part.

Seriously, I was going to marry that shower! It felt so incredible. If it served food, I'd never leave. It had almost given me another orgasm purely from the jets alone. That shower would come in handy living in a house of delicious men.

Looking at my closet, I decided to dress semi-cute for the evening, since the guys had only really seen me in athletic wear. Pulling on a pair of cute shorts, I wondered if they were too on the dangerous side of low and had, in fact, crossed into trashy. It was a very delicate line to toe.

Deciding to go with it, I grabbed a top that displayed a little midriff and combined it with a long boyfriend cardigan I left open. Everything was soft and comfortable while giving me a little sex appeal, or I hoped it did. I'd worked hard for my stomach muscles, so why not show them off?

I debated if I needed shoes since we were staying in, and eventually decided to go with my funny, no-show socks. I wasn't one of those girls who had sexy lingerie or undergarments. Nope, I had nerd merch. It was sexier, in my opinion. So I pulled on my 'I double heart Doctor Who' socks. Perfect.

Grabbing my laptop, I flopped into the massive armchair with my dog and began to do some basic searches. I wasn't sure what I expected to find this way that I hadn't found in the past five years, but for some reason, my mind felt that since I was in the right city, it would magically make new search results appear.

Sorry brain, the internet didn't work that way.

A few hours later, my stomach began to growl, and I realized the time. I hadn't found anything either, but I might have stumbled upon a few leads to look into later. But now, it was time for some food. My stomach demanded it.

Lucky had stayed with me the whole afternoon, curled up next to me. I hoped Ollie had told Elias I had him. He was my dog now, but I wasn't so cruel that I'd want him freaking out about him being missing.

I loved dogs and I'd always wanted one; it seemed my wish had finally been granted. Deciding to braid my hair to get it out of the way, I quickly pulled it to one side and it draped over my shoulder. I couldn't pull off the messy bun. It always resembled a bird's nest or something growing out of my head when I tried. It wasn't my best look. The Katniss braid, though. I could so rock that. Ah, the benefit of long hair.

It was close to 6:00 pm, so I made my way to the kitchen with Lucky in my arms. I knew he could walk, but I was having fun cuddling him for the moment. I could hear someone in the kitchen singing along with the radio. I stopped before entering, watching Soren dance around and sing while Matteo laughed at him. These guys were amazing. I'd definitely lucked out getting placed. We'd ignore the fact it was an error.

I hadn't connected with girls this way, not since Finley. When I'd told Charlie last night about my room-mates, he laughed for so long, I thought he was going to pass out. The old man found it funny too.

Though, the old grump thought it would be funny to end our call by telling me to use protection because he didn't want to be a great-granddad. Asshole, though, I did laugh at it.

Soren spotted me when he turned around, dancing toward me. He pulled me further into the kitchen, with one hand swaying back and forth. When he recognized what I was cradling, he lifted his eyebrow. Shrugging my shoulder, I enjoyed our dance around the kitchen. "Blinding Lights" was playing, and I loved this song. No matter how much I listened to it, I never grew tired of it. When the song ended, he bowed like a gentleman and then went back to what he'd been doing before our impromptu dance.

I handed the dog off to Mateo for a second so I could jump up on the counter. His face at the request was comical as he held the squirming dog out from him like Lucky might be radioactive. Lucky didn't seem happy about the arrangement either, though, so I quickly rescued them both. Lucky settled back into my lap, glad to be safe from the strange human.

A guy I hadn't met yet, stormed into the kitchen, zeroing in on my dog sleeping in my lap. He did not look happy about that fact, either. Oh shit, this must be Elias. He glanced up, meeting my eyes, once he realized Lucky was fine.

"Who the hell are you, and what are you doing with my dog?" he demanded, a slight British accent noticeable. His face was an impenetrable mask of disdain, and to say he wasn't pleased to see me sitting there with his dog in my lap was an understatement. I could practically see the fury rolling off him, steam billowing from his ears.

Well, too bad sweet cheeks. Lucky had chosen me.

While Elias stewed in his fury, I took the opportunity to look him over. He had to be around 6'2" in height and had thick chestnut brown hair that did that sexy, flopping thing. Not that he was sexy. Nope, not at all.

Elias' hair looked as if he had styled it into obedience. There wasn't a single hair out of place, probably afraid to be on the receiving end of his scorn. I could tell you from experience, it wasn't pleasant. His eyes reminded me of whiskey, and they swirled with scrutiny as he glared at me. He was rocking a little stubble along his jaw, but I had a feeling it wasn't normal for him as he was dressed very clean-cut. Elias wore gray pressed pants—nary a wrinkle to be found—and a light blue button-down shirt. Though, he'd rolled up the sleeves, putting his forearms on display, giving him a rugged sex appeal.

What was it about a man showing forearms that was so seductive? Seriously, it should be outlawed.

His skin was a golden bronze color, and as he flexed the muscles in his arms, I was transfixed by the movement. Elias should be a forearm model. Shit, was I drooling? I forgot my damn bib again.

When I finished checking him out, I realized I hadn't responded to him. He huffed at me in annoyance as he continued to glare. Oops. But, but… forearms! It was his own fault.

"Oh, sorry. He was about to run out the door, and Oliver told me to catch him. So, I did. Lucky and I became friends, and he spent the afternoon with me cuddling. Sorry if you were worried. I thought Oliver would've told you."

"Firstly, my dog does *not* cuddle. Second, it is quite rude to take someone's dog without letting them know. I spent the past hour looking all over the house for him."

As his voice rose, my usual bravado failed me. The confrontational tone he used and the apparent anger in his body triggered me, and I internally began to withdraw. I didn't understand what his problem was. I didn't take his dog on purpose, so why did he have to berate me? Plus, what was with him not using contractions? That was weird.

I cast my eyes to the floor, not wanting to experience his wrath any longer, trying to make myself disappear. I internally curled up in my mind to protect myself, trying to pretend I was anywhere but here.

"Elias, bro, take it easy. She didn't know. It's my fault, I meant to tell you. I knew Lucky was with her. Besides, if you'd asked anyone, we could've told you as well. I don't understand why you're attacking her," said Ollie, calmly walking into the room. Thankfully, it made Elias turn to him, removing his glare from me.

"I would appreciate in the future, *Ollie*, for your latest puck bunny to leave my dog the hell alone. I am appalled Lucky went with her. There is no telling what he witnessed. He usually has superior judgment than this," Elias huffed, crossing his arms. He directed it all at Oliver now, effectively dismissing me the minute he'd walked into the kitchen. If his words hadn't told me, his actions clearly stated how little he thought of me. His words stung, and it felt as if he'd literally slapped me across the face.

It dislodged me enough from falling into my panic, and I handed Lucky off to Mateo again, hopping down from the counter. The rest of the guys had inhaled sharply at his words, all focused on him. Elias, not realizing the big pile of dog shit he'd just metaphorically stepped in, kept right on talking.

"Secondly, when did we decide it was okay to bring arbitrary girls back to the house? I thought this was to be a safe haven? Why am I having to worry about running into some conquest—"

The slap rang out through the kitchen and Elias' jaw fell open as shock painted his features. The guys had tried to stop him, but he'd been too far stuck up his own butthole, and had stopped listening.

Rhett stood in the doorway, fuming, and I could almost see steam billowing out of his ears. If I hadn't intervened, I was certain he would've punched his best friend on my behalf. As angry as I was with what Elias had said, I didn't want to cause strife between the guys. They all had a close bond, and this was their safe place. Elias hadn't been wrong about that. I just hoped there would be space for me, too.

Discreetly, I shook my hand out at my side. *Damn.* That had fucking hurt. Elias' jaw was freaking hard. No one ever told you how bad it felt. Shit, I hope I didn't break anything. Reeling myself in, I faced the asshat.

"Listen here, you butt-munch, and listen well. First of all, I'm not some fucking puck bunny or rando conquest, or whatever other demeaning phrases you called me. Second, how dare you! How dare you judge me without even knowing me or who I am?" I held a finger up for each point, and my breaths came quicker with each one as I worked myself up for this confrontation. I could feel my panic beginning to return as well, edging its way in, and I knew I only had a short period before I would completely crumble. I didn't want that to occur in front of the entitled asshole.

"Third, you should respect women and not refer to them in such debased ways, asswipe. I'm surprised a woman would even kiss you with the way you talk about them. Lastly, you entitled jerk nugget. My name's Sawyer. That's right. Your fucking roommate! So, you better get real used to me being around since I fucking live here, too. Hopefully, that won't hurt your delicate sensibilities. Or even better, you can stay the fuck away from me. I felt bad for stealing your dog earlier, but now, I'm glad because Lucky deserves someone who will actually love him. You didn't even know he was missing until three hours later. Do fucking better! Recap for all the folks at home. Watch. Your. Fucking. Self. You. Big. Ass. douchecanoe!"

It was eerie how steady my voice remained throughout my speech, and I half expected spit to fly from my mouth. My face had to be crimson with the amount of rage I felt coursing through my body. My hands were clenched tight to my sides, my heart raced, and my breathing was erratic. Having said everything, I turned and slowly walked out the front door, needing to escape his toxic masculinity.

Damn. So much for me admiring all of my roommates. I guess odds were going to dictate that not all of them could be amazing.

After pacing for a few minutes in the driveway, I sat down on the stoop and took giant lungfuls of the cool air. As I started to calm my pulse, the door opened behind me, making me tense up again. What were they thinking of me? Were they coming to tell me it wasn't going to work and I needed to leave?

I feared the answers, but I was also curious who was brave enough to come out here after that disastrous display.

I was waiting for the verdict to come, to send me packing when a warm tongue licked my hand. Glancing down, I realized Lucky had followed whoever it was. Shit, did that mean? I tensed, hoping it wasn't Elias. I would literally explode if I had to look at him right now.

A tear dropped onto my leg, surprising me, and I realized I was crying. Dammit. I hated being a girl sometimes. Who else fucking cried when they were mad? Guys assumed tears were only because you were sad.

Uh, no fucker, I was angry, and it leaked out of my

eyes! It was biology. Stupid hormones. It didn't help that my hand still fucking hurt.

A body sat down next to me on the steps. I could feel their body heat next to me, but I couldn't bring myself to look. Their scent drifted over on the night breeze, and I inhaled. Citrus. Grapefruit.

Mateo.

Turning slowly toward him, I found him gazing back at me without any judgment in his eyes. This surprised me, and I continued to stare into his deep blue eyes, and they slowly restored some of my inner calmness.

"Are you okay?" he questioned quietly after a few minutes.

Shrugging my shoulders, I opted to remain silent, as I wasn't sure what to even say to him.

No, of course, I wasn't fucking okay.

I wasn't fine with what Elias had said or how it had triggered me.

I wasn't okay with how it made me feel. Not at all.

But mostly, I wasn't okay with how I responded.

He might've deserved it, but I hadn't been any better with how I reacted. It had been different with Oliver; we were teasing and joking around with one another. But Elias had meant every word he said. His vitriol hate had dripped from each word, piercing me in the chest, and now, I was hemorrhaging. He'd cast me aside so quickly, and I hated it because it made me feel inconsequential.

Mateo slowly lifted his arm and wrapped it around

me, pulling me into his side. I leaned into him and placed my head against his shoulder.

"You know, it's really unfair, them sending you out here. I can't be angry at you," I admitted. I even found myself smiling as I said it. Mateo turned his head into my hair and breathed in deeply. He spoke so quietly, I almost didn't hear him when he said.

"I know what it's like to respond in that way. I get it, Sawyer, and I don't judge."

He trembled as he kept talking into my hair, show-casing how hard this was for him to be vulnerable. His presence itself was soothing, and his scent melted into me, helping to lower my heart rate. I was learning Mateo would talk if he felt comfortable, so I wouldn't be the one to push him. He showed me how much he cared by trying, and that helped me not feel so alone.

"I have panic attacks. It's why I stopped skiing professionally. I couldn't take it anymore, all the pressure piled up, and... I made a dumb choice. I don't want to... I can't talk about that right now. But, I wanted you to know that I get it. When your body feels so out of control, you react to something without even realizing you're doing it. It's too late once you do, to dial it back. You're stuck in that emotion, and your brain isn't thinking. I didn't want you to sit out here and think we're judging you or think you're crazy. Elias was out of line, and we're all worried about you. So, whenever you're ready, we can go back in, and I promise no one will say anything until you are ready to do so."

His soft voice soothed me, and his words melted my heart. He didn't show much of himself to the world, and that was a crime. It was a loss because this man had a beautiful soul. He was kind and caring with a strength I hoped to possess one day. His kindness made me fall a little more for him too.

We sat on the steps until the sun disappeared, Lucky in my lap, and Mateo's arm around me. He kept his head turned into my hair the whole time. I wasn't sure if it was to hide some of his vulnerability while he talked, or if he was just obsessed with my shampoo. Whatever the reason, it was one of the most intimate moments of my life, and I'd never forget it.

sixteen

. . .

soren

FURY ROSE IN ME AS I STARED AT ELIAS. I COULDN'T believe the things he'd said to Sawyer. She wasn't any of those things. If Elias had taken one minute to talk to her, he would've realized that. Instead, he opened his mouth and crushed that beautiful girl's spirit. With each word he said, Elias had struck her in the heart. I watched each blow land, stealing something from her. Sawyer pretended they hadn't wounded her, but I knew the look. I was familiar with it in my own mirror. The pain was all in her eyes.

After she walked out, Elias dropped his head in defeat. "I fucked up," he groaned.

"You think?" Rhett fumed. I'd never seen him so angry before. "You better be glad she got to you first, or you'd be unconscious right now." Rhett glared at his best friend.

"You are absolutely right. I deserved that, and everything Sawyer said to me and more. Bloody hell, I'm such a wanker. Fuck, it's no excuse, but I let Voldemort get in my head yesterday." Elias hung his head in shame at his confession. It was obvious he was beating himself up now, but it didn't change the hurt he caused. At least, Elias knew he'd screwed up. He had a lot of baggage from his ex-fiancée, so I could sympathize that he might not have been in the right mind space. He needed to make this right, though.

"Maybe I should go apologize," he suggested, looking up.

"No," we all shouted at once. If it hadn't been such a tense moment, it would've been funny as we all reacted to stop him.

"I'll go," Mateo offered quietly.

None of us could deny he was the perfect option, so we let him go. He'd be able to calm her down, and she wouldn't be able to be mad at him. Logically, it made sense, but fuck if I didn't want to be the one who got to cheer her up. I'd been thinking about her all day, and I couldn't wait to spend more time with her.

Mateo made his way out the front door with Lucky trailing after him toward his new best friend.

"Great, even my bloody dog likes her better than me," Elias grumbled.

I couldn't stop the laugh bubbling out this time. The others soon joined in, laughing as they recalled how epically Sawyer had slapped Elias. Not to mention the insults were amazing as well. I glanced at his cheek, which now bore a very red and distinct handprint.

"Damn, she got you good, butt-munch," I chuckled out.

"Yeah, asswipe. That's going to leave a mark," Oliver retorted.

"I think douchecanoe was my personal favorite." Rhett smirked, not even trying to hide the fact he purposefully used it against Elias, but instead called him out about it.

"I think it would be best if I skip roommate bonding tonight and call it an early evening. I will apologize in the morning once she has had some sleep. Sorry, guys, I hope you can forgive me," Elias said apologetically. It reminded me that he was a good dude overall, just had royally stepped in it.

It was another thirty minutes before the trio came back in; Lucky, Mateo, and Sawyer. They all seemed better as they made their way into the kitchen. Sawyer looked embarrassed as she walked in, not making eye contact with anyone. I couldn't have that. She didn't need to feel that way; so, I did what I did best and made it light.

"We're making homemade pizza for dinner. What would you like on yours, Señorita?" I asked, making a little hip move. Sawyer's accompanied laugh was worth any embarrassment I might feel at myself. I smiled big at her and saw an appreciation in her eyes that I hadn't said anything.

"What toppings do you have?"

"Well, tonight for your dining pleasure, let me present you with your choices. We have all the meats, most of the veggies, and pineapple, if that's your jam," I replied in my best *Beauty and the Beast* imitation of Lumiere's voice.

"Hmm…. Let's do mushroom and Canadian bacon. Do you have that?"

"One Canadian bacon and mushroom pizza, coming right up! Please, have a seat Señorita, and we will be right with you."

I motioned toward the island with a big flourish, causing her to giggle at my silliness, but it achieved what I'd intended. She smiled, no longer thinking about what had happened earlier. I continued to sing and dance to the music as I made everyone's pizzas, and watched as Rhett discreetly handed her an ice pack for the hand she'd been cradling. Mother hen Rhett to the rescue as usual.

Once the pizzas were all cooked, we gathered around the island to eat. There wasn't a lot of talking as we all shoved food into our mouths. I was happy to find Sawyer relaxed more as the night went on. After eating, I suggested a movie since it was already late, and I could tell Sawyer probably didn't have the energy for a game tonight. She nodded enthusiastically at the suggestion. She sat in the middle of the couch with Rhett and I bookending her. Mateo chose to sit on the floor in front of her, leaving a disgruntled Oliver on the armchair, which made me chuckle.

"What do we want to watch?" I asked.

"Comedy!"

Laughter filled the room as we watched, and I was glad we'd gone with something lighthearted. Though, I watched as Sawyer ran her fingers through Mateo's hair more than the TV. He laid back between her legs, and I'd never been so jealous of hair with the way her fingers glided through his strands. At some point, I'd stopped watching the movie altogether and focused on her finger movements instead.

I shifted my leg against hers, causing her to inhale each time. Casually, I dropped my arm behind Sawyer on the couch and started to play with the small hairs on the back of her neck. Goosebumps broke out on her arms, and I swear I heard a soft moan. It instantly made my cock take notice. I shifted a little to rearrange myself, hoping it wouldn't be obvious, but Sawyer spotted me anyway and smirked back at me.

Rhett's hand was on her knee, tracing small circles with his thumb. His massive palm enveloped her entire thigh, but she didn't seem to mind his touch. Oliver became grumpier and grumpier as the night progressed, and we continued to touch her casually, leaving him out. I just smiled at him. *Sucks to be you, brother.*

When the movie ended, Sawyer headed off to bed, the rest of us following.

"Go Lucky."

I laughed as she tried to get Lucky to go into Elias' room, but he refused and eventually she looked at me, shrugged, letting him follow her to bed. I didn't blame the dog. I'd rather snuggle with her than Elias too.

Back in my room, I checked my phone and noticed I had a few missed texts.

Rey: Hey, how are things? How's the new roommates?

Cersei: Son, I have an opportunity. Call me.
Cersei: Don't ignore me. You owe me. I
made you.

I dismissed the ones from my mom on the screen. No, thank you! I wanted nothing to do with her, and I most definitely didn't owe her shit. If anyone owed anyone, it was her to me—my childhood.

Not wanting to let her in my mind, I deleted her messages and opened the texts from Rey.

ME: Hey man. The new roommates are cool. I
think you'll like them.
ME: So how is the fam? You managing?
ME: I kind of have some exciting news to tell
you too
Rey: Sweet. I can't wait to meet the new guys.
Fam is okay. Same as usual. Mom and dad
hounded us both on coming back home more.
They want me to meet with another skater that
they think will be a "great connection" and lead

me back to competing. They don't get it or listen.
It's exhausting.
ME: That sucks, man. At least you got your
obligatory visit out of the way for this year.
Speaking of family, you'll never guess who
texted me tonight.
Rey: Yeah, that's true. Thankfully. We just need
to find someplace to be for Christmas to avoid
them.
Rey: Who texted? What is your news?
ME: We can head to Aspen or something. Don't
worry, man. I'll get us some plans.
ME: My mom texted. I deleted them. She wants
me to do something for her, as usual.
ME: My news… I kind of met a girl….

It took a while for him to respond after that. Was he
upset? Was he jealous?

Rey: Oh yeah, really? That's cool.
ME: She's one of the new instructors. I think
you'll like her. She's funny, kind, and gorgeous as
fuck. I'm trying to get up the nerve to ask her out.
Rey: Wow. Awesome, man.
Rey: Hey, listen, I've got to go. Fam stuff. Talk
later.

Well, he'd gotten off quickly now, hadn't he? I
pondered if he was upset about Sawyer? If he only

knew, I wanted him to be part of it too. I needed to step up and find the courage to tell him how I felt. I didn't want him to be jealous, or worse, move on. I wanted him too. It wouldn't be as incredible if he weren't part of it. I began to imagine how awesome it would be to be with both of them and how she'd felt earlier.

Since I didn't wear boxers most of the time, finding them restrictive, my cock instantly sprung free when I lowered my zipper. I wrapped my hand around my shaft and began to stroke it. I envisioned what it would be like to kiss Rey finally. To feel him against me. My cock grew thicker as I imagined him next to me with his hand rubbing my cock. Suddenly, Sawyer joined my fantasy, and I pictured her sitting on my face as I sucked her clit. She'd be riding my face hard while rubbing her breasts. As the fantasy built in my head, I jerked my cock harder, feeling the precum at the tip develop.

Swirling my thumb against it, I spread it over my head. Sawyer continued to ride my face as I pictured Rey below me with my cock in his mouth. God, that was a hot picture with both of them. I quickened the pace and felt my cock begin to tremble as my balls drew up. Imagining Rey taking me deep into his mouth as his tongue licked along my cock with Sawyer riding my face as my tongue licked her wetness had me on the edge of orgasming. Fantasy Sawyer fondled her breasts and pinched her nipples and I was done for.

Fuck!

I came so hard at the thought, my cum shot across my stomach, legs and even landed on the floor. My breath came out erratically as I came down from that orgasm.

Damn, that was hot. I hoped I got the chance to make it come true someday.

After I'd cleaned up, I rechecked my phone, but there weren't any new messages from Rey. I'd have to talk with him when he got home. It was time I quit something again; it was time to quit being scared.

seventeen

sariah

A harsh smack against my cheek brought me to. "Ouch, what was that for?" I asked, rubbing my jaw to ease the sting.

My surroundings rushed into view, and I realized I was lying on the couch. My parents hovered over me, their expressions worried as they tensed their jaws, scrunching their brows. The past hour began to flood my memories as images of an intimidating man in the expensive suit sped across my mind.

His creepy smile. The goon. My parents frozen in fear on the sofa. The foreboding news. Leaving with Mr. Creep Factor.

Yeah, that was going to have to be a no, a resounding Hell No, in fact.

"Sariah, you fainted. Are you okay?" my mother asked.

Now, I was the one saying mother with a bad taste in my mouth. I sat up, causing both of my parents to step back. I knew deep down I couldn't be too upset with them for keeping this secret. I could see the love and concern reflected on their stricken faces as they hovered. They'd hidden it from me to protect me. I couldn't fault them for that; I was only sixteen.

"Yeah, Mom. I'm okay, just overwhelmed at the moment."

She visibly relaxed when I called her mom. Oh yeah, apparently, my parents had adopted me. My father shared that with me right before I fainted like a proper lady. Mom should be so proud.

"Can we start from the beginning again?"

"Sure, honey. Do you want anything to eat or to drink first?" Mom asked, falling into her hospitality role she did so well. It was these little things that confirmed they loved me. They hadn't done anything but show me love, provide for me, and indulge my skating obsession. They loved me, and I loved them. They were my parents, it was as simple as that, really.

"Maybe some tea?" I suggested. Mom smiled more at this, her love of tea and the classics shining through. It had to be why she always wanted me to act like "a proper lady." And well, when I was about ten, I indulged her, and we watched all the classics together one summer. We'd have afternoon tea every day and watch our next movie. It had become our tradition when we needed a pick-me-up.

"Of course, sweetie. I'll prepare it. I think I still have some of your favorite one left."

I smiled as she scurried off to the kitchen. I only told her it was my favorite because it was hers, and she'd never purchase something extravagant for herself. But if I told her it was mine, she would keep it on hand, allowing both of us to enjoy it.

No Lipton tea for us; we used the real deal. Mom had fallen in love with Teapigs on a trip to London and ordered it special from the UK.

It was these small things that demonstrated to me how much I was loved. I couldn't argue against that. And while I was disappointed they'd kept this from me, I didn't hate them for it. How could you hate someone who'd saved you and gave you a great life? Only a monster would.

While Mom prepared the tea in the kitchen, my father sat beside me on the couch and gently brushed my hair off my face. His touch was caring, and I leaned into his hand, needing to feel some comfort.

"Sariah, you've been our greatest achievement. I've been honored to be called your father for sixteen years. I only hope you'll still consider me that once you hear everything."

He had tears in his eyes as he continued to caress my head gently. I couldn't take it anymore and launched myself into his arms, hugging him. My dad gave the best hugs, and he didn't disappoint when he wrapped his arms tight around me. I could feel his tears hitting my hair, so I held on to him harder. This man was my father. I didn't care what he had to tell me or what genetics would say. There was nothing that would diminish my love for him.

"I love you, Dad."

"Oh, sweetie, I love you too."

We eventually pulled back, wiping our tears as Mom returned with the special teapot. I'd gotten it for her on her birthday a couple of years ago. It was a hand-painted china teapot that a local artist had made. It was a generic white pot, but the design was one of a kind. The artist had painted my mom's favorite flower, wisteria, and then wrapped her favorite quote from Pride and Prejudice around it. It was exquisite. Mom only used it on special occasions since it was delicate. It made me sad to use it today as I didn't want to ponder what its inclusion meant.

Mom poured us all a cup of the Rooibos Crème Caramel tea, and then we each prepared them how we liked. We had become tea snobs over the years, and each of us had a specific way to drink our tea. I cherished our family intricacies though; it confirmed our bond and connection, and ultimately, our love. I took a sip, preparing myself for the life-changing conversation.

"I don't know if you recall any of this because you were so young when I worked there, but when you were born, I worked for a shipping company, Latimer Industries. The man that owned that company, Jayce Latimer, wasn't a respectable man. I didn't know that in the beginning, though. However, once he pulls you into his circle, he keeps you there by providing your wants and dreams. I'm afraid to admit that in the beginning, I was weak and gave in and took what he offered, forgetting that everything comes at a price."

He paused for a moment to sip his tea, and I swallowed some as well, wanting to clear my throat. I didn't have a good feeling about where this was headed. He placed his cup on his saucer, and I noticed his hands shook.

"He introduced me to your mom." He stopped, peering at her across the table, love shining bright in his eyes. "When I met Kyla, I thought I'd hit the jackpot. She was beautiful, worldly, smart, and somehow, she found me attractive." My dad laughed at himself, and my mom smiled adoringly back. Taking her hand, you could see the love between them. It was practically palpable. It was so authentic, and I yearned for the same thing some day. My parents had always been an excellent example of a loving couple, and I was happy they'd found one another.

"Well," he started again, clearing his throat. "Once we'd been married for a year, we wanted to start adding to our family. Unfortunately, we weren't able to conceive." He stopped as they both shared their sorrow. "I was talking about my heartbreak one day to a coworker when Latimer overheard and he offered, once again, the thing I wanted on a silver platter, making all my dreams come true. By this point, I'd started to overhear things at the office, the strings attached to his gifts and the consequences if you didn't fulfill your end, but I was desperate to see my wife happy, and in my grief, I agreed."

Dad had tears streaming down his face at this point, and Mom clutched his hand in hers, focused solely on him. I could tell how hard it was for them to share this, and the last of my hurt at them for keeping it a secret dissolved instantly. My parents were good people, and they were given a no-win situation. Desperate people made desperate choices. And they were no exception.

"Latimer told me he could make me a father, that he knew of a couple who were expecting and weren't able to keep the baby girl. He offered to put me in contact with them and assist in the legal papers. Latimer assured me we wouldn't have to worry about the birth parents changing their minds. It sounded perfect, but in hindsight, I realized my grief had clouded my judgment because nothing that perfect was legal or without strings."

I sucked in a breath at that news. Oh, no, this wasn't headed in the direction I had anticipated at all, and I expected that it was going to be much worse. I placed my teacup back on the saucer. I didn't want it to be a casualty of my shock. Precious things deserved to be protected at all costs; my mom had taught me that. There weren't enough of them in the world, making them valuable.

My father took a deep inhale before he continued. "The day you were born was one of the best days of our lives. We were fortunate to be at the hospital when you arrived. We weren't allowed to meet your birth mom, which at the time didn't seem odd. We soon forgot about the strangeness because you were handed to us, this tiny bundle of tranquility. Well, that was until you opened your mouth. You looked up at me with those eyes of yours, and my heart was instantly lost to you. I vowed at that moment to do whatever it took to protect you. You became my princess, so we named you Sariah."

He smiled at me, and I returned it as a tear tracked down my cheek. Dad had often called me his little princess growing up, and I never recognized the significance of it. Tons of memories threatened to flood me at that moment, but I pushed them back, needing to stay present on what my Dad was telling me.

"The first few years were a whirlwind. You were an amazing baby. Always so happy and active. You had these big green eyes that would always make me give in to you whenever you'd look at me. When you turned three, Latimer approached me and informed me that he was calling in his favor. I was floored because, for some reason, I'd assumed I was exempt. Working there for so many years and never having to before, I foolishly believed I was above it all. I'd never agreed to owe him a favor, but instead of backing off, Latimer listed all the dreams he'd granted over the years: the accounts, the perfect house, the perfect wife, and finally, the perfect child. To say I was shocked is putting it lightly, as I never imagined he'd given me things only to collect a debt one day. It was stupid and foolish of me, especially after I knew him. I'd worked for him for ten years at that point and seen his business dealings, heard the rumors, and knew his reputation amongst the staff. All along, I was a pig he'd been fattening for slaughter."

The words dripped with self-loathing for himself and disgust for this man. My mom squeezed his hands again. Dad didn't respond at first, but eventually, he squeezed back. He looked at me with dread and utter devastation on his face. I knew the next words he said might break my heart.

"Latimer notified me I could pay back my debts from over the past ten years by doing one thing. Just one thing would wipe it all away. I thought I would get out of the deal lucky and that I wouldn't have to sacrifice too much. I was a fool, a naïve fool. Because what he wanted, the one thing that would wipe out all of my supposed debt to him… It was you, Sariah. He wanted me to give you to him when you were sixteen."

I sucked in a breath. What? No! This couldn't be happening. This wasn't right. This was *my* life, not some after-school special. Besides, I wasn't going anywhere. I wouldn't. Plans started to form in my head on the actions I could take, starting with calling the police. Because I needed to do something as this couldn't unfold, not to me. I just had my first kiss, for crying out loud. I was about to make the National team for Worlds. My life was amazing, and I wanted to keep living it. I didn't want to leave with some crazy old dude who assumed he owned me. Nope, not happening. It wasn't fair. I was a person; you couldn't own a person. Right?

"I can see the thoughts racing through your head, princess. Don't worry, I told him to go to Hell because there was no way in any situation I would hand over my daughter to him. Latimer was furious and didn't accept my response. He advised me that I absolutely would give you to him because you weren't my daughter to begin with. Fury ran through me at his words because, of course, you were my daughter. How dare he suggest such a thing! It didn't matter that we didn't share DNA. You were my daughter, and I had vowed to protect you against anything. I just hadn't known that it would be the monster standing in front of me at that moment." He sucked in another lungful of air, wiping his brow.

"I continued to refuse him for a month, stating I wasn't giving you to him. He insisted that if I didn't hand you back, then he would kill everyone I loved, starting with Kyla and would do it in front of me. Latimer told me that other things were at play here, and I was a pawn in a bigger game. He informed me that he'd only given you to us in the first place because he knew we'd take care of you. But that, unfortunately, your path had been laid out for you before you were even born. Latimer broke my hand that day by smashing it with a hammer. He expressed that he would continue to break something new each day if I didn't bow to the request. That was the night we packed all our belongings and moved here, to this town, far away from Latimer, or so we'd hoped. Fortunately, I had a… uh friend… who'd given us new identities, and we've been in hiding ever since. I'd hoped he would never find us, but I guess that was naïve, too."

I was trembling as tears streamed down my face. I didn't know if I wanted to hear any more. I didn't know if I could take it. At that instant, my mom's phone rang, startling us all from the intense moment. My mom got up to answer it, leaving my father sitting on the couch with me.

"I don't know if I can hear any more right now, Dad," I whispered. I didn't want him to think of me as weak, but I was at max capacity for news at the moment. Peering up at him, I expected to see disappointment written on his face.

"It's okay, princess. It's a lot to digest and part of why we haven't told you before now. Your mother and I didn't want to burden you with this. We wanted you to grow up happy and healthy, and selfishly, I wanted to appreciate the light you have for as long as I could. It was wrong, but I wanted to protect you from the truth for as long as possible."

Shaking my head vigorously, I rushed to stop my father's words. "You weren't selfish, Dad. Don't ever believe that for a second. I was shocked when you first told me, but I can't deny that my life has been happy and carefree. I don't know if I'd be the same person I am if you'd told me earlier. You and Mom have given me the best life. The absolute best, Dad. I wouldn't want any other parents because you are my dad. I don't care what any DNA test states, either."

My father gripped me in a fierce hug as we both

tried to manage our tears. He soothed me by rubbing his hand up and down my back over my hair in a comforting gesture he'd done when I was younger. "We can finish later, princess. I'm not letting R take you anywhere, I promise. We're going to have to run again, and I'm sorry about that. I know this will change your future and what you can do moving forward, but I refuse to let you leave with that man. I'll protect you with everything I have until the day I die. You can always count on me to do that."

We stayed together for a long time. After the phone call, my mom returned and joined us on the couch in a three-person hug. It felt comforting, making me feel safe and cherished.

I didn't know at that moment, though, that it would be the last hug I'd ever have from my parents, Kyla and Scott Brennon. Or that my dad's words would come true so soon.

eighteen

. . .

sawyer

Bolting upright in bed, my heart beat out of my chest as my breath left me in uneven puffs, and I tried to pull myself back into the present from the nightmare. Lucky looked at me as I gathered my bearings, watching me. He licked my nose and cuddled closer to my side. I couldn't help the smug smile that spread across my face when I recalled his owner's hateful words to me, and I no longer felt bad about stealing his dog.

Justice served, in my opinion, this dog was too precious for a crabby owner.

Shaking my head at myself, I should've been more prepared and anticipated the nightmare. It had been an emotionally draining day in a new environment. My barriers were weak with all the new things going on, not to mention facing off with the Queen Bitch, opening myself up physically to Rhett, and the emotional onslaught with Elias had thrown me for a loop. I'd only been here for two days, and I'd experienced more emotions than I normally would in a month in Iowa. It wasn't a bad thing per se, I was no longer hiding behind my shields to avoid my feelings, but I'd forgotten the toll these new experiences brought. Hindsight, meet my nightmare.

Glancing at my nightstand, the clock glowed mockingly back at me reading 5:30 am. Well damn, no point going back to sleep now. Thinking about it, I knew what would be the perfect way to spend my early morning Saturday. I could do with some self-care, and getting out of the house for a while sounded perfect.

The fact I also got away from all the testosterone and my own conflicted feelings, well, that was just a bonus.

If I headed into town now, I could investigate some of the leads I'd found yesterday and get some things I needed that I hadn't brought with me. Plus, with it being this early, I'd be less likely to run into people—I hoped.

After a shower, I dressed comfortably in jeans and a sweater, and headed out to the garage to check on my ride. Because my past being what it was, I wasn't a big fan of cars. Thus, I'd never acquired my driver's license. Instead, when I turned eighteen, I got a motorcycle license and purchased a used Vespa. Velma was my baby and perfect for getting around my small town in Iowa. Hopefully, I'd be able to use it for most of the year here without the snow hindering things. The Vespa should be adequate enough for taking me into town and getting around campus. I'd had it shipped here the week before I left, so I missed my baby.

Walking to the garage, I realized how odd it was for me to be attached to material things. I hadn't been since I was a teenager, but I did love my Vespa. It had been the first significant thing I'd purchased for myself. It was an older model I'd gotten from a kind older lady in town that Charlie had known. Her husband bought it for her years ago, but she couldn't ride it anymore due to her health. It was in great shape, and I'd gotten an excellent deal on it.

After I'd bought it, I'd visit her each week and share my tales of travels over a cup of tea. It reminded me of my mom in a way, and I'd enjoyed being able to share something in my life with her again, even if not physically.

Immediately, I spotted Velma, and I skipped to her, a squeal leaving me. Running my hands over the leather, I sighed in relief she was still in one piece. Pulling out my helmet, I clasped it on as I perched on my seat. The Vespa was mint green with chrome; and quite frankly, stunning. I loved every minute of driving her.

Like I'd assumed, there weren't a lot of people out this early in the morning, making the drive quick. I spotted a few stores as I drove into town that I wanted to check out, along with the library, a movie theater, a diner, a sushi restaurant, and even a Thai place. There were several ski rentals and clothing stores, unsurprisingly, but it also meant I'd never have to worry about needing any gear.

The library and diner had been part of the town for several decades, so I hoped they'd be an excellent place to start on my quest for the truth. On the third street I turned down, I spotted a colorful awning that looked promising. Thankfully, a couple parking spaces were open on the street, making it convenient. Hope bloomed in my chest as I took in the storefront, unsnapping my helmet. Yep, this was just what I needed.

Walking in, I was immediately accosted by the glorious smells of coffee beans, fresh baked goods, and the varying fragrances of caramel, vanilla, and cinnamon. This would be the perfect place to unwind. The interior was quiet, with a cozy atmosphere. Several short tables littered the sitting area with comfy armchairs, bean bags, couches, and loungers mixed around, offering a unique hodgepodge of furniture. Only a few people occupied the space, opting to sit in chairs, soaking in the comfort of the place. I had a feeling this would become my new favorite escape.

Walking to the counter, I quickly surveyed the menu they had posted. In the mood for some coffee this morning, I ordered a Caramel Macchiato. I wasn't a huge coffee drinker, but I appreciated a nice layered latte. Ordering a chocolate chip muffin, I felt giddy with my new chill spot. They even had my favorite kind of muffin—the toppers—where it was only the muffin's top. Pure genius.

Choosing the window, I plopped down into the oversized chair and realized I might never want to leave. This spot was perfect. It was semi-private but offered a view of the front window, allowing me to gaze outside and people watch. It was a favorite pastime of mine. My best friend and I used to make up stories about the passersby, and I found myself still doing it even though I no longer had a co-author for our tales.

Checking my phone, I didn't find anything that required immediate attention, so I put it back down. Daydreaming about a couple I saw outside; I was surprised when I felt someone tap my shoulder. Turning my head, I took in the guy standing over me.

He appeared to be biracial with a mix of African American and Latino, was of average height with chestnut brown hair that he'd shorn close to his head but allowed him to have a small faux hawk. His best feature were his eyes, which were dark chocolate and shone with a mischievous glint. He had a solid build, large biceps, and had some tattoos displayed. His smile was kind, though, and didn't set off my creep meter.

"Hi! I'm sorry, I don't mean to disturb you, but I couldn't help noticing you were new when you came in. Small town, you know, everyone knows everyone. You wouldn't happen to be an instructor at the school, would you?"

He spoke quickly, but kindly, and a little sheepishly all at once. He kept smiling genuinely at me, never giving me any weird feelings. Deciding I wanted to try making a new friend, I chose to be honest with him; especially since it was my thing now, you know, honesty.

"Well, I'm sure you already know the answer to that question." I smiled, kindly, letting him know I wasn't throwing shade. "I just started, or will in a few days, I guess, when classes start." I inspected him shrewdly as he listened. "I have a feeling you have an agenda, sir. No one with a smile like yours can be trusted." I cocked an eyebrow as I gave him my sassiest smile. His enthusiasm seemed to multiply even more if that was possible.

"Girl! Please tell me you're the one who threw down and challenged, none other than, the Queen of the Alphabets!" he exclaimed, glee practically dripping from his words. He even clapped his hands like a fangirl. I was beginning to think I'd misjudged his level of danger, afraid he'd spill the coffee in his hand all over me.

"Erm… well, I suppose if you are referring to Princess Adelaide. Then yes, that would be me. Tada!" I gave my best jazz hands at that. I was still confused, though. "But who are the Alphabets?"

I felt awkward suddenly, and not from the jazz hands, mind you, but that word of my epic fail in our meeting had spread already. Good to know the instructors in this place were a bunch of busybodies. So not cool.

"Squeeeeee!" the guy shrilled, causing my ears to ring. He could definitely give a tween a run for their money on that high note. His level of enthusiasm was odd to me, but I didn't necessarily hate it.

"Girl, You. Are. My. New. Favorite. Person!" He punctuated each word with a hip swivel, leaving me at a loss for words. Just who was this guy? Was I being punked? Did that show still exist?

"Can I sit? I'm going to sit. You're my new bestie, so it's all good." He continued talking, not expecting an actual answer, apparently. "The Alphabets are what I call 'Princess Adelaide' as you called her and her minions. You see, there's Adelaide Aldridge, the leader, and then her cronies, the Ashleys'."

"You're shitting me. Adelaide's friends have a group name?" I chuckled, expecting him to be joking.

"Oh honey, I never kid about gossip. Here's the down-low." He leaned closer, despite his voice being nowhere near a whisper. "First, you have Ashlee Berkshire—ice dancer, dietician, and doesn't particularly like Adelaide but likes to keep the peace, so she doesn't cause any scenes. Adelaide considers her inferior because she only "ice dances" and doesn't jump. Relatively sure she was only included in the group because she was named Ashlee, but she goes by Ash."

I scoffed at this, "Adelaide, thinks someone is inferior because of jumps, you've got to be kidding me?"

"Honey, no one can understand the mind of Adelaide! Nor would I want to try. Back to my story now. Ssh, or do you have more questions?" He raised his eyebrow at me in mock outrage, letting me know it was rhetorical, and I was to absolutely not ask anything else until he was finished. Miming zipping my lips, I got a wink from him before he continued.

"Next is Ashleigh Cabot, who goes by Leigh. She's our resident curling and bobsled instructor. Overall, she's not horrible but wants to fit in, so she goes along with Adelaide and can be susceptible to manipulation. Lastly, the worst of the three is Ashley DuPont. This 'Ashley' is what I refer to as the Basic Ashley Package and goes by, you guessed it, Ashley. She instructs cross country skiing and alpine jumps. She has no real personality and *always* goes along with Adelaide. I'm surprised she can breathe having her head wedged so far up Adelaide's butt." I laughed loudly at that, causing a few people to glance over, giving me a look. The guy kept talking though like I hadn't interrupted.

"They've been friends the longest, attending school together forever. She's the one to watch out for, as she can be mean and vindictive and is very insecure. I call them the Alphabets because not only do they go in alphabetical order, but they resemble that canned soup you eat as a kid, lukewarm and only minimally filling."

He finally took a breath, finishing with a nod to verify he was done. I tried to process everything he'd just shared with me, but my brain kept getting hung up on the details.

"You're telling me her friends are all named Ashley with descending last names in alphabetical order?" I stared at him in disbelief. It was comparable to asking if he was Santa Claus in my head because it didn't make sense. At all. How was this possible?

"Yep!" He exclaimed, popping his P. He was down-right giddy with eagerness. He reminded me of a puppy at that moment, endearing himself to me.

"And girl, you are the first person to ever stand up against her. It's *huge* news!"

"Great," I mumbled. Just what I needed, the Princess of skating gunning for me. Well at least I enjoyed his company, and while he was hot, I wasn't getting any flutters from the butterflies. Perhaps they'd finally calmed down, and I wasn't suffering from Altitude Delirium anymore. Regardless, it was nice to have someone I could just talk to as a friend with no ulterior motives.

He finally introduced himself as Wallace Benedict III and we spent the next hour talking about the school. Wallace disclosed that his name was too proper for him, so he went by Ace, which worked better with his personality. I had to agree—Ace fit much better. He was a natural flirt, and Wallace sounded like an old man. Throughout our chat, not once did I feel uncomfortable with his flirting. Mostly because I discovered he was an equal opportunity flirt, and it was just who he was. This was confirmed countless times as he batted his eyes at guys and girls who entered the shop. Ace hadn't lied, he did know everyone, and he greeted them all as they walked past.

Which led to Ace telling me how he was bisexual

and a self-proclaimed man-whore. He, of course, knew all my roommates and delivered a lot of smack for being "the lucky hussy to nab that house." Which made my face flame, and he didn't miss it. I enjoyed my time with him, and though I'd planned to have some alone time, it had been just as nice to decompress gabbing with him. Ace had a way of making everyone around him laugh and feel at ease. His knowledge of the town would come in handy as well, helping me to find info on people since he seemed to have his finger on the pulse of everything and everyone in this place.

When I'd hinted at my semi-relationship with Rhett, his eyes bugged out of his head as he slapped the table, jolting our cups.

"Girl, no one, and I mean *no one*, has been able to catch 'the monk' in the three years I've been here!" He jumped in his seat, the mugs tilting even more, and I made a note to wear a bib around him just to protect myself from the danger.

"Erm… I didn't realize it was that big of a deal," I whispered, now feeling unsure about sharing. I vaguely wondered why he called Rhett "the monk." Maybe it was because of his vow of silence? But Ace's shouting drew away my focus as I tried to not hide under the table from the embarrassment I felt by his reaction.

"Big deal, this is a huge deal!" Ace practically screamed the last part, not catching on to me hoping a hole in the floor would open and swallow me. His volume increased more, and panic began to rise in my chest. Bringing my hand to his arm, I was finally able to grab his attention.

"Ace, calm yourself, or I won't share anything with you ever again," I vowed sternly.

My inner self chastised my cockiness. This always happened when I started to feel comfortable or confident. I'd been lured into a false sense of security by his easy-going nature, in combination with the high of being honest for once in the past five years. I'd gotten too sure of myself and then utterly stepped into it, causing significant embarrassment and self-loathing for myself. Regret hung on my words as I started to backtrack internally. This was why I didn't have friends, it was too complicated, too hard to balance, it was too…

"Sorry, sorry, I promise to keep this tight-lipped. I'm envious of you, Sawyer. That man is delicious. You can trust me." His words seemed to be sincere, but part of me feared I'd made a grave error. Relaxing back in my chair, I tried to shake off my feelings. We talked for a little longer about our history in our sport and what led us to TAS. I kept mine vague this time, not wanting to go there yet.

Welp, so much for honesty; it lasted for an hour.

Realizing it was getting late in the day, and that I still needed to finish my tour and shopping before I headed back to the house before my date, I said goodbye. I wouldn't have time to talk to the locals, but it worked out anyway, meeting Ace. He just might be the key I'd been looking for. I exchanged numbers with him and promised to get coffee again soon.

Straddling the Vespa, I clipped on my helmet when the sensation of being watched steeled over me, the hairs on my arms rising. I stiffened at the feeling. No, I wasn't supposed to feel this here. I left Iowa to get away from this, this feeling of foreboding.

Starting to panic, I glanced haphazardly around at my surroundings. Of course, I didn't see anything sinister in nature. I never did, but it didn't mean the threat wasn't real. I didn't want it to ruin things, though, so I talked myself into following through with my errands. I didn't want to live in fear or let this sicko cause me to miss out on more of my life. I decided they could watch all they wanted, because I was boring as fuck. My new goal was to bore them into leaving me alone. It was a great plan, right?

I'd successfully found a cute outfit to wear tonight and gathered some groceries and necessities. I'd been able to shake the feeling of being watched and enjoy my time out by the second shop. Guess my plan to be boring worked. Take that, Veronica Mars. The drive and befriending Ace had worked to center me once again.

Arriving back at the house, I realized there were still about four hours before my date, so I decided to see what some of the guys were up to. When I walked by Soren's room, I noticed his door was open, so I peeked inside and found him lying on his bed with a book. Quietly, I knocked to get his attention.

"Hey." I smiled at him when he lifted his head in all his cute, rumpled glory.

"Hey back." He sat up, popping that dimple like it was no one's business. Those things were lethal and should require him to have a carry license if he was going to pop them out all willy nilly.

"What are you reading?"

"It's a new author I found, CJ Cooke. Have you heard of her?"

"No, I haven't. What's the book about?"

My question was met with a massive grin. Oh no, this couldn't be good. Lordy, the butterflies were making moves again.

"How about this be our first book for our club?"

"Sure, what's the title?" I couldn't help but laugh at his adorableness. Not to mention the fact he was reading while only wearing sweatpants. Shit, my heart began to have heart palpitations. It was a new symptom, and I needed to track them for the doctor. You know, if I ever got around to making an appointment.

"*Destiny Awakened* is the first book. It's about a kickass female who knew she had powers, but not really what she was. She had a pretty traumatic past but uses it to be strong and help others. She gets sent to a school for supernaturals and meets her fated mates. Lots of hilariousness, kickass attitude, and epicness follow. I think you'll like it, and it may bring some clarity to your own life."

He winked at that, causing me to wonder how he thought it would bring clarity. Granted, it sounded awesome, so I was definitely on board; it was just interesting how he phrased that—and had he said, mates? As in plural?

"Well, I can't wait to read it. What day do you want to try to have our club?"

"Let's shoot for Thursday evening. There aren't any practices then since Fridays are always challenge days."

"Sounds perfect."

I couldn't help the grin that spread over my face as I left his room—time to buy a book.

The dress I'd found earlier was a mustard-colored sweatshirt-type dress. It was the perfect balance of comfortable and cute. Plus, it had pockets. Anything with pockets was a winner for me. It was made from this buttery soft fabric that made me want to pet myself all night, and it also felt marvelous against my skin. So, while the dress was pretty simple, it did hug my body and hit mid-thigh. I decided to add my thigh-high brown suede boots. They'd give me a few more inches, which always helped when around Rhett.

Though, the way he'd picked me up with one hand the other day was downright sexy. Fuck, that had been hot! I needed to stop thinking about it, or I'd have to change my panties before I even left. I decided to keep my hair down with its natural wave. I wasn't a fussy girl, but I liked to look cute when I wanted. All the years of wearing performance makeup created an aversion to it in everyday life.

Somehow, I overestimated my time, and I still had about an hour before Rhett wanted to leave. Deciding to check on Mateo, I knocked softly on his door, but there wasn't an answer. Walking through the house, I searched for him. I checked in the front room and kitchen, but no one was there. A glance through the game room and movie room also came up empty.

Heading downstairs, I checked to see if he was in the fitness room. Since it had one of those two-way mirror things, I could see who was in there, but they wouldn't be able to see me. Shit. Stopping in my tracks, I thought about that more. Well, I hope no one got a free show yesterday. Oh well, there wasn't anything I could do about it now.

Looking through the window, I was surprised to stumble across a sweaty, tattooed chest with low-hung basketball shorts sitting precariously on his waist. The figure was doing bicep curls at the front. And I think I just discovered my favorite spot in the house. Hands down. All I needed was some popcorn, and perhaps my vibrator charged.

It wasn't until I'd stared at the sweaty chest glistening and the flex of his arms that I realized who it belonged to. The chest I'd lusted over was none other than Elias. *Damn.* Suddenly, I was thankful for the mirror I'd cursed a few moments earlier. My cheeks blazed with embarrassment as I scurried along the rest of the hall, avoiding my conflicting feelings toward him. Of course, the douchecanoe was sexy—just my luck.

Checking the sauna next, I was about to give up when I struck gold on the patio.

Mateo lazily swayed in a hammock that was stretched between two poles. He was wearing earbuds and had taken his glasses off. He looked so peaceful. I didn't want to disturb him, so I decided to leave him alone. As I turned, my leg bumped into one of the chairs, and this awful scraping noise sounded against the floor. Crap. Peeking over my shoulder, I checked to see if I'd been discovered and found his eyes locked on me.

"Oh, uh, sorry. I was looking for you but didn't want to disturb what you had going on. I didn't mean to wake you. I'll just go." I said it all quickly as I backed away, moving toward the door.

"No, wait!" He sat up, the hammock swaying more with the movement. "You were looking for me?" The way he asked broke my heart. This boy was the sweetest. I wanted to make whoever made him doubt himself suffer for putting those types of thoughts into his head.

"Yeah." I smiled encouragingly at him. I wanted Mateo to know he was valued, that even though he was not as outgoing as Soren, or as confident as Oliver, or hell, even as all-consuming as Rhett, he still had value. Mateo was unique because he was Mateo.

The smile he rewarded me with was pure and made

me want to weep. It made me horny, and I was positive now I'd need to change my underwear again before I left. The damn butterflies were traitors and had turned into horses, and they were about to clobber over my heart with the speed they were racing toward me.

Walking forward, I perched on the edge of the hammock close to him. It was pretty awkward, and I rolled into him unsteadily. Mateo reached out to stabilize me, and we chuckled at the uncoordinated movements a hammock seemed to create. My shoulder touched his and our legs pressed against one another, bringing us closer, allowing me to smell his grapefruit scent.

"I was wondering if you'd decided what you wanted to start with for our Marvel date," I finally said, peeking up at him. He blushed at the use of the word date.

"Yes, I worked on it this morning and made a list of the order I think we should watch them in as there are several different theories. It may take a few sittings to get through it all, so I hope that isn't a big deal."

"Not at all; I'm excited about getting to spend some time with you, Mateo."

"I've never had anyone be interested in the same things before, so let me know if I get too hyper about it. Just tell me to dial it in if that is the case," he huffed out.

"No such thing. I think your excitement is cute and shows me that it's something you enjoy. That's hot. I like being around people who exude passion, and that's you, you know." I smiled, bumping my shoulder into his. "Besides, I've seen quite a few of them but missed some of the newer ones. It'll be fun to get it from an expert." I playfully tapped his leg, my hand wanting to stay close to him.

Our heads had naturally turned toward one another as we talked, and somehow we seemed to be whispering. The volume became more hushed the closer our heads drifted together. Mateo's eyes peered intensely into mine, and I felt as if I could see his entire heart in them. Leaning in further, I gently pressed my lips against his. My brain shut off, and I went with what felt natural. At that moment, nothing else seemed as important as him and me.

Mateo didn't react at first, and I began to fear I'd misread the situation, pulling back. The slightest pressure was applied back to me, and my heart sang. I'd never been the dominant one in this type of situation, so I was unsure what to do next. Letting my body take over, I pressed against his lips more and ran my tongue over the seam.

Mateo gasped, allowing me to sneak my tongue into his mouth. He hesitated, and I started to pull back until I felt him gently prod my tongue with his. He mimicked my movements, and we quickly fell into a rhythm. After a few minutes, I drew back and pressed a firmer kiss to his lips. I realized I couldn't go any further than a kiss with Mateo until I understood what I felt. I'd never experienced this before; having feelings for multiple people at once was foreign to me. Even when I'd been hooking up with two guys at once, it never felt like this with both of them.

Honestly, I'd only felt this way for one person before. To be attracted and have feelings developing for three of them, well, maybe even four of them, was out of character for me. I couldn't deny that Oliver had started to grow on me like the fungus he claimed to be. Idiot—but a hot one.

Despite the fact we all lived together, which might create awkwardness down the line, I couldn't help how I felt. I could deny it, but I was tired of living that life. It felt good to be free and allow myself to feel real emotions, no matter how draining they were. It was a risk I was willing to take if it meant I could have something real.

Mateo was an extraordinary kind of person, and I didn't want to hurt him. But mostly, I didn't want to steal any of his light. He was a pure soul, and I couldn't do that to him if I weren't sure. So as much as it killed me, I stopped the kiss from deepening more. Staring into his eyes, I smiled. His face lit up, and the beauty there was astounding. My breath caught in my throat as he looked at me. Damn.

"You look lovely tonight," he said huskily.

"Thank you, that's sweet of you to say." I couldn't help but smile when I looked at him. "Are you ready for move-in day and classes to start?" I asked, bringing the conversation back around to a safe topic. We discussed how we felt about being new instructors and what we were looking forward to.

Eventually, I said goodbye, and we made plans to start our marathon. I promised myself I'd have a more precise answer for him by then. I couldn't lead him on; he was pure and precious. Regardless of whether or not Mateo saw it, I wanted to protect his light, even if that included from me.

nineteen

. . .

rhett

Stepping from the shower, I wiped the mirror clear that had filmed over from the steam. My dark eyes peered back at me, and I noticed how they seemed happier. I'd credit that to the amazing girl upstairs. Just thinking of her now brought a smile to my face.

I'd been furious with my best friend last night for what he'd said to her. I'd never been angry with him before. So when he saw my reaction, he knew instantly he'd missed something. Elias wasn't typically a jerk, but he'd fucked it up royally in that scenario.

The hard part was, it affected Sawyer more than I think she wanted us to know, and even seemed upset with herself over her reaction. I wasn't ashamed to admit her fire had been seductive, arousing a response out of me because she didn't need me to fight for her.

Sawyer fought her own battles, and that made me want to be by her side even more.

Toweling off, I stepped into boxers as I tousled my wet hair. Thinking about it now, I knew part of my attraction to Sawyer was her strength and why that was especially important to me.

My mom has always been my rock. But I hated to admit she'd been a weak woman for part of my life. Mom had allowed my garbage of a dad to take advantage of her and us. She never kicked him out or put a stop to his behaviors. He cheated so many times I'd lost count. In the end, she always took him back with his sorry ass excuses.

When my sister, Rowan, was diagnosed with Lupus at thirteen, he bailed for good, not wanting to deal with her illness. Sadly, it had been the wake-up call my mom needed. She changed her life and started her own business. Mom worked hard to create a healthy environment for my sister and finally stood up for herself. The treatment had been challenging for Rowan, but Mom had been there the whole way, showing me the importance of strength. I loved the woman she was now, but it had made me despise weak women.

I never wanted a woman to cower to me. It was difficult to begin with because of my size. I was tall, and my build was intimidating. Add in my prickly exterior, and most people left me alone, which was the way I liked it.

Though, I hadn't always been this way. In high school, I dated Molly for three years and thought it was forever. We were high school sweethearts, and as much as I denied it, I was a romantic and believed in happily ever afters.

In my youth, that equaled Molly, but I'd been naïve.

Rowan had been dealing with her illness for over a year when we graduated high school. Initially, Molly and I had talked about applying to colleges further away from our small town. We were going to start a life there and sail off into the sunset or whatever nonsense eighteen-year-olds spouted. Rowan's illness changed things, and I no longer wanted to be far away from home. My dad was gone, mom's business had just started, and Rowan was still learning to manage her illness. They'd needed me, and I needed them, honestly. I'd thought Molly understood and was on the same page as me. Our plan just needed to change a little so we could stay a year or two, and then we could get back to starting somewhere together.

Molly apparently hadn't agreed, and instead of talking about it, she just left.

One morning, I went to pick her up for the day, but when I pulled up to her house, her car was gone. I'd assumed it was at the shop or something, or maybe her mom had to borrow it. When I rang the doorbell, I wasn't met by my girlfriend, but by a look so pitying, I'd never forget it.

"Hello, Mrs. Collins, I'm here to get Molly. We're going with Rowan to the park today. Do you know if she's ready?"

"Rhett, Ummm. I don't know how to tell you this, honey, but Molly, well, she's gone. I thought you knew?"

"Where'd she go? Do you know how long she'll be? I want to get there before all the good spots are taken."

"That won't really be possible, Rhett, dear. Molly's in Korea. She took a job as an English teacher and will be going to school there. Molly left early this morning. She told me that you guys talked and had decided to take a break. Did she not tell you any of this?"

I shook my head, disbelief running through me.

"Oh, no." She started to fidget, looking uncomfortable as I stood on her doorstep, staring at her in heartbreak. So, I did the only thing a teenage boy could do. Pretended it didn't hurt.

"Oh, that was today? I thought it was tomorrow. I must've written it down wrong. Apologies, Mrs. Collins. I guess I better go then. Nice to see you."

Ever been broken up with by your girlfriend's mother? No? Well, I didn't recommend it. I never did make it to the park that day with Rowan.

At nineteen, my ability to cope with difficult things was limited. Meaning, I didn't make the best choices to get over my heartbreak. After six months of sleeping around and feeling completely unsatisfied, I vowed to myself to do better. I wanted more, desired more, and I wouldn't find it between the sheets.

I was determined to not have sex with someone until I felt it would develop into more—be more. It had to be worth the risk of my heart. Call me a sap, but I believed there was someone I could love and have it all with. Hopeless romantic to my core.

And as crazy as it seemed, I felt that about Sawyer from the moment she peered into my eyes. And I've only kept falling for her more and more with each moment I'd spent with her. I was confident she was someone I could have a real future with. All I needed to do was figure out if she felt the same. I wouldn't assume things anymore, not after Molly demolished my heart. Direct and blunt was more my style, anyway. If my self-imposed celibacy was going to be broken, well, I wanted it to matter. With Sawyer, I suspected it would.

Pumping myself up with a pep talk, I dressed in some black jeans, a maroon Henley, and a pair of black Doc Marten boots. It was casual, but so was I. Stepping out of my room, I spotted Mateo and Sawyer on the patio swinging in the hammock. I took a step toward the door when she leaned in, kissing him. It was a short kiss, but it didn't mean it hadn't been passionate. By the way they pulled apart at the end, it was obvious it had meant something to them.

But I needed to know what it meant to me.

Turning around, I made my way upstairs and thought about what I was feeling.

I liked Mateo. He was a good guy, if not a bit quiet and unassuming. It didn't mean I'd be willing to give up Sawyer for him, though. Suddenly, it hit me at that exact moment what I was forgetting, what I was leaving out in my reflection.

I hadn't been jealous when they kissed, nor angry.

Neither emotion had passed over me at all.

In fact, I think I'd been turned on. My pulse had quickened as I watched them kiss. What did this mean?

Maybe I didn't like her as much as I assumed?

Maybe?

No. Impossible.

I shook the thought violently from my head, not even wanting it to linger. I *craved* Sawyer. Just thinking about our time in the fitness room already had me hard as steel. Something else was at play here. I just didn't know what it was yet.

But I would figure it out. Sawyer was important enough to me that I needed to explore this more and find what it meant for me, for her, and for them.

While I waited for her to come upstairs, I decided to google. Google would have answers, right? I didn't know anyone else I could ask, and I wasn't ready to talk to the guys yet. I'd have to be blind, though, not to notice their combined interest in her as well. Oddly enough, I hadn't been jealous or angry when they were talking and flirting with her, or even touching her. Last night, Soren played with her hair in front of me, and it hadn't bothered me. So was I only attracted to her physically? That didn't seem right, either.

Questions swirled around my head as my google search populated with my results. Some of them were utterly ridiculous:

> *How to tell if your girlfriend is an alien*
> *I'm secretly in love with my cousin*

I swiped those away and filtered my search down. I'd been too general in my keywords. This time, some better options popped up:

How to tell if you are ready for a polyamorous relationship
Throuple, the new monogamy
Poly lifestyle and why it works
How to know if watching others be with your significant other means you're asexual or a voyeur

The articles had a lot of information, and I began to form some possible theories in my head. I was about to click on the last one when I heard her on the stairs. Saving the page to my collections, I cleared my screen and pocketed my phone.

I'd gone out yesterday and gotten Sawyer something for tonight in place of flowers. She was such a unique person that I wanted her to know it, and therefore, I didn't get the standard pre-date gift. No, Sawyer deserved creativity and thoughtfulness, and thanks to countless romcoms, I had that in spades.

When she turned the corner, I lost my breath for a second. Dressed in a form-fitting top, it hugged Sawyer in all my favorite places. I ignored fashion, but it fit her personality perfectly while looking sexy and comfortable. It was the embodiment of her. My tongue wanted to fall out when I noticed her boots. Those boots practically killed me on the spot. They encompassed her muscular legs and wrapped around her thighs perfectly.

I was fucking jealous of a pair of boots.

My doubt immediately cleared. There was no way this was only a physical thing. Not to mention I was more jealous of those boots than I'd been of Mateo. So, while her body got my heart racing and the blood pumping to a particular region, it was the look on her face and the emotions in her eyes that drew me in, causing me to risk it all.

Her smile was glorious, and I wanted to kiss her senseless right there. Deciding why the Hell not, I sauntered over. Heat had to be searing into her, my eyes holding all the promises of what I wanted to do to her. I probably even looked like I wanted to eat her. Which, let's be honest, I did.

Lifting her up a little on her toes, I brought her lips to mine. The thought she'd just kissed another guy wasn't even on my mind, nor was it unappealing. In fact, it spurred me on, even if I wasn't ready to admit that to myself. There was a stiffness going on in my pants that called me a liar. After devouring her, I sat her back down and gazed into her eyes.

"Hi," she squeaked.

"Hey, baby, I missed you."

"You missed me, did you? It's only been about twelve hours. I don't think even I want to be around myself that much." She laughed at her self-depreciation, but I could hear some fear that it was accurate. I couldn't have her thinking that.

Nope, not my girl. Because she was my girl.

"Any amount of time with you, baby, will never be enough. I'll always want more."

She sucked in a breath at my statement, and her doubt was replaced with heat. Not wanting this to get too out of hand this early in the date, I forcibly stepped back.

"I have something for you, I decided you deserved more than flowers that would wilt and die, and well, I got you this instead. I hope you like it, baby."

sawyer

Every time Rhett called me baby, my body involuntarily shivered with need. I'd always hated that term of endearment, but from his lips—Full. Body. Shiver.

I wanted to listen to him say that all day long. The kiss he'd just placed on my lips had been full of promise, not helping my heart that was full of uncertainty. When I was with Rhett, I only thought of Rhett. But the same could be said for Soren and Mateo. My heart was so confused. Rhett walked around to the wall and picked up something leaning against it and handed it to me.

It was a blank canvas.

"Um, thanks?" I wasn't trying to be rude, but really, what was I to do with a blank canvas? I was a horrible artist. The small tilt of his lips told me I hadn't hidden my doubt very well. *Damn.*

"It's a blank canvas, like us. I'm hoping we can add things together that represent our relationship. Words, cut-outs, songs, tickets, whatever really. I'd thought it could be a collaborative project and that I'd add the first thing later." His eyes dropped, almost like he was worried about my reaction.

I was speechless. No one had ever put so much thought into anything for me. Actual tears began to fill my eyes, and I blurted out the most cringe-worthy thing.

"I kissed Mateo."

Fuck! Why did I open my mouth? I've officially malfunctioned.

Send back for a replacement. Stat!

Repair order submitted.

I cringed and dropped my head, expecting his explosion of anger to be directed at me. His hand stroked my cheek softly, lifting my chin up. I squeezed my eyes shut tight, but the tears managed to leak out anyway. He wiped one away with his thumb with a gentleness that belied his size, that no one would expect from him.

"I know, baby, I saw before I came upstairs."

Snapping my head up, I wasn't sure what I'd find on his face. He was smiling softly at me, his eyes only showing adoration and heat.

Wait? What? How? Huh?

Shaking my head in an attempt to reset, I looked at

him to verify what I was seeing. Admiration and desire shone through, but now with a hint of amusement.

"I don't understand. You're not angry?"

"I'm not completely sure yet either, and I asked myself the same thing. But I'm looking into some info that I think might make sense. Let's not get into that tonight, and just focus on us." He stopped, moving closer. "But understand, I'm not upset with you. I've been looking forward to this date all day, baby."

"Okay. I can agree with that plan. I've been looking forward to this date with you as well, grumpy bear." He smiled at the nickname for him, causing relief and my heart to fall even more for this gentle giant.

"I love your gift, and I'd very much like for you to add something. I think it's an amazing idea."

Then it happened. My heart stopped.

Literally stopped.

Because apparently, Rhett had been holding back on me until now. My words made the most magnificent smile adorn his handsome face.

Rhett, the grump, no longer stood before me. No, this version of Rhett was pure light. He'd hidden this part away from the world and had just bestowed it onto *me*.

This guy, this *Rhett* standing in front of me now with his smile, that guy had just stolen my heart.

rhett

Her words allowed me to let go of my fear and doubts, and permitted me to hope. She wasn't Molly, not even close.

Sawyer was her own person, and she was the girl I'd been waiting for. She complimented me in the best ways and challenged me in others. I wanted to be that for her too—to be her strength when she needed it, and her pillar in the storms she battled.

I led her to the SUV, excited to get the date started. I'd been nervous about how she'd respond to the canvas and whether she'd think it was dorky or too much. Her response told me she cared. My face even hurt from all the smiling I'd been doing since she sauntered into my life. I didn't recognize myself in the rearview mirror when I backed out of the garage.

Pulling from my romance movie knowledge, I'd decided to create a unique and private date for us. Living in this town my whole life meant I knew the best spots and planned to use it to my advantage.

One of the wealthier families in town had an awe-inspiring garden in their backyard. I'd called Mrs. Monroe this morning and requested to use it for a picnic. I'd worked around her house as a teen and developed a friendship with her. I still visited her regularly to check in and made sure she was doing well. She was the only one living in that gigantic house and didn't tend to have a lot of visitors, despite being one of the town's founding families.

Mrs. Monroe had been excited when I'd told her about Sawyer and insisted on helping me in my master plan "to woo a young lady." She willingly offered up her garden, but I requested the gazebo that was set further back on the property. Mrs. Monroe even provided food, leaving me to "get that pretty young lady here." Her only request was to meet Sawyer at some point.

When we pulled up to the house, I could tell Sawyer was confused by our location. I'd kept my mouth shut as I opened her door and took her hand in mine. Linking our fingers, I led her around to the back of the house. Her gasp as she took in the garden had my heart racing.

The garden was full of flowers, and as it was getting darker, you could make out the several strings of fairy lights strung up. As if by magic, fireflies fluttered around us. I couldn't have planned it better if I'd tried.

"The lady that lives here is a friend of mine, and when I told her about my date idea, she was excited to lend me the use of her garden."

"It's beautiful. I love it."

"Come on, there's something else I want to show you." She followed me out to the path that led to the gazebo. When we got closer, she started to jump up and down, surprising me.

"Shut up! Are you for real right now? A gazebo? A freaking gazebo! Ahhhhhhh!"

Sawyer took off running, managing not to fall in her boots, and began to swing around the poles, jumping on the benches. I stood back, placing my hands on my hips as I watched her. Laughing, I enjoyed watching her enthusiasm. I honestly hadn't anticipated this reaction.

"Baby, what are you doing? I think you're going to give me a heart attack if you don't get down from there." I shook my head, laughing at her, walking closer.

"I'm living out my best life right now, Rhett. Don't ruin it with your mother hen ways. I'm recreating that scene from *Sound of Music,* where they dance in the gazebo to get out of the rain. 'I am sixteen going on seventeen'."

She kept singing to herself despite her voice being dreadful. Sawyer sounded as if she had a frog in her throat that was trying to escape. I couldn't help it and started laughing. Hard.

"I know I know." She laughed. "I can't sing. But I can't help it. I love it so much! So, get over it, grumpy. Put earplugs in if it bothers you that much." Sawyer stuck her tongue out at me, her voice full of childlike glee, and I couldn't help but do as she asked.

Shaking my head, I couldn't believe there was some-thing she wasn't good at, but it only made me fall for her more. How had she done that? Make something she was horrible at still be adorable?

Eventually, I was able to get her down, having to pick her up and swing her by her hips. Her squeal of glee penetrated my heart, and I knew I was done for. The move was fun and romantic, but I'd deny it if she ever asked.

A blanket laid on the floor of the gazebo, a basket in the center, narrowly escaping the fate of being a casualty of her leaping from bench to bench. As we ate, we shared stories and enjoyed one another's company. It was comfortable being with Sawyer in the best way. I wanted to tell her things about my life and know about hers. I didn't feel like it was a waste of time or that all my words would run out. I told her about my mom and sister and what it had been like growing up in this town.

"Wow, that sounds really hard. You were a good brother."

I shrugged, not knowing how to deal with someone praising me. Sawyer disclosed about losing her parents, being in foster care, and meeting Charlie. I saw how hard it was for her to share, but it warmed my heart she trusted me enough. Sawyer talked about her skating and what she loved about it, and how the accident that killed her parents had also destroyed her future.

I grieved with her when she told me that. I understood the loss of dreams and how devastating that could be. Sawyer continued to impress me with her outlook on life, despite the shitty things that had happened. It felt like we talked for hours in that gazebo as we discussed the things we loved and hated. Such as, fake people and onions for her and talking and raisins for me, causing us both to laugh.

"We better head back before it gets too late," I eventually said, not wanting to leave our bubble.

"It's hard to leave here. I feel so at peace. This place is perfect. Can we please come here again?"

"Absolutely, baby. In fact, I promised Mrs. Monroe we'd both visit her for brunch. She really wants to meet you."

"I'd enjoy that a lot. Thank you for bringing me here to this place. I haven't really been on a date like this, and it was lovely. I can't wait to add to the canvas now. Also," she paused, leaning up on her knees. "Thank you for being understanding about Mateo." She kissed me softly on the cheek, and then started to pack up. Grabbing her hand with my free one, I smiled at our height difference when we started to walk. Sawyer laughed but squeezed my hand in return.

"Can I ask a personal question?"

"Yes, Rhett. Of course."

"Is Mateo the only one you have feelings for?" She started to bite her lip, and I knew my guess was correct.

"No. I feel horrible saying that because you're amazing all on your own. I just, I also find myself attracted to Mateo, Soren, and possibly even Oliver." She had hesitated at the end, but I appreciated her honesty.

"I kind of figured, actually. I can tell the guys like you, too."

"Do you hate me? I'm the worst; you deserve to be with someone who can commit to only you. I'm sorry, Rhett." Tears had started to develop in her eyes again, and I hated seeing them.

"Baby, look at me. I can't pretend to know what

you're feeling. But I know what I feel, and I don't doubt my feelings for you or yours for me. I can see how much you like me, and maybe more importantly, I can sense it. We can figure all the other stuff out together. Because I know I want you in my life, and if that means something different than what I'm used to, then so be it. Traditional hasn't really worked out for me anyway, so maybe this is what I'm actually meant to have in my life. Let's promise to continue being open with each other, and we'll explore things as we go until we find a solution. I'm here with you, and I'm not going anywhere. You've already become important to me, and I know that you're worth whatever uncomfortableness I may feel. Though, I don't think it'll be as difficult as we're making it. Let's get the others together for dinner and see what everyone else is feeling, so that way we don't have to guess."

"Damn, Rhett. I think that's the most I've ever heard you say. You just keep knocking me over with your depth. I think you might be a piece of my heart I've been missing. You help me feel brave and I don't feel afraid to be myself with you. It's been a long time since I've felt that way, and I'm not sure you understand the momentous gift that is to me. You show me I'm sexy with just a smile, and now," she smiled, shaking her head, "you give me the space to figure everything out. I've been dreaming my whole life about meeting—"

Cutting off her words with a kiss, I felt my world settle into place around me. Here, with her, was my home, whatever that looked like. It didn't matter anymore as long as she was in it. Sawyer held my whole heart, and while it was probably stupid to feel that way after a few days, I didn't care because I knew deep in my bones, it was real.

Every rom-com I'd ever watched made complete sense at that moment. Molly hadn't even glimpsed the feelings I felt for Sawyer in just three days. Pulling back, I stared into her eyes as she caught her breath and knew I'd do anything for her.

Driving back to the house, we held hands as we sat in the quiet—both thinking about all the things we'd spoken between us. I felt content, and the silence was comfortable. Sawyer kept stealing glances as we got closer to the house, and I caught her licking her lips at one point.

Quirking my eyebrow, I hope she understood my message because I was rebuilding up my word count. I loved the look of amusement she got on her face at that move and wondered what the thoughts coursing through her head were right then. Pulling into the garage, I turned off the engine, and we both sat there for a few seconds, neither of us moving to head inside.

"I was wondering if maybe the date wasn't over yet?" Biting her lip, Sawyer turned to me with a question on her brow. Reaching over, I pulled her lip out from her teeth—no abuse against those pouty lips on my watch.

"Do you want it to be over, baby?" I somehow managed to purr out a few words. I'd no idea where the purr came from. Something about the level of passion coursing through me had to be responsible. Still, I didn't think she was complaining, not by her reaction to it. In fact, I believed she immensely enjoyed it if the quickening of her breath indicated anything.

I seemed to have short-circuited her brain. She pursed her lips, but no words escaped them. Sawyer's outfit had been tempting me all night, so I decided to strike. Sliding my hand under her dress, I rubbed my thumb on the inside of her thigh, eliciting a small moan to leave her.

"Baby, you've no idea the dirty things I want to do."

Moving my mouth to her neck, I gently bit her ear as I traveled further under her hem. Sawyer's legs parted voluntarily as more sounds escaped out of her mouth, but no words. Surprisingly, it seemed I had a million more words to use when describing all the debauchery I wanted to commit to her. The sounds she was already making were driving me wild.

"Hmm, tell, me," she gasped, squeezing my arm.

"I want to lick your body all over to start, but to do that, we're going to need to get out of this vehicle."

I brushed my thumb against the outside of her underwear as I talked, causing Sawyer to buck against me with a whimper. My own cock was rock solid now, straining against my zipper. Withdrawing my hand, I gave her a challenge.

"Last one to my bed has to make breakfast in the morning."

I took off, already through the door when Sawyer snapped out of her lust-fueled daze. I laughed the whole way to my room as I heard her cuss at me from behind as she stomped the entire way down the stairs.

"You're evil, grumpy bear. Don't think I'm going to forget this either."

Sawyer hadn't run on her way to my room. She knew I'd beaten her, so she punished me in return by taking her sweet-ass time. I quickly undressed down to my boxers and lounged back on the bed as I waited. My door slammed open, and whatever she was about to say died on her lips as she took in my boxer clad body.

Damn, she made a guy feel good.

twenty

. . .

sawyer

I'D FULLY INTENDED TO GIVE THAT MAN A PIECE OF MY mind, but all thoughts vacated the premises when I witnessed him lounging on the bed in nothing except his boxers—very snug boxers. Every inch of his chest, his abs, and that damn V were on display for my viewing pleasure. My mind crashed as every thought cleared from it. The only logical thing to do at this point was to attach to his abs like a barnacle. I could live on them and hang out all day petting them. I doubt he'd even notice.

Propelling myself across the room, I took a flying leap at him. For some reason, he was surprised by this gesture. Erm, hello? Did he not know me?

Instead of catching me like a normal person would, Rhett sat there staring wide-eyed at me, which of course, meant I bounced right the fuck off his rock-hard chest. Yep. I'd bounced back so hard I began to wonder if his chest was made from rubber.

"Ouch." I rubbed my head that somehow had managed to hit his chin and pectoral muscle in succession. I could see it now, black eye by pec. I was never going to live this down. I had to give it to him, though, because he tried really hard not to laugh. For a solid two seconds. Fucker.

"Baby, are you okay?" His voice was barely audible through his laughter.

"It's not funny," I pouted, rubbing my head. Rhett managed to get off the bed despite his laughter and bent down to where I laid on the floor. His body twisted in some Cirque du Soleil move that confused me because how that giant of a man pretzeled himself was mind-boggling.

"I'm sorry for laughing. Do you want me to laugh and make it better?"

"You just said laugh." Pouting more, I stuck out my lip, milking it. That was when I realized I was pouting like a damn four-year-old. At least I still had my clothes on because it would've been excruciatingly embarrassing if I'd been naked too.

"Did I? Slip of the tongue… Speaking of, I'd like to slip my tongue somewhere else."

His voice had that gravelly purr again, effectively curing me of my pout. But, I wanted to milk it a little longer. Besides, it was unfair he was fit enough that I'd literally bounced off him. He needed to pay it forward for his hotness and even out the field. Solid plan. Solid.

"I don't know." Biting my lip, I ducked my head, sniffling a little, positive I'd sold my doubt.

"Oh, well, let me show you then, baby."

Mission Accomplished.

Rhett swept me up in his arms and carried me to the bed. I'd never get tired of that move. Sigh. He laid me down gently, hovering over my prone body. His eyes were liquid sex, and I couldn't wait for what was next. He started trailing kisses up my neck and ear.

"Oh, and Sawyer, I know you were faking it just then, but it was cute, so I'll allow it."

His bite on my earlobe had me arching up off the bed. I wish I could say it hurt and hated it. But that'd be a fucking lie, as there was no way in hell I was stopping this fun. Fucking moaning like the wanton hussy I was, I embraced it. This man was devouring me, and I wanted to be consumed.

His hands slid down my legs, and he started to push my dress up as he dropped kisses over my exposed stomach. I loved how the stubble on his chin rubbed against me in such a scandalous way. My mind turned off, and all I could focus on was the feel of him against me. His big hands on me, his body pressed against me, his breaths fanning across my bare skin were erotic, and I'd never felt as desired by someone.

Rhett managed to push my dress over my breasts, stopping to lick my nipples peeking through the lace. I'd never imagined it could feel this good, this intoxicating. At that moment, I was thankful his room was downstairs because my moans echoed throughout the bottom floor. I wasn't embarrassed though, he deserved to know what he was doing to me, and I wouldn't be able to contain myself if I tried.

Rhett was all-consuming. His passion for me was the headiest thing, pulling me into a lust-fueled coma. Lifting me up to take my dress off, Rhett immediately tossed it, and my bra joined a moment later on the floor. He stared at me, taking my body in.

"Damn, baby, you're stunning."

His words traveled through me, settling in and taking root, effectively wiping out some doubt and insecurities I had. As much as I tried not to let what other girls said affect me, there was still a part that worried they were correct. With his gaze burning into me with complete sincerity, the heat in his eyes conveyed how much he liked my body. I accepted then that my body was mine and nothing was wrong with it.

My body was different, and it wasn't perfect, but it was mine, and it was beautiful. Taking hold of that confidence, I surged up to kiss him deeply. Pushing him back onto his haunches, I wrapped my arms around his neck, pulling him impossibly closer to me. My nipples rubbed against those impressive chest muscles, eliciting small tingles in my body. His pecs were now forgiven for almost killing me earlier. I pushed him further back in order to straddle him. My boots and underwear were still on, as well as Rhett's boxers, but it felt amazing, nonetheless. And quite frankly, pornographic.

His hands settled on the round globes of my ass, squeezing. One of his hands fit the entire length of my ass cheek, and his other hand slipped through the side of my underwear. Rhett wrapped his hand over my ass from the backside, teasing my entrance with his finger. I rocked on his cock, hitting my clit perfectly. In tandem with his finger teasing my entry, I was on the verge of going over. Rhett continued his assault on my mouth as his hand ran up my exposed back into my hair. Things were turning out much better now than it had started out, you know, with me laid out on my ass–and not in the enjoyable sense.

Finally, Rhett pushed further in, causing me to almost detonate. His fingers were long and thick. Combined with his cock rubbing me in the best spot, I was practically a goner. I started to kiss down his neck, leaving gentle bites in my wake. The urge to mark him suddenly surged in me, making me want to claim him as mine. I'd never felt that before, a sense of powerful possession. It wasn't ownership I was after, but purely wanting him. My intentions were to communicate to others my claim.

Because I did, I wanted this man badly. That didn't scare the crap out of me for some reason.

Okay, it did a little, but I told that stupid thought to take a hike. Rhett had shown me parts of myself I hadn't known. He gave me the space to feel strong, beautiful, and brave.

His moan from my bites ricocheted my own arousal up. What was it about a man's cry of pleasure that was incredibly hot and empowering? The power of seduction coursed through my body, heating my skin and pebbling my nipples. Knowing I caused this man to respond so intensely made the other things I'd worried about appear juvenile now.

"Baby, I'm so close. It's been a *very* long time for me, and I don't think I'll last long. But I want to come inside of you, feeling you around me." He stopped, shaking his head. "No, I *need* to be inside of you when I come."

Nodding my head enthusiastically, because I agreed 100%. Yes, let's do that! I was fully on board with this plan.

He lifted up on his legs, showing how mastering all those squats had benefited him. Rhett moved to lay me back against the bed, suspended over me again. At first, I thought he was about to do that thing, you know that thing guys in romance books do where they rip the girl's underwear off them? Preparing to yell at him, because in real life that move was anything but cool, and these were my favorite damn underwear! But I was taken aback by what he said.

"Is that Olaf on your underwear?" His voice was devoid of any emotion, and his focus was seared onto the snowman on my front.

Seemed I'd officially shocked him, because, yes, I loved Frozen. I didn't care what you thought about Disney movies, but a movie about an ice queen who lost her parents… Well, you could deduce why I liked it.

"I like warm hugs," I said, answering him with a shrug. "But don't even think about ripping these off me, Mr. Grumpy Bear. They're my favorite."

I grinned, bearing my teeth to him. His chuckle and lifted eyebrow brought my focus back to the fact that we were two layers away from being skin to skin.

Two. Measly. Little. Layers.

Slowly, Rhett pulled down my underwear, dragging them purposefully over every inch of skin. He moved off the bed, causing me to whine, but when I saw him shuck his boxers, I quieted. As he grabbed a condom, I checked out his ass. Damn, it was luscious and grab-bable. Definitely getting added to the *'Sawyer wants to lick' list*. I'd definitely bounce off an ass like that.

He turned as he was rolling on the condom, and my brain stumbled.

Holy Fucking Shit Balls!

Coo-coo Cachou with a side of crazy.

His cock was so small.

Haha, I made you panic there for a second, didn't I?

Rhett's cock was standing at attention, happy with me staring at it. I gulped as I licked my lips that had suddenly gone dry. I was both terrified and turned on simultaneously. Fuck it. Shrugging my shoulders, I decided I was going to own that monster. Rhett must've seen the determination fill my eyes because suddenly, he was laughing at my reaction.

"Baby, you're so fucking adorable. Damn. I can't wait to feel you. Now lay back and don't worry. I've got you."

With that, I did as I was told; the promise of this beautiful dick made me compliant. And believe me, it was magnificent. Stiff and rigid with a perfect head leaking small beads of precum. Despite him stating it'd been a while; he had definitely kept up the manscaping. Good for him.

"What about my boots?"

"Leave them on for a bit. I think you look hot in them. Plus, every time I see those boots, I'll remember this."

Damn, that smirking eyebrow of his did naughty things to me, but it worked for him. It *so* worked for him. I was beginning to feel subconscious about how wet I was now, and I wondered if I was leaving a mess all over his bed.

His kisses captured my attention and filled me with passion as he settled back in between me. I could feel his cock perched against my entrance, but it didn't enter me. Instead, Rhett took his time mapping out my lips, caressing my face, and peppering me with a million kisses. I was so lost in the haze that I didn't even notice when he started to push inside. The sensations over-whelmed me causing me to let out a loud moan.

"Fuck, baby, you feel incredible."

I could only nod my head at this point as he continued to push that beast he called a cock into me. He was filling me up so full, I wondered how I'd ever lived a moment without being this complete. Once Rhett was fully seated, he took a moment to gather his breath. His gaze bore into my eyes, the emotions swirling in his eyes brought out the purest gold flecks. The intensity of the moment almost caused me to cry. Rhett's thumb brushed over my cheek as he placed the sweetest, gentlest of kisses on my lips. My heart nearly stopped from that swoon-worthy moment.

He started to move in me as he lowered his other hand down to tug at my nipple. Rhett deepened his kiss, allowing his tongue to get in on the action. My breasts filled his hands as he fondled them, squeezing my nipples in combination with his short thrusts. Arching my back to meet him, I was surprised when he lowered his hand down to stroke the magic button. I'd never been one to have a purely vaginal orgasm, but I almost felt I could come with him. His cock hit every spot inside of me and filled me with an out of this world pleasure.

When Rhett touched my clit, my back lifted off the bed, and the most erotic sound left my mouth. He pulled back to check on me before he picked up the pace. Nodding to encourage him to move, he leaned back further on his haunches, grabbing my hips in his big hands. Rhett's thrusts became harder and deeper into me then. Wrapping my legs around his waist made our skin begin to make that purely erotic sound of skin slapping between grunts and moans.

By this point, we were both a panting mess, and our skin glistened with sweat. Rhett's eyes never left mine, making the moment tenfold more intimate. He was hitting my clit again with his pelvis causing me to vault over the edge. Stars, tremors, and goddamn angels singing exploded around me as I orgasmed.

I might've even blacked out. I didn't know at this point what I was even thinking. Tears were in the corners of my eyes, though. Have you ever had an orgasm so intense that your emotions were overloaded, causing everything to fire off at once? Well, that was what just happened—an emotional explosion.

Peering back up at him when I came to, his thrusts picked back up, almost as if he was waiting for that; he thrust hard one more time and erupted in an orgasm. His hands gripped my hips to him, sealing our bodies together. Rhett's head was thrown back in ecstasy, with his muscles rippling across his chest, his forearms flexing, and his legs holding both of our weight up. If I'd died right then, I wouldn't even care except for the fact I wouldn't ever get to experience that again.

Because I was pretty sure that sex with Rhett was better than Heaven. Better than cheesecake. Better than seasonal Oreos—which we all knew the Halloween ones were by far superior.

He laid beside me for a second, basking in his afterglow as he gently smoothed my hair off my face. I couldn't tell if he was searching for something or asking for reassurance in his gesture.

"Hi."

"Hi."

We busted out laughing, allowing our emotions to settle. If you didn't start sex off laughing and finish it laughing, apparently you were doing it wrong. At least for us, and that was all that mattered at the moment. We still had several things to figure out, but I knew that whatever Rhett and I had, it was unique in its own way because it was ours.

rhett

Disposing of the condom in the bathroom, I watched as she walked to the shower. Sawyer glanced over her shoulder as she started the water, checking me out in the mirror. I leaned back against the vanity, crossing my arms, smirking as I often did. Sawyer shook her head, dislodging my lust-filled eyes. She'd taken off her boots, and I laughed when I saw her socks.

Sawyer didn't give a flying fuck about sexy lingerie or trying to impress people. She was her own person. She wore and liked what she wanted.

Right then, everything made sense, and I resolved the niggling conflict that I'd do whatever it took to be in her life. If it meant I'd have to share, I would, because she made me feel like me again.

I hadn't always been a stoic or grumpy person. In fact, I'd been carefree and adventurous once. Life had taken its toll, and somewhere along the way, I stopped trying to feel emotions, to laugh, or enjoy things.

With Sawyer around, I'd laughed and smiled more in the past few days than I had the whole year, fuck five years, prior. Sawyer made me feel light. She made me want to enjoy things and yearn for more again. No longer was I stuck in the status quo I'd been trapped in, just going through the motions, but not really moving.

So, yes, I'd share her if that meant I got to be with

her. I would hold onto her with everything I had. Because I could see it now, Sawyer was my future, my forever. Our relationship might be headed in a different direction than I'd ever imagined, but it was time to think differently.

Stepping under the water, the shower was quick as we tried not to restart the passion still brewing between us. It was difficult not to touch Sawyer's body as she soaped up. I found myself getting lost at times as I tracked the water sluicing off her nipples.

After we dried off, I gave her my t-shirt to wear, so she didn't have to run upstairs. Selfishly, I'd wanted to see her in my clothes and smell like me. Sawyer hadn't balked at my request to wear my shirt, so I felt she wanted to as well. A small part of me didn't want her to go upstairs after sharing that intimate moment with her. I felt confident that some moments could be ours; sharing didn't mean we had to share everything. I was still learning the ins and outs of polyamory, or whatever this was, but I felt that was okay, good even. We needed to focus on the relationship developing between us.

Here, her smile was all for me, and I intended to soak it in.

Putting on a clean pair of boxer briefs, I slid back into bed as Sawyer snuggled up to me, laying against my side. She threw her leg over my own and it fit like the missing puzzle piece I'd misplaced. Now, with her where she belonged, I wondered how I'd ever function without her. Cliché, I know, but you didn't watch all those romcoms and not pick up on some cheesy romantic lines.

"Mmm. I love the way you smell. It's very you. Masculine, but sexy. What is it?" queried Sawyer.

"Something my sister bought me at Christmas. Berry something brand… Burberry, I think. I'm glad that you like it, I just wear it because I have it." I chuckled, causing her to join me.

That night, I slept soundly and content. This was something I wanted more of, and not just Sawyer in my bed and the 'out of this world' sex. I craved the intimacy, the connection, and the feeling of completeness.

It didn't mean she completed me. I was a whole person on my own. I felt complete in the sense that I'd gotten to the ending of one section of my life, and now was about to partake in the next part. There was no cliffhanger, no unresolved feelings, or conflict for me. Instead, it was now BS and WS, Before Sawyer and With Sawyer. That was what my life was now—With Sawyer.

twenty-one

. . .

elias

EVER SINCE LUNCH WITH VOLDEMORT, THINGS HAD FELT off and I no longer knew which way was up. The confession to my bosses, followed by the weird but exciting sexual escapade, had been a roller coaster of emotions for one day. Unfortunately, the weirdness just kept coming.

My voyeur experience days later still left me confused, but the royal fuck up with Sawyer had me all out of sorts. I was such a bloody tosser, and had really screwed things up. A day of self-wallowing about my wretched life still left me feeling miserable, and I needed to do something.

Perhaps a grand gesture was in order to amend things. I would be living with her after all, so I needed the house to be a conflict-free zone. Yes, that was my reason for wanting to apologize. Conflict-free house.

Thankfully, I was a competent chef and knew my way around a kitchen. Growing up, I attended boarding school overseas, which meant I was left on my own a lot for breaks. One term, I watched an excessive amount of reality TV and the cooking shows were my favorite. For some reason, it didn't feel as shameful indulging in them if I was learning in the process. Breakfast was my specialty, and I hoped it would help me ask forgiveness for my brutish behavior.

Walking down the stairs, Lucky followed me as I ran through the ingredients we had on hand. It seemed like omelets would be the best course of action. When I turned the corner into the kitchen, I was surprised to find it occupied.

Standing in front of the refrigerator, dressed only in a long t-shirt belonging to Rhett, was Sawyer.

Her bare legs were on display with her hair rumpled, flowing down her back. It was a whole look, and I was ashamed to admit I stopped in my tracks to thoroughly check her out. My eyes scanned every inch of her, taking it all in. The shirt draped off one shoulder in a way I knew wasn't intentional. Sawyer had loads of sex appeal, but seemed entirely unaware of it. In fact, it was just part of who she was, which to me, was even more enthralling.

She turned, finding me frozen to the spot, my eyes taking in every inch of her. A look of shock flashed briefly, followed by one of anger. Though, it was the last one it settled on that killed me—pain. It shifted something in me, and I knew I didn't want to be that guy—the guy who made her feel like crap.

"Hello, I um, I was going to make breakfast for everyone," I said nervously as it tumbled out of me.

"Oh, sorry, I didn't realize there was a schedule. Are there rules? Do we take turns? That would be efficient. I really should get a bullet journal."

She rambled as she fumbled to get her words out quickly, nervous in my presence. I despised myself even more for making her anxious because of me.

"No, sorry." I shook my head, waving my hand to calm her. "Sorry if it appeared that way. I hadn't meant to imply you were in the wrong. I was just surprised. Though, you do make an excellent point. It would be helpful to have a schedule. But actually, I was going to make breakfast as a gesture toward you. Uh, to apologize for my appalling behavior the other night. It was out of line, and I have no excuse for any of the things I said. I don't believe those things about women. I had a horrible day, but that's no excuse to be disrespectful to another person. So, I hope you will forgive me. Besides, I think the rest of the house likes you better than me already, so I'm certain they would boot me if you don't forgive me."

I tried to add some humor to my disparity, smiling as I hung my head sheepishly. Fortunately, it seemed to help. Sawyer relaxed as I talked, her shoulders lowering with each word spoken out of sincerity.

"Thank you, Elias, and I do, I accept. I appreciate you're making an effort to apologize. In my experience, people haven't admitted wrong, much less tried to do better. And when they do say 'I'm sorry,' it doesn't mean anything and the words eventually lose meaning." She fiddled with the hem of her shirt, unconsciously pulling it higher and showing me more leg. I swallowed, focusing on her face.

"Thank you, Sawyer. It means a lot that you would accept my apology. I hope I can prove to you that I am a decent guy."

"Breakfast is a good place to start." She smiled, gesturing to the fridge. "I'd like to help. I've no idea where anything is yet, so I've been staring into this fridge, hoping inspiration would jump out at me, but no luck yet." She giggled, her cheeks heating. "I'm supposed to make breakfast for Rhett after losing an unfair bet," she grumbled, "but well, I'm struggling."

Sawyer's sheepishness did something to me that I wasn't prepared to explore yet. I liked how poised and grounded she was, and how she didn't seem to be ruled by the opinions of others. Sawyer knew her self-worth, making it refreshing to have a conversation with her. Quite frankly, it was odd talking with a woman I didn't have to worry about only wanting me for sex, family money, or status. Sawyer didn't need me for anything, and there was something freeing about that.

Clearing my throat, I focused back on the task at hand, clapping my hands.

"Wonderful. We can knock this out quickly together. Could I ask one favor?"

"Sure." Her voice held worry and skepticism. Shit, maybe I should just deal with it.

Boners, the kitchen accessory you never knew you needed.

No, it would make things worse if she caught me sporting wood while whisking eggs. Sawyer would think I was a pervert. I needed to say something.

"Well, uh, this is awkward to ask. But in pursuit of me not burning the food, could you perhaps put on some pants?" Sawyer stared at me for a moment with a blank face as she digested my words.

"Sure. I'll change, but can you tell me one thing? From disgust or distraction?"

Shit. I never wished I could take back my words more than I did right then. I never wanted to cause her to doubt herself. My brain started to tell me to abort, but my mouth had other ideas.

"Distraction. Definitely distraction." I nodded enthusiastically. "I would also like to avoid Rhett giving me the black eye he threatened me with. If he found us cooking together and you looked like that, my best friend would choose you, and I'm not sure I can take that much rejection this early in the morning."

Now I was the one rambling due to my own nervousness. Why was I talking? I gestured toward her body up and down in a quick fashion, hoping to shut up. Sawyer turned to leave, a blush appearing on her cheeks. She stopped at the door, turning back.

"I don't know, Rhett might surprise you. And you should know I don't need a man to fight my battles.

You're wearing my handprint after all." Sawyer winked before sashaying her ass out the door.

Bloody Hell. Nope. I could not be thinking this way about my best friend's girl. I would not be a Voldemort.

A few minutes later, Sawyer returned in a pair of leggings and a long sleeve shirt, and I wanted to bury myself six feet under.

While she was technically covered now, it was worse.

So. Much. Bloody. Worse. And I only had myself to blame.

Her leggings were form-fitting, exposing her perfect sculpted bum. While her shirt was long-sleeved, it was the thinnest material known to man, likely from over-wear, making it practically see-through. When Sawyer turned, I almost had an aneurysm; you know if you could control those things. Her nipples poked through her top, pointing right at my dick.

Fuck, she wasn't wearing a bra. Her grin confirmed my suspicion, and I knew she'd intentionally chosen her outfit for the reasons I assumed. Sawyer was reminding me it wasn't my place to tell her how to dress. Well played, love. Point Sawyer.

"I hope it doesn't bother you, Elias, but Sundays are a no bra zone for me. Gotta free the tittie. Liberate the nip; you know how it is." She finished with a shoulder shrug as carefree as could be.

I had to give it to her, this was exquisite torture 101, and I would have to bear it.

Trying to ignore my body's reaction to her, we

started on breakfast. Sawyer mixed eggs together while I chopped vegetables. We found a good rhythm and worked in tandem. It was silent, but not uncomfortable, well not the silence anyway. I had to keep refocusing my gaze away from her nipples, or I might lose a finger.

The first of our housemates began to appear as we finished up.

"Good morning, beautiful girl!" bellowed a sleepy Soren.

He was mussing his hair, causing it to fall over his face in disarray. Soren wasn't wearing a shirt, only some sleep pants, and hadn't noticed what Sawyer was wearing yet. I was eager to see how everyone else would react to her "liberate the nip" movement. Soren sat at the island, still half asleep, when Mateo entered. He was more awake and dressed. He nodded, taking a seat at the island. Rhett and Oliver both entered from different directions around the same time. Oliver went to the fridge, and Rhett advanced toward Sawyer like a beacon. His comfortableness with her didn't go unnoticed by anyone. The whole kitchen was locked on Sawyer, to begin with, but it was odd to see Rhett hovering around a girl, surprising us all.

"Good morning, baby. You look beautiful."

Rhett wrapped his arms around Sawyer's middle and kissed her neck as he spoke to her. He appeared completely comfortable at that moment with her. It was a good look on him. She blushed, and I swear her nipples hardened, but I would never admit it, because then I'd have to admit I was staring at them.

Apparently, I wasn't the only one though, as every set of eyes in that kitchen zeroed in on her nipples. Rhett's smirk appeared to grow as he watched everyone's attention fall to her. It surprised me how he seemed intrigued by everyone's reaction instead of angry.

"Elias apologized to me about his behavior on Friday, and we decided to make breakfast together." Sawyer paused, and I had a bad feeling I was about to eat my words, again.

"However, I didn't realize there was a dress code for cooking, because apparently, your t-shirt that I was wearing was too distracting." Her voice started to turn into that sugary sweet tone that made it obvious she was being anything but sweet as sarcasm dripped from every word.

"I, uh, that's not how I—," I started, but was dismissed when she narrowed her eyes at me. Well, okay then. This was going to be fun. I sighed, hanging my head.

"It is Sunday, and everyone knows what Sunday is, right? Elias, maybe you could remind everyone?"

Her smile remained so sweet, it hurt my teeth. Oh wait, that was me grinding my teeth.

"Erm, well, I believe you mentioned you like to have a 'No Bra Zone on Sunday.' And… something about Free the Tittie and Liberate the Nip." I tried to be as blasé as possible, but it was comical, even if she was making fun of me. My lips smirked as the guys roared with laughter.

"I'm a fan of No Bra Sunday. Yes, to free the nip!" Oliver chuckled as he rubbed his own bare chest.

"Ha! But, here's the thing," Sawyer replied, and instantly the mood shifted when her tone registered. "My body is my body, and not here for your enjoyment. If I want to wear something that makes me comfortable. Then I can. If I want to wear something that makes me feel sexy. Then I can. Either way, it's my decision. You don't get to comment or judge. If you feel like saying anything other than 'You look lovely, Sawyer' or some equivalent, then keep it to yourself. Women have been judged by what they wear and blamed for it since the beginning of fucking time, and it's not okay."

She took a breath, centering herself, and my shoulders fell.

"If you slap my ass, it was your choice to slap my ass, not mine because my ass looked hot. Now, you can think whatever you want in your head. Lord knows I do that to you guys all the time. That's equal attraction, but it's never okay to make comments about my body or clothes as if it's a separate part of me. My body is me. My clothes are for me. And I am a person worthy of respect."

She motioned down her body, gesturing to her outfit. "Yes, I wore this to prove a point to Elias. But the flip side is I should feel safe to wear it without worrying about being degraded or assaulted, especially in my own home. So, remember, keep your thoughts in your head unless asked. Consent is sexy, guys. Thank you for coming to my TED Talk. Now, who wants what in their omelets?"

Sawyer finished with an air of confidence, and while we'd all just been put in our place, I hated to admit her whole speech was sexy as hell.

Bloody Hell. I was screwed.

twenty-two

. . .

oliver

Did you ever have a moment where you'd wish you could turn back about thirty seconds in time to stop yourself from saying something?

No. Well, I did all the time.

Why would I shout I liked nipples? You're an idiot, Oliver.

I regretted what I'd said instantly. Usually, it didn't matter because the girls I surrounded myself with weren't that bright and only wanted me for my status. In some ways, it was easier. I smiled, said stupid shit, girls laughed and I got laid. People didn't expect much from me, and for the most part, that was how I wanted it. If people weren't looking at me too closely, then they wouldn't see how fucking scared I actually was of failing.

My whole future had been clear—College star

drafted early to the Nashville Predators and played two years, starting my last.

To the world, I was Oliver Windsor, star and playboy hockey player.

But to my family, I was the outcast, the black sheep, the loser. I was the youngest in the family, with four older siblings—four successful older siblings. They'd gone into the family business and didn't understand why I'd want something different for myself.

Growing up in an environment where I was constantly bullied and picked on, I'd learned to hide who I really was. When I lost hockey, part of my shield went with it. This job allowed me to cash in on the shadow that was my career for a little longer. Because what I really wanted to do, well, most people would laugh at me.

I had a secret love affair with baking. I loved to bake all kinds of desserts and create pastries. It was my happy place, but I'd rarely shared it with anyone. It didn't fit the persona of who people assumed I was, and most of the time, it was easier being who they wanted me to be.

Except right here, right now, I wished I could shed my shields and be true to myself. Perhaps then I'd stop saying offensive things to people. Sawyer was the opposite of a puck bunny. It was obvious from day one, but my brain's filter to my mouth didn't get the memo.

Instead, I just kept doing what I usually did, making an ass out of myself. Only this time, no one laughed, and I ended up eating my words. Rightfully deserved.

This time I had company in Elias, and based on how tense breakfast was, Elias was still on her shit list.

No one said much as we ate. Rhett looked like a kicked puppy dog. I think he was beating himself up the most, not sure why though, since he hadn't said anything.

After we ate, I offered to clean up. Sawyer smiled at me, and I felt a little better. I decided to give in and do the thing I loved and make her some 'forgive me' macarons. They were difficult to get right and required precision, which would give me something to focus on.

I pulled out all the ingredients, setting them on the counter as I got to work making chocolate macarons with a chocolate ganache filling.

A few hours later, I felt better with my mind settled, and I had the perfect decadent dessert cooling. Cleaning up my mess, I hopped in the shower while they finished cooling. When I returned, they were flawless, so I put them in a box and headed to Sawyer's room. As I knocked, I hoped she'd let me in.

"Yes?"

"Hey Sawyer, it's Oliver. I brought you something. Can I come in?" I tried to sound confident, but it came out more unsure than I wanted.

"Sure."

Her response sounded forlorn, and I wondered if I'd already screwed things up too much. Entering, I found her lounging on the floor with Lucky. Laughing at the scene before me, I realized Elias wasn't getting his dog back. Sawyer peered up at me suspiciously, and it stung, but I couldn't blame her since I hadn't shown her the best sides of me.

"I uh, well, I kind of have a passion for baking," I said, sputtering. "I don't really tell people because no one would believe me, or they would laugh about it, but I wanted to share something with you. I love making macarons, so I made you some. Here, I hope you enjoy them." I couldn't bear to look at her and see rejection. Handing off the box, I turned to leave quickly.

"Ollie, wait." My breath halted. Her tone sounded light. I stared at the door, too scared to turn around.

"Would you like to sit with me and have some?" I spun around so swiftly I almost face planted on top of her. Fortunately, she laughed, something I could deal with.

"I'd love to." I smiled wide, maneuvering to the floor. She quickly closed a notebook and pushed it under some other things out of my line of sight. She opened the cookies, and I started to get nervous again as she took a bite.

"Oh my God, Ollie. These are amazing. Please bake me all the things! Give me all the treats! Forgiveness granted." She chewed, moaning around the dessert. Wiping the crumbs, she squeezed my hand. "I'd already forgiven you, you know, but I do love cookies, so extra bonus points." She chuckled, shoving another one in her mouth.

Pride, unlike anything I'd ever felt playing hockey, filled my chest at her words. With cookies and Lucky between us, we sat and talked for a bit, getting to know one another, and I realized that spending time on a personal level without the pressure of being fuckboy Ollie was nice.

"I have a confession to make, Oliver. I used to watch you play with my guardian, Charlie. We were both fans and would root for you each week. I had to stop myself from fangirling that first morning, so I overcompensated with my sass. While you were annoyingly hitting on me, I shouldn't have been so obnoxious about it." She paused, then grimaced. "Or stolen your bacon."

Her admittance shocked me so much that I stared dumbly at her for a few seconds. "No, Sawyer, you were right to call me out. Though, maybe the bacon was too far." I joked to ease her tension. Her small smile lightened my heart, and I didn't feel as much of a fuck up. Her words clicked in my head, and a smile spread across my lips. "So that morning, you knew who I was? My sexiness was too overwhelming for you."

It was hard not to full-on flirt, but hopefully, I could casually flirt without letting the jerk version of myself out. I was trying at least; it would take time. Sawyer's laughter soothed away the fear, settling some anxiety in me.

"I decided I needed to make sure you didn't take me for granted, so I decided to have fun with it."

"Well, it was a very memorable impression. I almost fainted when you started talking hockey, but now, I guess I know why."

We ate the rest of the cookies together as we talked, sharing about our families, but neither of us went into too much detail. It seemed it was a difficult subject for both of us.

After an hour, I decided to head out, not wanting to push the goodwill we had growing. I left feeling happier where we stood and feeling hopeful we could at least be friends.

I had no delusions a girl like her would ever see me as more.

sawyer

This morning had veered into a direction I hadn't expected. I'd wanted to torture Elias a little, but somehow it spiraled into me tearing into men on behalf of all of womankind.

Whoops.

While what I'd said was accurate, it wasn't fair to take out all my frustration as a woman on guys who'd been kind to me. After a tense breakfast, I'd retreated to my room to wallow. It felt like I was failing left and right, so I did what I did best and pushed them away.

It didn't help that I hadn't made any movement on the leads I'd found. Everything was sending me to dead ends, and I'd almost been found out. I'd barely been able to hide the notebook before Ollie sank to the floor. Close one.

Spending time with Ollie, though, had been healing.

I think he needed to show me a different side to him, and I needed to see it as well. Damn, those cookies had been amazing. They were magic in my mouth. Ollie helped assure me that I hadn't ruined things before the term even started.

Feeling better after some cookies, I decided to check in with Rhett. I couldn't find him on the main floor, and the training room was empty too. I knocked on his door to see if he was hiding in his bedroom, but I didn't hear anything. Assuming he was asleep or ignoring me, I turned around and sank to the floor. I didn't blame him. A beautiful moment between us had become smeared with poop all over it because of my big mouth. It was the ultimate code orange moment, so orange it was red.

Softly, I thumped my head on the door in hopes to wake him or annoy him into opening the door. I was surprised when I spotted Rhett exiting out of a room further down the hall. I hadn't been in that room, mostly because I hadn't known there was a door until he came out of it.

Now that I was facing him, I didn't know what to say. "Hey, I was looking for you."

"Sawyer, before you tell me that we're a bad idea and over, please, hear me out. I meant to show you this last night, but with everything, I completely forgot. I've been working for the past two days on something for you. Please, just come with me first."

I didn't understand what he was saying, why did he think I would break up with him? His use of my name had sent a pain running through me. I'd been sure he thought I was the crazy one and wanted to run away. Unsure of his intentions, I followed him anyway because I'd do anything to spend more time with him.

Perhaps this was their torture room, and he was showing me there. I had thought he was a CIA operative that first day! Eyebrow torture here I come.

Stopping as I walked into the secret room, I was left speechless.

It was a ballet studio. A fucking ballet studio. Shiny hardwood floors with mirrored walls stared back at me and across one wall stood a bar and a bench with a cubby area.

"You made me a dance studio!" I shrieked. Why was I shrieking? I tried again, lower. "You made me a dance studio?" This time it came out in a natural voice.

Rhett smirked and, of course, raised his eyebrows. At least he didn't seem pissed at me.

"No, baby, I'm not a carpenter or master builder." He laughed at his Lego joke. He had the nerve to laugh, which, of course, set me off. Jerk. Planting my hands on my hips, I waited for him to explain.

"I cleaned the room out for you. It's been collecting old equipment and furniture other roommates have left, along with some weird stuff I'm not sure where it came from. I'd thought you might want to have a place you could dance, you know, without Adelaide. It was just a thought. If you hate it, then it's no big deal." Rhett shrugged, looking unconfident.

Stupid boy. Clearly, he needed to be reminded of how much I liked him. Taking off at a run toward him—

conveniently forgetting how horrible it went last time—I squealed and took a flying leap into his arms.

The fact it worked, and I didn't gravely injure myself or my pride this time, was miraculous. The sensation of being caught in his muscular arms so effortlessly was sexy as fuck.

"I love it so much. I have no words, Rhett. No words. Well, that's not true, but thank you. I wasn't coming to break things off but to apologize for this morning. I didn't mean to go off on a soapbox and inadvertently ruin our morning after. I hope you don't hate me."

"Baby, I don't hate you. I don't think I ever could. I'm sorry you had to—"

The rest of his statement wasn't necessary, and I just wanted to be kissing him already. Shutting him up with my mouth seemed to work great.

Rhett and I spent hours christening that room. Several times.

It was now my new favorite place in the house. It seemed like men, I was starting to collect them.

twenty-three

. . .

finley

WALKING AROUND CAMPUS, I HOPED TO BUMP INTO someone I knew. It was Sunday evening, and the new school term started in the morning. I'd only been back for about thirty minutes, but I was bored, and a bored Finley was never a good thing.

My brother often gave me projects to occupy me when he'd notice the "Finley" look. He thought I didn't know he made up these fake tasks, but I did; I just didn't care. I was grateful to have a brother I was close to, a brother who cared and wanted the best for me.

Henry and I had always been close growing up. Probably due to being close in age since we were only a year apart, so we did a lot of things together as kids. Our parents were both busy with their careers, working late hours, forcing us to spend a lot of time with our neighbors. We didn't really mind, though, since Sariah was our best friend. I wasn't always reckless or destructive; that was only in the past five years.

Not wanting to think about those memories, I shook them off just like my therapist taught me: *'Stop, breathe. You are safe. You are in control. It's okay to feel angry. It's okay to feel sad. I don't have to give in to my feelings, though. I can choose to think differently.'*

I repeated it in my head as I took deep breaths, successfully shaking off the past's gloomy fog. People watching soothed me, so I made up stories as I meandered around. It was something I'd done with Sariah when we were younger. We'd make up stories about all the people and see who could create the most outrageous. We usually forced Henry to choose when we couldn't agree.

My brother would shake his head at us, but then pick things from both stories he liked, creating a joint narrative. He was good at that, weaving things together.

Henry had loved Sariah too, and we'd both taken her loss hard. I'd started to act out externally, as my therapist explained to me, and Henry withdrew internally.

Acting out recklessly without thinking gave me a way to feel something other than my grief. I'd started therapy two years ago when my parents were fed up with my behavior and threatened to send me to a rehab facility if I didn't get my act together.

So, for the past two years, I'd worked on controlling my anger, grief, and complete lack of control over the situation. I'd been fifteen with not a lot of power when she disappeared. I refused to believe she was dead like the authorities reported. There hadn't been a body, but they'd chalked it up to being burned in the fire.

I called bullshit.

Sariah and I were soul sisters. We were connected deeply, and I genuinely believed I'd feel it if she were dead. However, over the years, I started to doubt myself. Did I remember the connection as vividly as I thought I did? Maybe I was only kidding myself.

Henry and I had tried to find her with every resource we had to our names. He told me, a couple of weeks after she'd been missing, about the night she came to him. How Sariah made him promise not to look for her because of being in danger. I'd been really upset with him for keeping it to himself, but it gave me hope that she was still out there hiding.

So, I taught myself to code and hack so I could try to find her that way. Of course, that also got me in trouble, giving me skills that allowed me to do more reckless things. I wouldn't give up, though. I knew there had to be a trail somewhere. People didn't just disappear into thin air. Especially not after sending the emergency text code.

I'd been at my aunt's house, and she had a strict no-phone policy while we were doing "family engagement" activities, so I didn't even see my text until the next day. By then, her phone no longer accepted messages.

I chose to believe she was still out there and that

we'd find our way to one another again. I needed to consider it for myself, but also for Henry. He'd withdrawn into himself more and more every day, and I was scared if something didn't change, I'd lose my brother. I couldn't and wouldn't let that happen. I couldn't lose another person I loved.

Sighing, I kicked a rock, walking, deep in my thoughts. After being home for a weekend, I needed a distraction. The campus was starting to awaken with students and their parents, so I bounced along, concocting stories in my head of the families as they passed by.

As I scanned the crowd, the color gold caught my attention. A girl was standing outside the cafeteria, talking to Rhett. She was a short girl with long, wavy golden hair. It glittered just like Sariah's hair always had. I turned away to keep walking when I snapped my head back toward them.

Wait.

Sariah.

It couldn't be.

To have her walk back into my life after five years of searching for her would be surreal. I didn't get this lucky. It had to be a coincidence. Maybe I envisioned her by thinking about the past and now saw her in everyone? The girl turned just slightly, laughing at something Rhett said, and in the process, I saw her full profile. Sucking in a breath, I waited as my brain caught up with what my eyes had seen.

Taking off running at full force, I didn't even think.

This couldn't be real. How was she here? I needed to grab her and make sure she didn't disappear again. I didn't think I would survive it. Not now, not knowing we'd been right all along.

Sariah was alive.

I barreled into her like a linebacker, not realizing how fast I'd been running, barely righting us before we crumpled to the ground. Tightening my arms around her in a vise-like grip, I began to cry so hard I didn't think she even knew what I was saying. Loosening my hold, I looked up to make sure it was really her. You know, just in case I'd completely lost it, and I was hallucinating her now.

Sariah stood stock still, her face ashen, eyes huge as she stared at me with her mouth agape. Definitely real then. Wondering if she maybe didn't remember me—which hurt to consider—or perhaps didn't recognize me, I stepped back more, giving her some breathing room.

"Sariah, It's me. Finley. From Sugar Grove. Do you remember? My brother Henry and I were your neighbors. Your best friends," I uttered, thick with emotion. The whole time I was talking, she looked at me in fear. I didn't understand the fear. In all the times I'd envisioned finding her, this was never how I pictured it.

It was Rhett that interrupted my runaway thoughts with his question.

"Sariah? Finley, you crazy tornado, this is Sawyer."

As his deep voice spoke those words, the terror increased in her eyes. Suddenly, I felt her gripping my hands tightly. Sariah squeezed three times. *Our code.* I visibly relaxed at that. She did remember me. I saw the pleading in her eyes now to collaborate with whatever she had told him.

Sariah and I always could communicate with one another without saying a word. My brother hated it because we were usually talking about him. Even five years later, we could still do it.

Please, Fin, go along with this. Tell him my name is Sawyer. I promise you I have a good reason.

Okay, girl, but you OWE me a BIG explanation. I haven't seen you in five years, thought you were dead, but find you out here flirting with this hunk of a man.

I raised my eyebrow at that and then moved both up and down, exaggeratedly wiggling them at her. I squeezed her hand three times back. Sariah's face flushed red at my response, but her body relaxed when I agreed.

Years were nothing when you were soul sisters.

"Well, Finley, are you going to apologize to Sawyer?" Rhett mumbled grumpily. I swore I heard him mutter, "Don't embarrass me in front of the woman of my dreams."

This made me smile wider at his protectiveness of her. Rhett and I were complete opposites. He was quiet and intense. I was loud and always moving. But we both shared a secret...We believed in true love—hopeless romantics.

I'd caught him watching romcoms one night when all the other guys were out hooking up with people at the bar. Since then, we'd kept each other's secrets and often watched movies together because neither of us desired to meet one-night stands or booty calls. He portrayed this gruff exterior, but secretly he was a teddy bear.

"My bad, Rhett. I'm so sorry, Sawyer, for running into you. I hope I didn't hurt you. And Rhett, I called her Sariah because we knew each other when we were little. I couldn't pronounce the w, so Sawyer became Sariah for me," I responded confidently as the tale flowed from my mouth. I shook my head to emphasize my point and placed my hands on my hips in my power move. I arched my eyebrow at him, a move he taught me to do during one of our movie binges. Rhett shook his head but smiled, nonetheless. He might not admit, but he loved my dorky self.

"Okay, well, welcome back, I guess. How was your visit?"

"Eh, you know how it is. I'm glad to be back, though. I can't believe you know Sawyer. How did that happen?" I asked jokingly, wanting to embarrass him.

Rhett's cheeks blushed, and I knew I called it. Somebody had a crush. I couldn't wait to tease him about this. Smirking at my brilliance, I forgot for a second that I'd just found Sawyer.

"Well, funny thing….," Rhett said, tripping all over himself to say the right thing. Of course, leave it to my best friend to keep things real.

"What he's trying to say is that we've seen each other naked," Sawyer proudly announced and then winked at him. Rhett's face flamed red at the gesture and I'd never seen it do that before. Grumpypants was smitten.

I couldn't help it. I fucking lost it. This was too surreal, and I'd been hit with a case of slap happy. I forgot how Sariah, or Sawyer, often blurted out stuff and had no filter. Damn, I'd missed this girl.

I bellowed out another laugh so loud that I was holding my sides, slapping my leg, all the while tears streamed down my face. Slowly, the others joined in on my hilarity, and we all laughed and ignored the other people gawking at us.

sawyer

Finley. Finley was fucking here. I'd never thought I'd see my best friend again, not after that night when my whole world shifted. I couldn't believe I'd run into her at the campus cafeteria. Of course, I had to blurt out we'd had sex—total facepalm moment. I wondered how they knew one another. This was crazy. What were the odds? Was it just a coincidence?

Wait… if there's a Finley, does that mean there's a…

My breath stopped.

Turning back to Finley sharply, I almost fell over. She was already looking at me when I turned, and we communicated again with just our eyes. Smiling softly, she let me know the answer to my question with a small nod of her head. A tear developed at the corner of my eye, but I had to rein it in. I couldn't break down here because if I started crying, then I might not stop.

Henry.

Henry was here too.

My heart lifted at the thought of seeing him again—something I'd never dared to dream because the disappointment would've killed me. I'd been tempted over the years to find them, but I never wanted to risk their safety. With them here now, though, it seemed fate was putting us back together. My mission was still the same, but maybe I didn't have to do it alone now. I was *this* close to finding answers. I'd known this place was going to be life-changing; I'd just underestimated the depth.

A feeling of dread pulled in my stomach as I realized the risk this presented now. I had to talk to Finley and Henry before they said too much. No one, and I mean no one, could know that I used to be Sariah Brennon.

Rhett left us to run in to grab the food, leaving Fin and I to talk. I needed to speak to her, but now wasn't the right time.

"Finley, I promise I'll explain everything. I never thought I'd see you or Henry again. You don't know how happy it makes me. But until we can talk alone, please don't say the name you knew me as. It's imperative, you understand this. I'm Sawyer Sullivan. Here I have to be Sawyer Sullivan." My words rushed out in a frenzy, urgency at the forefront.

Fin nodded softly, squeezing my arm in hers. We kept talking and catching up on small things, and I discovered she'd come here after finishing fashion school to design costumes. She also assisted the tech department with social media for the school with online profiles for the students and any programs that needed tech support.

Talking to her felt like we were teenagers again. Back to when things were straightforward, and my parents were still alive, back when I didn't fear for my life.

I shook my head to clear it, now was not the time to go all morbid. Things were moving forward, and I was making it happen.

I would discover why my parents were murdered because it all led here—The Aldridge School.

Fin and I exchanged numbers before Rhett returned with the food. Things were better between us now, and I felt confident it would be better in the house.

We ended up spending the rest of the evening hanging out with Mateo and Soren watching Doctor Who. My plan to slowly convert them over was working flawlessly. I never saw Oliver or Elias the rest of the night, and apparently, the mysterious Rey had arrived home but had headed to bed while we'd been out. I guess I'd meet him tomorrow.

I'd slept alone, wanting to be rested for my first day, but I had the opposite result. I think I was already addicted to Rhett's dick. Though, as great as things were between us, I struggled with my attraction and feelings for Soren, Mateo, and Oliver. Elias was squarely on my shit list even if he did have nice abs.

Giving up on sleep, I decided to use the time to check out the dance studio before I had to be at the admin building for meetings. Yay!

Not. Meetings would be the downfall of the world, just you wait and see.

Entering the studio, I felt giddy, and slightly aroused if I was honest, as I remembered the day before with Rhett. I definitely needed to work out some tension, and push those thoughts away. I couldn't be horny all day long. I had students to teach.

Putting on some music, I danced. I loved dancing almost as much as I loved skating. Ice skating had a different feeling to it, though. I loved gliding and the feeling of flying that came with it. But dance was all about passion and emotion, and I had quite a few of those to work out. After an hour of dance, I felt spent, and headed back to my room to get ready for the day.

Checking my phone as I headed to my room, I wanted to see if Finley had responded back yet. The door that led to the bathroom Soren and Rey shared opened right as I walked up. Steam rolled out, clouding my vision for a minute. When it cleared, the most magnificent sight stood before me, clad only in a towel precariously wrapped around his waist. He was using another over his head as he dried his hair roughly. His head was cast down, so I took the opportunity to blatantly stare at his beautiful abdominal muscles. He had a couple of tattoos that took up one side of his chest. The biggest one was a huge tree covering his ribs, and the roots ran down into his waistband, you know if he'd been wearing pants. The opposite side of his chest was a detailed compass, and the third was smaller and harder to make out from this distance.

I must have zoned out for a second, hypnotized by the water dripping down his abs. It rolled over each one slowly, taunting me to lick. I subconsciously licked my lips as I continued to watch the water make its way all… the… way…. down. Another addition to the "Sawyer wants to lick" list, which was kind of a weird list to keep—even for me.

Realizing I was ogling my new roommate, who I hadn't met yet, as if he were a big slice of cheesecake, I snapped my eyes back up and made my way into my room. I didn't want him to realize just how long I'd stared at him practically naked. I was determined to make a good impression with at least one of my roomies, and he was the only one left.

I would have to revisit that image later of his water slicked abs when I was alone in my bedroom.

Yep, I was confident now that I was suffering from Altitude Delirium. The main symptoms were wanting to lick and impulsive hair touching. Yes, I needed to see that doctor before the symptoms became worse, and I'd have to move.

That would be a travesty because I couldn't bear to leave that shower. That shower was my soulmate. I would give my right kidney for that shower. Gah, it really was amazing. Sigh.

twenty-four

. . .

rey

When I'd returned from the weekend, I went directly to my room and crashed. Spending time with my family had been draining, and I hadn't had the space to recharge or decompress from them. To say the weekend had been difficult was putting it lightly. My parents were constantly demanding me to tell them why I didn't want to skate anymore. If I had to hear how much they'd sacrificed one more time, I was going to lose it.

It didn't help that I'd semi been avoiding Soren either. After his text about meeting a girl, I couldn't find the energy to be happy for him. Things were over-whelming, so I avoided meeting the new roommates, hoping that putting it off for a day meant it would be better once I'd slept.

Feeling rested, the sleep had helped recharge me to

baseline. It would probably be a few days before I felt completely energized and ready to step out of my bubble. Joys of being an introvert in an extrovert world.

My phone buzzed on my nightstand, and I glanced over at the notification. Sitting up in bed, I immediately realized I'd forgotten to charge it last night as the glaring 2% battery glared at me. Shit. There were a bunch of texts from my sister and one from Rhett. Wonderful.

Grumps: Give Sawyer a ride tomorrow.

Stinky Sister: Call me

Stinky Sister: Seriously, DUDE. CALL ME!!!!!!

Stinky Sister: 911!!!!!

Stinky Sister: Fine, have a heart attack. Don't say I didn't warn you.

Stinky Sister: BRO…. Just text me or call me. I promise it is not a fashion emergency.

She said it wasn't a fashion emergency, but it was always a fashion emergency with Fin. She had a misconstrued sense of what constituted an emergency. I'd been on the receiving end of her "emergencies" one too many times.

ME: Emergency, sure I've heard that before. I've been asleep since we got back. You know I crash after time with the rents. I have a busy day, so what do you want?

No immediate response back, which didn't surprise me since it was early in the morning, and Fin was a notorious night owl. Doubtful, she'd be up before 10 am. Throwing my phone back down, I stumbled out of bed, heading to the shower. I'd respond to Rhett later. Looking down, I realized I was still wearing the same clothes from the previous day. Gross. I could smell myself, and it wasn't pleasant—time to get my shit together.

My room was becoming an embarrassment of epic proportions. It was a new school term; perhaps it would be the kick to the gut I needed to pull myself out of the dark hole I could feel myself slipping into. I couldn't keep heading down this path and end up where I had last time. I wasn't sure I'd crawl out of it again.

The shower was invigorating and helped clear some of my melancholy. Stepping out, I opened the door that led to the hallway to let the steam out. Drying my hair with a towel, I paused when I heard the door across the hall, but by the time I removed the towel, no one was there. I shrugged it off; I'd meet whoever it was later.

Gathering my skates together with some workout clothes, I had a feeling I'd want to hit the ice later. There was a buzzing feeling under my skin now, promising a new choreo was itching to be developed. I had an inkling some of it was due to my tumultuous feelings for Soren.

I go away for three days, and he meets someone?

Fucking figured.

But would I let that be the end? Could I still tell him,

hoping he picked me? Skating would help me sort it out. Hopefully.

Picking up my phone, I immediately remembered I hadn't charged it when I showered and now it was dead. Shit. Welp, whatever my sister needed to tell me would have to wait.

Walking through the house, it didn't seem anyone else was around. I hoped whoever this Sawyer person was would find a different ride since my appointment with the school doctor for my yearly physical was this morning.

The appointment lasted longer than I'd anticipated. The school had added a psychological test after the last accident with an instructor. Seemed, the Board wanted to cover their bases, but that meant I'd missed more of my morning, and it was now lunchtime.

A great perk of the school was the well-stocked cafeteria with dietician planned meals for each student and instructor. Another way to maximize performance, but it benefited me, so I didn't mind. It meant I didn't have to think about it. Walking through the line, I chose one of my regular lunches and decided to eat outside, since the weather was still pleasant. The campus was actually tranquil with students in their classes. Soaking in the calm, I checked to see if my battery had charged any in the car—10% percent. Enough to send some texts.

ME: Hey, sorry, my phone died. You awake yet?

I saw the bubbles, but nothing came up. I hated that phones showed you when someone was typing. It was worse than wondering if they were going to respond as you watched them move and disappear. A million thoughts ran through my head during the few seconds as I waited for them to appear again.

Ugh, seriously they were evil. I couldn't take it anymore, so I ate my meal and scrolled through social media. Nothing interesting, but I clicked on a few of the local band pages to check when their next shows were. It looked like there was one this weekend. I'd have to talk with Soren. Maybe it was something we could do together and talk about things. I wish Shadows of Mayhem was coming back soon, that would be perfect, but scrolling through their fan page, it didn't look like they'd be near us anytime soon. Damn.

My sister's text started to come across my phone when it died again. Shit. I guess I shouldn't have scrolled through social media, but there wasn't anything I could do about it now. Finishing my lunch, I gathered my trash. Time to check out the ice rink and dissolve some of this energy.

sawyer

My first day had been filled with meetings of the typical boring administrative diatribe. If I had to hear, "We do this… blah blah… because we train the best… blah blah… We're the best!" peppy slogan one more time, I would bang my head against the wall. I zoned out after what felt like the fifth one which was probably for the best. Ha!

Instead, I was trying to figure a way out of this moronic challenge with the Princess. Her death stares were getting old, and I wanted her off my back. However, I didn't want it to appear as if I was scared of her. Because I wasn't, not of Adelaide. But I needed to play the slow reveal game and not tip my hand too soon. Mostly, I wanted to have a better picture of what I was up against before they knew who I was.

Lunch had been provided during the last meeting, not even giving me a breather from these fools. However, it meant I could head straight to the rink when the torture session concluded.

Thankfully, the rink was open, but I'd learned there was a sign up for time slots that I'd need to figure out at some point. It seemed anyone could be on the ice during the open skate, and sign ups were for private skate use outside classes. The individual's rank determined the amount of time allotted, the times of days you could use, and how many sessions per week you had available. It forced the students to do their best to utilize their resources efficiently, along with the instructors.

Currently there was an hour open before a private time slot, so I booked it to the rink, hoping to take advantage of students being in classes during this time. I desperately needed to skate. Living at a hockey rink for the past few years, I'd gotten used to skating to some degree daily. All this pent up aggression and sexual tension had me reeling for a way to let it out. If I was honest, I might need a dick workout, too.

Opening the doors, I found the rink empty. Lacing up my skates, I texted Fin.

ME: Hey! You have time today to talk? Does Henry know yet?

She texted back immediately.

FIN: Yes, yes, yes!! I'm done for the day. I just need to change and grab some food. I haven't been able to get a hold of Henry either, something about his phone dying.
ME: Okay, perfect. I need to skate. Meet up in an hour? I have SO much to tell you!
FIN: Yay!!!!!!! I'll meet you at your place. What's your house number?
ME: Well….. That's one of the things I need to tell you. Say, let's meet at Rhett's?
FIN: How am I not surprised that you have already found yourself in trouble? LMFAO

ME: Shut it! See you in an hour!

Feeling better now that I'd be able to talk to Finley, I made my way onto the ice. The sound system was Bluetooth, so I connected my phone and selected my 'Kick Ass Take Names' playlist. Music blared through the speaker, and I was off.

Skating always brought me peace and clarity. I felt more myself on the ice than anywhere else. Running through some old moves, I began to feel my body relax into the motions. Starting small, I built up my moves along with my playlist.

Toe Loop.

Camel spin.

The flip.

Upright spin.

The wind rushing by my face always exhilarated me as I felt my body giving in to the muscle memory.

Salchow.

Sit spin.

Lutz.

When I heard "Angels and Demons" playing, I knew I was on my last song. I decided to push myself and layout some more challenging jumps.

Axel.

Biellmann spin.

Nailed it! The adrenaline coursing through me filled me with pride at landing each of my jumps. Leaning forward, I placed my hands on my legs as I attempted to catch my breath. Damn, that had felt nice.

I heard someone near the railings and hoped it wasn't the Queen Bitch. After her continued glares and passive-aggressive digs at me for several hours today, I upgraded her to Queen Bitch, or QB for short. If it walked and talked, and all that.

Peering over at the side, I found a guy and not her. From here, I could make out long dark hair on top that swooped over his ears and eyes and appeared to be buzzed short on the sides. He had a real edgy look going for him. His eyes were dark as well from this distance. He kept staring at me, and I began to get worried. What if he was one of R's men?

I didn't remember this guy from the meetings this morning, so it couldn't be because of the whole debacle with Adelaide.

Suddenly, he began skating toward me so fast I wondered if maybe he was a hitman sent by Queen Bitch. Fuck, she was serious about being on top.

But then, as he came into focus, my brain malfunctioned.

Wait. Was that?

rey

Tossing my stuff in the locker rooms, I never got over how amazing they were. Thankfully, they were separate from the students and had a massage room, quiet room, conference room, and a massive soaking room with these Russian inspired banyas that were great for relaxing muscles.

Glancing at the room, I thought about using the banyas later, after I skated. I needed it to be a hard run, and the soaking sounded nice for my muscles. Running through the music, I focused on finishing the last bit of choreography for the senior pairs duo I'd been working with over the summer.

My main focus at TAS was speed skating, but I also assisted with the male skaters for both singles and pairs. I was known mostly for my cutting edge choreography and had been getting increasingly more requests. Choreography was becoming what I enjoyed the most outside of music, since pairs was no longer an option for me.

Exiting the locker room, I heard the music as I made my way toward the rink. I'd been hoping to have it to myself, hoping Adelaide, and whichever Ashley it was who skated wouldn't be out there on the first day. They weren't the type to put in extra work, but the song didn't sound like something either of them would choose. It was "Angels & Demons" by Jxdn, which struck me as interesting. It was a song I'd been thinking about using for a new piece. It was edgy with a hard rock feel to it.

Propping on the railing, I watched the skater glide around the rink. It was someone I didn't know. I hadn't realized they'd filled the Junior Instructor position. This had to be her. As I watched her skate, a sense of familiarity started to niggle at my mind. The skater was powerful in jumps, and despite the song having a hard sound, her moves flowed gracefully from one to the next.

She was intoxicating to watch and had a presence that demanded you pay attention. Sariah had been like that when she skated. When the song ended, the lone skater finished with a Biellmann move. Sariah had loved to finish with that move, too. Something about pulling her leg behind her head and spinning so fast made her feel powerful and free.

The realization that her memory didn't hurt as much to reminisce about today, shocked me to my core. Perhaps it was the sign I needed to tell me it was time to move on. It had been five years; I couldn't stay in this stasis pattern any longer. It was time to put the past behind me and live in the present, actually live.

Watching the skater gather her breaths, I could begin to make out her features. The tugging on my brain pulled again to grab hold of a memory, but it kept slipping away. My body subconsciously knew something as my heart rate increased, my breathing becoming ragged. What was going on? Who was this skater? Had I seen her at a competition or something?

When her head lifted, her gaze seared into me. I sucked in a breath, unable to formulate the words that crashed through my brain to get out.

No... it couldn't be.

My body propelled me forward before my mind caught up. My whole being shook as I skated onto the ice. She just stood there, shock covering her face. I kept expecting her to disappear or morph into someone else the closer I got. When I was halfway across the ice, she started to skate toward me. It became a race to see who'd reach the other first. My heart thundered in my chest, and I worried I might pass out.

We collided in a mass of arms and legs, but since we'd both been racing, we struck into one another with a mighty thud. Shit. We'd forgotten the basic rule for skating—physics.

Yep, physics. An object in motion and all that jazz yada-yada. Turned out, very important in skating.

Our momentum tumbled us to the ground, nearly knocking the breath out of me. Somehow, probably from years of practice, I'd been able to hold her tightly to my chest to stop Sariah from making an impact with the ice.

We laid there for a few minutes as we caught our breath, staring at one another with disbelief mirrored on our faces. Finally, I gathered my courage and pushed her hair off her face, where it stuck.

She was real. It wasn't some lucid dream. Tears streamed down her face, and I wiped them off as fast as they fell.

"Sariah," I sighed her name, the sound so foreign.

"Henry." Both of us barely breathed out the words, afraid to disturb the bubble we'd created.

Hearing my name pass over her lips again was surreal. Sariah's voice was different, but the same. It had rounded out some and seemed fuller, but her voice still made my insides tremble and my heart race. I didn't think, but acted on all the reunification fantasies I'd dreamed over the years and the one thing I'd wished I had done more of with her.

So, I kissed her. It didn't matter that it had been five years. It was Sariah. My Sariah, my Smalls, and I would always want to kiss her.

I'd known at seven years old, and I knew it at twenty-two. Kissing Sariah was how I wanted to spend my life. It was no different now. Her kiss felt similar but more intense, which might be due to five years of pent-up passion within us, but mostly, this kiss was desperate.

We both struggled to kiss every inch of one another, not wanting to miss any spot. It was messy, all tongue, and wet as our tears mixed with our saliva, but it was one of the best kisses of my life. She gripped onto my shirt with both hands so tightly, I was sure this shirt would never fit me the same. But who the fuck cared?

Sariah was sprawled out between my legs, and my dick started to notice. Just as I was beginning to consider taking this further, a door banged open, reminding us both that others were incoming. The cold of the ice was starting to penetrate my skin as well. Shit, it was cold. I slowed the kiss down, gently pressing them on her lips so we could catch our breath. I had numerous questions, but none of them mattered at that moment.

"Sariah, open skate time is up, and the private time

slot seems to be here. We should get up off the ice," I said softly.

She shook her head but began to get up, anyway. I instantly missed her presence. We both stood up, and instantaneously I grabbed her hand, lacing her fingers with mine.

In sync, we immediately began to skate as if we'd never stopped.

Compatibility made or broke a pairs duo. If you couldn't become simpatico with your partner at every level, where you could anticipate one another's movements, you'd never be great.

Sariah and I had that. It was part of why I never fit with anyone else. I couldn't fake this.

We made it off the ice as Adelaide came around the corner. I ignored her as usual and slipped on my ice guards. Sariah did the same, but apparently, Adelaide didn't get the memo.

"Oh look, it's Sawyer," she mocked in her fake nasally voice.

Sawyer? Wow, she was stooping to a new low to call her by the wrong name. I knew she was a bitch, but this confirmed it.

"Sorry, Ade. Did you want something? I'm sure I could schedule you in for some tips tomorrow. You should really work on your rotation on the double axel. Oh, wait, my bad, that's right; you can't land a double, only a single. Well, let me know if you'd want some pointers since I've been landing doubles for years. Tootles."

Sariah walked off like nothing, trilling her fingers over her shoulder. Adelaide started turning red, and I'd swear steam came out of her ears. Jogging, I caught up to Sariah and left Adelaide to herself.

When we neared the doors, we heard a scream of frustration from behind us. I turned to Smalls and we both busted out laughing as we headed into the locker room. If I hadn't been holding her hand, I'd swear I was still sleeping.

My Sariah, my Smalls, was back.

My smile spread over my face pulling muscles that began to hurt from disuse. I couldn't wait to tell Finley.

Oh....

Well, Fuck. I guess it hadn't been a fashion emergency after all.

twenty-five

. . .

sawyer

Henry. I couldn't believe he was here, holding my hand. The moment my brain caught up to the fact it was him, in this ice rink, it had been a competition to see who'd reach the other one first.

Somehow, Henry had been able to twist us, so we landed without cracking our skulls on the ice. Great guy, that Henry.

The rest was still kind of a blur. I remembered some kissing, some very wet, desperate kissing. I remembered feeling like I'd returned home as the smell of him infiltrated my senses. Henry had always smelled like fresh rain, and now that smell was washing me clean of my doubts, strengthening my resolve to keep fighting for the answers.

The kissing intensified as he pressed his lips harder to mine. His tongue game had sharply improved over the years. His hands caressed my face so lovingly, it had made me tear up. Henry massaged my tongue and gently bit my bottom lip.

A rush of need scorched through me, and I started to lean into him more, pressing my full body weight onto him. I could feel all of him, and he was no longer a teenage boy. No, this Henry was all man. Muscles held me firmly, and I could feel his pecs and abs muscles against my own chest.

Of course, just as it was getting good, Adelaide ruined it.

Though, it was probably a good thing, as I was about to fuck him on the ice. My brain was still too foggy with lust to make logical decisions.

Henry's hand held mine, making those damn butterflies go crazy. I'd need to have a talk with them. This was out of control; they had to be defective. Queen Bitch's shriek followed us into the locker room. Gah, she was such a bitch. She'd almost outed me to Henry out there. I hoped her face was purple again.

"Sariah."

Henry's soft voice brought me out of my ramblings and replayed the past few minutes. His voice held such devotion and sadness that it almost broke my heart. The love shone through his eyes, and it helped settle me that he hadn't forgotten me over the years.

On my darkest days, I'd cling to him and Fin, reminding myself that I still had people out there who'd loved me. My deepest fears had been that they hadn't cared when I left, that I'd imagined our connection and made it all up, and that they were happy to move on without me, relieved actually.

Well, stupid thoughts, you could shove it.

"Sariah, I can't believe it's you. That you're here. Does Finley know? She texted me she had something to tell me. Was it you?" Henry peered into my eyes so deeply. That piece of me that always felt home with Henry clicked back into place.

"Yeah, she does. She saw me outside the cafeteria last night. She actually tackled me, too. You Reyes sure are an enthusiastic bunch." I laughed.

"That sounds like Fin, but can you blame us? We've missed you so much, Sariah." Henry grinned so wide I was sure his muscles would be pulled tight.

"Speaking of, there's something I need to tell you. Fin too. I told her I'd explain everything. I'm actually meeting her now. Can you come?" I bit my bottom lip, anxiety racing through me. I wasn't sure how they'd react to the news. Henry reached up, rescuing my lip from my teeth.

"Of course, Smalls." My heart soared at his words. He still considered me to be his Smalls. *Swoon.*

We headed out of the rink and managed to avoid Queen Bitch. I didn't want to deal with her anymore today. I followed Henry to a car, noticing that he hadn't let go of my hand. I think I would be joining the perma-grin club with him around. I was okay with that. There were worse clubs to be part of, after all.

"What's your house number?"

"Well, that's an interesting story. Any chance you

know where Rhett lives? I told Finley to meet me there first." Henry gave me a perplexed look, almost like he was trying to solve a math problem but didn't have all the numbers.

"Yeah… I do."

Henry kept looking at me curiously, but I shrugged, pulling out my phone to update Fin.

ME: Funny story, I found Henry, and we're headed to Rhett's. See you soon?

FIN: Lol. I cannot wait to hear this story. I so wanted to be there to see his face. Did his head explode? Did he pee his pants? I bet he did. HAHAHAHA.

I chuckled under my breath. I'd forgotten what they were like together. I was glad that some things hadn't changed over the years. Henry and Fin were still Henry and Fin.

"What's so funny?" Henry glanced over at me as he maneuvered around the campus.

"Just Fin. I was updating her about finding you and that we're heading to Rhett's. She said she was sad she missed your face when you saw me. And asked if you peed your pants." It made me laugh even more when I said it out loud.

"Ha ha. She's hilarious. And yet she wonders why she's still Stinky Sister in my phone." Henry smirked at me.

I loved that they ribbed each other but never took it

seriously. They were the brother-sister duo I'd always wanted.

When I was younger, I'd begged my parents for a sibling. Now, I guess I knew why they never gave me one. We pulled up to the house and made our way in.

"How do you know Rhett?" Henry finally asked.

"He picked Mateo and me up from the airport," I answered simply. We walked into the house and found Fin already there at the counter talking with Mateo.

"Hey," I greeted them both, happy they were here. "How was your first day, Mateo?"

"It was pretty easy. Excited about getting on the snow tomorrow." His face heated, his eyes holding mine steady.

"We still on for later to hang out? I just need to touch base with these two."

"Absolutely, talk to you then."

"Looking forward to it."

His smile was so infectious that I smiled along with him. Motioning for Henry and Fin to follow me, ignoring their curious glances, I headed toward my room.

"Wait—" Henry started but was caught off by the fluff ball hurling toward me from Elias' room. My dog, yes, my dog, was happy I was home, it seemed.

"Wait… how do you know Lucky, and where are we going?" Henry asked, looking adorably confused.

"Um… yeah, that's part of what I need to talk to you about. Come on, let's go somewhere more private." I continued down the hall, holding onto my dog.

"Why are you going into my roommates' room? And how do you know that guy in the kitchen? What's going on here, Smalls?" Henry looked very concerned at this point, and I missed his smile and the happiness he had exuded earlier.

Come on, Sawyer, you could do this—Wait, did he just say *his* roommate's room?

"Your roommate?" I squeaked out.

"Yes, *my* roommate. Seeing as this room is mine." He pointed at the door across the hall from me. The one that had been shut. The one belonging to Rey.

"But I thought that was Rey's room…" I trailed off as the pieces began to click, and I realized that Henry was apparently Rey and that the hot body I'd seen this morning was the same body I'd been pressed up against only an hour ago.

Damn, when did Henry get tattoos? And I was right about my assessment; he was *all* man now. Starting to feel flushed again as I remembered the water dripping down his body, only a towel covering him, and the way he'd felt against me on the ice.

Drool. Yep, I was definitely drooling.

Covertly, I ran my hand across my mouth to wipe up any actual drool that might've been lingering there. When I didn't find anything, I looked up to my two best friends, who were staring at me with suspicion and humor. You could guess who wore which.

"Um, yeah, well, funny thing you see…. You know what. Let's just get into the room, and I can explain everything all at once. Stop looking at me that way.

Both of you," I huffed at them and turned to go into my room, hoping they'd follow.

Sighing, I placed Lucky down, rubbing my temples. A girl shouldn't have to drop life-shattering news the day after being reconnected with her long lost best friends. This was going to royally suck, but they needed to know. I couldn't carry this burden alone anymore. I realized that now.

Plus, I couldn't move forward in our friendship with any secrets. Time to bite the bullet. Hopefully, they'd still want to be in my life after this conversation was over.

I sat on the bed, picking up Lucky, and he immediately snuggled into my arms, beginning to snore softly. I was grateful for him, as it let me focus on petting him instead of seeing their stares. Finley sat in the armchair by the window, and Henry took the desk chair. It was now or never.

"First, I am Sawyer Sullivan. I live here. There was some mix-up in the housing office, and there weren't any other rooms open. Since I had my own bathroom, I just opted to stay here instead of living with the students or in a hotel room in the city. I met Rhett at the airport when he was picking us up. Mateo is the other new instructor, so that's how I know him. I think that answers all of your questions about the present."

I stayed staring at Lucky and the floor as I petted him. It was soothing, but I needed to suck it up, so I knew how they took the next news.

Raising my eyes, I looked between them both. They

were both quiet, intense, but no other noticeable facial expressions. Guess I needed to pull off the Band-Aid. Taking a deep breath, I said the words I hadn't uttered in five years.

"Sariah Brennon died in a car wreck five years ago. She doesn't exist anymore. In fact, she never did."

twenty-six

* * *

sariah

After I wiped my tears from my face, I grabbed my bag to head downstairs. It would be time to leave soon. When I entered the kitchen, I found my parents waiting for me. Silently, we headed out the back door in the dark, creeping along the fence line to the back gate. After walking down the street for about a mile, we stopped and Dad unlocked the doors of a random car, and we all got in. I had a million questions running through my mind, but now was not the time.

We drove from Indiana to Missouri before we stopped the first time. Dad took a lot of back roads and circled around, going in an odd direction to throw off our destination. The sun had started to come up when we stopped. It was weird seeing something beautiful and yet feeling as if my world was over.

Today was meant to be competition day, and instead, I was running for my life.

A pang of loss shot through me, and I wondered if I'd ever see Henry again; if it would even be safe to do so. As I recalled the look on his face when I left him, staring out of the treehouse, the words stuck on my tongue, and I feared there wouldn't ever be another chance to tell him how I felt.

We stopped for a quick breakfast, and then were back on the road. I was starting to wonder if this would be my life now. Driving in a car, ducking around corners, hiding who I was.

Since I'd slept for a significant portion of the drive, now I had too much on my mind and I needed answers.

"Dad, I think I'm ready for more if you are."

"Are you sure, Sariah?"

"Better now than never, I suppose. We can't really go anywhere." My surliness made him smile, and at that moment, things felt normal.

"Well, where did I stop?" he paused, considering. "Mr. Latimer had threatened to kill your mom and anyone I loved. I, uh, had someone I knew who worked on the less than savory side of things, but who I could trust. I reached out and set up a meeting with him. He provided us with the papers we needed to disappear. I'm not sure how they found us now. We should've been untraceable."

My dad seemed nervous as he pondered if we'd be

able to hide again. A feeling of dread washed over me, and I felt nauseous. Had we been found out because of my skating? Henry and I had started to get more attention lately due to Worlds.

"Once we'd settled and started a routine, I began looking more at the company and what they were involved with. The things I found were disturbing. I'd heard rumors of possible money laundering, but it seems it went even further than that. The company was actually a satellite office for the real mastermind. The larger corporation is known as the Council, and the people who sit on it are influential. The members have to perform some form of sacrifice in order to get a seat. Then they keep the others in line with blackmail. Similar to how the company worked, they prey on people's weaknesses, or hopes, by offering to solve all their problems. Once they have them, they demand repayment."

He took a breath at that, remembering his own time of falling prey to the dreams he wanted for himself and the cost of those—me. He swallowed before he started the next part.

"This part will be hard to hear, Princess, so let me know if you're not ready." Words wouldn't form, but I nodded.

"From my investigation, I... uh... I concluded that you were given to Mr. Latimer as payment for a seat on the council, and..." He hesitated again, not wanting to finish, and a sickening feeling settled in my belly.

"You were to be part of Mr. Latimer's human trafficking ring. He wanted us to raise you so that you were protected from the rest of the Council. Then, well… he wanted to break you and sell you to members of the Council to collect blackmail material. His experience over the years in the sex world had taught him that young, innocent girls were the most desired."

"Pull over!" I shrieked.

I'd barely made it out the door before I spewed my breakfast all over the concrete. My mom rubbed my back, pulling my hair away from my face. She handed me some water and a Kleenex. Mom was always taking care of me and anticipating my needs. She was the best mom I could've asked for.

"I'm so sorry, honey, I didn't want you to ever have to know this. This was why we were frightened yesterday when R was there. He wasn't pretending or making idle threats. Mr. Latimer feels owed and is wanting to collect what he believes is *his* property."

My body shook at my mom's words. I couldn't comprehend the level of corruption of someone who thought that way—to be okay with using a teenage girl for personal gain. Mostly, I couldn't understand how my biological parents had given me up for a seat of power. I was suddenly glad I'd been adopted.

Once I was calm, we returned to the road and were quiet for a while. Eventually, my mom turned on some talk radio to drown out the vast quietness of the car. Stopping that evening, we were somewhere close to the border of Missouri and Iowa. The contact we were meeting would only meet with dad, so mom and I grabbed some food and washed up in a gas station restroom.

My face was pale and stricken, heavy circles sat under my eyes. When we left the gas station, I felt like someone was watching me. But when I turned around, I didn't see anyone, and eventually, the feeling faded away. Dad returned to the car thirty minutes later with our IDs, a new car, and the name of a town somewhere in Montana we were headed to. Exhaustion caught up with me, and before long, I fell asleep in the back of the car, hoping to forget some of this awful day.

The sound of shattering glass, screaming, and tires screeching across the road woke me as the car tumbled off the road. The smell of something burning made me sick, and I struggled to hold back my vomit. It didn't help that I was hanging upside down, and I didn't know what had happened.

"Mom? Dad?" I whimpered out as my head pounded. My whole right side was in pain, and I was having a difficult time breathing. My wrist hurt, and my leg felt weird. I kept trying to get out of the seatbelt but couldn't figure out how, either from brain fog or inability; I wasn't sure. Suddenly arms grabbed me, and a scream erupted from my throat.

"Sariah, it's me, your dad. You're okay, sweetie. I'm going to get you out of here. We were hit by someone. I need you to promise me that you'll run when I get you down. Head west, and don't stop until you find some-where safe to hide. Promise me."

The fear in his eyes was staggering. I nodded my

head and instantly winced. Dad had to cut my seatbelt, catching me before I dropped to the floor. Someone was screaming near the front of the car, but I couldn't make out any other noises over the ringing in my head. My vision blurred, and I doubted I'd make it far in this condition. Wetness dripped down on me, and my whole body ached.

"Remember what I said, Princess. Run. Don't look back. I'll find you. Please, stay safe. I love you, Sariah. I would do it all over again just for the chance to be your dad. I love you so much," he cried. Tears streamed down his cheeks, mixing in with the blood from a cut on his forehead. I stared at the color, transfixed by the tracks.

"Sariah! Focus. This is very important. I need you to remember the following things for me, okay? Can you do that?" Dad urged me to answer, and I was able to focus on the fear in his eyes.

"Okay, Dad."

"The Aldridge School.... find... Abernathy. I believe..... Agency is..... You can trust..... I'm sorry.... I never.... you..... You 're.... ant... the.... cil. I think.... Reyes..... plan...... all.... long."

I couldn't make out everything he told me as my head kept spinning and ringing. He shoved my back-pack into my arms and pushed me, and I started west in a limp. I wasn't too far away when I heard the two worst sounds—gunshots.

They rang out, and the screaming stopped. At the sound, I stopped, but then fear overtook me and I jolted again in the direction he'd pointed. A sudden realization washed over me as I ran through the woods. I didn't tell my dad I loved him, and he had shouted one last thing before the gunshot, and it was repeating over and over in my head.

"It all starts there."

And, with that, I abruptly passed out.

twenty-seven

. . .

sawyer

Not able to look at Henry or Fin, I stared at the floor while I told my story. Some of my hesitation was fear for what their faces would portray, and the rest was I wasn't sure I'd be able to get it out if I did.

Finley had gotten out of her chair at some point, sitting next to me on the bed. She'd placed her arm around me, hugging me to her as I spoke. I didn't realize tears fell from my eyes until she handed me a Kleenex. Henry was the first to break the silence after I'd finished.

"That night... when you came to me... um... in the treehouse, that was when you found out everything?" he asked, his voice hesitant.

I nodded my head as I observed him. "It's why I

missed practice. R had stopped by, and then the conversation with my parents took place that afternoon. I spent the evening packing enough things to sustain me, but not enough to be noticed in case R had someone watching our house."

"Why didn't you tell me? Why didn't you have me call the cops?"

I could hear the hurt in his voice that I hadn't confided in him, but there wasn't a world where I would've told him. It was just too dangerous, too risky. I was glad after the wreck I hadn't, or they'd be dead as well. I knew it.

"I couldn't, Henry. I wanted to. I wanted to so much, but I'd seen my parent's fear when R was in our house. I'd met him and knew he wasn't someone to piss off. I didn't want to put you or Finley in harm's way. It was hard enough to say goodbye, not knowing if I'd see you again, but I had to hope that you'd still be alive out there. I didn't want your death on my conscience Henry. Can't you see that?" I pleaded with him to understand, my eyes begging him to believe me.

Henry opened his mouth, a rebuttal on his tongue, not accepting my reason when Finley stopped him.

"Enough, Henry. Can't you see how hard this was? For crying out loud, she was sixteen! She'd just been told she was adopted, a strange man wanted to take her away, and her life as she knew it was over. What did you expect her to do? When you were sixteen, you thought you'd marry Selena Gomez, and that baggy jeans with a studded belt were the biggest fashion trends. So, maybe cut Sawyer some slack? Don't judge her for her decisions. You don't know that you'd have made any different ones. Besides, it's in the past. We're here now. We're together. Let's be happy about that. We have her back, and I, for one, am grateful." Tears brimmed her eyes, but she didn't let them fall, holding her chin up strong. I squeezed her tight, missing her friendship and support.

Henry slunk down, appearing suitably chastised. I had to give it to Fin; she knew how to put him in his place when it was needed. Smiling at her, I was grateful this amazing woman was on my side.

Finley was fierce and I'd missed having a friend who unconditionally supported and understood you. Fin was that for me. Turning to Henry, I give him a small smile of encouragement.

"I'm sorry, Sa... Sawyer. *Fuck.* That's going to take some time to get used to, but Fin is right. I'm excited as Hell to have you back, and I don't know if I'd have made a better decision, or if there's even one. It's easy to judge when I'm on the outside. Please forgive me?"

I nodded, relaxing into Fin. My world was righting itself again. Henry opened his mouth, closing it a few times before he said what was bothering him.

"There's just a part of me that blamed myself for letting you go without more of a fight. It became this thing that grew inside of me. But," he sighed, "that's my issue, not yours. I'm sorry."

I sat up straighter, jostling Lucky. "Henry, no. Please, don't feel guilty," I pleaded with him. I didn't want him to carry any guilt. "I'd thought I would've been able to contact you once we were settled somewhere safe. But instead, I'd had to disappear into the night without a trace. So no, Henry. I don't blame you. I'd wanted to say more to you, but my need to keep you safe was stronger. I needed that to keep me going each night after. No matter how horrible things were, I would always think of you two. The hope that there were two people out there missing me who loved me, it saved me."

Giving him my most imploring eyes, I begged him to return to the Henry from a few hours prior. He relaxed, a tiny smile on his lips. It was a start.

"I feel like there's more you're not telling us, Sawyer. What happened after you left me? The wreck?"

That Henry, always so perceptive. Clearing my throat, I straightened my spine in resolve. It was time to relive that night again.

"After I left you, we gathered our bags and snuck out the back. My dad had arranged for a getaway car. Someone else left in ours to be the decoy. We'd made it almost two states over where we met Dad's contact. It was close to the Missouri/Iowa border, and he was giving us papers for new identities, cash, keys to a car, etc. It was after we left him that they'd found us."

I swallowed, remembering the crash, the sound of the glass, the tires screeching in the distance, and, worst of all, the smell. I took five deep breaths before I started again, trying to ebb away the panic that was threatening to overtake me. It had been five years, but the crash still affected me. It had been the worst day of my life.

"I don't remember much from the crash. I think I was sleeping in the back or something. When I came to, my dad pulled me out of the car and told me to run. He whispered, uh… some things to me before he turned around to go back and try to save my mom. But I heard the gunshots… two… and then the screaming stopped. I kept running until I couldn't anymore."

I stopped, needing a breath as I recalled my parents being murdered. The sound of the gunshot was still clear as day. The fluffball in my lap nudged me, licking my hand.

"I collapsed at some point, but someone found me and took me to the hospital. I woke up in Iowa with a broken arm, a torn ligament in my leg, three broken ribs, and a concussion. I had no name, no family, and no clue what to do. Fortunately, I'd been aware enough to tell them a fake name. I'd picked out Sawyer before leaving the house since it was similar enough to my name but wasn't obviously a girl's name. I'd hoped it would help me blend. When they asked me my last name, well… I panicked. I didn't know what my father or mother had decided on, but since I didn't have an ID, the lady told me to choose. So, I picked the last happy place I'd been."

Wondering if Henry would get the reference, I looked up and smiled at him. The treehouse in his back-yard butted up to a street—Sullivan Street.

"So, there in that hospital in Iowa, Sariah Brennon ceased to exist, and Sawyer Sullivan was born."

"What were the things your father said to you?" Finley asked.

I was hoping they'd skip over that omission, especially since I'd not told them all of it. I swallowed, not sure if I was ready for it.

"He'd told me some information about who my biological parents potentially were and a place to start looking." I was purposefully vague. I didn't think I was ready to share the news that could potentially destroy them too.

"Well, what was it?" Finley huffed out, her annoyance clear. She wasn't patient when she wanted something. Smiling inwardly, I was happy to see some things never changed with my best friend.

"He… um… he mentioned the name Abernathy and The Aldridge School. That it all starts at the Aldridge School."

They both stared at me for a minute, staying mute. I think I broke them. Great. But then they erupted at the same time speaking over one another.

"That's why you're here? To find your biological parents?" Henry asked.

"What the fuck?" shouted Finley.

Laughing at Finley because she never did anything half-assed. I sobered as I prepared to tell them this last part.

"It's the main reason I'm here, yes. I wasn't sure if I even wanted to find them or put myself back on R's radar for a long time. But eventually, I realized I was stuck. I needed to get out of Iowa, and I realized that I couldn't move forward in my life with this big unknown. This place provides me with a good opportunity to skate, find a new path, and start living my life. I was just passing the time in Iowa. But the most important reason for why I'm here… is to find out who killed my parents and make them pay."

twenty-eight

. . .

sawyer

It was silent for a moment as they digested my words. Finley squeezed my hand, her comfort oozing into me.

"Wow, Sawyer. That's intense. I cannot believe you've been dealing with this on your own for the past five years. You must've felt so scared and alone," she whispered.

God, I'd missed this girl. I pulled her into a hug, forgetting for a moment I had a dog in my lap. Lucky ruffed at us, effectively breaking the tension while reminding us he was there. Wiping my eyes, I glanced at both of them. I didn't see pity in their eyes, which I was thankful for.

"I don't know if I can talk about it anymore tonight. Can we take a pause here? I have something to do tonight anyway," I said, as I started to blush. Finley gave me a knowing grin, while Henry looked confused.

"Sure thing, girl! But I call dibs for Friday night. There's a house party I want us to go to, and you're my wing woman! No buts! You're going because we're in desperate need of some M&M time."

Finley stood up, wiggling her butt to the soundtrack in her head, giving me a wink over her shoulder.

"Oh, My God! How did I forget about M&M?" In sing-song voices, we both bust out the song we'd made as kids.

We're the Mavens of Mayhem,
Here to wreak destruction,
Because we're better than them,
So, let us give you some instruction,
We come in proud, we come in loud,
But we're sure to make you smile,
All the while we'll show you how,
To kick butt, in style!

I sat Lucky on the bed as both Fin and I'd jumped into the dance moves, hip checking one another at the end as we fell over in a bout of giggles.

"We were such nerds thinking we were so badass. But... yes, that sounds great, Fin. I could use some M&M time. Hopefully, the party isn't at Queen Bitch's house, though," I sneered.

"Uh-oh, have you already pissed off the princess?" Fin asked with delight as she clapped.

"Well, you could say that I've somehow inadvertently challenged her. In front of a whole room of people, including the Director, for, um, her position." I acted like it wasn't a big deal and brushed off imaginary lint off my pants. They both erupted at the same time. Siblings.

"What?" screamed Fin.

"Fuck, that explains her behavior earlier, at least," Henry mumbled to himself.

"Yeah, well. Me and my mouth." I shrugged my shoulders because what could I do at this point? Nothing. I just had to face it, or forfeit, and I wasn't a coward.

"Oh God. How I've missed your word vomit moments!" Finley exclaimed. I stuck my tongue out at her as she made her way to the door after giving me one more hug.

"Hey Henry, can we talk really quick before you leave?" I asked. I needed to clear up some things with him. I didn't want him to assume things based on how we reacted to each other when we reunited. I loved Henry, and I'd wanted to be with him since I was a teenager. To have this chance, to be together now, it was what I'd dreamed of.

But things had changed some now, and I needed to be upfront about my feelings. Too many secrets in the past five years had weighed me down, and I couldn't carry it anymore, especially when I didn't have to. The honesty thing felt so freeing, and I wanted to get behind this new outlook.

"Yeah, sure. Let me just go change. Say, five minutes?"

"Perfect."

"Well, I'll let you guys deal with that," Finley pointed, making a grossed out face. "Bye, girl, text me later. I'm so glad you are here. Remember you're not alone in this anymore. In fact, I'll see what I can find out. It just so happens, I have a very special set of skills." Leave it to Finley to quote movie lines as if it were her own while wiggling her eyebrows.

"You're such a goof." I laughed, my insides immediately feeling bright. I couldn't help but smile when I was around this girl.

As they both left, my thoughts began to swirl fast in my head, and I was practically dizzy when Henry returned.

He'd changed into some sweats and a t-shirt and was now barefoot. What was it about men's bare feet that screamed intimacy and sexuality? It also looked like he was a member of the 'drive Sawyer crazy club' by wearing gray sweatpants. Did they send out a memo or something? I wondered if there were dues, and who the president of said club was, probably Rhett. He definitely seemed like the president type—

"Sawyer." Henry waved his hand in front of my face, grinning at me.

"Dang it! I was staring, wasn't I?"

"Just a bit, but I don't mind. Stare away."

Well, when you were given the keys to the Ferrari, you drove the fucking Ferrari!

So, I stepped back, taking him in from head to toe, checking out every inch of his frame in detail. Henry had grown into a beautiful man: tall, at least 6ft, with lean shoulders and muscular arms. His waist tapered in from all the skating and his legs were well-defined. Henry had an edgy look about him, and it definitely worked for him. There were no complaints here. Nope. None, whatsoever.

I was about to scan again when something on his hand snagged my attention.

"Is that..." My breath caught in my throat.

"The rings we got before Worlds? Yeah. I never leave without it now. It was the only connection to you I had after you were gone."

This man was definitely going to make my heart detonate. I sucked in a breath. He was too much to take.

In all the years apart, I'd apparently dulled the memory of his appearance. It had been too hard to remember how much I cared for him and just how amazing he was. No wonder all the boys I'd dated fell flat. No one had been Henry, and my heart had never let go. Not until I came here. It seemed my body had known he was here, too.

Smiling at the boy from my childhood, I walked over to my dresser and opened the small box my mom had gotten me to keep personal mementos in. It was one of the few possessions I'd been able to take with me when we ran. Somehow, it had managed to survive the car crash.

Opening it, I found the tarnished and bent ring we'd

gotten and turned around to show it to Henry. "Mine eventually broke, so I kept it here to keep it safe. Whenever I was sad, I'd open this box and remember all the people who loved me. It was something that kept me grounded."

Henry smiled back at me and I hoped I didn't break his heart with what I had to say next.

"Henry, I wanted to talk to you about something."

I didn't know how to start the next part, and I bit my lip. Anxiety whirled in my stomach. I'd wanted this dream with Henry for so long, but now things were complicated. I had real feelings for the other guys. I didn't want to let them go, nor did I think I could at this point, but I also couldn't let Henry go.

Why did I have to want so much? It was going to cause me to be alone in the end. I just knew it. Hopefully, Henry would respond similarly to how Rhett had.

"Uh, well… wait, you go by Rey now?" I'd forgotten that everyone but Fin had called him Rey. That meant he was best friends with Soren.

"Uh, yeah. When you'd disappeared, I'd become kind of a rebel on the ice, and fans started calling me 'Rebelling Reyes,' and somehow Rey was born out of that." He shrugged, his embarrassment obvious about the rebel part of that story. Rey was fitting and hot, but I wouldn't tell him that.

"Okay, I'm just going to be straight with you, Henry. We've always been relatively forward with each other; we had to be as partners. I know that when I left, things with us were in a delicate balance. We'd just shared the most amazing first kiss, and I wanted so much more for us, but then R happened, and I had to disappear. It was too hard to hope I'd get to see you again or that you'd still feel the same way." I took a deep breath, trying to calm my racing heart. This was so much harder than I'd expected. The boy of my dreams was real again, but he was no longer the only boy in my dreams.

"At first, I kept a low profile, but as a year passed and then another... I started to feel comfortable that I wouldn't be found. At that point, I'd just met my guardian, Charlie. I finally had a stable and safe place. So, I started wanting other connections too, but I was heartbroken and missed you so much. I was naïve and thought that if I just started dating someone that I would be okay. I was wrong, so very wrong because my first time was horrible, and I regretted it. I decided then I wasn't ready to date anyone, so I started a friend with benefits arrangement. Two of my guy friends I wasn't romantically interested in but had physical chemistry with made an agreement. It worked out well, and I didn't catch feelings or anything." Henry looked uncomfortable, but I knew I needed to keep going.

"I don't know what your expectations are now for us. But I feel I need to be open about some things before this goes any further. I care about you too much to ruin anything. When I came here, I told myself to quit being so scared, stop keeping people at arm's length, and be open to possibilities. It seems that the universe, or fate, has a sense of humor because I was literally put across the hall from you, and well in this house in general."

I cleared my throat, feeling emotional suddenly. Being vulnerable sucked donkey balls, yuck. This was hard. Okay, Sawyer, time to pull up your big girl underwear and spit it out already.

"I do still have feelings for you, Henry. *Strong feelings.* You've always been in my heart. For the longest time, you were my whole heart." I took a breath, then said the part I'd been dreading. "I'm just not sure if that's the case anymore." Before I could say anything else, there was a knock on my door. Henry and I stared at one another on the bed. We both seemed confused and torn since we were neck-deep in emotions.

"Sawyer? Baby? Are you home? You aren't answering your phone, so I just wanted to check how your first day went," Rhett said through the door.

Shit. Abort, Abort. What should I do? Fuck. Awkwardness of epic proportions coming up.

"Erm, enter?" Why was I asking a question? It was my fucking room. I glanced at Henry, and he shrugged his shoulders. What Rhett said caught up to his brain just as the door opened.

His head tilted, his nose scrunching up. "Baby? Did he call you, *baby*?"

Rhett stepped into the room, stopping when he saw Henry and I on the bed. He nodded at his roommate. "Hey man, glad you're back. We missed you last night."

"Hey." Henry looked back and forth between us. "I'm confused. How do you know each other so well?" Henry looked more perplexed as the conversation continued. He kept glancing back and forth like a wind-shield wiper. Back and forth. Back and forth.

Shit, I really needed to say something. Speak! Gah, you know what that means? Put Sawyer on the spot, and well, code orange erupted.

"We slept together." Yeah, way to go there. That totally saved the day—double donkey balls.

"What? We haven't slept together, Smalls!" Henry exclaimed, jumping off the bed.

Whoa there, dude, no need to feel so affronted by that. Geesh. Rhett stared, arms crossed in amusement, giving me his eyebrow. Fucker.

"Nooo," I groaned out, placing my head in my hands. Then waving them between the three of us, I tried to pull my foot out of my mouth. "Not you and me. Fuck, why do I open my mouth? Rhett and I slept together. It's what I was getting to before Rhett knocked. Since I just dropped that bomb, I might as well finish. Henry, what I was going to say was that my heart doesn't belong to *just* you anymore. In fact, it's a confused hussy and wants to belong to four others as well."

I was so exhausted at this point I didn't even try to explain. I fell back onto the bed, covering my head with my arms. Hiding seemed like the perfect plan. Yup. Going with that.

"I'm guessing with Rhett not exploding at the news, that he knows you like others?" Henry asked calmly. Too calm.

I was too scared to look to see if we were about to

have a visit from Ragnry.

Henry was typically a pretty chill guy, but when he got mad, it went nuclear. Fin and I had named it his 'Ragnry' moments—Rage plus Henry. We were also thirteen and thought period humor was the height of wit. Thankfully, Rhett stepped in, taking charge of the conversation. Bless that man. He was no longer on my shit list.

"I know. Sawyer and I've talked. We hit it off from the moment we met at the airport, but then she was living here, and it was a serendipitous thing. I realized right away that I wanted to get to know her more. I can't fault others, or her for that either. But, it looks like I've interrupted something, so I'll let you two have your moment. I'm sorry Sawyer, for not thinking to tell you Rey lived here last night. Dinner will be in an hour if you want to join. I think Soren is making tacos."

Rhett pulled my arms off my head, lifted me up, and kissed me right in front of Henry. His lips lit a fire, but as soon as they were there, they were gone and he walked his sexy ass right out the door.

"What does he mean by others? Four others?" Henry stuttered. Crap. He'd hit Henry overload mode and was starting to malfunction. Thinking quickly, I grabbed his nose. Yep, you heard me.

Kissing worked for Rhett, clutching Henry's nose worked for him. He stopped immediately and stared at me with his mouth open. Then... the reaction I was waiting for happened.

He laughed, and it was fucking melodic. Gah, I'd

missed that sound. It brought a lightness to my chest and a warmness to my heart. I'd let go when he started to laugh since I didn't want to accidentally asphyxiate him.

"You haven't done that in years, Smalls." His smile was so broad it changed his face. He looked more like my Henry now. It hurt my heart when I thought of the pain he suffered because of me and how that must've changed him.

"Yeah, well, you haven't gone into overload mode in a while, not since you were fourteen, and I was thirteen… I believe it was about how you didn't understand why Olivia's skirt was so short, until one day you did, and your head about exploded. I think it was the first time I was jealous of your affection directed toward someone else." Smiling, I stared into his eyes, needing to see him now, not wanting to hide. I sighed, knowing I needed to tell him everything.

"I didn't plan to like four guys, you know. I just got here, and this place was my chance. My new opportunity and everything felt so light for the first time in forever. I connected with people, and I felt that I could trust someone for the first time since that day. And now, to have you here too, I feel that my heart is so full. I know I don't deserve it, and I feel selfish for asking. But I can't stop seeing Rhett, and I want to explore what is developing with the others too. But I can't deny that I hoped you would want to see how things go with us as well. I just—" I was rambling and babbling when he cut me off, smushing my lips together.

"Smalls. Stop. I don't need to hear anymore."

Well, shit. This was it. He'd tell me I was a slut and that he didn't want anything to do with me now. Why did this have to happen? To be reconnected with Henry after all these years the moment I started to fall for someone else?

Karma was a bitch.

I felt tears begin to fill my eyes. I'd been so close to being happy.

"Sorry, sorry, bad use of words. Don't cry, Smalls. Please, I can't bear it. I'm so happy to have you back. I want you to know that. I can't say that I didn't engage in sex with partners either, but I didn't give my heart away because I couldn't see past you." His voice took on a seductive and soft quality, as his hand gently held my cheek, swiping the few tears that managed to escape.

"Smalls, my heart has been yours since I was seven. I didn't know how to show you then or understand what it meant, but it was yours. And that night, my heart left with you. Every day since, I've been missing it —every day. I'm not the same Henry you left, and you're not the same Sariah. Hell, you're not even Sariah, you're Sawyer now. I would like the opportunity to get to know her. But especially for you to get to know me."

He gazed so deeply into my eyes, it felt like he was inside me. Henry might think he was different, but all I saw was the man he'd become, and I so wanted to get to know that man.

"Fucking hell, Henry. My life doesn't make sense

without you in it." His face morphed right before me, and a weight I hadn't realized was there, left at my words.

"I'd like to discuss these other guys, but I think I'm going to need more than a nose pull to stop from feeling overwhelmed today. Can we pick this up later?"

"I think that's the best idea. I'm emotionally over-wrought too."

Henry hugged me, and it was everything I remem-bered. My whole body relaxed into him, finding nostalgic comfort. Henry had always made me feel strong. He showed me trust and pushed me to stretch my boundaries. He believed in me even when I didn't. Being partners throughout the years had increased these traits in us. After a few minutes, he let go and made his way to the door. Before he left, he turned, looking at me.

"Just one more thing if that's okay?"

"Absolutely." My head nodded so fast I looked like a bobblehead doll.

"Who exactly are the other guys?" He had a weird expression on his face.

"Um... well, there's Mateo who you met earlier. Then there's a possible attraction with Oliver when he's not getting in his own way. I feel attracted to him, and there's a spark, but it's still new. And well, uh, there's Soren." He looked absolutely shocked but relieved at the mention of Soren.

"Soren, huh?" He smiled. Why was he smiling? "But not Elias?"

I rolled my eyes; I couldn't help it. "Ugh no. We haven't had the best interactions. Starting with Elias calling me a whore and then telling me what I could and couldn't wear. So, I don't think that'll be happening. But I've officially stolen his dog." I grinned so wide my face hurt, and I was sure I wore an evil smirk. Lucky was so *my* dog.

"He called you what?" Henry yelled but then shook his head. "You know what, never mind, I'll talk to the guys. My brain's too full right now. I don't even know where to start with what you said. I'll see you in a little bit for dinner?"

"Yes. Thank you, Henry. I'm so happy to be here with you."

"Me too, Smalls. Me, too."

The door shut, and the biggest wave of relief fell over me as I fell back on the bed. Pulling out my phone, I checked my messages and texted Fin.

Grumpy Bear: Hey, baby, how was your day?
Grumpy Bear: Are you home? Do you need a ride back?
Shy guy: I am open on Wed if you want to get together then.
Chill Bill: Have you started the book yet? Chapter 9 was badass.
Ace: Bestie!! How was your day, sweet stuff? How are all your hot roommates treating you? You ridden any yet?
Charlie: Hello, Sawdust. I just wanted to see

how your first day went. Do you have everything you need? Miss you, kiddo. This texting
thing is weird. Please, give this old man a call.

I laughed at Charlie. I couldn't believe he actually
sucked it up and learned how to text. I'd given him a
cell phone when I left, despite him saying he wouldn't
use it. Looked like I'd proved him wrong. It felt good to
have someone checking in on me. I responded quickly
to the other messages before I called Charlie.

ME to Rhett: *kissing face*
ME to Mateo: Wednesday works for me!
ME to Soren: I know!!! I loved her showing the
others up on her badass skills. Who was your
favorite character?
ME to Ace: Bitch, please. Like I'm going to tell
you the tea over text. You want the deets, then
you can buy me a beverage. I have a late
morning tomorrow. Want to meet at the coffee
shop?
ME to Fin: FIN!!!!! So many things to tell you
since you left. Believe it or not, I made a friend
the other day. Want to meet us tomorrow
morning at the coffee shop?

Then I called Charlie. It was nice to hear his voice—
home comfort. I hated that I didn't realize how much I
loved the old man until I was gone. He was my home. I
needed to make sure he knew it too.

twenty-nine

. . .

rey

As I shut Smalls' door, I had a difficult time wrapping my brain around the fact she was literally across the hall from me. I hadn't known where she'd been for five years, and then, poof, she ended up here, across the hall. The circumstances felt too coincidental, but how else could I explain it?

The timing and circumstances had me on edge, especially after this weekend at home. The info I'd discovered about my parents seemed too odd, and I was beginning to wonder if there was something more sinister going on. Did all of these pieces fit together? I'd need to share everything with Fin and Smalls soon. My head was too full right now to sort things properly. My phone buzzed with a message as I stepped into my room.

Grump: Sorry about earlier. We should talk.
After dinner?

I shook my head at Rhett's message; even in a text, he was brief.

ME: Yeah. That works.

The group text popped up then.

Message from Bros before Hoes:
Grump: Dammit, Oliver. Quit changing the names.
Cock Jock: It wasn't me!
Unknown Number: Um, hi?
Grump: Mateo, House chat. Guys only.
Unknown changed to Snowball
Hot for Teacher: Is there a reason it is just us guys? It's not wise to leave Sawyer out. I am already on her shit list.
Snow God: It was so Ollie, the green giant. You're the only one who ever says that phrase, bro. Nice try, though.
Cock Jock: I'm offended Snowy! I'd never do such a thing.
Snowball: I'm the dog from Rick and Morty. *wide eyed face*
Cock Jock: Ahhh... that's kind of cute. Though I'm sure whoever changed it was implying snow snow. But, hey... Let's go with that. *pouty face*

Hot for Teacher: Speaking of dogs… Anyone seen mine, the traitor?

Snow God: He's in the best spot. Sawyer's lap. Can't believe I'm jealous of a dog.

Broody Guy: Point Rhett? Can we get there?

Grump: Guys meeting after dinner. Sawyer knows.

Broody Guy: …

Switching out of the group text, I messaged Soren. I needed to talk to him. I needed to tell him I knew Sawyer, that she was Sariah, and not to say anything yet. I also had a feeling she might be the girl he was talking about, and if so, it changed things. I just needed clarification before we all sat down. I wanted to tell him how I felt; one way or another, it was time to get it out.

ME: Hey, sorry I didn't talk last night. I crashed. Heavy weekend. Can we talk after the other meeting? I have some things I need to get off my chest.

Soren: Of course. I'm finishing dinner, or I'd talk now. I'm glad you're home. I missed you, you know. You kind of shut me out the other night. Did you meet Sawyer yet?

ME: Yeah, she's part of what I need to talk about with you. Just, if you hear something later about her, make sure to not say anything out loud, but check with me or speak to me about it later. It's important. Okay?

Soren: That's not cryptic AF or anything. But yeah, sure.

ME: Thank you. I'm glad I'm back too. I…

ME: missed you too.

Soren: ……

My heart raced in anticipation; I couldn't believe I fucking said that. Fuck. The phone started shaking in my hands.

The fucking dots disappeared. Shit. Come back, dots. Come back.

But nothing ever returned, no message appeared. Shit.

I hung my head in defeat. Welp, it looked like I had my answer. Dread and disappointment lined my stomach. I thought we had something more, but I guess I'd just imagined it all in my head. Needing something to do to distract myself, I remembered my resolve to clean up my room. My suitcase still sat at the end of the bed where I'd dropped it last night. It was as good of a place as any to start.

I was placing my toiletries in the bathroom when I heard my phone ping. Trepidation filled my bones, and I debated if I should even look or just dismiss it, but I needed to know, even if it wasn't what I wanted to hear.

Soren: It's so good to hear you say that. I missed you too, Rey. A lot. I have some things I need to tell you also. I'm glad you want to talk. I've wanted to for a while. I just didn't know how to say anything. Now, quit hiding in your room and get your cute butt down here and help me set the table. *winky face*

Was I hallucinating, or was Soren flirting with me? What did he mean he had something to talk to me about, too?

A feeling of hopeful optimism filled me and, with a bout of zestfulness, I skipped off to the kitchen.

Fucking skipped!

My brain was malfunctioning with the thought of both Soren and Sawyer possibly in my life. So, with a smile gracing my face, I entered the kitchen. It was time to figure out how to flirt with a guy.

mateo

Staring at my phone for a while, I wasn't sure how to process the messages. What did he want to talk about? Did he know I kissed her?

I'd been waiting the past two days for him to punch me or something. It was obvious they had something going on, but then she kissed *me*.

I didn't know what it meant, especially since I didn't have much experience with girls. Scratch that, I had *no* experience with girls.

My life had revolved around training for the past

ten years. My youth had been spent on the road surrounded by chaperones and mostly older teammates. I didn't care back then because my focus had been skiing and nothing else.

But now, things were different.

Skiing wasn't my obsession anymore, and it seemed I was behind in things that most people had learned in middle school. I was twenty-one, and Sawyer had been my first kiss.

I didn't think she knew that, but she had been. It was everything I'd hoped it would be. It might seem weird that a guy would think about his first kiss, but I had. I would see other people kissing and wondered what it was like to have a partner. It didn't look very appealing with all that spit, but the moment her lips pressed against mine, I got it. My whole body lit up like a live wire, and I'd felt as alive as if I'd been at the top of the ski slope, ready to take off.

Sawyer had a way of making me feel seen, but I didn't think I could compete with Rhett. I didn't even know if she meant it more than a friendship kiss. Did friends kiss that way?

It hadn't felt like a friendly kiss, but I didn't have a frame of reference for either version.

Sighing, I closed out the game of Animal Crossing I'd been playing and wondered if Sawyer played. It was close to dinner, and the smells coming up to my room had me investigating.

In the kitchen, Soren and the last roommate, Rey, were laughing at something. Prepping myself to be more social, I decided to take a chance. Soren had been nice to me so far. It couldn't hurt.

"Hey, um, Soren, do you need any help?" Soren instantly made me feel at ease with his fun attitude. He was really good at that.

"Hey, Mate-o! Rey was supposed to be setting the table, but he's slacking. Want to whip him into shape? Rey, have you met Mate-o yet?" Soren changed my name each time we talked. I think it was his way of making me feel included, and I had to admit, it worked.

"Hey man, I'm Rey. Nice to meet you. Sorry I didn't introduce myself earlier. I was distracted by everything going on. Glad to have you here in the house, though."

His smile was genuine, and while I could glimpse some darkness in his eyes, he did seem pleased to have me in the house. The last bit of tension I'd been holding onto left my body at his words. Feeling accepted by others had never been this easy before. They might not understand what it meant to me, but I did. Vulnerability was hard for me, and this feeling of being valued was powerful, and I reveled in it.

"Nice to meet you too, and it's no problem. I know how hard it is to focus when Sawyer's around." I tried to bring some levity and smiled back at him. For once, I didn't feel like an imposter. He laughed, nodding.

Grabbing the plates, I headed to the massive table. When I'd finished, Sawyer was entering with Oliver, laughing about some movie. Watching her be carefree brought me a feeling of completeness, and she wasn't even with me. The realization that I felt the feeling of happiness at this moment shocked me.

It was hard to remember what happiness felt like. It felt foreign with the lightness inside my chest, but I decided I wanted more of it.

The rest of the house entered the kitchen and began to fix their plates as I watched them all. I found myself growing more confident with each day here, and knew this was the place I needed to be.

Dinner was a lively affair as everyone discussed how their first day went. Mine had been easy without the pressure to achieve a new personal record for once, or train until I couldn't move.

It had been the first time I'd skied since the incident, but it was also the first time I hadn't felt anxiety about skiing. Those two things within themselves were enough to make this job right for me. But if I also got friends who accepted me, who got me, and made me feel comfortable, well, then, that was exceptional. I liked exceptional.

After we all ate our fill, Sawyer excused herself to go have a date with her shower. I wasn't sure what she meant by it, but she seemed happy about it. I didn't miss that she kissed Rhett as she walked out of the room, but what was surprising was when she stopped by my chair next, kissing my cheek in front of everyone.

A blush rose to my cheeks, and I avoided eye contact, but when I glanced up, Soren smirked at me, but no one said anything. I hoped they weren't feeling pity for me, or that it was sad she'd kissed me. That would be devastating. I began to slip into my self-doubt as my thoughts circled me.

I'm not worth it. I'm not enough. I'm a failure. No one cares.

No, I wasn't falling into this trap again. I'd been down that path, and I didn't like it. I'd learned better now, and I'd felt accepted.

So, I stopped my spiraling thoughts and breathed like my therapist had taught me. Deep breaths in. Deep breaths out. Then the hard part, replacing the lies my brain told me.

Mateo, you are enough. Mateo, you are worth it. Mateo, you are not a failure.

I reiterated this to myself until I couldn't feel the negative weight of despair trying to slip back in. When I opened my eyes, I realized I'd closed them at some point. I was surprised to find the room was empty except for Rey. He watched me with a look of familiarity, not with pity, but understanding.

"I told them I'd wait for you. Are you okay to head in now? If you aren't, I can take some breaths with you. They won't be upset if you need more time. They would have all waited, but we didn't want to crowd you or make you feel embarrassed."

His voice was calming and reassuring, making me want to believe him. They hadn't been upset and only left because they didn't want *me* to be embarrassed. This feeling helped to reinforce that I hadn't imagined it. These guys did care about me and had accepted me. I wasn't alone any longer.

That statement sent a feeling of reassurance and gratitude through me.

"I think I'm good and ready to head in there. Thank you for waiting for me, and offering to wait. I'm not always good with new things, and my thoughts can be mean. I just needed a moment to remind myself." I decided to be open with him, plus it was easier to be vulnerable with one person.

"Not a problem, man. I get it. I've had some dark moments, too. If you ever feel you can't crawl out of it on your own, come to me, and I'll help. I don't care what time it is or what I'm doing, you can come to me. I've always pictured it as a pit in my mind, so if you're ever in the pit in your mind with no escape, I'll be your escape until you can see the light on your own."

"Thank you."

I had no other words. This guy had only known me for a few hours and was willing to do more for me than anyone in my family or life before ever had. I didn't think he understood what his words meant to me, but Rey had just fundamentally changed me.

And all he had done was care.

It was so simple but yet so powerful. Feeling confident from all the boost of good thoughts, I did something I'd never done before. I initiated a hug.

Thankfully, he didn't push me away or, worse, laugh

at me. He hugged me back and let me cling to him until I was ready to let go.

For a hug with a practical stranger, it was a great one. It'd been a purely platonic hug, but it was the first time I'd ever felt it was significant.

My therapist had once told me that hugs had healing properties in them, but that they had to last at least fifteen seconds to feel the effects. Honestly, I'd thought she was crazy because I had never experienced that before with my family. In fact, I'd often felt worse when forced to hug them. But maybe she was on to something.

This hug had been my choice, and I felt accepted by Rey. When we pulled back, some of the darkness from Rey's eyes was gone too, and he seemed lighter. Smiling, I reveled in the absence of anxiety that had been replaced with joy.

thirty

. . .

mateo

WHEN WE REACHED THE GAME ROOM, REY CLAPPED ME ON my back before sitting next to Soren. Deciding I wanted to be able to see everyone; I sat on the beanbag chair that faced the couches. Once I sat, Rhett was the first to speak. I'd noticed that while he didn't like to talk, he did because he cared.

The people in this house were like a family, and he'd fight to make sure they were safe and had their needs met. It had felt odd at first when he'd texted to see how my day was, but now it made me feel protected, and I looked forward to his nightly check-ins.

"I think we all have some things to discuss in regards to Sawyer." Everyone looked around the room, but no one spoke up. I shifted in my chair, causing the material to make that weird crackling sound. Soren chuckled, but there was no other sound.

Rhett sighed. "I'll start. I knew things would be different with a girl living in the house. I didn't know how different they'd be until I got to know Sawyer. So first, I have to ask, what do you think about her? What are your feelings toward her?" he asked.

I remained quiet, unsure what to say that wouldn't result in a punch to my face.

"Why are you asking?" Elias asked, skepticism in his tone.

"Because it's important." Rhett gave his friend a look that dared him to ask again. I was beginning to think this was better than TV.

"Are we having a dude gossip fest?" Oliver asked, laughing as he slouched down into the couch.

"Come on, be serious. I wouldn't ask if it wasn't important," Rhett huffed, crossing his elbows. He was being vulnerable and no one was taking it seriously.

"It's just weird talking about this altogether, isn't it?" Rey asked, looking around the room at everyone. Rhett finally seemed to be at the end of his patience, pulling out his true grumpy persona as his frustration rumbled out of him.

"Would everyone quit their complaining and just answer the damn question already? We aren't leaving this room until we do." Rhett had a total mom look going on as he looked at everyone, daring anyone else to speak out.

"Fine, she's fucking hot, dude," Oliver said, but immediately sobered. I hadn't gotten to talk to him much, but he seemed to have a cocky persona he defaulted to at times, but it wasn't his actual personality.

He sat up, trying again. "I mean, she's beautiful and smart. She's someone I enjoy talking to, and her passion for hockey is a huge turn on. But I'm not going to make a move, man. I don't stand a chance." His voice tapered off toward the end, but I could hear the vulnerability and sincerity threaded through it.

Rhett didn't have to say anything else as he glanced around the room, his eyes zeroing in on others to keep talking.

"Well," mumbled Soren, messing with his hair in a nervous habit. "I'll admit I've started to develop feelings for her. Sawyer's amazing, and I've connected with her on a level that's rare. I'd hoped to have the opportunity to explore things with her, and I'm not afraid to admit it."

"You know my answer," Rey said, sitting back against the couch. His shoulder brushed against Soren's when he crossed his arms over his chest and I watched as his cheeks tinted red.

"I'm not sure what you want me to say. She hates me, and I haven't given her a reason not to. I'm too broken to have feelings." Elias sighed, hanging his head.

Which left only me. Rhett's gaze swung to mine, making me swallow nervously under his intense stare. Words left my mind and I could only nod. Thankfully, he seemed to accept that and turned back to the group.

"This is what I'm talking about, you guys. We need

to discuss this because it's important. Most of you know I don't date. I don't do hookups, nor do I pursue girls. Sawyer, though, she's special. She's the future kind of girl, you know?" Rhett smiled, the action changing his whole face.

I looked around the room at the other guys and didn't understand their shocked expressions. It was like he said his real name was Santa. *Shock. Delight. Curiosity. Anxiety.* It all flitted across the guys' faces as they took in the mountain known as Rhett.

I soaked in their responses as I digested this interaction. Observing others was my natural state. It both helped me understand my surroundings and people. Since I was a shy, anxious, Hispanic kid, it hadn't done me any favors growing up. I'd only had one friend, and then skiing became my life.

"I'm happy for you, mate. It was about time you got out of that dating rut of yours." Elias chuckled awkwardly, finally turning to look at his friend. I noticed different emotions crossing his face before he hid them behind the 'perfect' mask he seemed to wear. Elias was the hardest to read because I never knew what was real with him.

"So, listen when I say this. Sawyer is worth a million other girls and then some. She's genuine, kind, funny, and sexy without even trying. She puts me in my place and shows me how big her heart is in everything she does. I can't deny that I've seen the way you've all watched her. Sawyer has a way of stealing the air from the room when she's there. You guys are my brothers, my best friends, and I want the best for you."

Here it comes, his claim on her and my subsequent heartbreak at never getting the chance to know what it felt like to fall in love. I hung my head as I waited for his killing blow.

"When I first spotted her, Sawyer's beauty took my breath away. But getting to know her, spending time with her, and laughing with her, it solidified my feelings. I might sound sappy, but whatever, I don't care. It's who I am, and I'm tired of hiding that part of me in a misguided effort to protect a misconceived measure of manhood."

He grumbled, and I realized I'd never seen him so passionate about something. He took a few moments, staring at the floor, gathering himself by inhaling deep before he continued.

"I intended to make her mine the moment I saw her, but things developed differently than I think any of us anticipated. And well, Sawyer is Sawyer. I'm not a fool to think I'm the only or best option for her. I'm humble enough to admit it."

He grunted and awkwardly laughed at himself—his voice hoarse from the excessive use. I wondered if I should offer him some water? He sounded like he could use it.

"What are you saying then?" someone finally asked, but it was so quiet I wasn't sure who.

"When I realized she had feelings for Mateo," he looked at me, "I was surprised because I didn't feel jealous. I witnessed a kiss between them, and instead of wanting to punch him, I was... um... Well, I." He cleared his throat, "Never mind that. The important thing is, I realized I wasn't jealous."

My breathing stopped. Was this it? I'd been waiting for him to punch me, but his words weren't computing with my brain. Wasn't he mad? Was he saying... wait, what was he saying? My mind had officially shut down.

"Wait, Sawyer kissed Mateo? Based on the other morning, I thought you and her were together?" Elias asked, looking confused and slightly panicked. Rhett gave his best friend a look, effectively shutting him down. Damn, I needed to learn that trick.

"Sawyer admitted to kissing him before I even said anything to her about it. She's not another Voldemort, man. She can't seem to keep much of anything to herself; she's an open book on most things. When they kissed, we hadn't gone out yet, so no cheating occurred. But she still wanted to be honest with me." Rhett huffed, pointedly looking at Elias almost like he was saying, "happy now?" Elias surrendered, lifting his hands, which seemed to appease Rhett to some degree, so he continued.

"Okay, so Sawyer kissed Mateo. Why are we all here? I'm not the smartest guy, but this conversation isn't making sense to me. You claimed her. Enough said," Oliver interjected.

"What I'm trying to say, but keep getting interrupted about, is that I didn't understand why I wasn't jealous. Curiosity got the better of me, so I Googled."

Rhett chuckled under his breath, causing us all to join him, effectively dissolving some of the tension building in the room.

Google. America's answer to everything.

"On our date, Sawyer confessed that she was unsure about her feelings because she had them for more than one person. I'll admit that it stung at first, and Google led me to some weird places, but it did help explain things. This isn't what I'd imagined for myself. But Sawyer's a fucking unicorn, man. I realized you don't let that go because it may be different than what you pictured. You all will have to figure out your relationships with her, but for the people who admitted their feelings and want to date Sawyer, well…" He raised his hands, pausing.

Rhett wasn't playing fair with his dramatic pauses. He had everyone on the edge of their seats, holding their breath. It was so quiet; I could hear the second hand of the clock ticking. He seemed to gather his thoughts as he shook his head, deciding what words he wanted to utter next. He cleared his throat before he dropped his bomb.

"What if we *all* dated her… at the *same* time? You guys are my brothers, my family, and I think it could work."

Rhett dragged the palm of his hands over his pants, attempting to dry them. It weirdly settled me to see a guy I thought of as confident, nervous. Whether it was from talking or the topic in general, I wasn't sure. Either way, it was validating.

The room seemed as shocked as me. No one said anything for a while. I'd thought he was going to challenge me to a fight, demand I quit talking to her, or even move. His style seemed more of a gruff, "I'm dating Sawyer. Back off" type of conversation.

"What do you mean, exactly?" someone asked.

"It's called a polyamorous relationship."

"How would that even work?"

I lost track of who was asking what as my mind whirled. Was this something I wanted? Was this something I could deal with? Slowing down each thought separately to not overwhelm myself, I dealt with them one at a time. If not, the thoughts would overrun my mind letting my anxiety take over.

Was this something I wanted? No sense denying my feelings for her. She made it easy to be me.

Was a poly relationship something I wanted? Honestly, I'd never thought about a poly relationship, but I hadn't thought against it either. So, it was a neutral thought.

Was this something I could deal with? In some ways, it relieved the pressure for me. I didn't know how to be in a relationship or feel I could be everything she would need. Not even being self-deprecating, but honestly evaluating my abilities. I did know that I felt accepted by Sawyer and these guys. When I'm with her, I felt I was enough.

Am I against this? I sorted through all the thoughts to find the logic:

I liked Sawyer.

I wasn't opposed to a poly relationship.

I liked the guys and trusted them.

I felt it would be good for me.

It would take off some of the pressure and keep my anxiety manageable.

All my thoughts led me to believe that I could do this, and I wanted to. I could have a relationship with Sawyer without fearing that she'd grow bored or regret her decision. Having the other guys to lean on and talk to about things would be good for me too.

Satisfied with my conclusion, I tuned back into the conversation finding it quite different than I'd left it. It seemed that my roommates could benefit from my self-talk method based on the shouting as they all spoke over one another.

"This is ridiculous!" Oliver said.

"Is this what she wanted?" Rey asked.

"Yes, but—" Rhett tried to respond.

"I'm all for this, guys. Reverse harem all the way, baby!" Soren cheered.

"You lot will trash her reputation, bloody Hell." Elias sulked.

"I am not having sex with you guys," Oliver said.

"That's not what—" Rhett tried again.

"What's the matter, afraid you won't measure up, Ollie bear?" Soren teased.

"Why are we discussing this without Sawyer?" Rey asked.

"She's–" Rhett started.

Having heard enough of them talking over each other, but especially not allowing Rhett a chance to answer, propelled me to do something. This wasn't productive at all. Jumping up from the beanbag, I let out the loudest scream I could.

"AHHHHHHHHHHHHHHHHHH!"

Everyone stopped, and blissful silence rang out. They all turned, gaping at me. Surprise etched on all their faces.

"Everyone, stop! Shut up and listen to me." Shockingly, they all did. Probably more from disbelief I was speaking up, but I accepted it anyway.

"I need you to listen to me with no interruptions. I'm going to break it down into three simple questions. If you can answer yes to any of them, then you need to think about this, really think about this. Don't let other things steer you away." I cleared my throat and took a breath. Being brave was getting more comfortable with them around.

"Deep breathing helps me when I'm anxious, so maybe you all could do some with me?" I left the question open, so at Soren's nod of encouragement, I continued. "Okay, deep breaths together: breath in, hold for five, breathe out." We repeated the sequence a few times before I noticed them all relax.

"Good, okay, the first question. Yes or No, only. Answer without thinking; just say the first thing that comes to your mind. Ready? If you'd met Sawyer in town, would you have wanted to date her? Don't think about the complications of how things are right now."

"Yes." Rang out through the room. We all turned to

Elias, who apparently even shocked himself with his answer.

"Bloody Hell, mates." I chuckled a little at his response. Preparing for the next question, I steadied myself.

"Great you guys, for the second question, answer it without thinking with the first thing that comes to mind. Do you trust the guys in this room?"

"Yes." This time was quicker for everyone to respond to. I couldn't help but smile, though, because that meant they trusted me. The guys started to relax more and I could tell they felt comfortable with their decision.

"Last question. Would you do whatever it took for a chance to date her if you had the opportunity?"

"Yes."

Again, it sounded out strongly around the room. Giving everyone a smug look, I retook my seat. I couldn't help feeling proud of myself for standing up to them and being the one to guide them in a clear direction. Some of my self-doubts that had clung to me my whole life began to shed away.

"It doesn't matter what I want. Sawyer hates me. I screwed up too much already. Not to mention, I'm still too fucked up from Voldemort to be good dating material."

Elias fell back, defeated. I didn't know who this Voldemort was, but she sounded like she'd shredded his heart. I felt for the guy. I knew what it felt like to feel inferior. I didn't think I'd ever had anything in common with him; he was so proper and put together. He exuded a poshness that not even my pinky finger had.

But at that moment, I saw it. His fear that he was the problem, that he deserved his ex's treatment. I mostly noticed the fear that no one would ever see him for who he truly was. I recognized that in myself, and for once I knew I could help.

"Elias, if you like her, keep trying. I don't know you very well, but I do know that every one of us is worthy of a chance. She's worth you giving her one, and you're worth giving yourself one. It just takes you stepping out of your fear and the pain you hide behind to see if there's something better and real there. Obviously, I don't know your ex or what the story is there, but I know it doesn't matter in the end unless you keep making it matter."

He examined me, digesting what I said. Each word seemed to land in his mind as he considered them. Sometimes, being the quiet one had its benefits. When you did speak up, people listened to what you had to say. Elias struggled to believe the words I said, to allow himself the chance to hope.

Hope was the scariest thing of all.

"Thank you, Mateo. I'll try to get out of my own way. You are right; it only matters if I keep giving it space in my mind." He nodded respectfully at me, and I felt as joyous as I had the first time I won a medal for skiing. I'd actually helped someone. Me.

Soren's snort had us all moving our gaze to him as he shook his head at Elias. "I just asked Sawyer if she hated Elias and whether or not she thought he was hot. Sawyer said, and I quote, 'I don't hate Elias. I think he's an ass most of the time, but I don't hate him. I think we could be friends if he let go of that shield he walked around carrying. And do I have eyes? Yes, he's hot as fuck with an ass I want to lick. Especially when his accent comes out. But that also means he opens his mouth and usually says something idiotic that makes me want to junk punch him.' So, there you go, Elias. Quit saying she doesn't like you."

Elias smiled. "She wants to lick my ass. I can work with that. Friends would be good for both of us. She thinks I am a twat all the time, and my record isn't great. Having a place to start is helpful."

Rhett cleared his throat next. "Rey, I know you have a history with her, but I hope you see that we care for her. I have no plans of going anywhere, but I need to know where you're at with this. That you won't steal her away from all of us at some point."

Confusion filled my head; what did he mean about Rey and Sawyer having a history? It seemed I wasn't the only one out of the loop, as confused looks filled the room.

"What do you mean they have a history?" Oliver asked.

"They grew up as neighbors, according to Finley. Sawyer and I ran into her last night, and it was like Fin had found her long-lost sister. She explained that they'd grown up together but hadn't seen each other in five years or something. I just assumed that meant Rey was close to her too." Rhett shrugged, presumably not really knowing the full extent.

As he talked, Soren whipped his head around to Rey so rapidly, he almost fell off the couch. There was evidently something I was missing here. For now, I was just happy that I would have a potential chance to explore things with Sawyer.

thirty-one

· · ·

soren

Throughout the meeting, I'd been feeling pumped. It seemed the two things I'd wanted, with the two people I liked, were coming true, or at least I hoped they were.

Rey wanted to talk, and I'd just been given the green light to pursue something more with Sawyer. Rey had admitted to missing me earlier, and it felt like more than just a friend missing a friend.

Taking the plunge, I'd flirted with him, and when he didn't freak out, I took that as a good sign. Things were finally unfolding in the direction I wanted for once.

The bomb Rhett just detonated, though, was wreaking havoc with my mind.

He couldn't be saying that Sawyer was Sariah? How was that possible?

I'd whipped around so quickly to look at Rey that I almost toppled off the couch onto the floor. Rey looked at me with an expression I couldn't decipher. My mind was racing; if this was who I thought it was, did that change anything? Was this what he wanted to talk about, not his feelings? But no, I was about to get my dream!

It was over as quickly as it came. I would lose Rey. I'd have to watch them fall in love while I sat on the sidelines pining for the boy I'd dared to love.

My calm demeanor vanished, and I silently spiraled headfirst into a panic attack. The others gathered up their things around me to head to their rooms, granting me the decency to panic in private.

My breathing became rapid as my skin grew clammy, my heart raced, and my hands shook.

Shit, Shit, Shit. I didn't know what to do. I was usually the calm one. I lived in the here and now and didn't stress over the things out of my control.

But, but, but… my brain misfired, and I could no longer formulate thoughts.

I felt pressure on my shoulder, and then a sensation ran through me as I recognized my hand being squeezed. A loud ringing muffled the sounds around me, making it challenging to distinguish voices. Unexpectedly, hands gripped my face, and gray eyes stared back at me.

I gazed into those eyes as a sense of rightness fell over me. I matched his breaths, in and out slowly. My surroundings started to return to me gradually: sound, smell, and then touch. The sensation of Rey's hands on my face began to register as I leaned into them.

When my breathing regulated, I watched Rey as I tried to find the answers to the questions my heart was asking. We were sitting so close now that he was nearly in my lap. He'd maneuvered himself there in order to grasp my face. When Rey realized I was back in the present, he didn't move, but stayed, holding my face.

"Are you okay?" His voice was soft and filled with concern. I didn't think I could use my words yet, so I nodded. Peering into his eyes, I felt myself relax more. Rey's eyes were filled with assurance, understanding, and affection.

"The others left before you started to show signs of panic, so no one else saw anything. I'm going to move back and let go now. Okay?"

Quickly, I clutched one of his hands, not wanting him to move. Rey merely chuckled at my gesture, but stayed put. A sense of relief washed through me as I replayed what else he'd said. Everything was muddled, but I was comforted to find no one privy to my panic.

"You know, I'm going to need my hands at some point, right?" Rey chuckled again. His eyes were lighter than I'd seen in a while. Swallowing a few times to gain my confidence, I nodded it was okay for him to let go. I kept my hand placed on top of his, so I linked our fingers together when he dropped his hand.

Rey's smile set my heart racing again, but this time in anticipation and a little bit of… hope? He still had a knee propped on the couch since he was turned toward me, and our entwined hands laid across it. He was so close to me; I could feel his breath fan across my face.

"I'm sorry you found out that way about who Sawyer is to me. It was part of what I wanted to talk to you about. I'd only discovered it myself a few hours ago when I saw her skating. It's been a whirlwind and surreal since. I mean… I even tackled her on the ice once I realized it was her. And then I proceeded to kiss the daylights out of her." Rey laughed again, his cheeks tinted a rosy pink. It was a good look on him.

"When we returned back to the house, Fin was here, and Smalls brought us up to speed on what happened. It's her story, so I'll let her share it with you. As soon as I left her room, though, I texted you… and well, then dinner. I hadn't meant to keep it from you. I hope you know that." Rey pleaded with me to understand, and I realized in that moment he was worried I'd be mad, not telling me to take a hike.

"I do, Rey. I understand, and I'm not mad. How could I be? You were just reconnected with your first love. It shocked me, and then my mind kind of exploded into a million pieces on what it meant, and if that changed things for me, well for us." Whispering the last part, I dropped my head and stared at our joined hands. Holding his hand felt natural, and I hoped it wasn't the only time I'd get to.

"I'm glad to hear you consider there to be an us," he said. His voice sounded hopeful, so I chanced it, and looked up.

Rey's eyes twinkled, his lip lifting up on the side. My heart took off racing at the beautiful man in front of me. Gah, he was so fucking gorgeous with his bad boy looks and dark, messy hair that swooped over his forehead. Though, it was his light gray eyes that lured you in with a promise.

"Do you want there to be an *us*?" I mumbled.

"I'd like to figure that out with you. I've been so confused about my feelings, not knowing what I felt or if it was real. I wasn't sure for a while. I did some research—"

"Of course, you did." I laughed, unintentionally cutting him off but amused with his behavior. Rey was always researching things. Him and Rhett had that in common.

"Yes, thank you, asshole, for that. I uh," Rey stopped, his cheeks heating even more. God, he was too cute with his blushing. I desperately needed to know what he had been researching now. "Let's just say that it was extensive and informative. The day I shared my songs with you, that was the day I solidified my feelings for you, that a piece of my heart belonged to you. But how does a person say that to their best friend?"

I couldn't help but take some joy in his uncomfortableness. He *was* my best friend, but his struggle to express himself to the object of his affections pleased me.

"I wasn't sure how to say anything or if you felt that way. When you texted that you'd met a girl, I'd never felt so jealous. I wanted to rage at you and ask how you could do that to me. I was struggling, but eventually, I acknowledged that I could only be mad at myself because I'd never said anything. Fearing the worst had only kept me in that negative place, and I'm so tired of being there."

Rey's hands visibly shook as he shared his vulnerability with me. It hit me like a ton of bricks, and I knew right then, that I fucking loved him. Rey had stepped outside of his comfort zone, taking what he wanted for once, and *I* was what he wanted. His courage was intoxicating and so damn beautiful. I couldn't hold my words back anymore.

"Rey, you beautiful, stupid man. I think I've been in love with you longer than I haven't. There is no version of my life where you're not part of it. I've hoped that there was more for us, but resigned myself to accept your friendship if it was all you could ever give me. It'd be enough because it was you."

I licked my dry lips, preparing myself for the next part. Rey squeezed my hand, giving me the encouragement I needed. I'd thought saying the 'L' word would've been the hardest part, but for some reason admitting I wanted a throuple was.

"When I met Sawyer, it was as if the universe showed me the perfect counterpart to us. Knowing now that she was your first love… I panicked, fearing there was no room for me. Everything flashed before me, and I saw myself alone as you rode off into your happily ever after, losing the boy I loved and the girl I'd hoped to. It was a reality I didn't know if I could handle."

A tear fell down my cheek, but I didn't care. I wanted him to see me. To peer into my heart and hear the truth I spoke. It wasn't time to hold things back anymore, we were laying it all out there, and it was my chance to be completely vulnerable.

Minimizing my feelings to protect myself was a false illusion. Because if I lost him, if I let my opportunity to share my heart pass me by, all because of fear, then my life from this point forward would be an illusion. A mirage of things I wanted others to see, but nothing would be real inside. Because how could your life be real if you denied yourself your heart? It was impossible.

"My greatest dream has been to meet a girl and for all of us to be together—a relationship where we could love and support one another. And now, it seems real. The other guys are a bonus because I know they care about her and us, too. I think we can become the family unit that we've all needed. So, I have to ask, Rey. Is there? Is there room for me to be with you and Sawyer?"

Everything hung on that moment. I needed to hear the words, feel his answer resonate deep in my bones, and clear away the secret doubt I'd held on to my whole life–that I wasn't needed.

"And you say I'm stupid," Rey grumbled. "Fuck Soren, I'm sorry it took me this long to see what I've been feeling for a while. Please, never doubt what I feel for you because you're the first person since Sariah that has breached my heart. You were the first person to show me that I'm still capable of loving someone, that I'm worthy of being loved. I've held so much guilt and anger over the years that it clouded my judgment, making it difficult to see our bond was more than just friends. I don't really believe in soul mates, but I know that my life is more with you in it—more beautiful, fuller, joyful, and calmer. I've never felt more acceptance, laughter, or… more love."

Rey paused there, leaving me hanging off the cliff like a notorious author I read. Waiting with bated breath, I was sure I'd pass out before he continued. Rey took a deep breath before starting again.

"Because yes, I fucking love you, Soren. I realized it before I left, and I knew that meant letting Sariah go. Holding on to her memory drowned me in the past, but to step forward, I had to surrender it. Of course, the fucking universe laughed at me and dropped her literally across the hall a day later. But I'm thankful I came to that conclusion before I found her so that you don't ever have to worry about my true feelings for you. You are just as important, just as necessary to my life."

His words croaked out, his own tear slipping from his eye. My heart was about to burst. He'd said everything I'd wanted to hear while reassuring my doubts. I really wanted to kiss him; I just didn't know how ready he was for that step.

"Only in my dreams have I dared to believe I could have you both. Life has been so cold and distant, and I've been afraid of getting close to anyone. But you, Soren, you pushed through with your smiles and willingness. You wouldn't let me close you out, and eventually, I let down my barriers, feeling everything again. It's overwhelming but amazing at the same time. I didn't understand that I was blocking out the good emotions by blocking out the bad ones. So, hear me clearly, Soren Stryker, with everything in my being, I want to be with you and Smalls. That would be everything."

Rey breathed out and I held myself from speaking, feeling like there was more he needed to say, and if I interrupted him, he'd never get it out. I'd learned these signs over the past year; when to give Rey space, and when to push himself to be brave.

"And I, I really want to kiss you right now, but I'm nervous as hell," he whispered. It had barely left his lips before my brain accepted it as a green light, and I went in for the kill.

Swiftly, I kissed him hard, jarring our bodies, missing most of his mouth in my excitement. Rey appeared stunned, and in my overzealousness, I'd practically jumped in his lap. Shaking my head, all I could do was laugh at myself. Welp, it was definitely a memorable first kiss.

"Okay, I no longer feel awkward. Nothing I do from this point on could ever be worse than that attempt to kiss me." The cute jerk had to go and point it out, but I didn't care. He was amused, and it was because of me.

"Can we try that again? Just not as 'excited puppy' this time?"

Still laughing at me, I grabbed his face and kissed him passionately this time. He quickly shut up then. I could get behind this method of persuasion. It was the best kiss of my life, with fucking fireworks and everything.

This evening had started with me trying to flirt, hopeful things might change, and ended with me kissing my best friend and now, hopefully, lover. The only thing that would have made this better was if Sawyer had been there as well.

sawyer

After my bath, I decided to run to the kitchen to grab some snacks for my reading time before bed. I hadn't meant to eavesdrop, but the emotional confession I'd witnessed between Henry and Soren was so pure it'd frozen me to the spot.

Their profession of love for one another was beautiful. I was happy for them, but for a moment, I'd been jealous and scared.

What did it mean for them and me? Did they need me or want me anymore? Was I just a space-filler until they found the courage to tell each other? But then Soren had said that he envisioned us all three together, and my lady parts exploded along with my heart. I didn't know what it meant for us all, or for any of the guys, but the freedom to explore it meant so much.

These guys had stolen a piece of my heart quickly, and I didn't want to give them up. I wasn't even sure I could choose at this point, because having to let go of anyone would destroy me. Deciding I'd spent enough time stealing their moment, I slunk off to bed, forgetting what I'd gone downstairs for in the first place.

Lying in bed, I processed the day with Lucky snuggled up to me. I didn't know how much more official I needed to make it, but he was my dog now.

Their conversation had me realizing I hadn't acknowledged that I'd also let my past keep me frozen. It was hard to digest, but I needed to. The knowledge of my birth had held me hostage, and ultimately, I'd become trapped in fear, never letting myself experience life.

No more. Sariah Brennon had died, but it was time to let Sawyer Sullivan thrive.

First—Tell all the people I cared about the truth. The *entire* truth.

Second—Start finding some answers. Quit half-assing it as a diversion to avoid the truth.

Third—Nothing would hold me back anymore. Not fear, not hate, not lies.

Sawyer Sullivan wasn't a wuss, so I needed to stop acting like one. I grabbed my phone and sent a text before I could chicken out in the morning.

ME: I want to call a house meeting.

ME: Can I do that?

ME: Actually, I'm doing that.

ME: Friday after class before the house party? It's important.

I had a few responses back from Fin and Ace confirming wanting to meet in the morning, and one from Rhett saying the talk went well and if I wanted to date the other guys, that they were on board. A feeling of happiness swarmed me as I read it.

I switched my phone to 'do not disturb' after that, I didn't want to see anything else tonight. I needed to soak in these feelings because I hadn't felt them in so long.

Acceptance.

Bravery.

Hope.

thirty-two

FIVE YEARS AGO

sariah

PAIN ERUPTED THROUGH MY BODY AS I WAS JOSTLED around at a quick pace. I could feel every part of my body radiating agony with each movement whoever carried me made. I could smell a faint scent of pine and Old Spice that was somehow familiar. Heavy breathing met my ears, along with my whimper.

"Shh Sariah, you're going to be okay. I'll get you to safety. You have to go into hiding until it's safe. I'll come to you then. I promised your dad I'd look after you if anything were to happen." I whimpered again at the news. "Shh, sweetie, it's not safe yet." I felt someone move my hair off my face gently as we continued. The pain was too intense, though, and soon all I saw was darkness.

Beep. Beep. Beep.

What the heck was that noise? Why was it so bright in here? It smelled funny, too. Did mom change the air freshener? She should really consider getting something different. This one smelled distinctly of old people and farts.

Taking in my body, I felt a scratchy fabric against my skin and a tug on my arm when I tried to move it. Something hard was on my wrist, my ribs ached, and I couldn't move my leg. What was going on? Did I fall at the competition and forget? Oh no.

A door opened, jolting my attention in the direction I assumed a door was. I couldn't see anything other than white light due to something covering my eyes, but neither of my arms were able to reach my eyes.

"Miss, it's okay. You're in the hospital. I'm going to remove your eye wrap okay? It might be bright, so prepare. One, two, three."

I felt something pull at the skin on my face as she removed the tape, and I could start to make out more shapes. As I blinked, more things came into focus. Feeling relieved I wasn't blind, I took in my surroundings.

I was in the hospital as the nurse stated. Where were my parents? If I had an accident during the competition, they'd be here, Henry too. Where was everyone?

"Miss, do you remember what happened? Can you tell me your name? You were brought in last night after being found outside the ER. You didn't have any identification on you." The nurse looked at me with kindness and some apprehension. I couldn't decide if she was scared for me, or perhaps, herself, which didn't make sense.

Starting to answer her, I opened my mouth, but the door opened, stopping me as a Doctor entered. The nurse nodded her head at him and then made a quick exit. Weird.

"Ah, it looks like our Jane Doe is finally awake. How are you feeling this morning? You were in pretty bad shape when you arrived here last night. Do you remember anything? How were you injured? What's your name?"

Was this a joke? Déjà vu? These rapid-fire questions were impossible to answer. He stared at me expectantly. Geez, at least the nurse had been patient. Opening my mouth again to answer, I was shocked when no words would come out.

"Ah, yes, let me get you some ice chips to help with your throat. Nurse," he bellowed out, and a different nurse entered with a jug of ice chips. I took a few, and instantly it helped soothe my throat.

The doctor prattled on about my injuries as I chewed. Something about having to be intubated was why my throat hurt, a broken wrist, injured knee or something, concussion, a few fractured ribs, a laceration, or something. I lost track of all the medical jargon as he talked. The doctor was really long-winded and boring, to be honest.

"Do you have any questions, Miss? Have you been able to remember your name so we can call your parents?" As the words left his mouth, memories slammed into me, and the machine started to go wild beeping. I heard some talking in the background, but everything blurred and then faded to black again.

I was beginning to be sick of fainting.

It must've been a few hours later when I awoke again. This time a different doctor and nurse entered my room demanding answers. I remembered every-thing now, but I told them I didn't know anything. It seemed the easiest way to stay hidden like my rescuer had told me to do. He was out of focus and almost felt like I imagined him, but I ended up at the hospital somehow, and I knew I didn't make it here alone, so he had to be real.

When they asked me this time, I acted indifferent and feigned amnesia, stating I didn't know who I was, where I was from, or what had happened. I reported that only my age and birthday seemed to be clear. The fact that there wasn't a missing person report for me meant they were left with no other option, but to believe me.

Eventually, I received a visit from a psychiatrist who ruled I had 'dissociative amnesia,' indicating some form of trauma occurred, causing me to lose memories asso-ciated with it which might return over time. He explained it was why I could remember my birthday as it was stored in the long term and how I knew things

I've learned, so I didn't have to relearn how to read or do algebra again.

Thank goodness for that; it was horrible the first time. Algebra that was. I mean, I hadn't actually lost it, but if they made me retake it at high school, I just might've given in to remembering. The psychiatrist explained that memories connected to the incident would be the hardest to retrieve due to the trauma. No shit, dude. He had no idea, but unfortunately, I remembered everything.

The next visit was from a social worker from the state. She told me that since there hadn't been any reports and no one had come to the hospital to claim me, I'd be going into the foster system. A pit formed in my stomach at that, but it was the best option and allowed me to stay hidden. Hopefully, no one would look at an orphan in foster care. It helped my amnesia story when I didn't even know what state I was in.

"What state is this?"

"You don't know? Oh, sorry, of course, you don't know. We're in Iowa, sweetie."

I merely nodded at her. We'd been close to the border before the accident, so that made sense. It also helped put more distance between me and the car accident. She kept talking about what to expect and when I would be getting out of the hospital. Her last question broke through my daydream by surprise.

"Miss, you'll get to pick a new name for yourself. What would you like it to be?" She actually seemed sad for me that I didn't remember my name.

"I think I like Sawyer."

"That's a lovely name. What about a last name?" Her smile about did me in. Kindness right now was unexpected after the shit show the past seventy-two hours had been. Tears and panic rose in me. I hadn't thought of a last name. Shit.

"It's a tough decision. How about picking something that you can remember? Maybe something or somewhere you remember being happy?" I started trying to think of things that would work and not incriminate me. Henry, nope. Finley, nope. Treehouse, nope. Ice, nope. Hmm… Sugar Grove, nope too obvious. Suddenly, it dawned on me.

"Sullivan," I said confidently. She smiled, nodding at my decision.

"Sawyer Sullivan. I like it, it has a nice ring to it. I hope it brings you many good memories, Sawyer." She squeezed my hand and then walked out after reminding me she'd be back the next day to take me to my new home.

I let myself cry once I was alone. I cried for my parents, who had done everything to protect me from the moment I'd been born. I cried for my friends, who were the best friends a person could have. I cried for skating and never getting to compete again. I cried for my childhood and future. I cried and cried with tracks of tears racing down my face.

Mostly, I cried for Sariah Brennon. Because she died two days ago, and I would never get to be her again.

My life from here would be filled with deception, darkness, and despair.

Now, more than ever, I understood why my dad had waited to tell me the truth. Because once I knew, I couldn't go back to the girl I was before. That girl had a future, family and friends, and faith in humanity.

I had nothing… barely even a name.

thirty-three

PRESENT DAY

sawyer

PARKING THE VESPA IN FRONT OF THE COFFEE SHOP, I hooked my helmet over the handlebars and headed inside. I needed to get in a better habit of wearing it again, especially when it snowed. Hmm, do they make snow tires for scooters? I would need to look that up because that could be handy to have. The image of me driving around in the snow as a scarf blew behind me had me beaming.

The drive had been peaceful at this time of the morning, and I'd enjoyed the mountain air. The mountains were calling to me, and I hoped I'd be able to convince Mateo to take me skiing soon. That sounded like an excellent plan.

Relief filled me when I entered the shop and didn't

feel watched today. I looked for my new friend, spotting him. Finley wasn't here yet. She'd texted early this morning that an emergency tech meeting had been called, so she'd meet me afterward. She was excited to meet my new friends and curious about who I'd already befriended in three days. I'd been surprised myself, but Ace hadn't really given me a choice. His tenacity had won me over, and made it easy to be his friend.

Ace and a girl were sitting in a larger area that contained a couch, fireplace, and two round chairs. They were sitting on the sofa together laughing, presumably at something Ace said. The girl was beautiful with Asian and Black features. She had gorgeous ebony curls that sat at her shoulders. Her eyes were brown, and her skin was a beautiful dark brown shade that highlighted her delicate and elegant facial features. She also had the best eyebrow game of anyone I'd ever met; they were definitely on fleek. Was that how that saying went? I laughed at myself because I still didn't know what it meant.

My chuckle drew Ace's attention, and he spotted me as I walked toward the counter. Gesturing toward the front, I asked if he wanted anything, but he raised his own cup before turning back to the girl. Needing some home comfort today, I decided to get some tea. I was surprised to find the shop had a good variety, so I selected an English Breakfast tea and a muffin top. It made my day even better when they handed me an actual teapot.

Taking my things, I started to walk over to my friend when I spotted an area around the counter I hadn't seen the other day.

"What's that?" I asked, pausing in my steps.

"That's the bookshop portion. There's a good selection and we host a book club once a month if you are interested," the barista said. "Here you forgot your muffin." His hand stroked over mine, shocking me. When he winked at me I almost spilled my tray, and a sound erupted out of me I was unfamiliar with.

I giggled.

Feeling mortified, I spun, careful not to slosh the tea all over me, adding to my humiliation. All things considered; it could've been worse. For instance, I could've blurted out something inappropriate, so I was happy to leave the incident with only a giggle.

Ace and his friend were rolling in laughter as I walked over to them. Shrugging one shoulder, I dropped my bag by the chair and sat my teapot down onto the coffee table.

"Oh My God, I can't believe that sound just came out of my mouth." I cringed, and they both laughed, sharing in my humiliation.

"Sawyer, this is my cousin. She's fabulous and needs a girlfriend who isn't stuck up Adelaide's butt or part of the Ashleys," Ace said, always laying it out there like it was.

Laughing at him, I waved awkwardly at her. Damn rogue hand again, still trying to get in on the fun. "Hi, I'm definitely not stuck up her butt. More like what she wishes came out of her butt. Ew. Gross. I can't believe I just said that. I need some tea so I can stop saying weird things, apparently." Fortunately, they both laughed instead of thinking I was too weird.

"You're right, Ace, she's hilarious. It's nice to meet you, Sawyer. Ace did forget to introduce my name as I don't really go by 'Ace's cousin,' believe it or not." We both snickered at that. "I'm Chloe Hughes, and this is my first year, too. I have the unfortunate luck of living with not one, but two Ashleys."

I grimaced, taking a sip.

"I know, I know, feel free to commiserate my bad luck as it means Adelaide spends a lot of time there." Chloe's eyes rounded so big she resembled the bug-eyed emoji causing me to almost spit out my tea which would've been a shame since Teapigs was not Lipton's, and it would be a crime against humanity to waste any.

"That is horrible! Feel free to escape and hang with me anytime."

"Does that invitation apply to me, too?" Ace asked, wiggling his eyebrows. I knew his request was purely to perv on the man candy I lived with.

"Absolutely, but hands off the roommates! I've licked them; they're mine." I laughed maniacally, and they giggled at me.

"So, what's your area of expertise, Chloe?"

"I'm a boarder, which means I get to stare at that yummy specimen of hotness that is Soren Stryker." She cooed and my cheeks blushed as I thought about the scene I'd witnessed between Soren and Henry last night, along with the view of Soren's abs the other morning in the kitchen. My eyes must've glazed over because Ace was suddenly snapping his fingers in my face.

"Earth to Sawyer, did you just get dicknotized?" Ace asked. I blushed, because yes, yes, I had just been dicknotized, or would it be abnotized?

"Um… Well, can you blame me? His abs are so pretty," I gushed, causing us all to chuckle even more. I was enjoying my time with them as I got to know more about Chloe. I discovered that Ace and Chloe were related by marriage; her aunt married his uncle or something like that. She was sweet with a hidden sassy side that I was beginning to see break through. She was definitely a girl I could be friends with.

When the door chimed open, it jolted us all with its sound since the shop had been slow while we'd been in there. Their reaction to the person instantly put me on edge, and I hoped it wasn't Finley. I loved Fin and would always pick her, so if they had an issue with Fin, then I'd have to say goodbye to them.

"It seems this place has started to let anyone in," a sneer from behind me said. Immediately, I knew it was QB and I was already so over this girl. It was 8 am and entirely too early to deal with her bullshit. Despite her insistence that we weren't worthy of the shop, she still stopped by our section to chat.

"Oh, hello, Adelaide. It's so lovely to see you here. Do you happen to know my companions?" I asked sweetly.

My favorite game was giving it to her in a kind voice because she couldn't tell when I was mean. Not giving her a chance to respond, I continued. "We were just talking about this amazing new move. Have you ever heard of the snowball or the Phelps?" I placed my fist under my chin as I turned to look at her.

"Oh my! Sweetie, you have something right there." I gestured toward her tooth with fake concern. Predictably, she fell for it and quickly swiped her tongue across her teeth before huffing to one of the Ashley's and gesturing toward the counter as they walked off in a huff.

Turning back around, I casually picked up my tea to take a sip while making sure to lift my pinky like the classy bitch I was. I was so living the meme life right now. Chloe and Ace were both stunned for about two seconds and then burst out laughing.

"Holy cow, you're my hero. I bow to you." Chloe mimicked bowing with her hands. "You insulted her with kindness, and she couldn't even retort. Like, I'm so stunned. I can't even form words. You stopped her right in her tracks and were so pleasant the whole time. Teach me your ways, master. Teach me, please, I beg you." Chloe gushed, beaming at me, and all I could do was laugh at her antics.

"Spending time in foster care, you learn the best ways to insult someone without getting in trouble with the parents or teachers. It really is an art form." I mimed brushing my knuckles on my shoulder to polish them as I smiled smugly.

Suddenly, my vision went dark as someone from behind placed their hands over my eyes. My body instantly tensed, and I berated myself for not sitting where I could see the door. This was the second time I hadn't noticed who'd entered the shop. I'd been slacking and falling into bad habits after years of nothing happening.

Trying not to panic in the middle of the coffee shop became difficult. The longer the hands stayed over my eyes with nothing said, the more my panic built. It rose increasingly and my breathing accelerated along with my heart rate.

Shit, Sawyer. Get this under control. I attempted to think logically as my anxiety began to overtake me.

Okay, First, Ace and Chloe aren't freaking out, so it shouldn't be anyone scary. Okay, deep exhale.

Second, the hands feel small and soft, so probably a girl's hands—another good point.

Third, Adelaide's upfront, so it's not her. I haven't managed to get on any other girl's shit list yet that I know of, so it's probably a friend. Another deep breath. This was helping.

Fourth, Ace and Chloe don't appear to know this person. That could be good or bad. Keep going, Sawyer. You're doing it.

Fifth, use your senses. What do you hear? What do you smell?

Noises returned to me but were hard to determine in the busy coffee shop. Smells of coffee and baked goods overwhelmed my nostrils, but I caught a subtle whiff of honeysuckle and I relaxed. I knew who it was.

"Zoom, Zoom, Zoom," I sang out once I had my breath back.

"We're going to the moon," was sung back as the hands dropped.

"Bitch, you frightened me." I gave her a pointed look, causing her to instantly wince.

"Shit girl, I'm sorry. I was so excited to see you and went into twelve-year-old Fin mode and didn't think. I didn't mean to scare you." She pleaded, a look of complete devastation etched on her face. Crap, I had to fix this fast, or she'd spiral.

"Fin, it's fine, I swear. I know you'd never intentionally scare me. I missed you too." I hugged her to me and squeezed tight. Fin deflated into me as she sucked in a deep breath of my smell as well.

When I'd been able to buy my own toiletries, I chose the same products I used before, returning a small part of me. Eventually, I remembered we weren't alone and probably being rude, but also, Adelaide was still lurking around and I didn't want her to ruin anything, so I stepped back and turned to the others.

"Guys, this is Fin. Don't mind us. We were neighbors growing up and haven't seen each other in about five years. We ran into one another the other day and are still adjusting to being back in each other's lives." I smiled at their curious but understanding stares.

"Fin, this is the amazing Ace and the cheerful Chloe. We must save Chloe as she has to live with two of the

Alphabets," I side whispered in case Adelaide was nearby. They all greeted one another, and Ace and Fin realized they had some friends in common. They'd seen each other around campus but hadn't interacted with one another before.

I enjoyed my tea while listening to them chat, and I realized how at ease I felt. These friendships had been so natural, and I was happy to relax into it. For once, I wasn't worried about having to leave in the dead of night or that I might be putting them in danger. I never realized the weight of lying to everyone in my life, which cemented my goal, to be honest with people. That feeling of determination from last night grew and took root in my chest.

Thankfully, Adelaide and two of the alphabets left without engaging with us further. They threw some shade at us as they walked out, but we ignored them, causing them to be even more pissed off if the sound of their huffs were anything to go by. While it might be cliché to think if you ignored your bully, they went away, it did work on occasion. Fortunately, this happened to be one of those occasions.

But I knew, just like with most bullies, I couldn't underestimate QB. She would come for me, and I'd need to be prepared when she did.

We stayed for about an hour until we had to leave for our classes. Throwing my trash away, I waved goodbye as I headed to the bathroom before I left. When I exited the coffee shop a few minutes later, the sensation of someone watching me ran up my spine. I was beginning to become irritated this kept happening. It was getting a bit ridiculous. Remembering my oath not to let fear hold me back, I shook off the feeling and headed out to my Vespa. Take that stalking fucker!

My footsteps halted when I spotted my back tire was flat. Shit.

I took it back! I was sorry, stalker.

And now I was bargaining with an imaginary stalker in my head. See-No-Evil monkey emoji right there.

Bending down, I saw that the tire had been intentionally slit with something sharp. Fucker. I didn't have time for this. Groaning in frustration, I tried to remember who could help me. Fin only had a car, so I called Ace to see if he was still near and had a bigger vehicle.

"Hey, Girl, miss me already?" Ace flirted.

"You know it, sexy." I laughed. "Hey, you wouldn't still be nearby and have a truck?" I asked.

"Oh, wanting some flatbed fun, eh? Just kidding. We're nearby, but Chloe drove her car. Why? What's up?" Worry laced his words and I knew he would be a good friend.

"It's nothing, just a flat. Don't worry about it. I'll call one of the guys. I just thought you'd be quicker. I'll talk to you later, okay?"

"Yeah, girl, let me know if you don't hear anything, and I'll head back in my truck for you. Okay? Go back and wait in the shop." Smiling at his care, a warm feeling filled me as I realized it had been a long time since someone had been concerned for me.

"I will. Thanks, Ace. You know, I'm glad you forced your friendship on me." I laughed.

"Ha Ha. I'm wonderful, and you know it. But seriously, let me know. Also, don't think you're getting out of spilling the tea on those hot roommates just because we weren't alone. Dish session this weekend?"

"Damn. I was hoping you'd forgotten. Ha! Yes, of course. Maybe we can do a slumber party or something. Ok, I better text the guys if I want to make it to my classes on time. Thanks again, boo."

We hung up, and I went back into the shop as he suggested. Sitting at the window this time, I texted the group chat. I hadn't checked all the messages from last night yet, but I didn't have time for that yet, so I scrolled to the bottom.

Fairest of them all:

Snow White: Hey, anyone able to come to the coffee shop and give me a lift back? Velma has a flat.

Grumpy: Shit, baby. Class for me. Velma?

Grumpy: Oliver. Quit changing things.

Dopey: I don't know what you mean, Grumpy. I'm innocent. Why would I call myself Dopey? But if I did… you have to admit it's inspired, right? Our very own Snow White.

Laughing at their messages, I hadn't even realized

my name had been changed to Snow White. Ollie, always with the jokes. Now, I was trying to figure out if I could pinpoint who everyone was based on their dwarf name. Rhett was obviously Grumpy.

Happy: I'm already on the slope, sugar cookie. You named your Vespa Velma, didn't you?
Mopey: I'm at the rink, but I can leave if you need me to. Leave her alone, Sor. I think it's cute.
Bashful: I'm free in an hour. But I don't have a car.
Doc: I have an open period. I can borrow the truck if you're okay with me picking you up.

I laughed at Soren. His new game was to give me absurd nicknames until he found one he liked or I wanted. It was funny in the meantime to see how creative he could get. My heart sank as I saw that most of them were busy. I felt that Doc was Elias, so it looked like it would be him or nothing. I could deal with him for a car ride, right?

Snow White: Thanks, Elias. I appreciate it. I'm at the coffee shop on Elm.
Doc: I'm on my way.
Grump: Baby, text when you're home. I'll fix your tire later.

Since I had time to wait, I decided to scroll through the rest of the messages from last night.

ME: Friday after class before the house party?
It's important.
Rhett: Of course, baby. Friday. It's set.

I should've expected Rhett to be to the point and then leave it. He was accepting like that. The other guys took it and ran with it, though. Shaking my head at their responses, I continued scrolling through them.

Soren: Good news or bad news?
Rey: I don't think she's going to tell you now, dork.
Soren: I'm not a dork. You're a dork.
Oliver: Soren, you're so a dork.
Oliver: But that's the way we love you, goof
Mateo: Works for me.
Soren: I'll show you goof Ollie Bear
Rey: But you're a cute dork.
Elias: It's a wonder she wants to date any of you; you guys are imbeciles. I'm going to bed. Friday night works for me, love.
Ollie: Ahhh, love you too, Elias. Kiss, kiss.
Rey: He doesn't want your kisses, Ollie.
Oliver: Says, who? I've never gotten any complaints.
Oliver: I think we need a competition to see who the best kisser is, don't you guys? I'm a great kisser.
Soren: I don't know if you'd be able to handle

the hotness. Besides, my kisses are reserved for two people.

Oliver: Ahh, finally admitting your love for me, Sor. I always knew my Jamie Fraser looks would pull you in Outlander style.

Rhett: ENOUGH. Stop hounding Sawyer. I suggest we talk about boundaries at this meeting as well. AND just because she said she was interested does not automatically mean she's going to date you. So, figure your own shit out and woo her yourself. And quit acting like buttmunches. Everyone go to bed.

Oliver: Whoa, someone poked papa bear. I think my phone crashed from all the words you just used.

Rey: Did Rhett just make a joke?

Soren: Yeah, it was you, Ollie clueless bear.

Soren: Yes, papa bear. Loves you. Kiss Kiss.

Rey: Sorry, Sawyer. Night.

Oliver: I'm still a great kisser.

chat name changed

nicknames changed

I couldn't help but laugh. Their personalities shone through the group messages, and it seemed Oliver changed the chat once everyone was off. Clever boy. I wondered if anyone else picked up on the flirting between Soren and Rey and if they cared or not?

Rhett's growly voice came across even over text and

had started to get my lady bits excited. Damn, that man's voice was liquid sex fire.

Yep, sex fire. Liquid sex fire. It was so a thing.

A truck pulled up to the shop pulling me from my fantasies. I recognized it from the garage, so I exited the shop to meet my doom.

"Hey, thanks for coming," I muttered, awkwardly.

"Absolutely, it's not a problem, love. Here let me get your Vespa," Elias said with a hint of caution. Gah, it was so awkward. I hated this.

As frustrating as the man was, something about the way he said 'love' had my insides going all girly. I was yelling at myself that it was only a British thing, but the butterflies didn't appear to care.

Fuckers. I wanted a refund.

I couldn't fault them though, stupid accent made me think the asshole was attractive. Watching him pick the Vespa up in navy slacks, a button-down blue shirt with rolled-up sleeves, and brown loafers was doing weird things to me. His butt looked really good in those pants, and they stretched perfectly over his bum. Either this was another symptom of my Altitude Delirium that I still hadn't seen the doctor about, or was it that marketing company again prying on my weaknesses.

Seriously, marketing people. You. Win.

The way his forearms flexed as he lifted and then pushed the scooter into the truck was mouthwatering. I stood there frozen on the spot like a dork. I probably even had drool on my mouth.

He shut the tailgate, brushing off his hands, and

turned, noticing I was frozen, and you know, staring at him.

"Bollocks, did I do something wrong? Was there a certain way to handle her?"

His frowny face was all kinds of cute. Crap. Nope, no, no, no. Just nope.

Internally, I shook my head at myself as I berated my thoughts. This could not be happening. I already had enough potential dick. I didn't need another one. Especially a very charming, but often infuriating one. Nope. Nuh-uh. Vagina, you're closed for business. No more room in the inn, closed.

I noticed the crease between his brows was getting deeper and I realized I hadn't answered him, so I immediately began to self-correct. Which meant, yup, you guessed it—insert code orange.

"No, you did *everything* right. In fact, I really liked how you handled her. I wonder what else you can handle with those forearms. Shit, I'm saying this out loud, aren't I?" I smacked my forehead. Literally, now I was the embodiment of the facepalming emoji.

Facepalming emoji was me. I was she. We were one.

I heard him chuckle, so I lowered my hand, and I swear, a faint blush stained his cheeks. His hair flopped in the wind perfectly, and it made me want to hate him because he was so stinking perfect, and he didn't even try. He embodied it from years of schooling, I bet.

"Okay, well, awesome. Can we go now? I'm pretty sure I've missed my first lesson already and don't want to make it two."

"Sure, yes, we can head back. I'll drop you off where you need to go, and I will take care of your scooter for you back at the house if you're fine with that?"

"That's very kind. Thank you, and thank you for coming to get me. I know you were probably doing something important or had time off, and you didn't need to spend it coming into town, so thanks. Wow, I just said thanks a lot."

My face burned with a bright red blush. Rushing to the door, I grabbed the handle, hoping I could save myself from further embarrassment. I wasn't sure if I liked it better when he was an asshole, or nice. At least when he was an asshole, I didn't feel so tongue-tied around him.

The ride back was quiet, but it wasn't as uncomfortable as I'd expected. It wasn't uncomfortable at all being trapped in a small space with his amazing sandalwood smell.

Fucking men and their delicious smells.

But at least we weren't fighting, maybe there was hope for us to be friends after all.

You hear that Vagina, *friends*. This was not Burger King, where you could have it your way. So stop it right there Vagina. Just stop.

thirty-four

. . .

sawyer

"AGAIN!" I SHOUTED FROM THE RINK RAIL. I WAS WORKING with Sarah and Candace today on double toe loops. They were both close to advancing to senior level for competition, and I really wanted to help them.

A sense of pride I hadn't felt in a long time filled me as they both landed the jumps for the third time perfectly. This was something I'd been missing. The kids were cute and all, but none of them were driven to do more with skating at that age. These skaters were giving me the same rush that competing myself did. Part of me envied they had their whole career still ahead of them, but I'd never take that from these girls. This was their moment, and I was happy to be part of it.

"That was perfect, ladies! Great job today. I can really see the difference already in your take-off position and landing. Next class, we can work on the double salchow, and then you should be ready to apply for the senior level testing." I grinned wide as I shared with them the next steps. Their own squeals of delight made my own mood rise.

"Thank you so much, Coach Sawyer. I've been struggling with taking off the back edge and landing back on the same edge. Your tips really made sense. I never thought I would be ready this soon to test for senior-level," Sarah said, gushing.

Candace was the quieter of the two friends and nodded along with Sarah. Class was over, so we headed toward the locker rooms. They both waved as we separated to enter our respective areas. Rolling my shoulders, the need for the sauna was calling my name. After a quick rinse, I stepped inside. Steam filled the room, and instantly sweat beaded on my skin. Ah, that felt nice.

After a few minutes, I started to get worried I'd get locked in here like every horror movie ever and decided I was ready to leave. No, thank you psycho, I was not making it that easy on you. Getting dressed, I headed out of the locker room and was surprised to find Soren leaning against the wall.

"Hey, beautiful." His smile had me going goo-goo, and I had to consciously make my legs move forward and not faint. Like a magnet, I was drawn to him, and before I knew it, I was standing in front of him. His hands landed on my hips and I tried to process what words were.

His bright golden complexion spellbound me, and I

forgot my name, the day, or even what planet I was from. There was no coming back from this disorder now. Altitude Delirium had fully taken over, for which the only cure was lots and lots of dick.

Not convinced? Look it up. Google MD right here.

"What are you doing here?" I asked, the words escaping in a husky tone.

"You see, this pretty girl I like happens to work here. I had an early afternoon, so I thought I'd see if she wanted to hang out."

"Oh? Is that so?"

"Yep." He popped that 'p' and his dimple at the same time. It was criminal. Damn him and his dimple.

"What would you do with this girl?"

"Well, I'm hoping I can kiss her."

"Oh?"

"Yeah. I think it will be a great kiss."

"The best way to know is to do it. That way, you don't have to wonder." I licked my lips, zeroing in on his.

"That's great advice. I'll try it out when I see her."

I'd started to lean in, but as his words permeated the lust, I heard his words. "Wait. What?"

He answered me with a hard kiss, filled with passion, and pulled me toward him. I eagerly followed, feeling his hands on my ass as my own hands greedily explored his chest, feeling his muscles bunch beneath his hoodie.

His tongue swirled around mine, gently massaging my own. He was a fucking excellent kisser, giving enough pressure to make you crave more. I was about to grind against him when catcalls sounded out behind us, pulling me from the moment.

Stepping back a little, I saw the heat in his eyes and that his lips were swollen and wet from our make-out. Giggles rang around me, and I turned to see my students walking past.

"Bye, Coach," Sarah said, winking at me.

I wanted to scold her, but at the same time, I couldn't really say anything since I had just wantonly made out with a guy in the ice rink. So, I just smiled, and you know, awkwardly waved. I'd come to accept it was my signature move at this point.

Turning back toward Soren's chest, I erupted in giggles. He hadn't released me when we'd been caught, so I was still pressed up against him, and my movement caused him to moan, spurring my giggles on more.

"Well, that's one way to end the class."

We both laughed and walked out, holding hands once Soren had sorted himself. These guys continued to take my breath away and I had never felt more secure in who I was.

The week flew by, and before I knew it, Friday was here. I had to reschedule my evening with Mateo and Soren, but was happy I'd gotten to spend a small amount of time with them. Classes had picked up, and I realized how much I needed to prepare beforehand, so I spent the last few nights skating and dancing.

I felt more confident going into this weekend and was looking forward to spending time with the guys. Assuming they still wanted to after the conversation tonight. A small part of me also felt I needed to be upfront with everyone before things progressed. I'd even avoided Rhett and Henry.

So, I just needed to get through this conversation first. The house party was at another hockey instructor's place. Ollie promised that Asa was a cool dude, and that it wouldn't be QB's territory. Hopefully, that meant she wouldn't attend. Fin was excited, though, and based off her behavior, I had a feeling she had a crush on the guy.

I'd asked her to come over before the meeting to help me get dressed and I wanted her to be part of it too. Finely had always loved to dress me, so she'd jumped at the chance to play dress up again. I didn't really love the idea, but it at least meant we got to spend some time together.

Currently, I was lying on my bed, making notes in my bullet journal. It had arrived today, so I was having fun putting my info into it. I had big plans for this journal to keep me organized with everything going on. Especially after finding out that in addition to my skating and dance classes, all the instructors rotated chaperoning events, parent seminars, and tours.

Blow me. That sounded excruciating.

Fortunately, the duties were only for two weeks

every three months, and each instructor paired up with one other person. My planner was already full, and I needed to add in possibly dating five guys along with hanging out with friends.

I was nuts. The last symptom seemed to have finally appeared. Delusions. I was delusional. Why did I think I could do all these things? Oh, right. Abs. I was blaming it on the abs. A knock at my door stopped my dirty train of thoughts.

"Come in," I huffed, resigned as I placed my head on top of the journal in a sign of defeat.

"Hey, homegirl, what's happening?"

"Hey, Fin. I think I've finally hit my limit. It's official. I'm delusional, and I'm suffering from Altitude Delirium disorder," I said, which only made Fin laugh at me. My best friend was laughing at me.

"Why's this so funny? I'm serious, Fin. Why did I think I could date five guys?" I cried as I banged my head on my journal. Her laugh broke off, and I looked up, confused why she'd stopped. I was met with the Finley death stare. Uh-oh. What did I do? How did I piss her off?

"What do you mean you're dating *five* guys!" she shrieked.

Oops. I guess I forgot to fill her in on that portion of my life. Abort. Abort.

"Oh, well, did I not mention that? Oops, my bad." Cringing, I tried to act as nonchalant as possible.

"Yes, biotch. I think you did. Care to explain?" She

was fuming and in full pissed off Fin mode with her hands on her hips, her foot-tapping.

"Well, long story short, Rhett picked me up, we made eyes at each other. Then I met Mateo and Soren. Things started to escalate with Rhett, but I was still confused because I had feelings for Mateo and Soren. Then I kissed Mateo. Went out on a date with Rhett. He saw me kiss Mateo, so we talked. I admitted my confusion and feelings. He told me that I was worth being with in whatever capacity that meant. We did the naked tango. Then Henry returned. While I hadn't progressed very far relationally with Oliver, the guys talked, and I'd felt a spark with him when he wasn't being a cocky asshole. Am I making any sense? I feel like I'm rambling, and I'm getting all sweaty thinking about it."

I started flapping my hands in front of my face. Oh shit. Oh shit. Oh shit. Was this real? Was I doing this? I finally looked up, finding Fin's mouth hanging open.

"What? What? Is something on my face? What is it?" I yelped, feeling around my body to see if I could find something.

"You're telling me that all the guys in this house have agreed to be in a relationship with you, reverse harem style?" Fin asked, her voice even higher than I thought it could go.

"Fin, I'm pretty sure all the dogs in the neighborhood heard you. We agreed to date, but nothing much has happened yet except for with Rhett. It's still very new... reverse harem, huh. Now, I get what Soren meant about the book," I mumbled to myself, stopping my train of thought.

Wapp. A pillow smacked me in the face, and I fell backward on the bed.

"What the hell, Fin!"

A pillow kept hitting me in the face over and over. I giggled as I tried to get away from her, but she'd sat on top of me, attacking me.

"Stop, I'm sorry. I'm sorry, Fin."

The pillow finally eased off, and I could breathe again. Glancing up, I found a smiling Fin staring down at me. Launching at her middle, I tackled her onto the bed as we dissolved into giggles.

"Gah, I missed you, girl."

"I missed you too, Fin." We stayed holding one another for a few minutes relishing in the comfort of our bond. Eventually, we moved and leaned against the headboard.

"Are you prepared for this meeting? And how do you plan to manage that many dicks, like where are you going to put them all? Ew. Don't tell me about my brother's dick. Though I am thrilled, you guys are together. I always shipped you two when you were skating partners." Finley swooned, sighing dramatically.

"You did? I was afraid to say anything. I didn't know how you'd feel about it. Um, did Henry ever mention to you that he kissed me two nights before I left?" I asked hesitantly.

"What? No!" Fin exclaimed, turning to glare at me. Damn, two glares in one day.

"Uh, yeah." I was blushing. Why was I blushing? "It was both of our first kisses. It was perfect. I didn't think I'd ever feel that way for anyone else, you know. I haven't been in a real relationship since then. I've just had causal things. Then, I met Rhett and all the other guys, and it was the first time I'd felt that spark, that something more was there. I'm scared, but I'm tired of being scared. So, I'm embracing my fear," I confided.

"Squeeeeee. If I didn't love you so much, I would so hate you right now."

"Speaking of, who is this Asa guy whose house we're going to?" I asked, bumping her shoulder. Her cheeks flamed and I knew I was right. She liked him.

"Oh, Asa. He's nice, I guess. He's on the hockey team. We had our rotation last year together, and we just clicked. He doesn't make me feel weird for all my tech speak or that I'm not girly enough. I don't know, he's sweet and listens. He kind of reminded me of you at first with how he made me feel. I uh, got into some trouble when you left. I started acting out. I even got arrested once." She cringed, displaying some embarrassment. She looked down at her lap, pulling the strings of the pillow.

"I'm so sorry, Fin. I hate that my life caused you so much pain, and I was helpless to do anything."

"Sawyer, I don't blame you at all. I was just worried and scared and not sure how to process those feelings. I'd gotten your emergency text and then couldn't reach you. When we heard about the car fire, I didn't want to believe it. My therapist told me that I was externalizing my pain, and until I dealt with my grief and anger, I wasn't going to be able to make good choices."

"I went to a therapist too for a while. I'm glad that you got help as well. My therapist helped me see that I was only responsible for me and that there were some good people I could trust again." We both smiled at one another.

"Asa didn't make me feel as if I were a freak. But I can't seem to take the next step. I don't know how to show him I'm interested. Apparently, you're the love guru now, so, please, do share. How can I tell him or get him to notice me differently? I think he likes me. I feel like there have been some instances where we've almost kissed, but then something would happen, and the moment would pass."

"I will help, however, I can, girl. You know I'm your wing woman."

"Thank you, you're the best! Let's get ready for this meeting and party. We both need to look fabulous, and fortunately, I'm even better at fashion than I was at fifteen." She flounced off the bed and did a very girly twirl. Laughing at her ridiculousness, I realized how good it felt to laugh.

Fin did my hair in some crazy hairdo. It looked amazing but I had no idea how she did it. She fixed it in two braids on the side of my head that entwined together in the back in some intricate French braid leaving the rest of my hair down. When she was done with my hair, she did my makeup in a natural look that I loved.

Since I skated so much, I didn't normally wear makeup since I usually sweated it all off. Unless it was for performances, which my mom always did for me, I didn't have much experience wearing it. I never really cared before because I didn't want to draw attention, but dating five guys made me want to put more effort in. Not all the time, that was ludicrous, but you know, every once in a while felt nice.

Fin's own makeup was more extreme. She did some crazy cat eye with her eyeliner, paired with a dark smoky shadow, bronzer, and dramatic lipstick. I didn't know what it was, but she told me while putting it on, thinking I would remember—crazy lady.

Somehow from my wardrobe, she put together a black lace camisole with an oversized cream sweater that sat off the shoulder, allowing the top of the black lace to peak out. She paired it with black skinny jeans that had holes in the knees and a cute pair of ankle boots. It looked hot but was comfortable, which had been a requirement for me.

Fin was right, though. Her fashion sense had improved. She had a good knack for making me look sexy without showing a lot of skin. She dressed herself in a cute striped romper with a pair of brown ankle boots. She was making a statement. Asa better watch out because the Finster was on the prowl.

We headed downstairs for dinner with the guys. They were all around the table already, passing out plates and the Chinese takeout boxes. All their heads looked up at us as we entered. I saw appreciation and heat in the guys' eyes, even Elias, which was surprising. Things had been better between us since he rescued me, but it was still overly formal, as if we were scared of saying the wrong thing again and ruining the relative peace we'd found.

There were a few catcalls and mentions of looking nice from the guys. Seemed they did learn from the last fashion disaster.

Dinner was quiet, though. They appeared to be worried about what I had to share, and I was nervous about what I'd say and their response. Sharing my secrets with everyone was going to be scary. But I wasn't backing out. The truth would set me free, or something like that, right?

We cleaned up dinner and moved to the game room since it was the largest room with seating for all of us. I sat on the couch between Henry and Finley. She held my hand for support. It was quiet. So quiet. Everyone stared at me, waiting for me to talk. Shit, why did I think this was a good idea? Ugh.

Get over yourself. Do it already.

"Thank you all for coming. I'm sure you're wondering what I would want to talk to you about. Well, there are some things from my past that I want to share with everyone. It's hard for me to say these things, so I'd like to ask that you let me tell it all before you ask questions." They all nodded, and Fin squeezed my hand three times, offering me comfort.

"You might know that I grew up next door to Henry and Fin. When I was three, my parents moved to Sugar Grove, and we lived there until I was sixteen. The day before Henry and I were to compete, a strange man came to our house. He only referred to himself as R and threatened my parents. R said he would be back the next day to take me somewhere. After he left, my parents explained to me that he was hired by the man that my dad had worked for before we moved to Sugar Grove." I paused, clearing my throat and took a sip of water Henry handed me.

"Apparently, I was adopted. My parents weren't able to have children, but my dad's boss offered to help them. His boss knew a family and said it would be simple. Everything was great for the first three years, but then his boss came to my dad and told him that he owed him a favor. That when I was of age, I was to return back to him—my dad's boss. My dad knew in that moment they were in danger. His boss threatened to kill my mom in front of him and everyone else he loved if he didn't give me over. So, they packed everything up, changed our names, and moved to the middle of nowhere in Indiana."

My hands shook, but I took another sip, needing it.

"Things were good there. I had a happy life. I loved skating, and we had a good future ahead of us. I had two best friends, and I was happy." I smiled at my two oldest friends. "That day R showed up, I learned about being adopted and why. My dad wasn't going to let R take me though, so he made arrangements for us to leave again. We left in the middle of the night and had made it almost two states over before they found us."

My voice started to shake with emotion, and I paused, taking a deep breath.

"My dad told me some more about the company he worked for. It was a shipping company called Latimer Industries, and he worked in imports. He'd heard rumors but had dismissed them while he was there. He looked into things more after we ran and discovered even worse things about the company."

I took another sip of the water. I'd been staring at the floor for the last part. I remembered my vow to be brave, so I looked up.

"The company was involved in a lot of bad things and used the shipping to hide a lot of their illegal activities. The worst thing they were involved with was, um, human trafficking of young girls. That was supposed to be my fate."

Fin gasped at that since I hadn't told them that part yet, and I felt Henry stiffen next to me.

"It gets worse, unfortunately. Latimer Industries wasn't where it stopped. There was someone over them that ran things—a Council. Several companies were part of this Council, and to get a seat on the Council, um, well, you had to do something. He didn't get to tell me too much more, just that a council oversaw things and ruled a lot of things in the world. Sorry if I'm vague, but it's all I know at this point. He met with his contact and had just gotten our new identities, a different car, and an address for a house. I'd finally fallen asleep when the wreck happened."

Taking another shuddering breath, I steadied myself for the hardest part of the story.

"I just remember my dad shaking me and telling me to run. He hugged me, and he told me," my voice started to tremble. "He told me that he loved me and that my biological last name was Abernathy, he left me with these words. 'It all starts at the Aldridge school.' The rest was jumbled together due to my concussion. I ran, but then I heard the gunshots. I kept running until I passed out. I came to once when someone was carrying me. I don't know who they were or why they helped me. We were on the Missouri and Iowa border when the car wrecked, and somehow I ended up in an Iowa ER. When I finally woke up, I had a concussion, broken wrist, a tear in my leg, a laceration, and some broken ribs. It took me a while to remember the wreck and that my parents were dead."

My hands began to relax now that it was over. Everyone listened to every word I said, waiting for me to finish. I tried to hold the tears back so that I didn't ruin Fin's makeup, but it was a battle I gave up as the tears started to fall silently.

"I was able to be aware enough to pretend I had amnesia and didn't know who I was except for my age. I was placed in foster care in Iowa and chose my new name, Sawyer Sullivan. A few days later, I remembered that my dad had said more when he hugged me. I've only guessed what the words were since everything jumbled and there was ringing from the concussion. Still, there was something about me being important, someone was safe, he was sorry he didn't tell me sooner, and that, um…" I trailed off, looking up, afraid the next part would ruin things with two people I loved.

Fin nodded trying to encourage me. I stared at her, watching her reaction. I trusted my best friend, but I also needed to know if she knew.

"The last thing that he said was, 'the Reyes' were a plant'." The two simultaneous gasps rang throughout the room, letting me know I'd been right.

Fin and Henry didn't know and had indeed been my friends. At least there was that.

thirty-five

· · ·

sawyer

THE ROOM WAS QUIET FOR A SECOND BEFORE IT EXPLODED into a cacophony of voices as a million questions were directed at me, making my head spin.

"Why didn't you tell us?"

"Are you safe?"

"I'm so sorry you experienced that."

"What did you mean about our parents?"

"Wait, where did you say the wreck was?"

"No one is fucking taking you."

"HEY! Everyone shut up! This isn't how we get answers."

I was surprised that it was Mateo who'd stood up and yelled at everyone. It was sexy seeing him take charge like that.

"Thank you, Mateo." I smiled my thanks at him. Rhett stepped up after that, shaken out of his shock.

"Okay, let's go around one at a time. Fin, you go first."

"I don't know where to start, actually. I have a million things running through my head. But something I'd forgotten the other day when you mentioned it, but you said that the wreck was on the border of Missouri and Iowa. That's impossible or doesn't make sense." Fin scrunched up her nose, thinking.

"Yeah, I remember seeing the signs when we stopped at the gas station, and I definitely have been living in Iowa for the past five years, so I'm sure that it was the border," I answered.

"Sawyer, the wreckage of your parents, was found two hours from Sugar Grove," she stated bluntly.

I wasn't expecting that news and stared, stunned for a minute. Everyone around me watched as I digested this new information. I hadn't ever looked up the wreck out of fear that it would trigger an emotion in me, or worse, allow them to trace it back to where I was somehow. But now?

"So, what does this mean? They moved the wreckage? But who? And why?" Confusion laced my tone as I tried to grapple with this information.

"I don't know. It's curious, but I don't think we'll get answers tonight, so let's put that on the back burner for now. Henry, do you have anything to add?"

"What do you mean by our parents? Because if they're connected to this... Yeah, my brain is stuck. So, I don't have anything else at the moment." He shook his head, and I patted his leg. I knew it would be a hard thing to hear.

We went around the room, most of the guys offered their support and sympathy. Being new to my history, they didn't have much to offer. That was until we got to Rhett—my protector. I couldn't help the feeling of belonging grow more.

"I have a few. Why put yourself in danger coming here? Who were your parents? Are you safe?" Rhett's concerned voice sent tingles down my spine not eliciting the response I bet he was going for.

"My name was Sariah Brennon, and my parents were Scott and Kyla Brennon. Or at least that was what I knew them as. I don't know what my name was before I was three." I stopped to take a deep breath for the next part, knowing he probably wouldn't agree with me.

"It might not make sense to you, but I had to come here. I was drowning in fear in Iowa. I constantly felt as if someone was watching me. I was scared to make relationships, and always felt alone. There was this hole inside of me that needed the truth—an unanswered question of who I was—and it was never going to get discovered in Iowa." I pleaded with my eyes for him to understand, to see me. His bore into mine with intensity. It felt like days passed before he gave a slight nod. Exhaling, I continued.

"It might be dangerous, but you all make me feel brave and that I'm no longer alone. I want to know who killed my parents. Maybe figure out who my biological parents are and why they gave me up. Those were the things that propelled me to apply and accept the job. But since I've been here, a bigger part of me has returned, and I realized that it was just as important in me deciding to come here. Skating again in this environment has reminded me how much I love it. How it was more than just something I was good at, but something that brought me intense joy." Clearing my throat, I refocused myself to finish his answer.

"Danger. I'm not sure because my inner radar has been off for years. From that day, I've felt like someone watched me, but I don't know if it was just my paranoia after five years or actually real. I'm just over feeling this way, and I'm ready to face things head-on. I'm so tired of not knowing if anything is real."

I was surprised to find a new tear trailing down my cheek. Most of the guys nodded in understanding, while others gave small smiles of assurance. Only one held out with no change of expression, and I was surprised to find it was Oliver.

"Ollie?" I asked, but to my surprise, he shook his head, standing to leave the room. My heart sank at his departure, but Soren drew me back with his question.

"Why tell us?" he asked.

"I'm done living two lives and never fully engaging in either. Sariah Brennon died that day, and Sawyer was born, but I never let Sariah's ghost go. I held onto her, afraid that my memories of my parents would go as well. But I'm tired of lying to people and feeling that I can't be myself. The deceit was crippling me. You guys have been the first people I've met who I feel I can trust, and I wanted you to know the real me. Not just the version I showed you. I didn't want my past to be a barrier between us; especially, if things progress."

I'd hoped my honesty and sincerity were obvious, bleeding through my words because they were my truth. Soren's smile eased my heart at his easy acceptance.

"Thank you for trusting us enough to share." His face showed so much kindness, I got lost for a second. Elias asked a question, bringing me back to the room.

"Where are you starting with research, Sawyer? Can I help?"

Surprise etched across my brow, and I quickly cleared it. Elias still noticed if the pain in his eyes was anything to go by. I was touched, though, that he was willing to jump into my madness.

"I don't know where to start, so any help would be appreciated. I just know the name Abernathy, and this school were connected, or I guess the place where it all starts." He gave me a small nod before switching over into thinking mode.

"Sign me up for the tech, it's my expertise, and I'll try not to get arrested this time!" Everyone laughed at Finley, causing the mood to shift back. I glanced over at my best friend and mouthed "thank you" and she grinned back. Life had been empty without her exuberance.

"I think we've all had enough for the night. Let's pick this back up later. We can devise a plan and figure out our roles. But for now, we kick back, dance, and let go at this party. I think we can all use it. So, who's the DD, and what is the plan of attack?" Soren asked, bringing the excitement back to the room. He rubbed his hands together as he looked around at all of us.

Everyone started to discuss the party and who was driving, and what time we needed to leave. Soren was right, nothing more could be done tonight. Instead, we needed to have some fun with one another. It was time to dance with my boys, and while that made me excited, a small part of me wondered what Oliver was thinking and if I'd already lost him.

elias

My mind turned over everything Sawyer had shared with us. The number of things she had experienced in the past five years was astounding, but I didn't believe she had told us all of it. Not that she owed any of us. Her story was her story, and I would let her keep her secrets.

Even if my need to know everything was screaming at me.

Since the day I'd met her, I had been more curious than I ought to be, and now, I'd just volunteered to help her before I thought it through. But I did want to help her, despite the pit that had formed in my stomach that I might not like what I uncovered.

I wouldn't let it stop me though. Especially since research was something I excelled at. My brain thrived on knowledge and solving a puzzle, and even though we were at a party I was itching to get started. In fact, I was not in the party mood at all, but it made it easy to agree to be the designated driver for my friends.

So far, I hadn't spotted Voldemort, so doubly good. Currently, my gaze was fixed on Sawyer as she danced with Finley and Wallace. I wasn't sure of what her relationship with Wallace was, but it didn't appear to be sexual. There was a sense of familiarity between them that confused me. She wasn't like that with me, and I really didn't know how to take it.

We'd been formal and polite since the first two disastrous conversations, and I hated to admit I missed her fire.

"You can say you like her; you know. It's not a crime."

I turned to the voice that had settled against the wall with me. My best friend thought he was bloody brilliant, as if it was that easy to admit I might like someone. Pfft.

He sipped a beer, keeping his gaze fixed on the blonde dancing. He was sunk, but I knew he'd readily admit it. He was a romantic like that. Once he made a decision, he was all in.

I didn't have that luxury. Things were too jumbled, too complicated for me to like someone as pure as Sawyer. Because she was—I could admit that—and I was afraid my baggage would dirty her beyond recognition.

So, deny and deflect. Something I was rather good at.

"What are you going on about, man? I'm just trying to figure out her relationship with Wallace. When did she meet him?"

"Sure. If that makes you feel better. They met last weekend at the coffee shop. They're just friends. No need to worry, you know, if you were checking her out." He smirked at me nonchalantly. *Wanker.*

"I am not *worried*. Should you not be, though? Is she not *your* girl?"

"You already know how I feel about her. You were there." Rhett gave me a pointed look, lifting his eyebrow, making me really want to shave it off. His mastery over those things was uncanny. It was truly unfair, and I hated my best friend a little at that moment.

"A mature relationship communicates openly."

He grinned smugly at me. Now, I wanted to punch him. Maybe I could let one slip next time we trained together. He definitely deserved it, the tosser. Scoffing at him as I shook my head, I turned back to the dancing trio. Now she was joined by some of the others, and I found my jealousy simmered at that. I wasn't jealous of my housemates, just Wallace.

Some seductive song came on, and she paired off with Rey and Soren. Rey was at her back with Soren at her front. Rhett and I watched them dance, and I had to admit it turned me on. Based on how Rhett adjusted himself, I wasn't the only one.

He at least got to be with her, kiss her, touch her, taste her—Fuck, I wanted her. I hadn't wanted anyone for more than sex since Voldemort had crushed my heart. But was I ready for this? Could I be someone other than the version she'd met?

The doubt that I couldn't, stopped me short. Perhaps it would be better to focus on helping her first. That might help me show a different side of me, that I wasn't the douchecanoe she believed me to be.

I would need to be prepared for the possible backlash, but it was time to quit hiding in the shadows. If Sawyer could be brave and vulnerable, then I could offer it to her in return. She was worth any uncomfortableness I might experience from being vulnerable.

My family wasn't a subject I spoke of, but it could be what I needed to assist her. I only hoped she wouldn't think worse of me when she discovered the truth.

soren

Sawyer's arms hung around my neck as she danced with me along to the sexy song that blared through the room. Placing my hands on her hips, I pulled her closer to me. One of Rey's hands landed on top of mine, and it felt electric to be holding her like this together.

His other hand wove around to her stomach, inching lower as the song played. Her hair was pulled over her shoulder, offering her neck for him to kiss and nibble on as her hands played with the hair at my nape, sending tingles through me.

Watching Rey with Sawyer was erotic. He was so comfortable with her, and their bodies moved together gracefully, hinting at their shared history. This entire scenario felt almost as if it had been plucked out of one of my fantasies, and I had to remind myself that the room had other people in it.

My dick didn't seem to care, though. Nor did Sawyer based on how she continued to grind into me, pressing her body against mine. She was so close that her pear smell intoxicated me as I breathed in. I didn't think I'd ever look at the fruit again without getting aroused.

One hand dropped from my neck and worked its way down my back. Holding my breath, I waited for what she did next. The tight squeeze of my ass had me jolting into her. I was already hard, but at her squeeze, I almost came. I needed to stop this, or we'd all hate ourselves tomorrow. The song ended, thank fuck, and the bigger challenge was disengaging from them.

"Hey, let's get some air and water," I suggested.

They both nodded their heads in acknowledgment and followed me to the back deck. This house was as magnificent as ours, but theirs had a spectacular backyard. There was a big deck with string lights, a large seating area with multiple sectionals, several fire pits, and an outdoor kitchen and bar.

We headed there to grab water. Even though we had a DD, I didn't think any of us had more than one drink. Athletes didn't often drink during training, and it seemed like the habit stayed for most of us.

We spotted Mateo and Oliver by a fire pit and headed in that direction once we had our water. Sawyer held my hand as we walked, and I reveled in how it felt in mine. It was small and soft, and I loved the way it fit. When we got closer to the guys, I stopped her for a second, causing Rey to stop with me. He'd been walking on the other side of her and looked at me curiously.

"Hey, before we go over there, can we talk to you about something? We wanted to earlier, but it didn't seem like the time." Sawyer nodded as she smiled sweetly at me. "Okay, well, I don't know if you're aware, but Rey and I have feelings for you, and each other. We want to be with you and one another. How do you feel about that?"

Peering into her eyes, I hoped to see acceptance, but feared I'd lose my dream before it even started. She stepped closer to me, her hand cupping my cheek.

"Soren, what you two have together is beautiful, and I would never dare to interfere with that. I was nervous you wouldn't want me, so I'm happy that there's room for me too. You should be able to be with whoever makes you happy." She stepped closer as she pulled my head down and whispered in my ear. "I think your love is sexy as fuck, and I hope you'll include me."

The bite she delivered to my earlobe had me moaning out loud. The fucking minx.

"Not fair," I growled as she stepped back. Sawyer just turned and swished her hips as she walked toward the fire pit. I knew she was doing it on purpose, but I didn't care. Her ass looked amazing in those pants. She glanced over her bare shoulder as she neared the pit and winked.

"Fuuuucckk," I drawled out with a groan. At least Rey joined in that time. I turned toward him, beaming. "That's our girl, man." Rey chuckled at my enthusiasm but didn't deny it.

"What did she say to you?" he asked, curiously.

"She um, said it was sexy as fuck and that she hoped to join with you and me at some point." I groaned, and he moaned, causing us both to chuckle.

Each time I looked into his eyes now, I saw joy instead of pain. He was coming back to who he was meant to be. I saw it now. The light, the love, and passion he had to share. It had always been there, but he'd hid it away, afraid of allowing others to see it.

Grabbing his hand, I wanted to feel more connected with him, and was happy when he didn't drop it, squeezing it back. I wasn't sure how he felt about holding hands in public, but he didn't seem to be embarrassed or weird about it, even though this was new. Instead, Rey took it in stride and owned it.

I didn't think he knew he did that. He was unflappable at times, and it was reassuring to know I was part of it. Part of him.

Walking over, we found the rest of our roommates had joined them. Sawyer sat next to Mateo, and I noticed he seemed to be coming out of his shell each day, and I knew Sawyer was a big part of it. He was a cool dude, so I was glad he felt comfortable to be himself.

None of the guys said or did anything when they saw Rey and I holding hands. It made me appreciate them even more. We truly were a family, accepting one another for who we were and seeing the best in one another. I didn't have this growing up, so having it now was everything.

I didn't think it was possible to be happier than I was at this moment. It was the small moments that mattered. Sitting around a fire, laughing with your friends, and being comfortable with who you are, that was bliss.

Feeling loved and accepted was an imperative part of life. Gold medals, money, and adoring fans faded away. But this, this was everlasting and worth more than any gold medal.

Ollie made a joke, and we all laughed, and I felt it. Family.

Though I noticed, he was doing his best to avoid looking at Sawyer, and I wasn't sure what was going on there. Sawyer kept glancing at him, trying to catch his eyes, and each time he avoided her, her face fell.

Finley walked up with Asa a few minutes later,

helping to shift the focus off Ollie. I didn't know Asa that well, but he seemed like a cool dude. Fin saw Rey and I holding hands and smiled at us, lifting my spirit even more. I didn't know why I was worried about her accepting us, Fin had always felt like a little sister to me, and I knew she would be okay with it, but there was a small part of me that feared she wouldn't.

She introduced us all to Asa, going around the circle, when my phone vibrated for the tenth time in my pocket. Pulling it out, I checked it to see what was going on since everyone I texted was around the fire pit. A bunch of texts from my mom appeared, and I began to delete them without reading. The last one had me pause, though.

Cersei: If you don't give me what I want, then I'll just take it. You might not like how.

Fuck, she was escalating. I needed to get a handle on this, but I couldn't do anything about it tonight. It was officially tomorrow's problem.

Tonight, I just wanted to enjoy the company of my best friend and our girl.

thirty-six

...

sawyer

Despite how the night started, it was a fun evening. Well, except for Oliver avoiding me. I was trying to forget that part, though. I'd enjoyed dancing with the guys and getting to chill with them without worrying about jealousy. Being free of the lies had lifted my burdens, and I felt more like the girl I'd been long ago, back when I'd been ignorant of who I really was.

Being around Henry and Fin again helped with that, reminding me of who they saw me as. Not the person I'd been pretending to be, or living as, but me. They accepted me as who I was and I wasn't made to feel ashamed for it. It was liberating, making me stronger.

Chatting with Mateo was a lot of fun, so I'd asked if he wanted to hang out after the party. We'd decided to have our movie night since we'd had to reschedule earlier in the week.

Sitting next to him around the fire pit, I was attempting to flirt with him, but I wasn't sure if he understood my advances or didn't know what to do with me.

For my own pride, I was going with not knowing how to handle me, so I decided to help him out.

My hand rubbed his leg, and he seemed happy about that. He smiled, and nervously put his arm around me, so I leaned into him. Okay, now, we were getting somewhere. Smiling at him, I hoped to ease some of his shyness, and I realized how much I loved how different the guys were.

Rhett said what he wanted and took it.

Mateo was quieter and needed direction.

Henry was sweet and passionate, while Soren was playful and sexy at the same time.

Oliver was still working on letting his mask drop enough and not be the cocky asshole I'd met the first day.

We were just on the flirting stage, but it was fun, and he made me feel beautiful. When I told Charlie about sharing a house with him, he had his first fangirl moment. It was quite cute. I bet if I got his autograph, Charlie might pass out. Christmas this year was going to be a hoot.

Elias, on the other hand, he was still a mystery.

Things were better between us, but almost like we were two strangers or too polite to really say anything. We were both so proper around one another that it was starting to feel rigid. I needed to be the one to drop it, I knew it, but he was trying so hard that it made it worse. His carefulness toward me only made me feel more ashamed of how I'd responded to him initially. I needed to take ownership of my own feelings and recognize that he hadn't deserved my apathy.

It was apparent now that there was more to him than that horrible first impression. Besides, I had stolen his dog, and he'd let me. So, I couldn't be mad at him forever. Feeling resolved about Elias, and hopefully the beginning of a friendship with him, I turned and kissed Mateo on the cheek.

"What was that for?" he asked, looking down at me. From this angle, I could see his cheeks turning red. Shit, he was too adorable with that blush. He pushed his glasses up, another nervous habit I'd noticed.

"Does it have to be for anything? I just felt like doing it, and now I can. Is that okay with you?" I asked, observing him. Now, I started to worry that I'd crossed a line. We hadn't gotten to the boundary talk earlier, and maybe PDA was an issue for him. Or perhaps he didn't want others to know we were in a relationship. Crap, I was already messing this up. Shit. We needed to have that talk before I ruined things.

"Whatever you're thinking, stop. I liked it. I'm just not used to girls kissing me. That's all. But I'm glad you feel like kissing me. Please kiss me whenever, or wherever you want."

His voice had taken on a smoky quality that was doing things to my insides. When had Mateo gotten so seductive? I didn't miss his little flirt there either. He was becoming more and more comfortable with himself, and I was glad I had a front-row seat to it.

"Oh, wherever you say?" I teased, leaning forward.

His reply was just a smile and a blush. Cheeky devil. I was thinking about kissing him on the lips this time when Fin walked up to us with a guy.

"Hey guys, I don't know if you know Asa Walsh or not, but I just wanted to introduce Sawyer to him."

The guys all shouted out a "Hello" and I stood up to walk closer to them. I was excited to meet the guy that had caught my bestie's eye. He was tall and muscular with blonde hair. He was attractive, but I didn't feel a spark with him, which was reassuring. I didn't need my Altitude Delirium spilling over onto him as well. Fin would murder me. Legit murder.

As I got closer, I made eye contact and was startled for a second. His eyes were a very unusual color of green. His smile was kind, though, and he seemed happy that Fin was introducing him to us. Bonus points for him.

"Hi, I'm Sawyer Sullivan. Fin's bestie." I put my hand out to shake his. I could have manners when needed.

His hand was larger than mine, which wasn't unusual for guys, and warm and comforting. He had a friendly vibe about him that I liked. His smile was open and inviting, and I felt like he was probably a decent person. I was glad that my bestie found someone worthy of her.

"It's nice to meet you, Sawyer. Have we met before,

though? I feel like I know you already, but I guess that's just because of Finnster here." He shook his head as he looked at me before smiling over at Fin. She blushed, and I couldn't help but give her shit for it. After all, what did besties do best if not stir the shit, and I had a lot of time to make up.

"*Finnster*, is it? Well, I just heard about you today, but it was all good things, *very* good things, so no worries. She did mention how—"

I was cut off by a hand slapping over my mouth, as Fin held it there, blocking me before I could get the rest of my sentence out. She gave me a look with her eyes that screamed, "Shut the hell up bitch!" but also appeared to barely be holding back a laugh, so I helped her out. I was a great friend like that.

Licking her hand, I caused her to let go—gross, I know. But always effective.

"What, Finn?" I said in mock outrage, feigning hurt. Her face turned tomato red. I kid you not. I was so getting it back from her later, I could see the plans developing in her mind already, but I couldn't stop at this point.

"I was just going to say how you mentioned being excited about this year's hockey games. That's all. Geez. You act as if I am so uncouth. I would never tell him you were called—"

Another hand covered my mouth, but this time it was Henry's. He was a good brother, but I wanted him to be a good boyfriend right then. *Traitor.*

When he dropped his hand, Fin and I burst into

giggles. Fortunately, Asa joined us. His voice was infectious and comforting. Thankfully, despite me trying to embarrass her, they decided to join us around the fire pit.

Ollie got up and hugged Asa, but avoided making eye contact with me. Hanging my head, I stopped trying to engage him here as he was obviously evading me, so I returned back to my seat. Only, now there wasn't enough, so I went to sit on the ground.

Rhett pulled me to his lap when I walked by him. His legs were massive, so he worked well as a chair. Looked like my dream of being a barnacle was getting closer to coming true as I settled back into his embrace. He placed his head over my shoulder and breathed me in, making me swoon on the spot. Having been worked up all night already, it didn't take much for him to get my lady bits sparking. I was trying not to squirm, but he was making it difficult.

"Baby, I've missed you this week. It feels like forever since we've been together. Can you stay with me tonight?" The way his voice rolled through me was intoxicating. I almost gave in, but remembered a promise I'd made earlier. This close to him, his smell wrapped around me and I had to swallow a few times before I could answer him. I found it increasingly hard not to shift in his lap or rub my legs together.

"Um, I promised Mateo I'd spend some time with him when we got home. But I could be persuaded to spend the night with you if that's what you were asking. We didn't talk about the boundaries thing either, so we should do that tomorrow."

"Good point. Yes, let's do that over breakfast. And yes, please visit me afterward. I will take any cuddle time with you." Fortunately, he moved back after that and just held on to me, helping to cool my jets.

Ace and Chloe came over to join us at one point as well, and I relished in the amount of friends I was collecting. Ace had a girl with him, but I didn't catch her name. She seemed shy compared to his over-exuberant personality. I couldn't tell if it was just a hookup or something more. It was a toss-up with him. The knowledge that I knew people made me feel warm inside.

My world was expanding, and it was thrilling.

We spent the evening laughing and sharing stories around the fire. I needed people like this in my life that reminded me of the things that were important enough to fight for. I thought pushing people away had been the right choice, but I think it only made me weaker, not stronger. I might not have had people in my life that could be used against me in the past, but I also didn't have anyone to lean on.

This group here, they gave me strength in spades. No matter what happened from this point forward, I know I made the right decision coming here and opening up to others.

This wasn't something you could fake. Real friends, they were invaluable.

mateo

Sawyer and I were hanging out in the media room after the house party.

Alone.

I'd been nervous, but it was going well so far. We'd returned from the party around 10 pm and decided to start our Marvel movie marathon with Captain America.

"I'm glad that we're spending time together. It's easier when there aren't a lot of people around," I mumbled, but she didn't appear to notice, or care.

"You do better around people than you think, Mateo. People are drawn to you and your quiet nature. You make them feel at ease and that they don't have to put on fronts. That's a powerful thing. You aren't going to be Soren, so don't try to be Soren. The world needs introverts just as much as extroverts; they just make introverts feel bad about it. It's one of my pet peeves, actually."

She laughed, and I swore her laugh was magical. "I'm a sociable introvert, though, maybe not really because I'm socially awkward and blurt things out all the time. But I do like to be around people that I know. Afterward, I need time to recharge and have my alone time. People suck out my energy." She shrugged, like it wasn't a big deal. But to me, it was. She understood me in a way no one else ever had.

"I like being around you. You make me feel confident to be myself."

I smiled over at her, finding she'd moved closer to me. I loved this room; it was comfortable with a lot of different seating options—recliners, massive bean bag chairs, a daybed like lounger, and a few Moroccan pillows. It was fun and inviting, and I enjoyed each moment in here.

We'd found an old-fashioned popcorn machine in the back along with a soda machine. These houses were self-sustainable, making it where no one needed to go into the big city, ever. The entertainment system was state of the art and made my geeky side very excited. The room had surround sound with a media player that connected to your phone via Bluetooth.

You downloaded an app that connected to a media library that had every streaming service. It was excessive and a bit ridiculous, but I would definitely take advantage of it.

Taking a chance again, I slid my arm around her and she leaned into me, resting her head on my chest. Her hair smelled amazing, and I breathed it in small doses so as not to weird her out. Sawyer was warm and soft against me, and while I was freaking out internally, I felt I was managing well on the outside. At least I hoped so. I didn't want her thinking I was pathetic.

Moving my arm more, my hand dropped to her hip, so I rested it there. I could feel where her sweater and jeans left a slice of skin for me to rub. It was good to know her clothes were rallying for me by making it easier for me to touch her. Feeling brave, I rubbed my thumb over the exposed skin, and she shivered. A part of me I'd never felt before filled with pride at her reaction to something I'd done.

"Are you okay with this?" I asked in a barely there whisper.

Her smile and nod gave me the courage I needed to go for it. When she peered up at me, I felt the heat simmering in her eyes spurring me on. I knew it was important for me to do this, to make the first move to show her I wasn't a total disaster. Our faces were so close at this point, so I only had to lean forward a few centimeters to press my lips to hers.

This kiss held more passion than the other one. That one had been hesitant and sweet. I wasn't sure at the time what it had meant, but now... now, I knew she wanted me and it made me heady with desire.

Following her movements, I put my emotions behind my actions this time. Sawyer licked at the seam of my lips, urging me to open for her, so I did. It had been a foreign feeling the first time, but I was able to mimic her rhythm and follow her direction.

It became a dance as we kissed one another. My breathing grew ragged as my heart rate increased, my body heavy with arousal. I started to unintentionally grip her hip harder as we devoured one another. The simple act of kissing her made me feel weak and I wondered if more would kill me.

Her hand glided into my hair as we kissed, and a sound escaped me that I hadn't known I could make. Her fingers in my hair felt addicting, and I leaned into the kiss more, which caused my glasses to go askew as they pressed into her face. Laughing, I pulled back for a moment to take them off. Fortunately, I could still see well enough without my glasses because I'd hate to miss out on Sawyer.

"Here, let's put them somewhere safe," she offered, and placed my glasses on top of her things, then turned around and leaped at me.

"Oof," I grunted as I caught a knee to the stomach. Before she could feel bad about it, I grabbed her hip, propelling her forward to straddle me. I was pretty impressed with myself for that move. I might be a geek and inexperienced, but I was also an athlete. Strength and agility were ingrained in me, allowing me to pull off that feat. Her gasp of surprise, followed by her megawatt grin, made it worth it.

"That was sexy as fuck, Mateo. You always surprise me."

She'd landed on my dick, which was now making itself known to her. I started to feel embarrassed, but her rocking motion shut me up. Sawyer began to pepper my neck with kisses, making my head fall against the headrest as she continued to grind on my hardness.

My mind was in a state of bliss, so when she nipped at my ear, I nearly jumped up off my seat. My cock jutted at her movement, causing me to moan obscenely loud. I didn't have time to think about it when she did it again. This time I could feel her smile against my neck as she tightened her hands in my hair. I was jealous of my hair as she yanked on it. My hair had never had so much attention before. Feeling brave, I pushed my hand under her shirt, but when she stopped it, I felt like I'd fucked up.

Getting ready to apologize for crossing a line, I was surprised when she yanked her sweater over her head, leaving only the black lace shirt she had on under it. Her nipples pebbled through her shirt, and I couldn't take my eyes off of them. When I eventually looked at her, I almost drowned in the amount of desire there. How could she feel all that for me? I couldn't believe it.

"Are you okay?" she asked hesitantly. My heart had taken off at a gallop at her husky voice.

"Yeah, I uh." I swallowed, trying to gather my words. "I'm not as experienced as most guys my age. I'm not really sure what to do." I felt embarrassed to admit it, but I didn't want her to think I was terrible either, or didn't want her. I would much rather she knew and showed me instead.

"That's not a bad thing, Mateo. We'll go at your pace, okay? Just do what feels natural. What you think you're comfortable with. Don't worry about crossing a line with me. Consent is important, so just know that right now, I'm giving you consent to explore what you want, and you don't have to feel hesitant about it. But don't compare yourself to the others or feel you have to be on the same level because I don't, and I don't want it to be that way. I just want us to be us."

I blinked when I realized she wasn't judging me or upset about my lack of experience, which helped. I didn't feel as clumsy anymore.

"Thank you, that means a lot to me. I would like to, um…" My face heated at my embarrassment of having to say it out loud.

"You know, I had a teacher once who said if you can't talk about it, then you're not ready to have it. Just trust yourself and me, and we'll figure it out." Sawyer smiled, normalizing the whole thing for me, helping me not feel weird. I liked how she did that.

"I like that. It makes sense. And… I guess I want to go there with you someday, but I'm not ready for that right now, but I don't want to stop. I'm enjoying what we are doing."

Surprisingly, I was able to look at her the whole time I was talking without feeling embarrassed. It solidified my feelings for her and what she was starting to mean to me.

"I'm more than okay with that. Would you feel better if I took the lead, or do you want to explore what feels good to you?" Sawyer asked, giving me control instead of making me feel inadequate, proving she was who I needed, making everything natural.

Deciding to answer her question with an action, I moved my hands up her ribs as I began to kiss her neck. She started rocking on my lap again, her words drying up. Dragging her shirt up with my thumbs, I lifted it over her head, allowing my fingers to graze her body. Goosebumps rose on her skin, followed by a shiver. I took that to indicate it was a good feeling.

Sawyer sat before me now in just her bra with her necklace dangling above the swell of her breasts. The most glorious pair of breasts. Granted, they were my first real breasts, but I felt strongly that they were still the best. Her bra fastened in the front, so I unsnapped it, and then I was granted an even better view. Her breasts spilled out, captivating my gaze. Swiping the straps off her shoulders, I was transfixed by her chest.

"Wow," I mumbled.

I was utterly entranced by them, so I took my thumb to touch them. Rolling the pad over the tip of her nipple, I watched how they pebbled. The pink color stood out against her creamy skin, and I couldn't stop touching them. Both hands got in on the action, and I started to understand the appeal of boobs. They were seductive as fuck, and when Sawyer arched her back, bringing them closer to my face, I almost died.

Now they were taunting me, so close that my tongue flicked out on its own accord tasting her nipple. She moaned, and it made my dick twitch. She picked her movement back up, and I felt good that I was affecting her this much. Massaging her breast in one hand, and playing with the nipple in the other, I began kissing up her neck, sucking on her skin.

"Yes, Mateo. Mmm. Keep doing that," she rasped.

Transferring one hand back to her hip, I slowed her down some, or I'd make a mess in my pants. Going back to her lips, I took her mouth, and we began to kiss passionately again. I was getting better at this kissing thing. Tracing my fingers at the top of her jeans, I slowly unsnapped the button and lowered the zipper. The feel of her underwear against my hand was oddly erotic.

Breaking my kiss, I wanted to watch what I was doing as I traced my finger against her underwear. I noticed that she was wearing Harry Potter underwear, which surprisingly made it hotter; this girl was the perfect balance of sexy and nerdy.

Dipping my finger in, she encouraged me to keep going with her movements, so I did. My fingers met her soft curls before I felt her warm heat. Rubbing my fingers on the outside of her lips, she let out another moan. I did this a couple of times and pressed one finger in deeper. I was following her movements as I slid inside her and began to move back and forth.

"Fuck. Gah, that feels good. Yes, please don't stop."

Her rocking started again, and Sawyer showed me where to place my thumb. She demonstrated the pattern she wanted me to do, and then let go. I continued to rub circles with my thumb as I kept my pace with my hand and felt her grip my finger with her walls.

Inserting another finger, I filled her fuller as Sawyer rocked on my dick in such a way that I almost couldn't concentrate on what I was doing. I felt her hands on my shirt, and she raised it over my head. I pulled my hand out for a minute to help her get my shirt off. She began to trace the muscles on my chest and pinched my nipples. It felt so good.

"I never thought that would feel this good," I moaned.

I pushed her pants down to get more leverage and inserted my fingers back inside her warm pussy. I rubbed the palm of my hand on her clit, moving two fingers quickly in and out of her. Her own hands continued down to my jeans, and then she was unzipping them. I felt her hand on the outside of my boxers as she rubbed me. Just that felt amazing, and I didn't know if I would be able to handle her hand for long.

"I'm getting so close, Mateo. I want to feel you too and come together. Please," she begged of me. She put her hand down my boxers, and I felt her hand wrap around me. It felt so incredible when she touched me, and I threw my head back in a moan.

"Fuck." I breathed out, which apparently made her giggle. I lifted my head back up and peered at her.

"I've never heard you cuss before, so it must feel perfect then."

"Incredible," I mumbled through another moan. We quit talking after that as we both continued to grind on one another. Sawyer squeezed my cock and ran her hand up and down from the base to the tip. She rubbed her thumb over the head and squeezed more, making a small bead of precum coat her fingers.

For some reason, that was sexy as fuck. She rode my finger so hard, she was rubbing herself against my palm. I moved my other hand back to her breasts and began to knead and squeeze. I twisted her nipple, and it seemed to start a reaction in her. She increased her speed on my dick, and I began to feel my balls draw up.

"I'm about to come," I muttered.

"Me too, don't stop, don't fucking stop."

We didn't stop, thankfully, and kept pleasuring one another until we both erupted. Sawyer detonated first, but I followed shortly after, as the warm cum coated my stomach. She rested her forehead against mine as we stared at one another, smiling. She was so beautiful, and I couldn't believe that she just let me touch her and bring her to orgasm. If that had been this incredible, I couldn't wait to see what else we could explore together.

"Thank you, that was amazing," I breathed out as I kissed her temple.

"Of course, Mateo. It was incredible, and I know it'll just keep getting better."

We stayed staring at one another, cuddled up like that for a while until we realized the movie had stopped playing, and the "Are you still watching" screen had popped up.

We both laughed at that because obviously, we weren't watching, thank you, Netflix.

We cleaned up as best we could and got dressed. She grabbed my shirt instead of hers and smirked at me, but I kind of liked it, so I didn't care and walked back to my room without one.

At my door, she kissed me one more time before she headed to her room. I knew she was going to see Rhett next, but it didn't make me jealous. I just had the most mind-blowing time with her, and that was what mattered.

Before I got ready for bed, I took out my journal and wrote down my feelings for the day and any irrational thoughts that had popped up. I wrote down the good things I experienced as well. It was something my therapy taught me to do. Sometimes we got so bombarded with irrational and negative thinking that we forgot the positives. Having a journal helped show a journey of small accomplishments that could help defeat any negative thinking.

It was also an excellent way for me to get my feelings out without them becoming overwhelming to the point where I did what I did last time. The anxiety could overrule my mind if I wasn't conscious about it.

Today, I had a lot of happy things to write, and the negative thoughts didn't seem to be as bad. It was a nice feeling, and I celebrated the small improvements because it was those moments that would help me see my progress forward. My life was coming alive, and it had more than just skiing in it. Feeling at peace when I went to sleep, I had the best dreams.

thirty-seven

. . .

rey

Waking up next to Soren was different, yet exhilarating. It was the first time I'd had a man in my bed. Scratch that, *anyone* in my bed. When I hooked up with others, it was just that, a hookup. No sleepovers, nothing. I'd never shared my bed with anyone outside of Fin and Smalls, but that was when we were young.

Things between Soren and I were still developing, and I wasn't sure what roles we were with one another, or if that even mattered. Like was he a top? Was I? How did you know? It was all confusing to me. I just knew he was part of my heart, my breath, my future.

Currently, Soren was playing big spoon to my little spoon, and I didn't hate it. In fact, I enjoyed it, a lot. His arm was draped over my ribs, his hand resting on my stomach—my bare stomach. I could feel his breath on my shoulder as he inhaled and exhaled, stirring tiny bumps on my skin.

I'd been awake for a few minutes, basking in the feeling of his body against mine. More importantly, his cock nestled against my ass, feeling its hardness. Thinking about it made my own dick harden. We hadn't talked about what we were ready for with each other yet, and so far, we'd only kissed the night we confessed our feelings. We'd fallen asleep after watching TV last night in pajama bottoms, but the material was thin enough to feel everything.

Wiggling back a little, I felt his dick nestled into my ass cheeks. The feeling was new, but damn erotic, causing me to gasp at the sensation of it. My dick stiffened more, and I casually rubbed my hand against the outside of my pants, offering a little relief. That was when I noticed the breaths on my neck had sped up and a soft kiss was placed on my shoulder.

"Good morning, hot stuff. It seems you're feeling adventurous. Hmm? Just how adventurous are you feeling, babe?"

The hand on my stomach became firmer and began to drift down further. Soren scooted closer to me, and his hardened length pressed into me more, stealing a moan from my lips as my head was thrown back. Soren used the opportunity to nuzzle into the crook of my neck. His hand dropped on top of my own, and he began to move with me.

"Well, Rey babe, what's it going to be? I need to hear you; I don't want to rush this or mess anything up if you're not ready." He cautioned between the small kisses he planted on my neck.

"Sor, I'm ready. I am so ready. Please… show me." I wasn't sure if he could make out what I said between my moans, but he seemed to get the gist.

His hand began to move over my dick while he rocked into me. Kisses were planted on my neck before he sucked at the skin. I tilted my neck back, straining for our lips to meet. Kissing Soren was so different than any girl. His lips were firmer and more aggressive. Soren pushed my hand out of the way, taking charge as his hand slipped into my pajama pants, palming me.

"Gah, that feels so good," I moaned as my ass rocked harder against him. Giving in to my desire, I reached back to rub his dick over his pants. It was a bit awkward, though, so I rolled over, so we were face to face, staring at one another for a moment. His bed hair was sexy, tousled over his head, his golden curls in disarray. I desperately wanted to pull it.

"Hey," I cooed, grazing his jaw. The feel of his stubble beneath my palm roused a deep desire in me. Moving in, I kissed him this time. It was slower and sensual as Soren allowed me to take some control. His hand grabbed my ass cheek as he pulled me closer. The effect caused our dicks to rub against one another. We both moaned out in unison at the sensation.

Sliding my hands down his chest, I traced the outline of his muscles, feeling their firmness against my palm. As I traveled his body with my hands, I sneaked around to feel the muscles in his back. They flexed beneath my touch as I roamed his body. Stealing his move, I slipped my hand in the back of his pants, surprised for a moment when I felt his ass cheek, forgetting his penchant to go commando.

Soren's ass cheek was firm and round. As I gripped it, I rocked into him more. I was able to graze his balls with my hand from the back, eliciting a loud moan from him. Our kissing became frantic as we madly grabbed at one another. Without even needing to speak, we started to shuck our pants off, freeing ourselves. I took in Soren's cock, and was momentarily shocked. I'd known him for over a year, and I'd never known this.

Soren had a fucking Prince Albert piercing. Shit, that was fucking hot.

"Holy fuck, dude," I said huskily.

Soren borrowed a move from Rhett and fucking smirked. I wasn't used to seeing this side of him with a cocksure smile on his face. It made my insides melt. Fucking melt. Soren stole my heart with who he was, but now, now he was robbing my essence.

If I hadn't known I loved him already, the look on his face confirmed it.

Focusing back on the desire in the room, I noticed we were about the same size, but with his being a little longer and pierced, while mine was girthier. Having explored one another's bodies thoroughly, building arousal, we went right to the main attraction and began to work one another over. It was such an odd sensation, feeling another hand on me that wasn't small or feminine. It was better because it was Soren's, and it felt intoxicating. Using my thumb, I rubbed his piercing. The moan he released nearly sent me over the edge.

"Rey baby, lay back. I want to taste you."

Not one to say no to that, I did as he said. Soren placed kisses down my body as he made his way to my dick. It stood at full attention, waiting for him. As Soren licked the tip, tingles ran up my spine, distracting me. When his mouth swallowed me whole to the base, I nearly died. Soren just fucking deep throated me, and I'd never felt anything that good before.

"Fuck," I stuttered, not sure how I was even formulating words at this point. Nothing I'd said was voluntary as my body took over.

Placing my hands in Soren's hair, I moved it out of his face so I could watch him. He was such a beautiful man, who just so happened to be giving me intense pleasure at that moment. One of his hands snaked down to grab my balls as he fisted his own dick. Soren timed his thrusts with his mouth. It was erotic watching him pleasure me and touch himself.

"Damn, that feels incredible. It's sexy as fuck watching you touch yourself too."

My voice made Soren glance up at me. The moment he peered into my eyes, I felt the most intimate connection with him. This was what I'd been missing; no one before had ever looked at me like *that*.

I couldn't hold back anymore and I threw my head back in a long moan, coming hard. Soren took it all with a deep swallow. He released my dick with a 'pop' once I had stopped shooting the warm liquid down his throat.

Kissing the tip, Soren left me to grab some tissues. I hadn't realized he'd cum when I did. I couldn't help but watch his ass cheeks flex as he walked away, revealing a dimple in one of his cheeks mirroring his other one.

"Your ass is cute." At my chuckle, he turned and winked, making all my insides warm. His winks were deadly.

Falling back against my pillow, I grabbed my phone off the nightstand to check the time. It was still relatively early, so when Soren returned, I convinced him to cuddle with me. Being with him like this, enjoying one another, was everything I'd always wanted but was too scared to ask for.

"So, how was your first experience with a guy?" I didn't miss the hesitancy in his usually confident voice.

"It wasn't an experience with a guy. It was a moment with you. And that moment was everything," I reassuringly professed.

"I never thought I'd get to have that with you, so know that I'm here with you. I'm in the same place, and this means everything to me as well," Soren affirmed, tenderness in his voice.

I never realized how touchy feely he was, but I wasn't complaining since I got to be the recipient of his touches. We laid there peering at one another as we talked. His hands continuously grazed my arms, my neck, my hair; his gentle touches filled me with love. This simple act between us felt intimate. We were invested in each other and wanted to know what the other was doing instead of it being a conversation filler.

"I'm excited about spending some time today with Smalls. I haven't gotten to see her much since I found her again. Part of me worries she'll disappear again. It's dumb, but I'm waiting for the other shoe to drop because things are too good at the moment," I confessed.

"It's not dumb. Your feelings are your feelings, but Sawyer's here. She's not going to disappear, so enjoy the time with her instead of worrying about 'what ifs'. Besides, I'm jealous you get time with her. I want to get to know her more. The moments we have spent with one another have been unforgettable, but I still want to know her. Damn, this girl makes me babble." Soren chuckled.

I knew he was right, though. I could worry about disaster striking and waste time, or I could actually enjoy it. I decided to enjoy it.

"At least we have book club tomorrow. I'm excited to talk with her about the book," rambled Soren.

Basking in listening to him talk about the story, I relaxed in the comfort of lying here with him. We were completely at ease naked in each other's arms. I never thought this would be my life, but now I couldn't imagine it any other way.

Well, except for Smalls being here. Then, I'd never want to leave the bed.

oliver

The water rushed over my skin as I rested my head on the shower wall. My head was pounding from the amount of beer I'd drunk last night. It was the only thing I could do to stop from blurting out my truth.

Several times I'd thought of taking up one of the girls at the party for a quick fuck, but then Sawyer's laugh or smile would stop me. I couldn't do that to her. We might not be anything, but if I wanted there to be, then I needed to respect her.

Just thinking about her now had my cock standing at attention. Fuck. It had been several weeks since it had gotten any attention. Maybe if I gave it some, it would stop causing me as many problems.

I stroked it from tip to the base in a long drag as I squeezed tightly. Thoughts of Sawyer filtered through my mind as I remembered how she looked that morning in the kitchen when I first saw her. She'd been so full of light, and fierce in a tiny package. She had her own natural beauty that shone through in her personality. Her voice sounded like butter and I wanted to bathe in it.

I stroked faster as I imagined her tracing the top of her shirt that day, caressing her breasts. My eyes had been fixed there, and I hadn't even cared when she stole my bacon. It'd been worth it.

My grunts echoed out through the shower as my climax built. Faster, I stroked and squeezed as I pictured her ass in those shorts she wore the other day with her cheeks nearly hanging out and how much I'd wanted to grab them. Thinking of squirting my cum all over her ass, I erupted hot, thick jets against the shower wall.

Fuck. That had felt amazing. I could only imagine what Sawyer would feel like.

Not that I'd ever know now.

I didn't think I could do this. Not now that I knew her past.

This was unfair.

Quickly I dressed, wanting to do something to distract myself, so I headed to the kitchen. I loved to eat and could never get enough. Being a hockey player, I burned an obscene amount of calories, so my intake was massive. Thoughts continued to race in my head as I rummaged through the fridge. Things were spinning out of control, and I didn't know what to do.

This couldn't be happening. Not her, not this.

Fuck. I needed to make a decision or I'd lose everything.

sawyer

Waking up next to Rhett filled me with happiness. I'd missed this over the week since I'd been holding myself back some until things were more figured out. In the end, I'd only deprived myself.

I loved that each relationship would be different,

and at its own pace. So I couldn't punish other relationships that were further along. Being cognizant of it would be an important first step in making things equal with my guys.

My guys.

That was the first time I had called them that, but I liked it. I liked it a lot, actually.

Deciding to get out of bed before Rhett, I wanted to have a redo at making breakfast, especially with the boundary relationship talk looming this morning. Slipping on pants this time, I pulled my hair back before heading upstairs. Elias wasn't in the kitchen, but Oliver was. Perfect. We needed to discuss last night.

"Good Morning, Oliver," I said, hoping he'd talk about his reaction last night.

"Uh, hey, buttercup," Oliver's face was strained and he seemed to have fallen at my use of Oliver. Waiting to see if he'd say anything else, what he'd just called me sunk in.

"Say what now?"

Willing to let the tension slide, I wouldn't push him. I knew how that felt, so I would wait until he was ready to talk about whatever was going on with him and his out of character behavior. At least he wasn't avoiding me anymore.

"I've decided to join Soren's quest in finding the perfect nickname for you. We're racing each other to see whose you like the best first. It's a competition but not a competition."

"Because that makes total sense," I deadpanned. He

nodded his head in the affirmation, not picking up on my sarcasm. Well two, or in this case three, could play this game. Challenge Accepted.

"Want to help make breakfast, beefcake?"

Oliver was stunned for five whole seconds before a raucous laugh erupted out of him. Mission Accomplished. It was good to hear him laugh.

Oliver agreed to assist me, and we decided to make French toast and turkey sausage links. Each time I opened the fridge, I marveled at the food here. They ate healthily, but it was also flavorful without being diet food.

Oliver turned on some music as he started bopping away to a movie soundtrack. Apparently, in addition to his baking love, Oliver loved musicals. His voice wasn't bad, either. We were dancing and singing to *The Greatest Showman* when the first inhabitants of the house emerged.

"How do we rewrite the stars," sang Henry when he stepped into the kitchen. He took me into his arms as he danced around the kitchen, singing to me. I couldn't believe I'd forgotten how well he could sing. We continued dancing, falling back into our old dances effortlessly, moving together reflexively.

Since the last time I'd seen him, he'd grown in height, making his reach and flexibility better. I started to think about the difference it would have in pair skating. When I realized where my thoughts were headed, I shut it down. I couldn't go down that line of thinking.

It was too dangerous. I couldn't compete anymore. I

knew that. So, thinking about it wasn't helpful. It would just make me sad all over again.

Soren and Oliver clapped for us as I did a dramatic bow. Thankfully, Oliver had taken over at the stove, saving the French toast from burning while I danced. Soren hugged me from behind, snuggling into my neck, and watched me work. I liked this cuddly side of him.

"What's shakin' bacon?" he murmured into my neck, unaware that I was clued into his new game.

"Not much, stud muffin," I said naturally. He lifted his head and peered over at Oliver, who was shaking, trying to hold in his laughter next to me.

"Um, thanks?" Soren sounded so unsure now, and I'd never heard that from him before. Oh God, I'd shaken him with my response. I couldn't hold my laughter in anymore and lost the bread I was dipping into the egg mixture. Taking pity on him, I clued him in on my involvement in their nickname challenge.

"It doesn't matter; I won this challenge. History for the win," Henry proclaimed as he fist-pumped the air causing us all to laugh.

So far, this morning was off to a better start than last week. A sigh of relief escaped me as we finished up the French toast. Slowly, the rest of the house awakened and stumbled into the kitchen in various forms of untidiness. I'd completely won in the housing department, getting to see them in their natural habitat—raw sex appeal on display for my viewing pleasure.

Sign me up. All. Day. Long.

Starting in on the meal, several murmurs sounded

around at how good it was, making Oliver and I share in a satisfied smile. It felt nice to not be causing a scene and taking care of everyone. Rhett did it so naturally that we took it for granted that it wasn't his actual job. We were all adults and capable of pitching in. When it looked like we were all finishing up, Henry cleared his throat. It seemed he would take the lead, and I smiled at seeing part of his confidence returning.

"We didn't get around to discussing boundaries. Does anyone want to start?" When no one said anything, Rhett spoke up.

"How about I list some things I read about, and then we can all say yes or no." Rhett had grown so much since the first time I met him. I didn't think it was that he was more confident now, because I didn't think that was ever the issue. Instead, it was more that he cared, that he wanted to be more involved or more willing to make an effort. It made me get heart-eyed emoji each time he used his words as more than just a means to an end. He was demonstrating to the house his care for them.

If I wasn't already falling in love with the guy, this simple act would've kicked me over the edge.

It was quiet around the table for a while; I wasn't sure if everyone just didn't have any issues or if no one wanted to be first. Rhett broke the silence again.

"PDA. Thoughts on PDA in public, and um, at home? Sawyer, maybe you should tell us what you think first?"

Everyone nodded in relief, happy to have some

direction. Smiling at him, I nodded my thanks for him considering my thoughts. Thinking it over, I tried to put myself in different situations and how they'd make me feel.

"Um, well, I'd say I'm okay with PDA. Obviously, it should be mild and respectful of the situation. I don't want to be grinding on someone in the middle of the campus, but kissing goodbye or holding hands I'm good with."

I nodded my head at myself feeling confident about my decision. Agreements sounded around the table. Okay, this was going well. I didn't know why I'd been nervous about this. I guess it was the first time we were all together, affirming to me they wanted to date me or see if there was something more than the physical attraction.

I looked around the table, pausing. Shaking my head, I knew it was not the time to get distracted by abs. Though, they were making it difficult. Very difficult. Especially when Mateo and Elias were the only ones wearing a shirt.

Fuck, I needed to avoid looking, or I'd start drooling right at the table effectively grossing them all out and stopping this relationship before it started.

"Good, what about things here at the house? Things wouldn't necessarily have to be as… mild," Rhett stammered, shifting in his chair, drawing my attention to him.

Was he? I think he was getting hard thinking about it. *Interesting.* Seemed Rhett might have a hidden exhibitionist streak. Of course, I'd become pecnotized as I thought this, so I didn't hear the question directed at me.

"Sawyer?"

"Hm?"

My apparent stare-off with his pecs hadn't gone unnoticed like I'd hoped. Well shit. My cheeks flamed as I focused on the question. Everyone chuckled around the table, but for once, I didn't mind. It was comforting.

"I'm good." More laughter rang out through the room. "What? My lady bits are a hussy, and if you start kissing on me, I'm not liable for the happy fun times that follow. You've been warned."

"Did she say lady bits?" Oliver whispered.

"Why is that a warning? Sounds more like a challenge, to be honest," Soren taunted.

"There will be more than happy times, Smalls," Henry purred.

Like fuck. When did Henry become so seductive? Damn boy.

I think I was panting as I stared at him, the possibilities running through my head. More laughter rang out, causing me to realize I'd lost focus *again*. Could you blame me, though? Seriously, it wasn't fair.

"Laugh it up fuckers, and I'll go find Bob."

Feeling pleased with myself, I leaned back in my chair, crossing my arms over my chest. Ha! Take that, ridiculously good looking roommates. The laughter abruptly died, causing my smugness to grow.

"Who's Bob?" Elias and Henry asked. Oh, right. They hadn't been here that morning.

"Don't ask," Oliver mumbled to them, only making me grin wider. Good to know I had something to use as a threat.

"Okay, back to the question. Focus everyone; this is important. I don't want things in the relationships we have with one another to be damaged. So, while this is uncomfortable, it's important," Rhett reprimanded us all.

My smile dropped as I realized he was right. He was considerate of everyone's feelings while making sure I knew my consent was important. I wondered if he knew how sexy that made him.

"I already told you all how the kiss I witnessed turned me on. So, it wouldn't upset me to see you kissing the other guys, Sawyer, and I wouldn't be opposed to… uh at times having others join us." His cheeks tinged red from his confession, but it made me hot and bothered too, so I wouldn't call him out for it.

"It doesn't bother me either. I also feel I need to make something else clear if it wasn't already, but Rey and I have feelings for one another and want to date each other and Sawyer. Definitely hope there are some threesome fun times." Soren looked over at Henry when he had mentioned them dating, warming my heart. I loved that they weren't hiding their feelings anymore. "That being said, threesomes outside of us I haven't thought about, so I'd like the option to revisit it later. Figuring out the dynamics between us three will be overwhelming enough for the time being."

He was always so sincere and thinking of others. Soren had the biggest heart under all that goldenness.

"I feel the same as Sor," Henry replied, grabbing Soren's hand under the table, "this is still new for me, and I'm getting my head wrapped around it. I'm honestly still surprised I haven't been more possessive, but I love you guys, and I guess I understand having feelings for two people, so I get it. But, I'd like to revisit the inclusion of more as well."

My face was starting to hurt from smiling, but I felt excited for them, identifying their feelings and making a statement in front of their roommates.

"I don't have a horse in this race, but I hope you continue to give me a chance to be your friend," Elias said honestly.

I felt a tiny bit disappointed at his response and could feel the butterflies pouting. Just great; first, my vagina was giving me grief, and now my imaginary butterflies. My body was revolting against me. Wanting to distract myself, I spoke up before thinking through what I was saying.

"Liberate the nip!" I pumped my arm in the air like a moron as peals of laughter rang out around me. Perfect segue way I guess. "Elias, I uh, just want to say that the morning about the clothing thing, it had been out of line, and I took my frustration with all mankind out on you. So, in the spirit of fun, I do think Sunday's should be free the tittie day. So, no bra for me, no shirts for you guys! What do you think?" My face flamed at my suggestion, but I'd effectively distracted myself from feelings about Elias. They all sat stunned for a moment; then, more laughter rang out.

"It is done!" Soren pronounced as he imitated a judge and made a gavel hitting the table motion.

"And on that note, Mateo, do you have anything to add?" Henry asked, redirecting the conversation back to the topic. Thank you, Henry, for keeping us on track and not chasing all of my weird tangents. At least he was used to The Sawyer Show.

"Um, well. This is embarrassing, but if anyone needs to be privy to this information, it's you guys. Sawyer knows this, but I'm not as experienced. It didn't bother me last night to see Sawyer with you guys, but I don't think I'm confident enough to do more than hold her hand or kiss her in front of you all yet, so that's my line at the moment."

I smiled at Mateo; he'd shared something he felt made him less than others, but he did it and didn't have a panic attack. He beamed back, and I knew he'd grow more confident before long.

Oliver was the last one, and he was sitting next to me. I'd been worrying about what he'd say because things had been weird last night, but he'd seemed okay while making breakfast.

Peeking over, I noticed he looked shy all of a sudden, and it made me feel nervous. Things had started off weird between us, but I couldn't deny the spark. Oliver made me feel accepted and was constantly making me laugh. I knew there was space in my life for him; I only hoped he did as well. He turned, a sheepish expression on his face as he dragged his hand over the back of his head.

"I don't know what to say. Things are… complicated. Can we talk about this on our own Sawyer?" Oliver sounded resigned, and it didn't fill me with butterflies, but dread.

"Of course, Oliver. We can talk later. But I just want to say that each of you are different, meaning each relationship will develop at its own pace. It feels surreal that you guys are interested in me enough to want to date me. I don't expect you to race or try to win me over. That's not the point of having a relationship like this, but more to not feel that we have to compete. I like what we're all creating."

I smiled on the outside, but part of me crumbled inwardly. Since I'd shared my history with Oliver, something had changed. It reminded me that we were all fighting invisible battles. I just hoped I could be the pendulum shift for him, whatever that entailed.

"I'm good with doing what feels natural and not having to police ourselves in the house. If each of you has your own boundary, then I'll go with that. Remembering each other's comfort zone will be helpful, so if I'm in the movie theater with Mateo and someone comes in, they just leave and not say anything if we are sharing a moment. But if I'm in the fitness room with Rhett and someone comes in, check with us and see how we are feeling? Does that make sense? We have to be respectful of each other and not push the line by being open and communicating about it at the same time."

Everyone nodded as I finished, and I felt very mature at that moment. Rhett took up the mantle again, and I wondered what else he could want to ask.

"I guess that just leaves a few more details. These, I guess, are more ground rules than boundaries, so I'll just say them, and we can discuss if we have anything to add." We all nodded, not really knowing where he was going with this.

"Okay, first was protection. What are our thoughts on protection with Sawyer? Sawyer, what are your thoughts?" My cheeks went red real fast. I didn't know why. But the question threw me off. Clearing my throat, I tried to figure out what I wanted to say.

"Well, um, I have the implant, so on that front, I'm covered. I haven't had sex without a condom, and I was tested before I came here with a clear report. Um, I don't know why I'm so uncomfortable with this when it's a vital thing. Hmm… well, I guess I don't want to say not to use condoms because birth control is only 99% effective, but I also don't want to say we always have to. Maybe, it's something I should discuss individually?"

"That's fair, baby, but I might suggest that if we enter the idea of not using them, then we all show our tests. And if it wasn't clear, this relationship is only the people at this table. Meaning, no other girls or guys, nor should there be any hooking up with others outside this table unless discussed as a group. I think that should be the first ground rule, but if we're all committed to one another and have clean records, it would be okay to go without, but it's ultimately a couple's decision. How does that sound?"

Rhett had such a way of sounding possessive and diplomatic all at once, and to think I thought he was a grumpy pants when we met. It was just his intense nature to protect that made him look severe at times, I realized.

"I'm good with that and feel it's important to state, so thank you," I affirmed.

"Okay, last ground rule, if there are any feelings of jealousy or hurt by another member, then we go to them and talk it out. We don't talk to the other people about it first because that only creates division. This is the exclusion of the throuple, you guys may have different rules since you three are in a relationship together, but as a whole, we keep our relationship drama with one another, which brings us to how we present this to the outside world. What do we say? Do we need to say anything?" Rhett had a perplexed look on his face that was annoyingly cute. Pulling my attention back to his words, I thought about how I could reply.

"It will affect me the most, as unfair as that is, because I'm female. I'll be called names by other girls, and I'm sure other guys will think it means I'm easy and open for business. We can't let whatever they say come between us or bother us. I'm going into this fully aware.

The thing is, living the way I have lived, experiencing the things I have experienced, the queen bitches of the world don't scare me or bother me. I've had to hide who I am for the past five years, and it's exhausting. I don't want to live that way anymore. I came here to thrive, and part of that means being authentic in who I am and who I'm dating. If you're uncomfortable, then tell me, and I will be more aware outside of the house, but I can't promise I won't mess up at times because to feel free for once in my life is very empowering, and I don't want to be shackled by deceit anymore."

My breath came out quickly, and I realized how passionately I felt about the topic. It was true. I was tired of hiding who I was.

"I agree with that. I'm not ashamed to be with you and Rey. I want others to know," Soren boasted.

"Same for me. I need to tell my parents, or well, maybe I don't, depending on what their involvement was in your life, but I may tell them before I make it Facebook official, but otherwise, I don't give a fuck what the world thinks. I haven't for the past five years. They already think I'm a rebel, so it fits with my persona." Rey shrugged.

"It may be hard for my family to approve, but I don't want to hide my relationship with you, Sawyer. Being here and meeting all of you has been the best thing for me. I'm not going to hide you or be ashamed. You guys make me feel... normal." Mateo admitted softly, but we all heard him. It made me curious if there was something else he wasn't saying.

"Baby, I told you that you were mine on our first date. I've already claimed you, and I have no plans of stopping." There was that damn gruff voice that made my panties wet. Every. Single. Time.

"Does anyone else have anything to add?"

"Actually, I do." They all looked at me weirdly, not expecting me to say anything else.

"I want to make sure I'm spending time with all of you, so please let me know if I've neglected you. Relationships are important to me, and I want to do them well, so just be honest." Everyone looked happy that I said something and agreed readily.

"Perfect. With that, I'm stealing Henry this afternoon, and then tomorrow evening, I have book club with Soren. I created a shared calendar and will send it to everyone to add things so we can all have time. I want to do a group thing at least once a week too, please."

I smiled like I was begging, and they all just chuckled at me. Embarrassment aside, I felt the conversation was successful, and I felt like a proper adult. Winning.

thirty-eight

. . .

rey

Smalls wouldn't tell me where we were headed, only to pack a bag since we weren't coming back until the morning. Soren could tell I was a bit nervous and told me to enjoy myself as he kissed my cheek and slapped my butt.

Smalls gave me directions as I drove, but I still had no clue where we were going. It was an area I'd never been to before and I realized how much I hadn't ventured outside of campus. Pulling up to a massive treehouse was not what I'd expected. I sat there stunned for a few moments while she bounced in her seat, giddiness exuding out of her as she clapped.

"Isn't it the best?"

I didn't know how to feel. I was overwhelmed she'd found such a perfect place to bring me to. It made me realize I had nothing to worry about because she was still the same Smalls in all the ways that mattered. She'd matured and had more depth to her now because of her life experience, but she was still kind, compassionate, and giving.

"This is incredible. How did you find it?"

"Ace helped me. He mentioned going to one, and I couldn't get it out of my head. I wanted to find something to ground us again, and the treehouse was always our safe place. I felt we needed a bit of that together." Her vulnerability shone through, and it was beautiful. I guessed I wasn't the only one who was nervous about how to act.

"It's perfect, Smalls. I'm mad that I didn't think of it."

"Come on, let's check it out. I had the rental place leave us groceries too, so we should have everything we need."

She started to walk up the stairs, but I grabbed her wrist and pulled her to me. She curled back into my arms, instincts taking over from years of skating together. She looked up, and I devoured her mouth. Putting all my feelings into the kiss, I wanted her to know how much this meant to me and how much I'd missed her. She responded in fervor as I pushed her back against the car door. My hands cascaded all over her body, taking her in. It was as familiar to me as my own in some ways.

When you lifted someone and skated with them for as many hours a day as we had, you got acquainted with that person's form. It had been awkward at first, especially as we hit puberty, but over time it became as natural as breathing.

Now though, I took her body in an all new way, tracking all the ways she'd changed. Her muscles were firmer, her frame solid as she matured into her body, and she had more curves than before. Maybe my favorite developments were that her ass was plumper, her breasts rounder.

Sawyer responded to me in kind as I traveled all over her, mapping out her new form, her hands doing the same to my body. When my hands reached her ass, I squeezed her cheeks and lifted her. Smalls wrapped her legs around me, grinding against my hardness.

Not wanting things to escalate too much out here, I carried her towards the stairs. My brain started to think and I realized it sounded like a hazardous decision. So, I stopped walking and slowed down the kiss.

"Smalls, I want this to continue, but I don't trust myself to carry you up those stairs and not kill us both. If I injure you, then I'm pretty sure Rhett will kill me. So, to avoid that, let's push pause, grab the bags, lock the door, and take that tour."

She laughed at me as I explained this, which helped ease my frustration for having to stop. "You're right. Rhett *would* kill you."

She hopped out of my arms, winked, and walked over to the car as she slapped me on the ass. This girl, she was the girl I fell in love with and yet so much more —Smalls 2.0.

We carried our bags up the stairs and entered the

first level. This treehouse was built around one colossal tree mingled in with a few other trees. It was three stories, with the bottom floor being an open deck area with rocking chairs and a hot tub. The second floor was the living space with a small kitchenette along a wall of windows to the west side. The top floor was the bedroom with a small bathroom. I wasn't sure how they got electricity and running water up here, but I was glad for it.

The bed sat under a sky-light, giving it a view of the night sky. The parts of the tree that were visible throughout the treehouse gave it all a rustic effect. The floors were a light natural oak wood with the same wood paneling on the walls; it was beautiful in a significantly grown-up treehouse way. We set our bags in the bedroom and gazed out the picture window. The view was incredible, with trees all around on one side and the mountains on the other. It was calming and I could stay forever.

"So, do we want to pick up where we were, sort out some food, play a game, talk, test out the hot tub, all of the above?" Smalls asked in a flirtatious voice as she turned to me.

"Definitely all of the above. Let's sort out some food and then maybe take a dip in the hot tub?"

"That sounds perfect."

Lunch was some sandwiches and fruit, light but filling. We sat out on the deck, enjoying nature. When we finished, we changed into swimsuits and headed to the hot tub. I hadn't been in a hot tub in a while, but never with someone I was dating. All the fantasies that ran through my head were making me hard.

Smalls wore a cover-up, so when she took it off, all thoughts left my head. She was wearing a green two-piece where the top straps crossed over her chest in an X shape and then tied around her neck. The bottoms had an extra strap wrapping around her belly in the same pattern and tied in the back. I was sure it was decorative, but it made her look like a present, and I wanted to unwrap her.

She'd hooked up her phone before we came out here, so music played softly in the background. We both stepped into the water, just peering out toward the trees for a while, soaking in the stillness. I didn't think I'd felt this calm in a while, not since the last time I was in a treehouse with her.

"I miss skating with you. This morning when we were dancing, it reminded me how much I loved being a duo. All this time, I thought my grief with skating was because I wouldn't be able to skate professionally, but I think it was because I wouldn't be able to skate with you. When we were on the ice together, I felt so sure of myself, of my place in the world, and like I could do and take on anything."

Her voice was melancholy, so I pulled her over to my lap, needing her to be closer. I needed to touch her, scared she'd evaporate into thin air. Her legs bracketed my thighs, and she put her arms around my neck as she stared down at me.

"That peace was stolen from me that day in so many

ways. R broke my innocence by introducing me to things, and people I wish I didn't know existed in the world. My parents broke my idealism by breaking my trust. I realized they weren't as perfect as I'd always viewed them. I thought my dad could conquer anything, but I saw their humanity, weaknesses, and fallibility that day. I understand why they didn't tell me, and I'm glad they didn't, but that childhood view of the world was stolen from me. The world became unsure and frightening. I witnessed horrible acts of violence and began to see danger in everything. It kept me safe, but it also made me void of emotions and connections. It broke my spirit. But the worst was losing you and Fin. It broke my heart."

Tears streamed down her face and mine, and I tried to give her the strength she needed. I never thought about what she must've been going through. I only thought about how I missed her and how it affected me. Fuck. I'd been so selfish. I'd been punishing myself for something I had no control over, while this beautiful girl had been trying to survive, and had to do it all alone.

"When I first came here and started to meet people, I felt myself coming back to life, the pieces clicking into place. I felt my heart start to heal. I was trusting people and being vulnerable. I could dream of a future. I didn't realize until I found you and Fin again how much I needed you. There's something I've regretted for the past five years."

"What?" I asked, smoothing her hair back.

"It was not telling you how I felt. Five years have passed, but I still feel it as strongly as I did then, and I know it will only grow from here." She paused, tears shining in her eyes as she smiled at me. "Henry Alexander Reyes, I love you so much, and I don't want to go another day without you knowing that. Loving you was one of the only things that kept me from giving into the darkness."

Needing to kiss her at that moment, I didn't wait to hear if she had more to say because she'd said the only thing that mattered to me. *Smalls loved me*. Kissing her deeply, I held her head in my hands, capturing her lips. After a few minutes when we needed air, I pulled back, gazing into her eyes.

"Sawyer, 'I don't know middle name' Sullivan, my Smalls. I love you so hard. Losing you destroyed me in a way I didn't know was possible. I hated everyone and pushed them away because I felt empty without your presence. You added so much life to my days, that I ached when you weren't there. I hate how selfish I've been these years. How angry I've felt when you were fearing for your life. I am so sorry, Smalls."

I was crying now in sadness and relief. I hated how I'd wasted the past few years because I was angry, not honoring the sacrifice she'd made.

"Rey, you're allowed to feel how you feel. It happened to you just as much as it happened to me. It affected us all differently, but it doesn't dismiss our own experience. I don't want you to feel bad. I don't need your apologies. You have nothing to apologize for. We were both kids, figuring out the world, there wasn't much we could've done differently, and I know you were doing everything you could do." She wiped my tears, offering me comfort.

"Don't you see? Being here now with everyone, that's where I'm meant to be. We're a unit. We all need each other, and I'm glad that I'm here, as hard as it has been on my own. I love the man you are and the man you'll be and that I get to experience it all."

How was she able to say the right thing? She didn't make me feel wrong for my feelings but validated them.

"God, I love you," I said.

"And I love you."

Our kissing became frantic as our bodies urged us to physically demonstrate our emotional connection. Her hand slid over my chest and shoulders, gripping for purchase. I was doing the same to her as I roamed her body. Breaking away to take a breather, I started kissing down her neck as she rocked into me. Our swimsuits were not much of a barrier between us, and I could practically feel her already on me. I slipped my hands under her top and tried to figure out how to unhook it —breaking away from her to focus more on this bizarre contraption. There seemed to be both a hook and a bow that were causing me problems.

"Smalls, this suit is hot on you, but how the hell do you get it off?" I laughed, causing her to join me.

She quickly unhooked the straps, and they fell forward, giving me a peek. When she unhooked the main part, I was stunned speechless. Maybe it was because I'd thought about what Smalls would look like naked for such a long time, or perhaps because she was the perfect woman for me in every way, but looking at her breasts was like seeing a double rainbow.

Somehow, I got distracted away from her breasts when she began to suck on my neck, biting my earlobe. The bonus was it brought her closer to me, allowing me to suck on her nipples. My tongue swirled around the peak as my hands grabbed onto her hips, pushing her down onto me more. Needing to touch her, I slipped my hand into her bottoms and found her wet for me. Her moans set my skin on fire as she rocked, chasing my finger.

Her hands traveled down to my cock, and she managed to release me out of my swim trunks as she started to move her hand up and down my length. Teenage me stopped for a moment to watch her hand, feeling all of my fantasies come to life at that moment. It was more erotic than I'd ever imagined.

"Henry, oh my God, I need you. I need you so much right now. I trust you if you say that we don't need a condom. I don't want to stop or get out."

My brain wasn't processing what she was saying at first. When it finally caught up, I looked up and saw the desire heavy in her eyes and wondered if it was reflected in my own as well. I nodded my head yes so fast I probably resembled a bobblehead.

"I've always used one, and I had my physical at the beginning of the week and got the report back I was clean."

As I finished my words, she lifted off my lap and lowered herself back down in one go. We let out groans as she sank onto me. I wasn't sure if it was the water, going bare, Smalls, or all three together, but it was the best feeling in the world.

She used my chest to brace herself as she started to move up and down on me. My hands gripped her hips as she undulated. Water sloshed everywhere, but neither of us cared. I could feel her twitch and slide over me, and it was divine. Her nails dug into my shoulders, and I knew she must be close. I moved a hand to her nipple and rolled it between my fingers, pinching it until I was sure it stung. With my other hand, I moved lower and rubbed her clit through the part of her bikini bottoms she had on, using the material to provide some friction. She started to move more erratically as she tightened around me, and I had to hold myself back from coming as she orgasmed.

When I felt her settle, I stood as water fell over us. Sawyer wrapped her legs around me, and I placed her on the edge of the hot tub to gain more leverage, with the water no longer slowing our movements. She braced her hands behind her, and it pushed her breasts upward as I began to move in her at a quicker and rougher pace. She felt amazing against me, and when our eyes connected, I saw the love pouring out of them. It sent me crashing as my orgasm took over.

We stayed connected for a few moments, both catching our breath. As she readjusted herself, I slowly pulled out of her, already missing the feeling of her. I noticed how bright her eyes were, and I felt the last of the darkness that had clung to us both dissipate around us.

sawyer

We spent the rest of the night cuddling and laughing. Tracing the outline of the compass tattoo as I laid on his chest, I remembered that there had been a third one I hadn't been able to make out that day in the hallway. Sitting up, I examined his chest, looking for the smaller tattoo.

You almost didn't notice it because his compass and tree tattoo were bigger and more detailed. But it was there, directly over his heart. It was a small ice skate and etched on the blade was Smalls. Sucking in a breath, I glanced back up at him. Henry had been watching me as I'd searched his chest, so when I peered into his eyes amusement and love blasted back at me. A small tear fell, and he wiped it away gently, smiling softly at me.

"I wanted you with me, always."

If you think I didn't jump the man after that, well you haven't been paying attention.

After our lovefest, we dressed and went outside to take in our surroundings. Sitting on the deck, we caught up on what had been going on in our lives the past five years as Henry made s'mores. As he readied the marsh-mallow, it seemed he'd finally gotten the nerve to ask me about my time in foster care. I'd been dreading it, but knew he would want to know. Preparing myself to share parts of the past I wished were forgotten, I opened myself up and dropped the last wall between us.

"There were some homes that were better than others. I had a good home for about six months, and I got to go to therapy. But then their son was home for winter break, and he tried to touch me when I was asleep. I woke up before anything happened, but my therapist had to report it when I told her. The family didn't want to believe their son would do that, so I was removed. A couple of lecherous fathers would get too close or say things, but I survived it overall. It was more the constant state of being on guard, feeling like a burden, and being separate from everyone else. I missed belonging. I was too nervous and withdrawn to make friends, and I didn't trust any adults. It was mostly just lonely and grieving, but I had to pretend that I wasn't because I wasn't supposed to have my memory. When I met Charlie, things changed."

"That's who you were with before you came here, right?"

"Yeah, he became like a surrogate grandfather for me. He lost his wife, and they didn't have any kids. He owned the ice rink, and I met him when I was applying for a job. I bugged him until he caved. He started noticing me always being there, eating there, and wearing the same clothes. I was embarrassed that it was that obvious, but he told me he had a proposition for me. At first, I thought I'd lose my job because this old man would ask me for sex, and I was going to have to leave. He saw the look of horror on my face and roared with laughter. He told me 'No offense, little girl, but you're not really in my age bracket, and I don't find shrimp attractive'."

I did my best Charlie impression, causing us both to laugh as I told the story. For the first time in a while, the smile on my face didn't feel forced, but genuine.

"He told me that he had a house that was too big for just him, and I would be doing him a favor if I came and kept him company. He needed more help around the rink, and if I was willing to teach some beginner classes, I could stay with him even after I turned eighteen. I was seventeen at the time, so it was appealing. I'd been trying to save as much as possible for the inevitable cut off, but was nervous how I'd survive for long. We did it on a trial basis, but we both knew it was so that I could get some power back. We established a routine quickly, traded making dinners, kept one another company, and helped fill the loneliness. It was the first time I felt safe and that I could trust an adult. But also, that there were good people out there. Charlie saved my life in a lot of ways."

I needed to make sure I checked in with him more. He was alone now, and I didn't want him feeling that way. He was my family.

After stuffing myself with marshmallows and

chocolate, we headed to the top floor. We laid on the bed staring up through the skylight and watched the stars. It was so peaceful, and the view was comforting. Out here, without the light pollution, we could make out so many stars. It was incredible.

The evening had been just what we both needed. An opportunity to reconnect, establish us again with one another, and have the space to focus on only each other. Henry and I had been such a significant part of one another's life, that losing each other had substantially more consequences than either of us could have ever predicted. Coming here brought us back to a place of security and safety. Getting to tell him how I felt had finally lifted one of my biggest regrets, and I felt freer.

Each day I was shedding the darkness and lies, and I was starting to shine as brightly as I had before.

That night, we made love and explored each other more fully without the frenzied desire we felt earlier. Being with Henry was everything I always hoped it would be and so much more. I had a feeling I was going to need the strength these relationships were filling me with in the months ahead.

I'd vaguely mentioned to the guys about feeling someone watching me, but I hadn't shared that it had happened twice here in town. It was time to start finding answers before there was nothing to be found.

thirty-nine

. . .

soren

My excitement was bubbling over, so I decided to make lunch to use some of my energy. I was looking forward to book club and finally spending time with Sawyer one-on-one. Now, I just had to make it until it was time.

Humming to myself, I decided to make enchiladas. Oliver joined me in the kitchen as I was cutting the chicken.

"Hey, man. What's up?"

"Oh, um, would it be okay if I baked?"

"Knock yourself out."

He didn't say much else as he pulled out ingredients, and I realized I was worried about him. He'd shut down on Friday night and fallen back into his cocky guy persona after Sawyer had shared her story. It seemed odd, and I wasn't sure what was going on with him, but I hoped he'd feel comfortable enough to talk to me if he needed to.

At least he was baking. He was such a different person when he baked, and I enjoyed seeing that version of him. Oliver started singing along to the music as he stirred his ingredients. Pulling out my phone to record him, I sent it to Sawyer and Henry. I had managed to keep myself from texting them all night to give them time, but figured now would be acceptable.

ME: Hey BAE. Tell sugar tits I say hi as well. Check out Ollie. *video*

ME: How did it go last night?

ReyBae: Those are horrible. Try harder. LOL. It went well. We talked and shared. I told her I loved her. I still feel like I'm dreaming, but I don't want to wake up if I am.

ME: Wow, breaking out the I love you twice in a week. I'm so proud, man. I just want to squish your cheeks. You decide which ones.

ReyBae: HAHA. Jackass. Good thing I love you too. And… I think I could get behind that. Pun intended.

ME: My charm is part of what makes me so loveable. Admit it. And I like flirty Rey.

ReyBae: I'm pretty sure it is your hot body. Oh, wait, that's what makes you fuckable.

ME: Fuck. You're going to make me hard if you keep flirting with me. Besides, you're the lickable

one. I can't wait to lick you both. See you
soon, boo.

ReyBae: You're ridiculous but looking forward to
seeing you and kissing you. Missed you, babe.
Sawyer says, nice try, but sugar tits doesn't cut it,
boo bear. Her words. And she agrees that I'm
lickable, but so are you. You'll have to wait and
find out the rest.

Laughing at their flirty conversation, it felt good to
hear that he missed me. A small part of me had worried
he'd realize he didn't need me now he had Sawyer, and
sail off into the sunset without me. I hated that I'd felt
insecure, but it was validating to know he was in this
with me just as much as I was.

His confidence and his attitude about everything
was sexy, and I loved how he was embracing his sexuality. He didn't care what others thought, and I knew
firsthand it felt amazing. I was proud of him for
opening himself up more and more.

The timer beeping broke me out of my reverie and I
found Oliver still dancing and singing as he baked,
making me chuckle. He just smiled, winked, and kept
going.

"You doing okay, man?" I asked Oliver. He tensed at
the question, his back going ramrod straight.

"Yeah, man, everything's perfect," Oliver said, but it
fell flat.

"Well, you know I'm here if anything ever isn't
perfect, right?"

I didn't want to push him, but I needed him to know he could come to me. He nodded and his smile seemed sincere. I had to accept it for now. We both went back to cooking and dancing around the kitchen. Sometimes you just had to be the friend who accepted you and gave you space. I could be that for Oliver.

Sawyer and Rey returned as I finished setting the table. The four of us sat down and enjoyed the meal together. The other guys were busy, so it was quiet for once, but enjoyable. Rey and Oliver headed off after we cleaned up, leaving Sawyer and me to have our time together.

"So fun size, your room or mine?" I waggled my eyebrows, causing her to laugh.

"Let's go to mine, honey bun."

Laughing, we headed to her room. When we walked in, she pulled blankets out and placed them on the ground with some pillows, making it a comfy spot. Before I could close the door, a white furball dashed into the room and pounced on her. Sawyer giggled as she played with Lucky, who gave her kisses all over her face. I sat down next to her, close enough our legs and arms touched. I was still figuring out my boundaries with her and didn't want to mess up, but I needed to be close.

"Did you finish the book?"

"Yes! It was so good. I'm so glad you picked it. I love Aria and her kick-butt nature. I need to channel her in my own life, I think. I do find it funny that you picked a reverse harem book and told me it might help me figure out things. Were you trying to give me a hint there, Casanova?" She narrowed her eyes, teasingly.

I loved the way she played with me. Her enthusiasm and energy were uplifting and positive, and I craved being around her. I didn't think she even realized she pulled us guys in so effortlessly.

"I have no idea what you mean there, snuggle butt. I just happen to be a fan of that genre. No love triangles." I was the mask of innocence as I stared at her. She looked at me quizzically but decided to let it slide.

"Who was your favorite character, and why?" I asked her.

"Well, there are a lot of great characters in the book. Her mates are sweet and protective but let her do her thing. Madame Nines was the type of grandmother figure you want to have in your life. Caleb was support-ive, and I kind of felt like he liked her a bit, not sure how that will play out. But I think I loved the Elites the most, Britt especially. That ending, though…"

We talked about the book for about an hour, and it was one of the most fun conversations I'd ever had. We discussed themes, things we'd liked, things we wished could be different, or how we would have acted in Aria's situation. It gave me a good representation of who Sawyer was and how she viewed things.

You could tell a lot about a person based on what they read, what they clicked with, and how engaged they were. Books were a way to escape and do the things we couldn't do in our own lives. It was exciting to find someone as passionate about books as me.

Deciding to open up, I wanted to share my history with my mom and past. She had shared hers, making it unfair with how much we all knew about her, but she was still learning about us. Snuggling with her in my arms, I told her my tale.

"I didn't have the best childhood growing up either. My mom was not your typical mom figure. She was always owing someone something and wasn't responsible enough to keep a job or a functional relationship. She would jump from guy to guy, hoping it would be the one to save her and give her everything she needed. Mostly she wanted someone to worship her and provide for her, so she didn't have to do anything, but she could never manipulate anyone for that long. So, she would have to sell our stuff and even her body at times if it got her what she wanted. I was six when she realized she could also sell… me." I cleared my throat as I prepared to share a part of my life I hated.

"At first, it was just doing modeling and commercials. She became a tyrant, though, and constantly focused on my "career" as if a model was what I wanted to be at that age. This went on for a couple of years. I hated it, but she manipulated me into believing that it was the only way for us to have a home, food, etc. She told me she was saving my money for me, and I would get it when I was older. I didn't know until later how much of a liar she was and that she was spending all my money to support her drug, gambling, you name it habit."

Sawyer grabbed my hand and interlocked her

fingers with mine. She squeezed them and let me know she was there.

"I was on a shoot for a ski resort, and some of the other models were going skiing. I tagged along because Pamela was not known for her parenting skills. She was usually off drinking, getting high, or sleeping with someone. I was about ten, I think, at the time. One of the older models had a brother a few years older than me, and he helped me get the right gear and showed me how to board. It was an eye-opening experience. I wanted to do more of it. At first, Pamela didn't want to hear about it and didn't want me to quit modeling because it gave her the life she wanted. Then she overheard someone say how much of a natural I was and how I was primed to go to the Olympics. She saw dollar signs then. Suddenly, I wasn't modeling, but boarding."

I squeezed her hand, taking a breath.

"It didn't matter to me, though, because I loved it so much more than modeling. I made a team, and I started to get faster, better, and braver. With more practice, my confidence bloomed, and I made flips and tricks that people twice my age couldn't do. When I was fourteen, we traveled with the club. There was… one night, I was taken to a room, drugged, and then returned a few days later. I don't remember all of what happened because I was so out of it, but the things I do recall are… horrible." My voice started to crack as I recalled the men and women's voices in that room and the things they were saying, though most of it had been in a foreign language.

"Pamela didn't even know I'd been missing—mother of the year there. I didn't say much about it because I just wanted to forget it and thought if I ignored it, then I could pretend it didn't happen. Boarding wasn't as fun after that though. I used it for a while to block out things, but the pressures continued to increase to be the best. When I was sixteen… it happened again. Someone drugged me and took me to a hotel room, but I was more aware this time. I fought against them and remembered their faces. When I threatened to tell my mom or an adult, my captors threatened to kill my mom. I didn't like my mom on most days, but I didn't want her to die. They said they'd hunt me down and ruin my hopes at a career in snowboarding. So, I stayed quiet." I braced myself to continue.

"It wasn't until I was eighteen and on my first Olympic team, I discovered more about what my mom was doing behind the scenes as my manager. She was getting endorsement deals and making bets on the side. She was taking my money and gambling it in high stakes. At first she was doing well, but eventually, she began to lose. Big time. I won a gold medal that year, but it was worthless. It didn't matter anymore. Everything that I was, I hated." A tear escaped my eye and Sawyer wiped it away from my face gently.

"I spent two more years being destructive by drinking, partying, and sleeping around with people. I tried to cope, but nothing made it go away. Things with my mom just got worse. When I turned twenty, I was at the point where I didn't even want to live anymore. Fortunately, a friend recognized my despair and checked me into an inpatient facility. I stayed for twenty-one days, and it was both the hardest and best thing for me. Needing to heal from my past wounds, I connected that my mother was toxic and not capable of loving me, that my worth was not measured in my looks, my skills, or my success. I continued therapy for a year and was finally able to look at myself in the mirror and not hate who I was. Happiness and joy returned to my life, and I sought it out in everything. Deciding I needed to quit competing was a big step for me. Realizing that I didn't want or need it was freeing. I'd only ever wanted to board. I didn't care about being the best."

She smiled at me, giving me the courage I'd needed.

"I got linked up with this job three years ago. They were excited to have the great Soren Stryker on their team, but I was just glad to be able to do what I love in a healthy environment. I'm twenty-four now and the joy of molding kids to think differently about sports brings me more happiness than my gold medal ever did. Teaching kids they have options and not letting themselves become consumed by something fleeting is everything. This job has brought me best friends, and it brought you and Rey to my life."

I stroked her face, pushing her hair back. Her skin was so smooth, her hair so soft. Sawyer peered at me, listening, allowing me space. Nowhere on her face did I see judgment or disgust.

"I don't like the things that happened to me, and I

wished they hadn't, but I do like the man I am today, and if I had to go on that journey to be this person, then I can accept that. I hope I can be the difference in a young person's life to show them a different way, that sports aren't going to make them truly happy until they're first happy with who they are."

She kissed my cheek, holding my face.

"Thank you, Soren, for choosing me as someone worthy of sharing with. I hate the life you had to lead, but I'm glad you're here. I think the person you are is amazing. From the moment I met you, you made me feel at ease. You calmed my spirit. You accepted me and made it your mission to make me laugh. I haven't laughed this much in a long time. I love what you do for Henry, too. I see how you look at him and how much you love him, and it makes me happy that he had you in his life, especially when I wasn't. Thank you for loving him and helping him be the person he is. You're a beautiful person inside and out, Sor."

I think Sawyer kept talking, but I kind of tuned her out because I was too focused on her. Her smile, her laughter, the way the light hit her hair. I couldn't stand it any longer, and I went in for the kiss. At least this one went better than Rey's.

She responded back immediately as I devoured her mouth. Hands started to roam on both sides, and it felt incredible to be touching her and be touched by her. I pushed her down onto her back and deepened the kiss. Her legs parted for me, and I fell between them as I continued to kiss her.

Starting to get distracted by all the sensations, I focused on her hands as they roamed over me. But the feel of her breasts pressing against me and the way her core hit me perfectly kept drawing my attention back. The roll of her hips had me gasping as I stopped kissing her to get some air. Sucking down my neck, she licked the outline of my collarbone. I never knew that could be so erotic, but damn, it was turning me on.

Rocking into her this time, I caused her to moan into my shoulder. She tugged at my shirt, and together we managed to get it off. Her eyes roamed over my skin, her desire clear. I puffed up a little at her appreciation.

She traced my muscles with her fingers and began to trail down them with kisses. I started to move my hands to unbutton her shirt, but I was met with another shirt when I got it undone. Why did girls wear three shirts? Seriously, it was like their own defense system. Shirt after shirt after shirt to make it harder for guys. I must've groaned in frustration when I wasn't met with what I sought immediately.

Laughing at me, she sat up and pulled one shirt off her shoulders and the other one over her head. So complicated. But then I was granted my treasure. Her breasts sat perfectly in bra cups, winking at me with their seductiveness. Needing to know how far we wanted to take this, I broke my eyes away from her hypnotizing mounds and stared into her eyes.

"Sweet pea, I hope you know I want you so bad, and I am in this with you 100%. But I need to know how far.

I don't want to cross any lines." Her smile was breath-taking, and I almost didn't catch her answer.

"I kind of like that one." She blushed. Seeing this confident girl also be shy was fucking adorable. "I'm in it 100% too, dreamboat. I don't want to put limits on us; how about we go with what feels right."

"I think that sounds like a brilliant plan, sweet pea."

Her smile sealed the deal, and I locked that one away. I started to wonder if I'd beaten Oliver when my brain shut off because she'd just removed her bra and… boobs. Boobnotized. Boobnoozled.

sawyer

Soren's story was heartbreaking, in a way, but also beautiful and filled with hope. He'd found his way out, and he was one of the best people I knew.

The way he was staring at my chest made me blush. Taking his distraction as a win, I pounced. I took him by surprise and landed on top of him, straddling his chest, laughing as I peered down at him.

"Hello."

I loved that we were always laughing. Even in inti-mate moments, we still had fun, making it even more intimate. I lifted off him so I could discard my pants and panties. So far, I hadn't lost any panties to any underwear-ripping men, and I wanted to keep it that way. I shimmied out of them and tossed them. They landed on Lucky, and I realized he was still in my room. Not sure how I felt about Lucky being a voyeur, I decided to let him out.

"One second," I said as I scooped up the little dude and held him in my outstretched arms. I didn't want his paws anywhere near my naked flesh. Ouch.

I opened the door as I ducked behind it and let him out. He didn't look happy and even huffed at me for good measure, but he eventually trotted back towards Elias' room. Sorry dude, but a girl's got needs.

I headed back to Soren and expected him to be naked, but instead, he was lounging with his hands behind his head, as if he didn't have a care in the world.

"Figured you would have had your pants off. Those things can't be too comfortable."

I gestured toward the outline of his penis in his pants. He shrugged. He fucking shrugged like it was no biggie.

Fine, I could play this game.

I kneeled down and slowly released his zipper. His smirk made me think I might have played into his hand. Oh well, I still got to look at his abs and that delicious V thing he had going on. Snowboarding did him good. I was almost too distracted by his abs that I missed his cock springing from his pants.

"Wait, what? I'm confused. Why am I confused?" I mumbled. Oh yeah. Soren wasn't fucking wearing any boxers. He went commando. Why was that so hot? To top it off, his dick was fucking pierced.

Damn. I was drooling. Pretty sure I was drooling all over it. I licked my lips, and his smirk grew wider as I stared, hypnotized by his beautiful cock. Seriously, it was gorgeous.

Deciding that I needed to see the whole thing, I yanked the rest of his pants off. I wanted to touch it, but I was afraid now that I had stared at it for too long. I needed to regain some balance here. I straddled above his snake charmer of a penis and leaned down to Soren. My tits were in his eyesight now, and I felt more relaxed.

I kissed him, and he came alive. His hands were roaming my body, my ass, and he pulled me into him. His kisses became deeper and passionate as he took my mouth. He dragged me against his hardened length, rubbing the piercing over my clit. It felt so good. He broke away from the kiss, and I whimpered at the loss of his lips.

"Sawyer, sweet pea, I need to taste you. I want to feel you on my tongue. Please, sit on my face."

I stared at him for a minute, sure I'd heard him wrong. He wanted me to sit on his face, but why… then I got it.

Seriously, I shouldn't be that slow, but I'd never had a guy ask me to do that before, or give me oral sex, so it was kind of a new thing for me. He began to get nervous with my delay, so I moved quickly and braced my knees on the side of his face.

"Like this?" I asked nervously.

"Lower, you won't hurt me." I trusted him and

lowered more until I felt my pussy come into contact with his hot tongue. Fuck. That felt amazing. I needed to get in on this more. Holy Hell.

His tongue swirled around, going in and out so that I couldn't even concentrate on what he was doing. I started to massage my breasts as I rocked on his face. His hands gripped my ass hard, and he moved with me forward in motion. A loud moan left me as my door opened. I opened my eyes, not even caring at that moment that I was in the throes of passion, just hoping it wasn't somebody I didn't want it to be, like Ace or Fin. Fortunately, it was Henry.

He stood stock-still, not sure what to do at first, stunned at what he'd walked into. I smiled at him, nodding my head for him to enter. He shut the door, locking it this time. Yeah, I should probably remember to do that, though I didn't hate this interruption.

Henry walked over with confidence as he took us in. Soren didn't appear to know Henry was here yet, as he still went to town on me and I'd never felt that Lizzo lyric more at this moment, "I'm not a snack but a whole damn meal."

Soren apparently felt that way as he continued to eat me out. Henry stopped in front of me, kneeling to kiss me. He took over my breasts for me and began to tweak them the way I liked. I helped him out of his shirt as I ran my hands over his chest. He whispered in my ear as he started to lick my neck.

"I want to surprise Soren; I don't think he knows I'm here. Are you sure you're okay with us being together and doing things in front of you?" He pulled my face up to watch my face and eyes.

"So much. I think your love is hot. Please join us."

He kissed me once more on the lips as he got up and moved around to the other side of me, closer to Soren's dick. He took off his pants and joined us in our nudity. I was trying to twist my head, so I could see what he would do while enjoying what Soren was doing to me.

An orgasm started to build just as Henry took Soren's cock into his mouth. Soren sputtered for a second, surprised by the move, no doubt. I didn't want to lose my momentum, though, so I rocked on his face to encourage him to keep going. He gripped my ass tighter as he pulled me down harder.

If I thought he was going to town before, now that he realized Henry had to be with us, since I was obviously not the one sucking his dick, Sor showed me just how much he was enjoying his meal.

It took no time for my orgasm to return, and I was tightening around him and trying not to squeeze his head with my legs. When I finally came down, I lifted to see Soren beaming at me as he licked his lips, his face covered in my juices. I wanted to be embarrassed by how wet they were, but his movement only made me feel sexy.

"Fucking delicious," he rasped at me, then moaned as Henry went deeper on his dick.

"Fuck, I think I'm in heaven. Am I? Did I die from Sawyer's cream? If so, it was worth it." See, laughing.

This guy was always making me laugh, and I loved it. Henry popped his head up and smiled at Soren, too.

"No man, this is our reality now."

Soren pulled Henry up by his neck and kissed him, and I shivered at it. Fuck, that was hot. I'd imagined it, but seeing it, seeing them both naked with their dicks rubbing against one another, was fucking erotic. Henry leaned back and pulled me in as well, kissing me. It became a blur after that of who was kissing who, whose hands were on who, as it all just felt incredible. I ended up straddling Soren, who grabbed a condom from his pants pocket. After he rolled it on, I sank down on him.

Henry kneeled by Soren's head, and Soren took Henry's cock into his mouth as I started to move. I could reach Henry as well, so I kissed him since Soren's mouth was occupied with his dick. Soren put his hand on my clit, and before long, I was orgasming again.

A few minutes later, Henry was as well down Soren's throat. Soren sat up once Henry pulled out of his mouth. He grabbed my ass and began to fuck me faster, thrusting up into me. Soren wrapped his arms tight around me, pulling me to his chest. He took my mouth in a passionate kiss, and I didn't even mind that he'd just had Henry's cum in his; in fact, it turned me on.

Soren continued to thrust into me at a fast pace while kissing down my neck, licking the curve of my collarbone. He moved to my shoulder, where he sank his teeth into me as he thrust up, coming. There were so many sensations all at once that I came again.

Three times. Fucking unbelievable. I sagged against him as we both came down from that orgasm.

Henry was there with some towels and washcloths that we used to clean up before we all stumbled to the bed. We curled up around one another and slept peacefully.

Best book club ever.

forty

. . .

sawyer

THE WEEK MOVED QUICKLY AS WE SETTLED INTO A ROUTINE. My relationships seemed to be doing well, and I managed to spend time with everyone. Oliver was still hiding something, and it had begun to affect our relationship. I didn't want to push him, but if he didn't open up, it would affect our progress even as friends, since there was a significant roadblock preventing us from getting closer. It seemed I wasn't the only one feeling it either, as some of the other relationships he had in the house seemed strained, too. And Elias and I still tiptoed around one another, afraid to wake either of our tempers.

On Monday, I learned that the challenge with Queen Bitch would take place this Friday. We were to prepare a short program length-wise but could add whatever jumps and moves we wanted. Typically for competition, there were requirements for each program, but the committee gave us the freedom to pick our best moves at a two-minute and forty-second length. Scoring would be based on the level of difficulty using Olympic scoring.

I wasn't nervous because I knew I was a better skater than her, but I didn't know if I should beat her. My life would no doubt become more difficult if I did, and I didn't know if it was really worth it to win. I was still debating it during my last skating class on Thursday when shit hit the fan. Oh, how I wished that was just figuratively.

The Junior level girls in grade ten were working on upright spins and were practicing the scratch spin. Another instructor was on the far side of the ice, working students on single jumps. In total, there were five students and three staff, as a medical intern was also present.

At first, I thought the smell was just some old equipment. The downside to being the lower level skaters meant we had to use the oldest rink. It was small, cluttered with a lot of old equipment, and not as updated. There were big fans placed around the rink to help circulate the air because the temperature gauge only went to one level, so they helped keep the air moving and the ice frozen. But all the old equipment had a rather musty smell that seemed to always linger.

But as the class went by, the smell got stronger until it was obvious it was in fact... well, shit. Everyone had stopped skating, looking around, wondering if someone pooped their pants or farted on the ice. Skaters weren't modest about their bodies or bodily expressions. It could be gross, but it was just the way it was when you spent so much time together. You couldn't hide the fact you had natural bodily functions, so everyone embraced it—no need to feel embarrassed if you had to take a poop because we all did.

We all looked at one another and no one owned up to it, which was odd. By the time we realized something was fishy, the first splat hit the ice. We all stood in shock until it started to hit the ice faster, and then it hit a student.

That was when the screams began, and everyone rushed to make it off the ice while not being hit with flying poopsicles. The smell was overwhelming, and I tried to help the girls off the ice, cover my nose, and dodge the counter strike. I got hit a couple of times, fortunately only on my clothes and not my face. A few people started vomiting, and it was a literal shit show.

Vomit and poop covered the ice, and I stood there gaping, stunned at what was happening. I couldn't fathom it. Who? Why? This was so childish. The other instructor had been able to make it off the ice and call someone; and when the fans finally got turned off by maintenance, we all sighed in relief. The director made his way into the building, handing towels to us. I looked around at the girls, still trying to figure out how this had happened. We were stunned, silent, not sure how to interpret the last fifteen minutes. If we hadn't been standing with shit on us, I would've believed it had been a nightmare. This kind of thing didn't happen.

The director apologized to us all and ensured we would have extra ice time on one of the other rinks while this was cleaned up and investigated. They would have to redo the whole ice floor and clean all the fans since it was a biohazard. We were instructed to shower and destroy our clothes as well, letting the school know so they could replace them.

I felt sorry for whoever had to clean up this mess.

When I opened my locker, a note fell out. My face screwed up, not knowing what it could be. Opening it, my mouth fell open.

Motherfucking ice-cunt prima donna bitch. It was time to have a cuntversation with her. Nobody flung shit at me and got away with it. She'd just awoken the bear.

Game. Motherfucking. On. Bitch.

You skate for shit, so now you can smell like it. You will NEVER beat me, skank.

When I told a few of the guys that night what Queen Bitch had done at practice, they'd been livid. Henry offered to run through my program with me after dinner. So, we spent a few hours tweaking things. It had felt easy falling back into skating with him. He'd improved with his choreography. I was impressed. If I hadn't already wanted to jump his bones, watching him create magic like he'd done definitely sent me there. In fact, if I hadn't been determined to shove QB's face in my victory, I would've jumped him on the ice. But instead, he gave me some useful tips on things to change in my routine, making me feel prepared to kick some ass.

Classes weren't in sessions on Fridays due to challenges, and they had to reschedule some since we were down a rink. It also happened to be the first staff challenge for ice skating, so it had turned into a big deal. The school wanted to take advantage of it to foster the concept of challenging and encourage students to push themselves.

Honestly, I was surprised the school was being so open about the challenge since it included QB, but I figured they assumed she'd win, so there was no harm. I was about to shove that notion down their throat. Jackasses.

Henry had explained how the judges were selected, so I was pleased they were outsiders with no affiliation to the school and would vote without bias. The school had underestimated me; everyone always did, and it was time to show them.

QB opted to go first and smiled smugly at me as she took to the ice. I didn't know what she was so smug about. I was about to wipe her with the shit she'd put on the ice. Her program was very robotic, and while technically challenging, she lacked passion, grace, and power. Her most challenging jump was a double flip jump, and I wasn't sure if that was because she was that confident or if it was all she could do. Surely, she was more advanced if she was teaching at the elite level? Hadn't she competed last year? Where was the lutz or axel? Could she not even do a single axel?

It was my turn to take the ice, and as my song started to play, I tuned out the world. I'd chosen "Elastic Heart" by Sia. It was meaningful to me and a great performance song. I started slow with a few small jumps and moves, but as the music built, so did I.

Double toe loop

Double flip jump

Double Lutz

Landing them was such a rush that it boosted me to keep building. I was feeling cocky, and that was my mistake.

Never deviate from your program. Basic 101 skating.

But I let my arrogance get the best of me and decided to throw my double axel to show off and shove it in her face. I hadn't practiced it but was running on a adrenaline high and assumed I would be fine.

I wasn't.

I mistimed the jump, didn't complete my rotation, and landed on my ass. Feeling stupid and mad at myself, I got up, wanting to show my students the importance of continuing even when you fell. I finished my program still confident in my performance but angry at myself for letting QB get in my head and do something reckless. I could have hurt myself more than just a bruised bum. I could have re-injured my leg and lost skating for good. I needed to get a hold of this anger and not let her get to me. I had more important things to concentrate on now.

I waited by myself, ashamed of my actions in the kiss and cry area, while the judges spoke and added their scores. My program start point was higher than hers, so it depended on how much they deducted for my fall, the incomplete rotation, and deviation.

Her scores came across first. 72.05.

Damn. They scored her higher than I'd expected. Holding my breath, I closed my eyes and did some deep breathing, not wanting to see the scores until they were up. The shock that rang out through the rink didn't tell me which way it went. I peeked open my eyes and almost didn't believe it.

73.05. I'd beaten her by one point.

The shriek of outrage she let out confirmed it as well. Holy shit, balls. Yeah, I went there. Hey, if you got covered in shit, you might as well own it.

The director came over and congratulated me, telling me what it would mean starting next week. It hit me then that I'd be losing my students. A pit developed in my stomach, and I knew what I needed to do. Cutting him off, I interrupted him.

"Sir, as happy as I am to prove I'm the better skater, I have to decline the position. It would be unfair to my students that I've already started to work and build a rapport with. I came here to teach, not to advance myself; I would only be hurting them by accepting."

He paused, regarding me, before he nodded. "I understand Ms. Sullivan, and I appreciate your commitment to your position. I wonder if maybe I might persuade you with something different then? We want the students to see your challenge as a positive pursuit and that hard work gets rewarded. There is an exhibition in a few months. Would you be persuaded to perform during it?"

I didn't know what the angle was for having me perform, but I couldn't deny I'd missed competing. This could be a chance to skate at a lower intensity compared to a competition. The physical therapy and training over the years had helped me become stronger, but I'd always been too scared to put myself out there in the public eye again, but I no longer had that fear.

"I'd love that. Thank you for understanding."

"I've also heard a rumor that you and Mr. Reyes have been practicing together; any chance you guys would want to do a pairs routine? I have it on good authority that you have a history with Mr. Reyes."

I started to get a cold chill. Did he know I skated with Henry as Sariah, or was he assuming it was a different time? How did he know this? Cutting my thoughts off from spiraling, I thought it over. It could be a good opportunity, but I didn't know if I was ready for it.

"Can I get back to you on that? I'm not sure if we're up to par to perform, but it's worth considering," I answered, trying to maintain a blank face while internally freaking out.

"Splendid. I look forward to hearing from you. I have one more favor I wish to ask then."

Tensing, I nodded. "Sure, go ahead." Apprehension built in me as I realized he was asking a lot, which made me uneasy. I hadn't got any weird vibes from him before, but something about him was off today.

"Would you be willing to hold a jumping clinic every month on the weekends? That way, the Senior Level students can still get your expertise and instruction on jumps, but you don't have to leave your students. Since it's outside your normal work schedule, you would be compensated for the time. How does that sound?"

He was looking far too eager and excited about this proposition, but I didn't feel I could say no. Nothing felt off about it, and I did want to help the students. They shouldn't be punished for QB's lack of skill.

"I can agree to that, but I'd like a few tickets for the expo as well."

"Absolutely, we can most definitely provide air travel and housing if needed for your guests."

Wanting to accept this so Charlie could come, I agreed, even though Director Donnelly seemed so smug. I wondered if he was happy because he got me to commit to his terms, or because I wouldn't cause a huge deal and make him move QB to my position?

In reality, I'd probably saved him a massive headache. I convinced myself that was what his reaction was about, and not something sinister.

The guys were waiting for me after leaving the

locker room and congratulated me ridiculously loudly, and I couldn't ignore the fact that it felt nice. I'd worked hard for something, and even though I was reckless and made a mistake, I still had people to support me. This was the part of my life I'd been missing.

We headed back to the house, and I invited Chloe, Ace, and Fin over. Fin had Asa with her as well and we decided to order pizza and do a game night. It sounded fun, and I loved that I had this many people in my life to celebrate with.

"Baby, are you free in the morning? Mrs. Monroe has asked us over for brunch. Would you want to go with me?" Rhett asked as we were setting up the games.

"I'd love to join you. I have training now with Henry to see if we can put something together for the expo, but if it's brunch, I can make that work."

He smiled big, that dimple peeking out, and I flashed back to when I used to have to count his smiles because they were so few. Now, he graced me with them at will, and I loved that I got to see them whenever I wanted.

"Okay, who has played Werewolf before?" Mateo asked, taking charge of the group. It was hot seeing him feel confident and comfortable in who he was. More and more each day, I saw him relax into himself and shed anxiety. Only a few people raised their hands, which made his smile widen.

"Excellent, it's fun to play with newbies. Okay, here

are the rules…" Mateo explained how the game worked and the roles we might get.

We all had a lot of fun, laughing at each other's attempt to hide our identity or convince others not to put us on trial. Mateo did great as the narrator and weaved a rich story for us all. We played for several hours and settled into a comfortable friendship with one another. It was good to see Ace and Chloe getting along with the guys. Ace flirted with everyone, which was hilarious. I knew he was just being himself and not trying to steal my men, so I laughed along with everyone. It was funny to watch some of the guys react to his flirting too.

Asa fit comfortably in our group again, and I felt that his and Fin's relationship would be developing soon. They'd sat next to each other all night. He waited on her, bringing her drinks when she was low, and I thought I even saw him hold her hand at one point. They were so cute, and I was happy for my friend. Asa had a friendly personality, and we discovered we had a lot in common. I joked that Finley was dating the male version of me, which made us all laugh. Asa took it all in his stride, and that said a lot about who he was as a person.

That night I went to bed feeling full.

Full of community, belonging, and connection.

Full of purpose and accomplishment.

Full of acceptance and love.

Full of hope.

forty-one

. . .

rhett

Mrs. Monroe was excited to meet Sawyer for brunch. She'd asked if we would be able to visit when I'd been out here to check her yard. She hadn't stopped talking about how much she was looking forward to it the whole time I was there.

Sawyer and Rey returned to the house after training around 9 am. She wanted time to change and bake something before we had to leave. I told her it wasn't necessary, but she wanted to make a good impression.

Rey and Sawyer both seemed lighter when they returned last weekend, and it had been growing all week. I missed having her to myself at night, but seeing how much she radiated with the others made it worthwhile. That was how I was able to deal with any jealous feelings. I could see how much she needed all the guys in her life. I wasn't egotistical enough to think I could be her everything. That was something romance movies got wrong.

Love wasn't about being the only person in their life, or completing someone. No, you had to love yourself enough for that.

Being in a relationship made your life fuller. You got to share your life with someone, and it was an honor to be part of it. Every one brought out different things in others, and since no one was perfect, it was unreasonable to think one person would meet all of another's needs. It led to a lot of unsatisfied and unhappy relationships.

I had my family, friends, students, and the guys to round out my life, and now I had Sawyer. She made me softer, and I hadn't realized how rough I'd started to become. And Sawyer needed a lot of people in her life. I knew I couldn't be them all, but I was glad I was one of them.

I found myself excited about brunch. I thought they would get along well, at least I hoped, and it seemed they could both benefit from a relationship with one another. Mrs. Monroe could possibly be a good source of information for us, too. She had been in the area for a long time, and her family had some connection to the school. It was at least somewhere to start.

When Sawyer finished baking muffins with Oliver's help, I watched as her face fell a little. I think she kept hoping he'd open up, but he was still keeping his distance emotionally. It was beginning to wear on

Sawyer. I needed to talk with him and see if it was something I should be worried about or not.

She'd been quiet the whole way here, and as we approached the door, I noticed she was shuffling her feet nervously.

"What's wrong, baby?"

"I just want to make a good impression. I don't have a good track record with adults, but I know she's important to you."

I smiled at her, so enamored with her wanting to connect with someone close to me. Sawyer was so compassionate, and I hoped to help her see that in herself.

"Baby, you being here makes me happy, but you don't have anything to worry about. You'll love her, and she'll love you. Just be yourself. That person is amazing."

Her answering smile made me feel as if I'd won the lottery. I knocked on the door, and the butler answered the door. Yep, Mrs. Monroe had a butler, but he was more of a companion at this point. His family had worked for her family for generations, and they were close friends. He was the only staff at the house now. The best part was that his name was Alfred. Yep, just like Batman. I often asked her if she had a secret identity and she would just smile and say, "You never know."

"Welcome, Mr. Rhett and Miss Sawyer. Please come in. Madam is waiting in the sitting room for you." He directed us to the room Mrs. Monroe was sitting in. She looked up from her tea when we entered and smiled at Sawyer, helping to ease her tension.

"Hello dear, please have a seat. I'm so happy that you were able to join me this morning."

"Thank you. It's so wonderful to meet you. Your house and gardens are beautiful, Mrs. Monroe."

"Please, dear, call me Aggie." Sawyer smiled and nodded her head as she sat.

"I made you some muffins to thank you for your hospitality."

"That was so kind of you, dear. I do enjoy a good muffin. I shall have Alfred add them to the brunch spread." She nodded for him to take them, turning back to us. "So, tell me, how do you like Oak Crest Peak, dear? I assume this is your first time here, yes?"

Sawyer smiled, nodding. "You would be correct. I love it here and find myself very drawn to the mountains and all of the nature. I grew up in a flat place with cornfields, so Oak Crest Peak is very picturesque by comparison."

"Rhett tells me that you're an ice skater?"

Sawyer relaxed more, falling into the conversation easily. "Yes, I love it. I've been skating my whole life, but unfortunately, an injury made it where I couldn't compete anymore, but I'm happy that I still get to skate and train others. Skating is air for me, and without it, I don't feel like myself."

"I remember that feeling, as well. To skate is to feel both powerful and beautiful, to be free and strong." Her smile was one of fondness. I hadn't known she was a skater. Maybe she did have a secret identity.

"What kind of skater were you?"

They talked for a while about skating and the differences between the different types. I sat and listened to them share a passion. I'd hoped Aggie would be a good friend for Sawyer, and it seemed I was correct.

We moved into the dining room for brunch when Alfred came to gather us. The spread was extravagant, and I could tell they'd gone to a great deal of effort to make us feel welcomed.

"Oh my, this is such a great feast. I don't quite know what to start with!" Sawyer exclaimed, and by the smile on Aggie's face, she was pleased with her reaction.

We dug into the food with enthusiasm. I didn't normally eat this big of a meal, but it was a special occasion, and I wanted to share in the enjoyment with Sawyer. After we finished, Aggie asked us to walk around the gardens. Sawyer was happy to oblige so that she could see more of them. They'd become quick friends and were walking arm in arm as I trailed behind them. I tried to find a way to bring up my question but decided to just get it out, as I didn't think there was a delicate way to do so.

"Aggie," I started, when the woman cut me off.

"Tsk, Tsk, Rhett. I do not remember giving you permission to call me by that name." She looked at me so sternly I couldn't tell if she was joking or not.

"I apologize, ma'am. Mrs. Monroe, I was wondering —" cut off again before I could finish.

"Please, dear, call me Aggie." She grinned so wide at me that all I could do was shake my head and continue.

"I was wondering, since your family has lived here for many years, do you know of most of the families that have come and gone from the area?" She looked at me curiously before answering.

"Of course, my family has lived here on this very estate since the town was founded. We are the longest founding family to remain here; most of the others have died out or moved on over the years." She looked at me, trying to figure out where I was going with this; Sawyer was as well.

"Well, Sawyer was told her biological family might have some ties to the school. I thought that since you are such an expert, you might know of them?"

Sawyer's face morphed into a look of understanding, quickly followed by hope when she realized my line of questioning.

"You flatter me, dear, and I do know most of the families that have lived here over the years. I'll help if I am able." She grabbed Sawyer's hand and squeezed, giving her some comfort. We were almost back to the house, so we headed back to the sitting room. As we sat, Aggie directed her attention to Sawyer.

"What name are you looking for?"

"My adopted parents told me that to find answers, I should come to this school and find out how the name Abernathy connects to it. That it would lead me to some answers."

For a moment, I almost believed that Aggie had

paled at the name, but it flickered off so quickly, as she nodded in concentration, taking a few minutes to answer.

"There was a family here by that name. Were you given any other information?"

"No. Do you recall anything about them? Where they might have gone? How were they involved in the school?"

"They had two sons, I believe. I'll have to look through some of my things from that time before I can give you any definite answers. I want to say that the children attended the school a couple of years apart. The family moved afterward, and I haven't heard the name much since then. Can I get back to you at the end of the week? I will look into it more for you, dear."

Sawyer seemed excited to have some connection, but I didn't miss how Aggie deflected and the flash of fear on her face when she heard the name. I didn't have a good feeling about this.

Sawyer hugged her, and they exchanged numbers as we left. They wanted to do a weekly chat and tea. I felt good that my idea of connecting them seemed to have been a success, even if the history hadn't been a slam dunk.

At least there was that going for us. I just hoped that whatever made Aggie react in fear didn't come after my girl.

But if it did, then I would be there to protect her.

forty-two

. . .

soren

Deciding to spend the morning on the slopes had been a terrific idea. I hadn't had any alone time to board all week, and I craved the sense of serenity I gained on the slopes. After a few runs and some dips on the ramps, I headed back down the mountain. The school had snowmobiles and sleds to transport students outside the ski lift. It was kind of like a snow golf cart. It was nice, though, and I appreciated not having to find my way up here. As I made my way down, I checked my phone to see if there were any messages. I'd texted Fin and Rey to check in with them, both for different reasons.

With Rey, I wanted to see how things had gone with Sawyer at practice today. But with Fin, I needed her hacking skills. My mom continued to send threatening texts over the weekend from different numbers after I blocked her. I needed to get to the bottom of this before it became a serious problem—time to go on the offensive.

FIN: I have some free time around lunch. You
want me to come to you?
ME: I am heading back now, that works. I'll
make you some food, squish.
FIN: Sounds yummy Sunshine.

Laughing at our exchange, I was glad that Fin had become a sister to me. I called her squish for "my squishy" because I always wanted to pinch her cheeks and squeeze them. She called me Sunshine because she thought I looked like the guy from that movie, *Remember the Titans* because of my hair. Getting to spend one on one time would be good. I wanted to pick her brain on my new relationship, too.

Scanning, I realized Rey had replied as well.

ReyBae: It went well, man. I think we will be
able to get something together. She is so incredible to skate with again. I have to convince her to
compete. I want to skate with her more than just
this expo for the school.
ME: I'm sure you know some ways to be
persuasive.
ReyBae: Well, you sure seem to think so. You
couldn't stop sucking me off last night.

ME: Well, your dick is amazing. I think I want it in my mouth every day.

ReyBae: Maybe, we can try something else too…

ME: Are you ready for that? I don't want to rush you boo.

ReyBae: Nothing with you is rushed. You make me feel safe, and I trust you. I want this with you, Soren. I love you.

ReyBae: I miss you already. You headed back soon?

ME: Yeah, just finishing up and headed down the mountain. I'll see you soon. I invited Fin over for help with my mom.

ReyBae: Okay. See you soon, babe. I can't wait to kiss you.

The blush that spread across my cheeks was unexpected, but I liked it, especially when it was because of Rey. He'd been different since Sawyer's resurfaced, and I was glad I got to be part of it. I still had to pinch myself that I could kiss him whenever I wanted.

Fin was sitting at the counter as I came into the kitchen, chatting with Mateo and Rey. I walked around and kissed Rey on the check, catching Fin grinning at us as Rey blushed. Pulling away, I started to walk around to start on lunch when Rey grabbed my hand. Looking down at our fingers, I looked up, questioning what he wanted.

"I said I wanted to give you a kiss; that was barely a peck, babe."

Something about the way he called me babe set fire to my body. I grinned and turned back around so that he could give me the kiss he was wanting. This one was passionate, surprising me since his sister was here. It was just another indication he was ready to be himself and no longer hiding. Before it went too wild and crazy, I drew back and kissed his nose. I shook my head at him and went to the fridge. Fin, though, had to be the little sister that she was.

"Ahhh, Soren and Henry sitting in a tree, K-I-S-S-I-N-G."

She sang way off-key, making us all laugh along with her. Sometimes she was too adorable to be mad at.

We ate a simple lunch of bowtie pasta in a vodka sauce. It was one of my go-to dishes when I needed something filling and quick. Mateo headed off to his room after lunch, so the three of us went to my room.

"Fin, I'd like to see if we can find out any info on my mom. She's harassing me with texts, and even after I block her number, she gets a new one. Her threats are increasing, and I'm worried she may do something drastic if she doesn't get her way. I just want to be ahead of it and know what we're dealing with."

"Of course, Sunshine. Let me see your phone. There aren't any naked pics from my brother, right? Or you? I don't really need to see that." Her face was too funny not to poke some fun at her.

"Loads, you know how we are. Just don't look in the folder titled afternoon delight." I gave her the straightest face and her mouth hung open, gaping at me.

She moved my phone between two fingers, trying to touch it as little as possible. Rey was cracking up on the bed, shaking with silent laughter. She finally felt the bed move and turned toward him. When she noticed his chuckle, she whipped around so fast; I thought she was about to do a 360 turn.

"First, ew. Second, I'll get you back for this when you least expect it, Sunshine."

"Bring it, Squish."

Now we both laughed. This was what I loved about Fin, she helped me feel like I had a normal childhood instead of the shit show mine was.

She plugged my phone into her computer, and I sat next to her to watch her work. However, it was pretty dull after a few minutes, so I scooted back toward the headboard with Rey, and he snuggled into me before falling asleep. Perfect, I could get some reading time in.

I pulled out my kindle and began reading the second book in the series for book club. The first book had ended on a cliffhanger, and I had a desperate need to know how things would work out. It had been about thirty minutes when Fin kicked my foot to gain my attention.

"I think I found something, and it doesn't look good." She bit her lip; a classic Fin move for when she was nervous. My stomach sank, apprehension flooding me at full force. I wanted this woman out of my life, but she was like a cockroach that wouldn't die.

"What is it? I can take it." I swallowed, leaning forward.

"You might want to see it."

I moved Rey's head to a pillow and climbed out from under him to get closer to Fin at the end of the bed. What I saw on the screen, though, froze my insides. Fuck. Mother, what have you gotten yourself into now?

sawyer

The ride back was quiet as we both digested what Aggie had told us. I couldn't believe that we had already found a clue, and it hadn't been that hard. Seemed that this might be easier than I'd anticipated, and I would find out who my biological parents were soon. The feeling of relief and dread filled me at once.

There were a couple of cars in the drive when we pulled up to the house. One looked like Fin's car, but the other one was unfamiliar. Rhett and I headed to the front door when it opened abruptly from the other direction, revealing two people I wasn't expecting to see together. Standing there frozen, I took in their body language, trying to make sense of everything.

"Why am I not surprised to see you here? I guess the rumors of you whoring yourself out to the whole house weren't exaggerated. Just watch your step, hoe. I'm not going to let you ruin everything. I will get my prestige back, and you will pay for embarrassing me."

Venom dripped from every word Adelaide spewed as she pointed her long fingernail at my chest. Almost at the same time, Rhett and Elias unfroze and moved. Rhett pulled me back, and Elias shifted in front of Adelaide, Queen Bitch herself. The level of hurt that hit me at his action surprised me. The last dredge of hope I had that things would change, blew away. I could never like someone who was associated with girls whose main goal was to destroy others. We all wore crowns; no need to knock them off.

QB continued to scream and stomped her foot like a two-year-old, but I'd zoned out. I hadn't been prepared to see her vileness here, in my safe place, and it had thrown me off. She triggered my anxiety of confrontations and threats, and before I knew it, I was being thrown back into a flashback. Before everything went dark, though, I looked at Elias, devastation etched on my face, tears streaming down.

"Why?"

It was all I managed before I collapsed into Rhett's arms.

Screams were all around me.

Smoke.

The sound of glass shattering.

I kept rolling, and rolling upside down and never stopped. Hands grabbed me and pushed.

I was running and running.

Leaves and tree branches whipped past me; some smacked me in the face.

Blackness and pain surround me. Arms carried me. Someone was talking to me.

Words mumbled.

Beeping. Beeping. Bright lights.

Feeling scared and alone. Shaking and hiding in my bed. Under the covers, hoping no one came into my room tonight.

Yelling. Lots of Yelling. Dishes breaking. Constantly moving.

New faces. Bullying. Screams all around me.

Everything whirling past me faster. Faster. Faster.

Images blurred around me like a kaleidoscope.

Then I heard it, as faint as the wind…

"Find your brother."

elias

Music blared through the fitness room as I punched the bag in front of me. Sweat dripped off my head and onto the floor, letting me know I'd been down here awhile. I'd hoped Rhett would be back by now so we could spar, but it didn't seem like it was going to happen today.

Cleaning up, I headed to my room to shower. The water felt magnificent on my muscles, and I was glad

I'd upgraded the shower last year. Wrapping the towel around my waist, I stepped into my room to grab clean clothes. What I didn't expect to find there was Voldemort on my fucking bed—naked.

"What the fuck, Adelaide! You taking the piss? Ever heard of privacy? Or I dunno, personal space? You are not welcome here. *Ever.*"

"Come on, Eli. I know you're just playing hard to get. But the game's over. You got me. Come on. I'm hot and ready for you."

I tried not to gag as she spread her legs, rubbing her hand over her pussy. Squeezing my eyes shut, I grabbed some clothes out of the dirty pile and threw them at her. Grabbing some clothes out of a drawer, I raced back into the bathroom to dress quickly.

She could not be here; this was not good.

Panic threatened to overwhelm me, but my background fell into place, and I put my 'proper' shield on. It felt odd now, having been able to take it off recently, and I didn't realize how good it felt until I had to put it back on. It felt awkward now, almost like it had shrunk in the wash and it no longer fit right.

Exiting the bathroom, Adelaide still laid on my bed, trying to seduce me as she masturbated, thinking I wanted to see that. She was fucking deluded. Now, I was going to have to wash my bedspread. Better yet, I would burn it.

Lucky hid under my desk, not wanting to be anywhere near the vile bitch. Me neither, buddy, me neither.

"Eli, come help me. You know you miss this," she moaned, but even that sounded fake. How had I never noticed this before? Nothing Adelaide had to offer me sounded remotely enticing after meeting Sawyer. Adelaide was superficial and manipulative. She only cared about herself and her image. She didn't care about me, but what I could do for her. I saw that now.

"You need to leave. If you're not dressed and out of my house in two minutes, I will call the police and your father. I am over this bullshit. This has to stop. Now."

She huffed as she grabbed a trench coat, apparently arriving only wearing it. Good, my clothes wouldn't have to be near her. Thankfully, Sawyer wasn't back yet, or this would've been so much worse. I'd heard from my housemates and the students about the showdown between them, and I didn't want to give Sawyer the wrong impression. Sawyer didn't deserve to experience Adelaide's wrath. I might not be a good match for her, but I didn't want anyone to hurt her. She had been through enough.

It was clear Adelaide was only here because she was jealous and insecure. Everyone was talking about her losing the challenge, and now Adelaide needed to prove herself without help from her parents for the first time. She was trying to find leverage wherever she could. It was amazing how clear I could see, now that I wasn't blinded by lust and false promises.

Finally, I got Adelaide to the door. When I opened it, I was shocked to discover none other than my best friend and the girl who was too good for me—Sawyer and Rhett.

Sawyer's face paled when she took in Adelaide and what she was clearly wearing, or not wearing, in this case. My hand on her arm and our proximity didn't help my case. It looked bad. I knew it did from her perspective. Quietly freaking out in my head, I was frozen as I tried to figure out how to explain this. Unfortunately, it meant I missed Adelaide spewing her hatred at Sawyer. She stood there frozen, no sign of the girl I'd grown to know over the past weeks.

Rhett and I both snapped out of our dormant states as Adelaide started to push her finger into Sawyer's chest; that was not okay.

Moving, I grabbed Adelaide and placed her behind me to stop her from accosting Sawyer. Glancing up, I saw Sawyer's face, and it broke the rest of my broken heart.

Bloody Hell, I was the worst.

Her face was ashen, pale, and a lone tear dropped down her cheek as she peered up at me with a look of utter heartbreak, effectively crushing me.

"Why?"

The amount of devastation in that one word would haunt me for the rest of my life.

Rhett caught her as she fainted, giving me a look that conveyed I was to deal with the trash as he carried her inside.

Adelaide was still ranting, but I was done listening. I couldn't let her do that again. I must protect Sawyer;

she was the one who was worth it. Adelaide did not deserve my politeness or respect anymore. Time to be harsh and hope she got the message.

Grabbing her arm, I hauled her to her car, practically dragging her along the way. I wrenched open her door, shoving her inside. I wasn't one for violence against women, so I stopped myself from inflicting pain, but I really wanted to make her hurt as much as she'd hurt me, and now Sawyer.

"Adelaide, I've tried to be polite. I've tried to be nice, but you're not getting it. So, listen to me carefully because this is the last time I am saying it. I don't want you. I don't love you, and in no world would I ever marry you, much less touch you, ever again. You're bloody mad, you hag! Stay the fuck away from my friends and me, and yes, that includes Sawyer, who is one hundred percent a better person than you in every way. Show up at my house again, and I will call the police and have you arrested for trespassing. Keep doing it, and I will get a restraining order. I am done. I am so done with you and your rubbish. Do us all a favor and just fuck the hell off, okay?"

Somehow, I managed to say all that without raising my voice. I hadn't completely ignored my upbringing.

Slamming her door shut, I walked to the house, not even glancing back. Things with Sawyer needed to be fixed. I owed her that. She was important, and I wanted her to know that before it was too late. Even if I could never be with her.

forty-three

. . .

sawyer

Sitting up suddenly, I almost head-butted Rhett, who was bent over me. My heart raced, and my breaths came quickly as I recalled what I'd just remembered.

What the hell did that mean?

Someone grabbed my arms and shook me a bit, breaking through my thoughts.

My eyes snapped up to Rhett, who said something, but I couldn't hear him over the blood pounding in my ears. He was replaced by Mateo, who started to mimic breathing, so I matched him, following his breaths. As I began to come back down, I could hear yelling in the background. I tuned it out to focus on Mateo's blue eyes, which were filled with concern and understanding.

"Dulzura, are you okay?" His gentle voice grounded

me, and I nodded my head. "Can you tell me what happened?"

"I, uh, had a flashback." My voice held shame, and I dropped my head. I started to ask him what he called me when his hand lifted my head back up.

"Do not feel bad, Dulzura. It's part of you, but it's not you. Are you okay now? Do you need to talk about it?" I smiled at the warmth from him, and I accepted what he was saying. I wanted to dismiss it, but I heard the truth in his voice.

"I'm okay now. I remembered something, though. I'm not sure what to do with it yet." I mulled it over. Had I heard that right in my head? Did the person carrying me actually say that? "Also, what does that word you called me mean?" His cheeks went from white to crimson so fast, I worried he was having a heat stroke.

"I uh, well, I um," he stammered out sheepishly, embarrassed. Assuming it must be a term of endearment, I didn't want him to feel uncomfortable, as adorable as it was.

"It's okay, you can tell me when you're ready," I reassured.

Being grounded back in reality, the arguing in the room reached my ears. From my position on the couch, I was unable to see anyone else in the room. Sitting up, I turned and was momentarily shocked to find who it was—Elias and Rhett.

Rhett was blocking Elias from entering the room, even though he kept trying to get around the giant grump. The heartbreak I'd felt earlier resurged when I saw him there. Elias noticed I was sitting up and instantly pleaded with me.

"Sawyer, I promise you. It's not what it looked like. She is my ex-fiancé, and she showed up unannounced, let herself in, and tried to seduce me. I was escorting her out when you guys returned. Nothing is going on with her. I'm sorry for what she said. Please, believe me."

The emotion was thick in his voice, and to deny that would be unfair. The truth and pleading on Elias' face broadcasted his truthfulness, but I'd be lying to myself if it still didn't hurt.

I didn't know if I could forgive him; even if he hadn't necessarily done anything. He'd still been the cause of my hurt.

Right?

Shit. I had to forgive him. I couldn't hate him for someone else's choices. It hurt, but we weren't dating, and I knew he had a past. I'd just been surprised it was her. Elias and I were still getting to know one another, so I had to give him the benefit of the doubt. It would definitely push things back for us. I didn't know if we would ever move past friends. Especially with how my other relationships were developing quicker.

All of this flitted across my mind as I stared at him blankly. Eventually, I gave him a small nod, and he relaxed, his body sagging with relief.

Rhett took this as his cue to stop guarding the door and returned to me, clapping Mateo on the shoulder and squeezing it in thanks. A look of appreciation passed between them. Rhett, my protector, acknowledged Mateo's strength in that situation, and it only made me fall for him even more. He wasn't trying to push him out, but made space for both of them. I didn't know if he realized how easily he did that.

"How are you, baby?" He rubbed my shoulders, sliding his hands down to grasp mine. I'd noticed how he continually touched me lately, and I loved every moment of it.

"I'm okay now. Sorry if I scared you. I wasn't expecting her, and she triggered a flashback. I don't do well with things that I'm not prepared for, and then her confrontational tone and body language in my home, it sent me spiraling." I sucked in a breath. "The flashback had me remembering something new, though. I'm just not sure if it's accurate or my mind playing tricks on me." I bit my lip in concentration as I thought it over.

"I'm here if you want to talk about it, but I also understand if you need to keep it to yourself until you figure it out."

Could this man make me swoon anymore? He kissed me softly on the lips, cradling my head in his hands. The warm feeling that settled in me didn't scare me anymore. I could admit that I was halfway to loving him. Thanking him for catching my ass, so I didn't bruise it more, I left them to decompress and headed to my room to journal.

A few minutes later, I threw my journal on my bed. Words weren't wanting to come out of me today, but I still felt unsettled. I needed to do something active, so I put on some workout gear. I heard Fin in Soren's room as I passed, but I wasn't ready to talk to them yet, so I walked softly by to the stairs.

No one was on the main level, and I made it to the basement without running into anyone. I saw Rhett and Elias in the training room sparring. Watching them for a few minutes wouldn't harm anything, I convinced myself. Sweat dripped down their chests, and I was transfixed. Every time I saw Elias without a shirt, I forgot my middle name for a minute. He was so pretty until he opened his mouth—such a shame. It was the tattoos that always took me by surprise, though.

Watching them go back and forth, I wondered what kind of boxing they were doing since I kept forgetting to ask. It looked like some type of intense fighting style which I was clueless about, but I could get behind a sport that had guys looking like that. Fuck, those shorts. Biting my knuckles, I almost groaned out loud. Shaking my head, I tried to clear it so my lust wouldn't overtake me.

Once I could think again, I headed to the dance studio. My dance studio.

Contemporary dance was a perfect way for me to process my feelings without avoiding them. It was all about fluid movement through the expression of emotions.

I turned on my 'heavy hearts' playlist and warmed up with some stretches. Going through the movements, I replayed in my head what I'd remembered.

Was it real, or did I make it up? Did I really have a brother? How did they know? Who were they?

Getting nowhere with my thoughts, I stood to start dancing. Music was such a huge part of dance for me. I felt the music, and I felt the moves. Beginning with some simple dance moves, I did a plié and a chassé. I fell into the music and found myself as I moved. "Surrender" by Natalie Taylor began to play, and I succumbed to the dance.

Assemblé. I saw my father hugging me. I saw his lips moving. I could focus on what he was saying better.

Grande Jeté. The man came more into focus. He looked familiar. His voice. His smell.

Pirouette. The day my parents told me I was adopted. My father disclosed, "They had a girl they were giving up."

Arabesque. "Abernathy... Aldridge School... I'm sorry, I didn't tell you... Find your brother."

The song ended, and I collapsed spread eagled on the floor, trying to catch my breath as I focused on the memories.

Sitting up, I gulped some water, but I knew, I knew it was true. I hadn't imagined it.

Holy Shit, I had a brother.

finley

Soren and I stared at the screen, trying to process what was going on and what this meant. We became unfocused on our surroundings, so we both jolted when Sawyer busted through the door, panting and sweating.

How long had she been back? What time was it, anyway?

My mind spiraled because it wasn't able to put all of the information together to make logical sense. *The mind could not compute. Must shut down.*

I felt like a robot, and my motherboard was malfunctioning. Sawyer, of course, had to test my limit.

"I have a brother."

"Hilarious, Sawyer," I scoffed, and turned back to the screen. Was she serious right now? I'd grown up with her, and she'd been an only child.

"I'm not joking. IhadaflashbackwhenIsawAdelaide-andElias…."

She kept talking, but it was so fast at this point I couldn't follow. Soren was still focused on the computer, and I wasn't sure if he was even aware Sawyer was here.

"Slow down, girl. I didn't catch anything you said, and we're kind of dealing with some earth-shattering news ourselves." She finally took in the room and noticed Henry asleep and Soren frozen.

"Soren, what is it?"

He jerked his head up, his eyes widened when he

took her in, and I was right; he hadn't noticed her enter. Crap, this was really affecting him.

"Sawyer. Is everything okay? I'm sorry, I didn't see you there." He was speaking, but it was almost as if he was speaking from another body because it had none of his usual zest for life or personality. It was a flat, devoid voice. Sawyer, finally reading the room, realized that something was going on with him and walked carefully over to the bed, sitting next to him.

"Soren. Talk to me. I can tell something's going on. How can I help?" She grabbed his hand, smoothing it.

"I don't know if you can. My mom's been sending me texts. You know my history. We don't have a good relationship. So, I started blocking her, but she's been finding ways around it. I asked Finley for help to figure out what she'd gotten herself into so that we could be prepared, but I don't even know if we can. I'm not sure what's going on completely, but it doesn't look good."

"Hold up, did you say Adelaide was here with Elias?" her words had finally processed through my filter, and I blurted it out before she could answer Soren. Fuck, this has turned into a massive pile of shit.

"Yes, I—"

"Never mind," I shook my head, dismissing it. "We all need to be present. I'll wake up Henry, and call a meeting. Let's put all our heads together. This is getting too complicated, and we're missing pieces."

I stood, shook Henry, and grabbed my computer to head to the front room. They stared at me as I left with looks of shock on their faces at me taking charge. I shook my head and began knocking on doors as I walked past. Fucking hell, this was crazy pants.

"Family meeting. Urgent. Meet in the front room."

I knocked on the three doors up here and then headed downstairs. Rhett was in the kitchen, so I veered there to grab him.

"Rhett, family meeting."

He turned at my voice, saw my face, and then nodded. Man, I must look hella serious since that was four people now who hadn't even questioned me. I needed to take a picture to remember this look for later, for when I needed people to listen.

Placing my computer on the coffee table, I flicked on the TV and cast my screen to it. I blacked it out for a moment, not wanting people to see what was on it until we talked. They started to trickle in, taking seats around the room, giving me curious looks.

"We have some information to cover, and instead of texting or playing the telephone game, I thought it best to just talk all at once. Anyone have an issue with that?" No one said anything, so I continued. I was kind of digging this power play here. I braced my hands on my hips in my power move. Time to shine, motherfuckers.

"First, I think Sawyer needs to share. It seems there was a visitor earlier?" She nodded her head, but it was Elias who spoke up instead.

"Adelaide showed up unannounced and came into the house on her own. She tried to seduce me. I turned her down. I was leading her out of the house when Rhett and Sawyer returned. We were all in shock, so

Adelaide was able to say some things before we reacted."

"She said some things that triggered me, and I had a flashback. When I woke up, Mateo was there to help me calm down. I wasn't sure at the time if it was real, but I went to the studio and danced through it. I, uh, I was able to remember more of what my dad told me that night. He told me…find your brother."

Okay, so she *had* said that earlier. That was a colossal bomb I wasn't expecting.

"Do you know what he meant by that? Did they have another child somewhere? Or did they know if you had other siblings?" Elias asked, already trying to process the new info with his mega brain.

"I don't know. I don't think my adopted parents had another kid based on what they had told me, but I could be wrong. I think that he was referring to my biological parents."

We all sat and thought about that and what it could mean for her. I was still pacing in front of the TV with my hands on my hips when I stopped and turned toward them all, ready to share what I'd uncovered.

"Soren, do you want me to update them on what we found?" He nodded his head, still with that blank look on his face. I hoped he was going to be okay.

"Sor asked me to help him stop his mom from harassing him. She's been sending threatening texts for the past week, and they've been increasing in frequency and aggression. I was able to trace the phone she was using back to the IP address and locate her current location. That was the easy part. I was then able to piggy-back off the internet she was using at the time and hack into her phone log."

I clicked on the TV this time, showing her recent call log and messages on the screen.

"Oh my God." Sawyer's hand covered her mouth as she started to process what was on the screen.

Call Log:
O. Abernathy
O. Abernathy
L. Rojas
O. Abernathy
Unknown number
Blocked number
O. Abernathy
Aldridge School mainline

Messages:
O. Abernathy: Bring me the girl, and your debt is cleared. Do not fail, or you will not like the conse-quences.
Leon Rojas: Your son is cozy with her. I've been watching them all. Use him to get to her.
Leon Rojas: You're running out of time. He's not happy. You won't like me when I'm angry. You have been given a free pass because you promised to deliver.
Unknown: Tick. Tick.
Unknown: I wonder what your son will think when he finds out you sold him when he was younger? That

you're the reason he was molested, and it was all for drugs? Good thing he was older when your gambling debts were out of control, or I'm sure you would have done it again.

Blocked: You've gotten in too deep; I can't help you this time. You're running out of options. Tell him the truth, and you might be able to save one thing.

Everyone stared at the screen in shock, disgust, and fear. It was written over each of their faces. Sawyer immediately went to Soren and sat in his lap, wrapping him in a hug. Henry grabbed his hand and locked their fingers together on his other side. Soren finally seemed to respond as he placed his head into the crook of Sawyer's neck and tightened his hold.

I had a bad feeling things were only going to get worse. Somehow, someone with Sawyer's biological name was connected to Soren's mom. The how and why were still unknown. I needed to do some more digging. I went to shut my computer when a new text came up on the screen. Except it was a picture. We all waited as it loaded with bated breath.

Unknown: *pic attached*

Shocks rang out as the picture appeared on the screen. Surely that wasn't?

Squeezing my eyes shut to erase the image, I missed the last text that came through until I heard more gasps.

Unknown: I'm watching you. Bye for now. Enjoy my gift.

The screen went blank, and I scrambled to it, trying to stop whatever the other person was doing to my computer.

"No, No, No," I screamed as I frantically typed in commands. Finally, I got the computer to accept what I was telling it and gained back control, but I knew it was too late. The hacker had already copied my hard drive. Good thing I didn't have anything on this computer, but it wasn't good.

Not good at all.

Someone knew we were looking, and they were much better at this than I was. Shitsicles.

I was calming down when the angle of the picture registered. It had been a picture of Henry, Soren, and Sawyer in the throes of passion. As much as I didn't want to see that, I realized a fundamental fact.

The picture was taken from inside her room.

forty-four

. . .

mateo

Everything was spiraling, and I was trying to manage my anxiety as the past few minutes unfolded. When the picture flashed on the screen, I was immediately hit with arousal, but I had to stop that train of thought.

Shaking it from my head, I realized instantly that the picture had come from Sawyer's room, meaning that someone had placed a camera there. Jumping up, I took off for the stairs. This was something I could do, something I could help with.

Entering her room, I found the angle the picture had been captured from. There was a bookcase, her desk, and an air vent that could be possible places. Searching through the bookcase first, I pulled out all the books and shook them. Nothing.

Next, I went to the figurines on the top of the bookcase, a snowflake, a necklace, and an antique jewelry box sat next to a framed picture. I opened and picked up each item carefully as I inspected them, but still found nothing. I checked behind the bookcase for any cracks in the wall, but it was nothing but a standard bookcase.

I moved to the air vent, using my phone flashlight to shine into the slots. I could only spot dust. There wasn't anything hiding in there. That meant then it was either on her desk or whoever had placed it, had already retrieved it.

As I started to inspect the desk, I heard feet coming up the stairs and then entering the room. I kept up my search, assuming they'd finally realized the same thing and came to inspect.

"Check the laptop if you don't find anything else," Fin offered behind me.

"I've checked the bookcase and the vent, but I think it has to be from this area based on the angle." I mumbled, picking up things and checking behind and under them.

"Agreed. Though, I am surprised you know this stuff." She didn't sound suspicious, just curious. Good.

"Playing too many video games and movies." I shrugged my shoulders as I continued to search the desk, unable to meet her eyes.

There was only one place left, and I didn't want to violate Sawyer's privacy anymore. I turned to Fin and shook my head as I picked up the computer, sighing. I headed out of the room and she followed.

When we reentered the room, Rhett and Elias were talking loudly about what steps to take. Rey and Sawyer were sitting on the couch where they were the last time I was here, but Soren was gone.

"Where's Soren?" Sawyer and Rey just kept staring at the ground, worrying me, and it was Elias who answered.

"He stepped outside."

I didn't like the sound of that, but I needed to ask her permission to look at her laptop more, so I left it.

"Sawyer, I think it was from your computer. Do you mind if I look at it? I didn't want to violate your privacy."

She smiled at me weakly and nodded her head, twirling her necklace. I couldn't believe I called her sweetheart earlier, but at least she didn't seem to know much Spanish. It had slipped out before I was even aware. I'd been eating a snack in the kitchen when I saw Rhett carry her pale and lifeless form by. I'd never felt so scared before, that it popped out of me in relief, revealing my true feelings when she'd awoken.

Fin sat down with me on the floor, and we placed the computer on the coffee table. I checked to make sure there weren't any unknown networks on her laptop, but it seemed clear for the moment. I would have to see if Fin could add a better firewall later. I headed to her temporary folders and checked there first. It seemed they had been deleted or removed as nothing out of the ordinary was in there, so I moved on to her trash.

Checking there gave us the answer we were looking

for. They'd either forgotten to empty the trash or wanted us to know if we got this far. First, I disabled her webcam, realizing they'd used the school's open network to get on her computer, spying through her webcam. And boy had they spied. There were over a hundred pics in the trash bin.

I looked to Fin, and she shook her head, letting me know to keep the sheer amount to myself. I didn't want to freak Sawyer out. There were pics of her coming out of her shower, some of her crying, reading, talking on the phone, playing with Lucky, sleeping, and then the more intimate ones of her with Soren and Rey.

It was a complete violation of her privacy. I selected all the photos, only leaving the one we saw, and I permanently deleted them to save her some dignity. I just hoped they hadn't saved or downloaded more of the photos. When I looked up, Sawyer was looking at me, waiting to see if I found anything.

"They took it through your webcam, and then airdropped it to themselves." Her gasp of fear let me know I'd done the right thing by hiding the rest from her. "I've disabled your webcam and put you on a closed circuit. But we'll want to make sure you have a stronger firewall. In the meantime, stay off Wi-Fi or turn off your computer when you're not using it."

She bobbed her head, but I could see fear lurking in her eyes, and I worried she'd have another flashback. I jumped up and kneeled in front of her, clasping her hands.

"Hey, it's okay. None of us are mad or ashamed of

you. Fin and I will fix it, and they won't be able to do it again. We should probably check all of our computers and update them." She nodded, a tear falling down her face. "You don't have to sleep alone if you don't want to. Don't let them take your safety. You are safe here. We got you. I got you. Okay? You are not alone in this, not this time."

She smiled softly, and I saw some of the tension leave her body. The past couple of hours had been a fucking whirlwind for me, so I could only imagine how it had been for her.

"Thank you, Mateo."

"Where's Soren?" I asked again. I had a bad feeling about this. Every comic book nerd knew you didn't separate the party. Bad things always happened when one person was left vulnerable.

"He went out front. I'll check on him. It's been a while now," Rey said, standing.

I hoped I was wrong, but I feared that things were about to get worse. Perhaps it was my own anxiety kicking in, but something in me eased as Soren walked into the room a few minutes later with Rey.

I sat back with a sigh, relieved to see him. He didn't look okay, though. His head was hanging, his shoulders slouched, and his hands were in his pockets—the total opposite of how I'd come to know him. I didn't like it, and it set my anxiety off again.

We needed to get a game plan together. That would help everyone. I was about to speak up when Elias beat me to it. I sat back, comforted again. I felt relaxed with this group, but it still took a lot out of me, and the past thirty minutes had drained me. I was happy to pass the torch.

sawyer

Mateo had eased my anxiety when he told me that no one was thinking badly about me. I'd started to feel shame and violated like I had in foster care. I was beginning to fall back into that dark place, but he pulled me out of it. Mateo surprised me every day.

After Soren returned, Elias stood up to address everyone. "Okay, game plan time. We're only spinning our wheels here, not knowing what direction to go in, so we'll figure out a plan. What are the things we need to do? Let's list them. I find that lists help keep my thoughts straight instead of letting them run around in my head."

Elias kept talking and appointing people to get things, and I had to admit, it was sexier than I'd have expected. But Elias, in full teacher mode, was hot. It was a fantasy coming to life right in front of me. I suddenly felt terrible for all the pubescent students that had to deal with the crush they surely had on him.

Fin grabbed some paper and appointed herself secretary. We started to list the things we needed to figure out, all joining in and throwing out ideas.

We listed everything that was going on and then broke them up into subgroups to simplify it more, and we agreed to focus on two things first:

Who could my brother be?
And how did Abernathy connect to Aldridge?

These would give us the answers we'd need. Elias was right, breaking it down had helped ease the overwhelming feeling.

Everyone was tasked with asking their parents, other instructors, or townspeople to see if anyone remembered an Abernathy. Elias was going to access the yearbooks and see if he could find a trail that way. Fin was going to look more into things on the dark web.

We all had jobs to do, which helped us feel useful.

I headed to bed that night wanting answers, but feeling more confident about getting them now. I was even more glad that I'd told them because their help was getting me further than I had been on my own. Plus, their support was keeping me standing.

I didn't sleep in my room that night, opting to stay with Soren and Rey. Soren seemed so lost, and I was worried about him. I hoped my comfort would help bring him back to himself. It wasn't until I fell asleep that I realized Oliver hadn't been present all afternoon. What was going on with him?

No one had had any luck yet, and it was already Wednesday. I was starting to feel restless again, unsure if we were moving in the correct direction or not. Elias had requested the yearbooks from a storage facility, so it would take a few days for them to arrive. Rhett had asked his mom, but didn't seem to find anything useful.

I was starting to lose hope when I heard back from Aggie. She wanted to see if I was free for dinner that night, as she had some new information for me. Excited to see her again and hopefully get a lead on my family history, I'd readily agreed. The first step in uncovering any other information just might happen tonight. I hoped I was ready for it.

Knocking on her door at 4 pm, I smoothed my dress down. She joked that it was old people's dinnertime, but I didn't care because it meant I didn't have to wait as long. Alfred opened the door again and led me to the dining room, bypassing the sitting room this time.

"She's waiting for you in the dining room, Miss Sawyer." He bowed as he left, and I almost wanted to curtsy back. He was so formal, it made me want to return it.

Reminding myself this was not *Downton Abbey*, I entered the dining room. No one was there, which surprised me since Alfred had said she was waiting for me. I glanced around the room at the pictures on the wall, taking in all the people she'd met over the years. Aggie was a freaking legend.

I was scanning past one of Aggie on a podium when a photo captured my eyes. That couldn't be? I leaned closer, trying to make sense of what my brain was telling me.

Mom?

"I didn't recognize you at first when we met. But as you told me about your life, I had a sinking suspicion, but I didn't want to believe it. I hadn't seen Victoria in many years and had only heard from her twice in the past twenty-two years. The first time was the day she got you. She sent me a picture saying she was so happy to be a mom." Aggie smiled wistfully as she recalled the memory, but my brain was malfunctioning. Wait… she said Victoria. Who was Victoria?

"You said Victoria. I don't know anyone named Victoria." She smiled softly as she walked over and pointed to my mom standing next to her. Aggie looked to be in her forties, and my mom was bright-eyed and young. I guessed about my age, maybe a little younger, around eighteen or nineteen. It was clearly my mom, though, with her long hair and bronze skin, her Brazilian heritage shining through.

"That's because her name *was* Victoria. She attended this school. She was an amazing ice dancer. She was projected to go to nationals, but she didn't show up when it was time for her tryout. I never did get her to tell me what happened. I was a mentor back then to some of the students, and I'd clicked with Victoria. We kept in touch after she left school. When you told me your parents' names were Kyla and Scott Brennon, I didn't think anything of it, dismissing my curiosity. But then I saw your necklace as you left, I couldn't push the feeling away anymore. I gave her that necklace when she graduated from school here. She was clever, your mom. Do you know what Kyla means?" I shook my head no, still shocked that my mom's name wasn't Kyla.

"She was sneaky, that one. It was her spirit that had always drawn me to her. I could tell she had a lot going on off the ice, but she kept it to herself. She was so beautiful and strong when she skated, trying to find her place in the world. Kyla means victorious. She was sticking it to whoever she was running from. Kyla didn't tell me anything else until, I believe you were three or four. She sent me a cryptic text telling me she'd always valued me in her life but that she had to go away and didn't know if she would be able to contact me again. She was happy with where her life led her because she had you, and you were her greatest victory. That was the last time I heard from her. That is, until about five years ago, when I received a package in the mail addressed to me with no return address. When I opened it, there was a letter on top of a box. The letter was addressed to me, and the box just said, "To my daughter."

I started to feel faint. How was this possible? I grabbed the back of the chair and sank into it, not sure if I was prepared to hear the rest, but knowing I must.

"The letter was vague in case it was intercepted with no names besides my own on it. It said, *'They have returned, and we're no longer safe. If my plan works, she will be though. She's what matters. One day she may find her way to you. She will need to know to be careful and perhaps do what I was not able to. The Council must be stopped. Thank you for your kindness. It has often helped me push through the fear and pain to do what I must. Help her if you can. She's going to need it. Look for the tiny dancer."*

She handed me the letter, speaking it from memory. When I opened it, a wave of nostalgia washed over me —my mom's handwriting. I couldn't believe this. I never expected to have anything of hers again after the car wreck. I only had her necklace because she had told me to wear it that night. It was a silver ice skater. She'd always worn it and said a special person had given it to her to remind her to follow her dreams. But I was her dream, and she believed that was why I loved to skate. She had never let on that she skated. Everything I'd believed about my mom, and that night, was now being called into question. I wondered how much I even knew about my parents. This was bigger than I'd even anticipated.

We decided to skip dinner and reschedule for another day. She realized my brain was overloaded, and I needed some time. I took the box with me, not ready to open it there, and headed back to the house. I wasn't sure if I even wanted to open it alone.

Driving back to the house, I zoned out on my Vespa. Rhett had fixed my tire last week, and this was the first chance I'd had to drive it again. As I took the road back to campus, I replayed everything from earlier in my head.

Taking a turn, a big truck came at me too quickly and I didn't have time to react. I swerved the Vespa off the road, trying to keep control as I careened down the hill toward the stream that was rushing toward me.

I pulled the emergency brake, but nothing happened. I had a choice to make. Stay on and let the water break my fall or take a chance and dive off, tuck and roll style.

It rushed through my head as the water grew closer. I decided to take my chance and dove off. Here goes nothing.

forty-five

. . .

finley

Tapping the key on the computer, I entered another command to see if I could find any new info on O. Abernathy. We were assuming it was connected to Sawyer's biological parents or would lead us to them. The school records weren't digital back then, so I was having to go through scans of old paper records. We knew they either had to have attended, or be connected in some way to the school.

Too bad there wasn't a directory we could just look through. Elias was hoping the yearbooks would give us a clue. There wasn't much on the name as someone had done a great job covering their tracks. There was a link to a corporation, but no picture or other identifying information. If we had to, we could stalk the company, but it wasn't really practical since it was located in Massachusetts.

Growing frustrated, I decided to run one more search. I could set it up to scan, so I wasn't having to sit here and watch it. As I typed in the last key, a knock came at my door. "Come in," I hollered, finishing.

Asa poked his head in, and I got this girly feeling in my stomach. I hadn't felt this way about a boy in a long time. Things had been relatively slow between us, but it seemed the other night they were starting to progress forward. Asa had seemed comfortable with my friends, and he and Sawyer got along, so I was happy with that. They were my people, and without them, nothing mattered, so I was glad he clicked.

Smiling at him as he sauntered toward me, I couldn't help but check him out. He was so clean-cut and All-American in his looks with his boy next door charm. His smile got me every time, too. Damn him and his perfect teeth. His blonde hair and green eyes made him look like some kind of Adonis.

"Hey, Fin. How's your day going?" He smiled, and the whole room lit up.

"It's better now."

"Ready to go to the coffee shop?" I swore his cheeks blushed a little from my response. Maybe he was just as nervous as me, and I needed to give him more signs that I was interested?

He came and stood behind me, peering at the computer. I didn't hide it, figuring he wouldn't know anything or what it regarded anyway. I'd learned acting suspiciously was more suspicious, but people tended not to question things as much if you acted naturally. I smiled upside down, leaning my head on his abs. I was so jealous of my head.

"Yep, I'm just finishing up one thing for Sawyer, and then I am all yours."

He grinned down at me and I wondered if he was getting a little flirty. He glanced at the screen, scrunching up his nose a little as he peered at what I had in the search: O. Abernathy. Gathering the courage to push the boundaries a little more, I was confused by his question when his eyes returned to me.

"Is there a reason you are searching for my father's name?"

My mind went blank. What. The. Fuck.

"Your *father's* name? O. Abernathy is *your* father? But that isn't your last name!" I shrieked. I was spiraling and asking questions so fast I was surprised he understood enough to answer.

"Yeah," he sighed, "unfortunately, that jackass is my sperm donor. Not really a father figure. I have my mom's last name, Walsh. My father mostly ditched us once I was born. He only checks in when he wants something from my mom or me. I try to avoid him as much as possible."

No, it couldn't be.

"When is your birthday?" I held my breath.

"It's actually next month. October 10th. I'll be twenty-two. Why? When's yours?"

I couldn't answer him because my head had just exploded.

Rapid-fire explosions.

Holy Fuck.

Holy Fuck.

Not only was Asa Sawyer's brother, but he was her fucking *twin* brother.

Shit balls.

oliver

My shoes hitting the treadmill echoed off the walls of the workout room. I'd been avoiding using the fitness room at home all week, finding myself here. It was getting tiring, keeping this secret, and having to wear this mask all the time that everything was okay.

What was I going to do? How did this happen? I kept replaying the words she'd shared in my head as the fear coiled in my veins.

Because my father worked for Jayce Latimer, for Latimer Industries.

It was the family business after all.

Of all the fucking companies that her dad had to work, it had to be *that* one. I thought I'd escaped it when I'd chosen hockey. My family had made me the black sheep, and I was okay with that because it got me out from under their thumb. But now I was getting pulled back in.

I'd been debating all week if I should leave it alone and just wash my hands of it. No one knew. I could just keep it to myself, pretend I didn't know and go on my merry way.

The 'Oliver' of a couple months ago, pre Sawyer, might've been able to do that. To use the shield, to not care about anything, or let anyone in. To fuck his way into an early grave, all the while smiling that life was hunky-fucking-dory.

But the person I was becoming, the person who'd met Sawyer and started to be changed by her magic... That guy couldn't pretend. So, I had to decide.

Did I tell the truth and hope she didn't hate me?

Or did I forget about them all and just walk away?

My watch beeped, alerting me to my workout finishing. As the treadmill whirled down to a slow crawl, my mind landed on the only option I could make. With my decision solidified, I jumped off the treadmill and headed to the showers. The decision was easy once I recognized what I had to lose.

Pulling out my phone, it was time to send a text.

epilogue

. . .

unknown number

The text came through, vibrating on the bar top. Placing my tumbler of whiskey down, I read the message.

555-9384: It's done.

Pocketing my phone, I picked my glass up and tossed it back. Swallowing the last of my whiskey, I threw some bills on the bar and walked out. Squinting as my eyes adjusted to the sun, I headed in the direction I'd parked my car in this small tourist town. Once there, I took out my phone and pressed call.

"Report."

"They were successful in running the girl off the road. Status is still unknown, but it should at least scare her enough to back off or leave. If not, then we'll advance to stage two."

"Good. The boy?"

"Seems to still be unaware at this time."

"Have you uncovered the Agency spy yet?"

"Not yet, but I have some ideas. I'm planting some bugs and following a few of the guys to see if I pick up anything. I'll find the spy and take care of them."

"Make sure you do. I can't have them getting to her before I do. I have plans, and I'm tired of waiting. I'm owed *that* girl, and I will have her; however, I have to get her."

"Understood, sir."

"You don't want to fail me again. Where are we with Pamela?"

"She continues to send threats but isn't getting any reply. They hacked into her phone to trace where she was calling from, but I don't know how much information they gathered before I shut them down. I left them with a picture to scare them to back off. There are still a few of the instructors we can use against them as well if they don't start to comply."

"Make it happen. I'm growing impatient. Abernathy cannot have the upper hand on the council. It will not bode well for either of us if he does."

blocked number

Wunderkid: I've connected with the target. She seems unaware. It doesn't feel right lying.

Agent B: The mission is to get close, not have opinions or feelings about it. You've been trained better. I will reassign you if you can't keep your emotions out of it.

Wunderkid: No feelings. I was just making an observation. I can do the job.

Agent B: Status update on uncovering her biological parents?

Wunderkid: Nothing has been discovered yet.

Agent B: Keep me informed.

Wunderkid: Understood. I will need to fortify her equipment when I get a chance. We can't have the Council hacking them again.

Agent B: Good. Will the friends be a problem?

Wunderkid: No, I have it covered.

Agent B: You might just redeem yourself yet.

Wunderkid: Thank you, sir.

Wunderkid: Fuck, the police scanner just reported a scooter accident off Pearcrest Grove. How many scooters are in this town?

Agent B: Not many. She must have gone to visit the old lady.

Agent B: I didn't think she would make that connection so quickly. We cannot afford to underestimate her again. We must keep her safe. I haven't worked all these years to keep her alive and away from him to have her end up there now. I brought her here because it's time she knows, but she needs to remain alive for our plans. Head to the hospital and give me an update on her status. We might need to increase security if they're going to make attempts on her life.

Wunderkid: I'll follow the ambulance and increase my time around her. She won't know I'm guarding her.

Agent B: Affirmative. Report in tomorrow at the same time.

Wunderkid: Yes, sir.

Tossing the burner phone on to the seat, I buckled myself in as I contemplated Wunderkid's update. Things were escalating quicker than we'd anticipated. She needed to discover her lineage and what it meant.

Hopefully, Aggie would have given her a push in the right direction, or I would have to insert myself. *Again.*

I'd been doing it her whole life in order to keep her safe, but especially in the past five years. Every decision and move I made was to lead her here. She was finally at the right place.

And now, I just needed her to uncover the truth.

The plan was in motion and she was the key.

To be continued in Shattered Secrets
Turn the page for bonus chapters

thank you for reading

Thank you for picking up Damaged Dreams. This has been re-edited and professionally proofread. While there have been some changes, the core of the story is still the same, just with some polishing.

The whole series is being re-edited and will be published in a boxset with a new bonus story. So, stay tuned for all the exciting things. Including Fin's story this summer that will be releasing in a duet, and in the fall, a brand new hockey series.

I would love to hear what you think of this story, by either writing a review, joining my reader group, or sending me a message on social media.

acknowledgments

Warning… cue the tears and grab the Kleenex. I'm about to get sappy.

How do you tell someone thank you for reaching in and touching your soul? I've stood on the sidelines most of my life watching others be brave. I've been a great cheerleader and friend along the way and have lived vicariously through other people's moments, happy to share with them. But there was something inside of me wanting more but scared to believe I could ask for it.

Serendipity is a real thing, and somehow in this crazy world, I met a friend who fit me as perfectly as a puzzle piece. Because of some random comment on Instagram, a true friendship was born. From there, I began a journey I never imagined for myself, writing. Words will never convey how much your support and love mean to me. Thank you for encouraging me, thank you for believing in me, and thank you for fixing all my million tense mistakes. Besties for life, Cat, you're never getting rid of me now!

Okay, Em, if you're not crying yet, you can start now. Becoming friends with you has also been life-changing. You are probably the sweetest person I've ever met with a heart of golden sunshine. Thank you for making me laugh when I've wanted to scream, for loving these characters as much as I do, and for always being willing to do whatever I need. You've also saved me on my tenses, and until you tell me to go away, I'm keeping you! Your claim on Soren has been noted.

This book wouldn't be possible without the love and support of my husband. Thank you for supporting me, believing in me, and allowing me to take this chance. You are my rock, and I wouldn't have even started this without you. But mostly, thank you for always answering my random questions of "what's the word for?" And while I hope you never read this, know this, I love you to the moon and back. Always.

There are a million other people who have helped me along this journey, from Instagram and Facebook. I've met a lot of authors who have effortlessly given me countless advice and a supporting comment. Readers and bookstagrammers who have cheered me on even before they have read a single word. So, thank you, from the bottom of my heart. Every one of you had helped me when I needed it, and I hope I can do the same for you. That thing you want to do, that secret dream or hope, I'm here to tell you that you can. Step out from the cloak of fear and embrace a future of unimaginable greatness.

I've officially entered motivational poster territory, but if you need someone to encourage you, I can be that for you. Reach out, comment, or message me because you never know where that one connection can take you.

also by kris butler

beauty and the cleats

#baseball #standalone series #heartfelt

The Cleat Retreat (Blake's prequel)

The Pitch Slap (Blake's book, MMFMM)

No Balking Way (Bryce's book, MMF)

Whiff it Real Good (Ledger's book, MM)

lux brumalis (completed)

#hockey #girlboss #nonbinary sibling

3 guys, no MM

Penalty Box

Dead Lift

Breakaway

the council series (completed)

#figure skating #secret past #dark elements

7 guys, lots of MM with bi-awakening

Damaged Dreams

Shattered Secrets

Fractured Futures

Bosh Bells & Epic Fails

The Council Boxset

the order duet (council spinoff)

#secret agency #spy + hacker games #fashionista

4 guys, light MM (in book 2 at the end, and bonus)

Stiletto Sins

Lipstick Lies

The Order Duet Omnibus

dressed to kill shared world (standalone)

#female assassin #quirky & curvy #twins

4 guys, no MM

Raven

f*ck steal kill (standalone)

#morally gray #bestie unalivers #sassy

3 guys, biawakening, (FF in Joy's chapter)

F*ck Steal Kill

dark confessions (completed)

#mafia #therapist #foster kids + dogs #tattoos

5 guys with MM

Dangerous Truths

Dangerous Lies

Dangerous Vows

Reckless (Cami's Novella)

Relentless (Nat's Novella)

Dangerous Love

Truth Lies Vows Love: The Complete Series

tattooed hearts duet (completed)

#tattoos #penpals #music #curvy fmc

3 guys with MM

Riddled Deceit (Part 1)

Smudged Lines (Part 2)

Open Road (Road trip Novella)

Tattooed Hearts Completed Duet

music city diaries (tattooed hearts spin-off)

#motorcycle club #age gap #TW #cam girl

4 guys, no MM

Beautiful Agony

Beautiful Envy

Beautiful Unity

vacation romcom

#romcom #social media experiment #besties

3 guys, no MM

Vibing

sinners fairytales (standalone)

#Rapunzel retelling #dance #TW

3 guys, no MM

Pride

about the author

Kris Butler writes under a pen name to have some separation from her everyday life. Writing has become her second love, providing a safe place to normalize mental health through her characters. Kris enjoys writing emotional books with flawed characters, sassy heroines, and all the book boyfriends she loves to drool over. You can find her at home most nights reading with her husband and furbaby, trying to maintain her nerdy sock collection, or playing tabletop games with her friends. Kris loves to talk with readers about her books, even if it's just them yelling at her for that cliffhanger. If you enjoyed her book, please consider leaving a review. You can find her in her reader group or on social media.

Join my newsletter
Join my reader group
Check out my website